Invaders in Our Town

The Battle of Gettysburg Through the Eyes of Some Who Lived It.

8/27/17

A Novel about the Battle of Gettysburg

by James M. Faber

Maps by Albert Pan

Dedication

This book is dedicated with love to my wife, Jennifer, and also with love to my parents, William H. and Norma C. Faber.

To my wife who endured with great patience this project of mine for the last year or so, who was active in listening as I read each chapter to her upon its completion, and how she offered me tips as to how to make it interesting to the readers of the story.

To my parents who instilled in me a great love of this country and a great appreciation for the sacrifices and the pain the past, and present, citizens of it, both military and civilian, had to make in order for it to become the great country it is today. And, especially to my dad who also instilled in me a great interest in the Civil War, explaining early on in my life how the history of the country was really shaped by it, how it grew from it, and how it had to suffer and had to endure the hardships created by the war in order to preserve this new experiment of freedom for all of its citizens.

The author and his son Jim at Gettysburg on July 5, 2013 for the 150th Commemoration. (Photo by Servants Old Tyme Photos, Gettysburg, Kevin Servant Owner.)

About the Cover

"The Diamond" was painted by Mr. Brad Schmehl and is used on the front and back covers with his permission. A copy of "The Diamond" can be purchased by contacting Mr. Schmehl at www.bradleyschmehl.com.

The painting depicts a scene when the Confederate Army first enters and occupies Gettysburg on June 26, 1863. It is named "The Diamond" because that is what the townsfolk called their town square. The scene occurred around three o'clock in the afternoon, and is included in this book starting in Chapter 27. The north direction is toward the left side.

The painting includes several interesting features, which are listed below, starting from the upper left:

1. Confederate troops are marching into the town square from the north along Carlisle Street.
2. Supply wagons are parked on the northeast and southeast sides of the square.
3. A pair of horsemen with a small remuda of horses, located beneath and to the left of the flagpole, are members of Elijah White's 35th Virginia Cavalry Battalion, later in the war to be nicknamed "White's Comanches". The horsemen commandeered the horses from local farms to serve as cavalry mounts.
4. A Confederate soldier is lowering the American flag, to soon be replaced by the Confederate flag.
5. Confederates are moving an artillery piece through the town square.
6. Confederate troops are marching Union prisoners from the Pennsylvania Militia, captured earlier in the day from a battle west of town, while townsfolk look on.
7. Confederate troops are marching to the east toward York Street.
8. A group of six Confederate officers, four on horseback and two dismounted, discuss their next move.
9. The two officers watering their horses at the trough located at the lower right are from left to right, General John Gordon and General Jubal Early. Note that Early is bent over in the saddle from the pain of his rheumatoid arthritis. They are speaking with some townfolk.
10. Three Confederate soldiers stand in front of JL Schick's store. One cleans his boot from the mud, while someone, perhaps Mr. Schick himself, looks on from the upstairs window.
11. Off in the distance, in the center of the painting, the Globe Inn can be seen as the fourth building, with white columns, on the left/north side of the street.

About this Book

This is a story of some of the civilians who lived through that horrible, but very essential for the survival of these United States, three days in July of 1863; the Battle of Gettysburg. The story begins about a month before the beginning of the battle and is concluded on the day of the battle's completion. The events, and the brave and extraordinary actions, taken by the people of Gettysburg after the armies left, leaving behind their carnage, both human and animal, and destruction is the subject of another story and therefore is not a part of this one.

This story is built around **actual** people who lived in Gettysburg, and who experienced the horrors of this battle. It is told through two different sets of characters, the primary characters and the secondary characters. The primary characters:

John Charles Will, Mary Virginia (Ginnie) Wade (it is worth noting, for clarity, Miss "Ginnie" Wade is the same person as the famous "Jennie" Wade. Miss Wade was mistakenly referred to as "Jennie" in a newspaper article after her death. This mistake was never corrected and so she became "Jennie." This article, and the subsequent usage of Jennie, occurred after the timeline of this book; prior to which she was referred to as ("Ginnie"), Matilda (Tillie) Pierce, Fannie J. Buehler, John L. Burns, Barbara Burns, Martha Gilbert, Elizabeth (Old Liz) Butler, Samuel Butler, Elizabeth Salome (Sallie) Myers, Annie (Culp) Myers, Reverend Joseph Sherfy, John Wentz, Sarah (Sallie) Broadhead, Joseph Broadhead, and Professor Michael Jacobs.

The secondary characters, who compliment the primary characters:

Charles Will, Mary Wade, Samuel Wade, James Pierce, Elizabeth and Jacob Gilbert, Francis Ogden, John Rose, John L. Tate, Mary Broadhead, and Henry Jacobs.

It also includes several soldiers, who were from Gettysburg, primarily John Wesley Culp, who enlisted in the Confederate Army and fought with the 2nd Virginia Infantry Regiment, part of the Stonewall Brigade; and Johnston (Jack) Hastings Skelly, Jr., who mustered into the 2nd Pennsylvania Volunteer Infantry for 90 days and then was mustered into the 87th Pennsylvania Volunteer Infantry. Culp and Skelly were boyhood friends and shared many of the same friends while growing up in Gettysburg. And, their exploits during the time covered by this book were intertwined.

Several other soldiers from Gettysburg were included as they became part of the story told about Culp and Skelly. On the Union side they were

William (Billy) Holtzworth, William T. Ziegler, and William Culp, brother of Wesley. On the Confederate side Henry Wentz, son of John Wentz.

Two more soldiers, both from the Confederate Army, Benjamin S. (B.S.) Pendleton and William Arthur, were included as they were Wesley Culp's best friends in the Rebel Army.

The author has introduced several fictional characters to assist in the telling of this story. It should be understood that any similarities of these fictional characters to any real person is purely by coincidence. These fictional characters, in order of their appearance in the book, are: Samuel Jones, Confederate spy (a composite character of a real person witnessed by John Charles Will); Matthew Franklin, storekeeper at Fahnestock Brothers Store; Silas McGee, the drunk tannery worker and adversary of Samuel Jones; Charles Milton, Confederate soldier and adversary of Wes Culp; Catherine Butler, sweetheart of Wes Culp; Isaac and Ester Moses, free black folks from Gettysburg; Lieutenant Phillip Greene, Confederate soldier; and several minor characters whose full names were not used.

The story is mainly told by the words and expressions of these characters. This is made possible by the imagination of the author, strengthened by the author's research into each of them from the vast amount of information available concerning the battle and the people who lived it.

Acknowledgements

This was not possible without the extreme helpfulness of Mr. Timothy Smith, Chief Research Historian of the Adams County Historical Society; Mrs. Linda Seamon of Guided Historic Walking Tours of Gettysburg, Pennsylvania; and Mr. Scott Mingus, an expert who has written many books about the Civil War. **All** of these gracious people provided valuable historical prospective. The author would also like to express extreme gratitude to my mother-in-law, Mrs. Royce Brazo, and to Ms. Janice Miller and Mr. Kyle Kincaid who provided valuable comments and edits to the writing. Their comments were critical in making this book read well.

Many of the buildings and residences referenced in this book are well preserved. Where it enhances the story, photographs taken by the author and by Ms. Seamon, are included to breathe a little real life into it. These places are available for viewing if the reader plans a visit to Gettysburg in the near, or distant, future.

Finally, the author would also like to recommend the following books, listed as suggested reading, which were excellent references about the battle and about the people of Gettysburg.

Suggested Reading

1. *Gettysburg*, by Steven W. Sears; Houghlin Mifflin Company, Boston/New York, 2003.
2. *John L. Burns: The Hero of Gettysburg*, by Timothy H. Smith; Thomas Publications, Gettysburg, PA, 2000.
3. *Witness to Gettysburg: Inside the Battle That Changed the Course of the Civil War*, by Richard Wheeler; Stackpole Books, Mechanicsburg, PA, 1987.
4. *Days of "Uncertainty and Dread": The Ordeal Endured by the Citizens at Gettysburg*, by Gerald R. Bennett; Higgins Printing Company, Harrisburg, PA, 1994.
5. *Days of Darkness: The Gettysburg Civilians*, by William G. Williams; Berkley Books, New York, 1990.
6. *The Jennie Wade Story: A True and Complete Account of the Only Civilian Killed During the Battle of Gettysburg*, by Cindy L. Small; Thomas Publications, Gettysburg, PA, 1996.
7. *Notes On The Rebel Invasion Of Maryland And Pennsylvania And The Battle Of Gettysburg, July 1st, 2nd And 3rd, 1863*, by M. Jacobs; The Times Printing House, Gettysburg, PA, 1909.
8. *Recollections of the Rebel Invasion and One Woman's Experience During the Battle of Gettysburg*, by Fannie J. Buehler; Gettysburg Star and Sentinel Print, Gettysburg, PA, 1900.
9. *The Second Battle of Winchester June 12-15, 1863*, by Charles S. Grunder and Brandon H. Beck; H.E. Howard, Inc., Lynchburg, VA, 1989.
10. *Adams County History*, Published by Adams County Historical Society.
11. *At Gettysburg, or What a Girl Saw and Heard of the Battle*, by Mrs. Tillie Pierce Alleman; W. Lake Borland, New York, 1889.
12. *The Ties of the Past: The Gettysburg Diaries of Salome Myers Stewart 1854-1922*, by Sarah Sites Rodgers; Thomas Publications, Gettysburg, PA, 1996.

Preface

The bullet cleared the barrel of the gun no different than the hundreds, maybe thousands, of times a bullet had done from this very same rifle. A rifle that had seen lots of action before, but within the last three days, had been fired more than in the last year. The soldier who discharged the rifle knew how to shoot. He always did, from the time he was a little boy in Louisiana, and he was an expert marksman. He could aim the rifle and hit a target from a distance of hundreds of yards.

And, now he was firing the rifle, exchanging shots with enemy soldiers who were as good as he. Some of his opponents had higher ground, occupying the hill just outside of town, and therefore he was at a slight disadvantage with those. He was not used to being at a disadvantage. It made him a little uncomfortable, edgy, and for the first time in awhile, afraid.

Some were below his perch on the second floor of the house he occupied, those being across the road and in and around a house and a fence. There were plenty of enemy soldiers to fire at, and there were plenty firing at him. He found himself shooting then immediately seeking cover to reload the rifle. He was not confident of hitting his target, or any target. He couldn't be exposed to fire long enough to be sure. They were too good.

The bullet from this shot headed southeasterly, searching a target. Originally it had been meant for a soldier, one of the many who were firing at him from around the house across the road. But the rifle had been discharged too soon to be accurately aimed, so the bullet instead headed directly toward a civilian house, further south of its intended target.

Moments before the shot, a young lady just finished her breakfast and was in the midst of her morning prayers. She was very religious, so her daily prayers were an important part of her life, and especially today, as the great battle continued around her right outside the house she was staying with her mother, sister, and new-born nephew. Bullets continually struck the house in the last three days, but more reached the boys fighting the battle outside. She never imagined such an event of death. It was horrifying. So, she prayed to God to keep her family safe. She was so very afraid, and prayed for courage. When she finished her prayers, she went to the kitchen and set about her work.

At the same time the bullet was in flight toward the house, this very same young lady was kneading dough to bake bread for the soldiers. They had great appetites, and it was some of the only food they had eaten for the last two days of this great struggle. It was a difficult chore because the need was great and the ability to satisfy this need was limited. But, she had done this most of the day before, and she would do it today. She knew they were now dependent upon the little bit of nourishment this freshly baked bread gave them, and so she would do it. Never mind it was safer in the cellar. This bread was what she could contribute.

The bullet continued its flight toward the house and then slammed into the side door, that door being the one facing north and toward the shooter from Louisiana. The door wasn't sturdy enough to stop it, merely slow it down slightly. Once inside the house, the bullet passed through an interior door separating the parlor and the kitchen. This door was partially open, so the bullet hit it at an angle. Like the side door of the house, the kitchen door wasn't made to stop it either, so it passed through entering the kitchen.

The young lady was working the flour mixture, kneeling at the dough trough, concentrating on getting the right mix to prepare it for baking. It was early in the morning and the sun was just beginning to warm the day. It was going to be another hot, early-July day. She thought about that and what horrors this day would bring. How many more soldiers would she see dying on Culp's Hill, between the hill and this house, and just outside this house? She was thinking also about how she could help her mother take care of her sister and her sister's new baby. She was thinking about all these things, when the bullet found her.

She didn't feel it really. She just lost her balance and her hold on the dough trough, and slumped to the floor. It didn't hurt, but she knew she was dying as her face was on the floor, and her back was warm, with blood she guessed. Her mind began to race. She thought of what she had said to her mother and sister earlier, only moments ago, that if anyone was to die in this house, it should be her. She was comforted by this thought, as the Lord takes people when He is ready. Today, He was ready and so was she.

Her sense of time and reality became different. She could see her mother next to her, calling her name. Or was she? The sounds her mother made and her movements were so different; slow and confusing. She became cold and tired all at once. Her eyelids closed, but she was still here. Familiar thoughts began to flood her mind. Things of times ago. Of her older sister when she was just a young girl, teaching her how to make bread. This thought briefly brought her back from her drift, thinking about the bread she must make for the soldiers. But, as with the rest of her thoughts racing through her mind, it didn't last long.

She thought about her mother and the kind, warm days of walking along Breckenridge Street toward the west end of town when she was very young. She thought of that awful day when her mother told her that her four month old little sister had died, and the heart-breaking funeral. She thought about her father, how she would sew for him and help him with his tailoring business. How he had been thrown in prison for stealing money he claimed he found, and once he was released how he had changed, become insane, so much so her mother had to have him sent to the Alms House, never to return. She thought of her neighbor, Maria, how much she loved her, like a second mother, and the many times she spent at her house having tea and telling her deepest thoughts and secrets. She thought about her closest friends, Wesley, Jack, and Wesley's sister Annie, and the times they picknicked on Culp's Hill during the summers.

And, she thought about Jack. How she missed him and why it had been so long since she heard from him, or even heard news of his regiment. She just visited his mother and found out nothing new. She loved him so, and because of her love for him, her thoughts stayed with him. Why didn't his mother approve of them? Approve of her? Was it because her father was a Southerner, or that he was insane? Was it because she was a bit jealous of her and Jack? After all, he was very, very close to his mother, even ensuring he had her permission before joining the Pennsylvania boys in the army. Or was it something else? Her thoughts began to drift, and the answers to these questions were too difficult for her now to figure. She longed for him to come home so they could get married and begin their lives together. This thought brought peace and joy to her heart. She sensed it was beating ever slower. Time was short, but she had thoughts only of Jack. It seemed to her hours she laid there, thinking of so many wonderful thoughts, but in real time it was only short seconds.

Then, darkness closed in on her, but she could make out a light. A light full of warmth, full of belonging, and full of love. She was home. She breathed her last breath and then she was gone. So young and so full of life, yet gone from this earth.

Invaders in Our Town

The Battle of Gettysburg Through the Eyes of Some Who Lived It.

A Novel about the Battle of Gettysburg

Part 1

Before the Invaders Came

In early June 1863, the Confederate Army of Northern Virginia was on the move north toward Maryland and ultimately Pennsylvania. General Robert E. Lee decided this was a critical point in the war for independence from the United States. His army was winning battles, most recently the Battle of Chancellorsville, but the victories were relatively meaningless toward ending the struggle, and were very costly in both men and supplies. The loss of General Stonewall Jackson at Chancellorsville was of particular damage to Lee and the army, as Lee lost his best lieutenant.

At the same time, the Rebel army was losing in Mississippi, as the Union army laid siege to Vicksburg. All attempts to break the siege had failed so far and Confederate President Jefferson Davis was beginning to accept the loss of the city as inevitable. Davis and Lee strategized that a bold maneuver was necessary to counter the bad news from Mississippi. So, in mid-May Lee began planning the Pennsylvania Campaign: an invasion of the North. A great victory in the North would not only make up for Mississippi, but more importantly, put extreme pressure on the Union, which may result in the commencement of peace talks.

Lee decided on June 3rd as the day to begin the move north and at 11:00 AM, the order arrived from General James Longstreet's Headquarters. General Lafayette McLaws's division of Longstreet's corps was the first to begin the march, starting the Pennsylvania Campaign.

During the last days of May and the first couple in June, the Confederate Army was rampant with rumors as to where they would be going, and these rumors, or at least the discussion of a move north, was not lost upon the newspapers in both the North and the South. Hence, the citizens of the North were constantly alarmed and afraid of the potential invasion by the Southern Army. Where would the invaders bring death and destruction?

The citizens of Gettysburg lived with constant fear of such an invasion as they knew Maryland was only a few miles to the south, and the way the war was going, the ability of Union forces to stop an incursion into Pennsylvania was questionable at best. No one slept well awaiting the arrival of the invaders.

June 4, 1863 Gettysburg, Pennsylvania

CHAPTER 1

Samuel Jones is a spy. Not the normal spy whose job it was to report on troop movements, rather Jones is a spy who precedes the army into unknown lands. It is his job to understand the land; understand and report how the local communities could support an invading army. He would do this by preceding the army by a few weeks, scouting the countryside, looking for, mapping, and quantifying, supplies and goods the army would need to survive in this enemy country. He was sort of a forager. And, he did this by experiencing life in the towns and villages, making friends, seeking potential business partners, understanding the folks who lived there. He knew that interacting with the town, acting the part of an interested and enterprising visitor, would yield him the best information he could pass onto the Army of Northern Virginia, to assist in the invasion of Pennsylvania.

Jones was relatively new at spy work. He had begun this career venture only a couple of weeks or so ago, when the rumors began of the Southern invasion of the North. He read it in the *Baltimore Sun* and thought of an opportunity where he could be of help. But, even though he was new to it, he also knew he was very good at it. His way with getting to know folks, strangers, was inbred in him. He was an actor, plain and simple, so it was second nature for him play the part of a traveling businessman. It was a part he really liked to play. And, the result was getting and reporting information vital to his country.

Jones fancied himself a good stage actor, having acted in many plays, beginning with playing the part of Buckingham in *Richard III*, in August of '55, at the Charles Street Theatre in Baltimore. It was during this play Jones came to know the Booth family very well, particularly young John Wilkes Booth, who played the Earl of Richmond. Jones continued acting with the Booths in several plays at the Holliday Theatre in Baltimore. During this time, he shared many conversations and opinions on the politics of the day with Booth, particularly when the Southern states seceded from the Union and formed the Confederacy. Booth was more of a fanatical supporter of the cause, as he called it, but Jones was more practical.

The majority of their conversations centered on what they could do to help their country win its independence. They both had agreed the course did not include enlistment in the army, as neither was the soldiering type, so they thought. That would have to be the last option, and only if the war

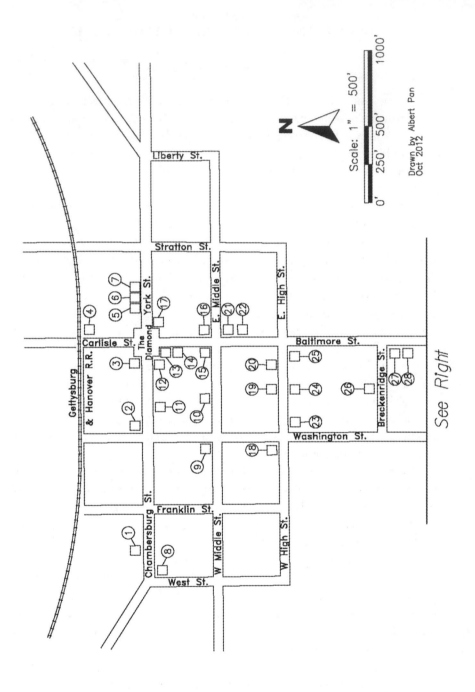

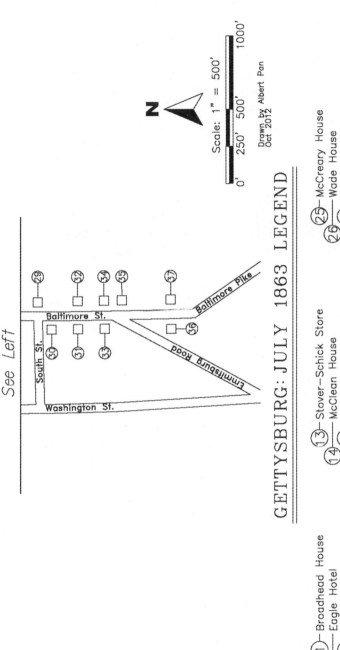

Scale: 1" = 500'

0' 250' 500' 1000'

Drawn by Albert Pan
Oct 2012

See Left

GETTYSBURG: JULY 1863 LEGEND

1 — Broadhead House
2 — Eagle Hotel
3 — Eckert's Corner
4 — Railroad Station
5 — Bank of Gettysburg
6 — T. Duncan Carson House
7 — Globe Inn
8 — Burns House
9 — Jacobs House
10 — Skelly House
11 — Christ Lutheran Church
12 — Bank

13 — Stover-Schick Store
14 — McClean House
15 — Fahnestock Bros. Store
16 — Fahnestock House
17 — Wills House
18 — Foster House
19 — Myers House
20 — Catholic Church
21 — Kendlehart House
22 — Buehler House
23 — Eyster's Female Academy
24 — United Presbyterian Church

25 — McCreary House
26 — Wade House
27 — Pierce House
28 — Shriver House
29 — Winebrenner Tannery
30 — Sweeney House
31 — Rupp Tannery
32 — Winebrenner House
33 — Rupp House
34 — McCreary House
35 — Welty House
36 — Wagon (Battlefield) Hotel
37 — McCellan House (Jennie Wade Dies)

was going against the Confederacy. Thus far, the Confederacy was winning, so this course was not necessary. Then a couple of months ago, Jones decided being a spy was it. Booth, however, did not share his enthusiasm for this adventure, so off he went on his own.

His first experience as a spy was just ten days ago in Chambersburg. He spent two days there, learning about how much coffee, sugar, bacon, meat, flour, wheat, and most importantly about the town's business and how much cash would be available for confiscation once the army arrived. When he was done with his stay, he completed his report, rode for two days to the Confederate encampment of General Jubal Early, and presented it to the general. General Early was impressed by the thoroughness and detail of his report, listened intently, and remarked:

"Mr. Jones, Aye see your services can be of much value to me and my Division as we move into Pennsylvania. Aye want you to continue your work, and report all of what you find directly to me as my aide."

"General, I am at your service, sir," Jones replied.

"Good. I would like you to rest up and then start off toward Harrisburg in the morning, stopping at towns in between. Find out all you can and then find me and report it."

Early then paid Jones the sum of 50 Confederate dollars, plus some silver coins, which could be of use for any expenses he would have. Jones was pleased indeed knowing this was what he could do best for the Confederacy and the war effort, and it was also very profitable for him.

So, here he was in Gettysburg, having arrived in town today, around ten o'clock in the morning. It made sense to Jones to stop in Gettysburg, as he noticed on his map the town was the wheel hub of many roads. These roads connected Gettysburg with Chambersburg to the west, Carlisle and Harrisburg to the north, York to the east, and Baltimore to the south, and were aptly named for these destinations. It was perfectly set up for business, and should be a wealth of supplies and money.

He rode his horse into town from the west on Chambersburg Street, and headed into the Diamond, the town square. From the Diamond, he rode east onto York Street, and found himself in front of the Globe Inn. Tired from his travels riding most of the night, he got off his horse, removed his travel bag, and handed the horse over to the boy in front of the inn. He entered looking for a bed to sleep in, a meal, and a beverage.

After paying for a room for the night, he rested awhile. He then went downstairs and he found himself a table. Jones was in his early thirties, tall at five (5) feet ten inches, with shoulder length blonde, graying hair and blue eyes. He dressed in a black ditto suit, with the waistcoat and matching trousers, a loose fitting coat, and some would say it was larger than Jones should be wearing. The outfit was complemented with a black bow tie, a white shirt under the waistcoat, and a black bowler hat that fit snuggly on his head. He had a silver pocket watch tucked neatly into his waistcoat. These were his working clothes. He also had a set of traveling clothes much less businesslike. He sat on one end of the bench seat and removed his watch to check the time: noon.

John Charles Will ran the day-to-day business of the Globe Inn. He was in his mid-twenties, average height, dark hair, and blue eyes. He was dressed in gray and white checked trousers, a white long sleeved shirt, collar turned up, red braces to support the trousers, and black congress boots.

His father, Charles, was the proprietor of the Inn, but due to his advanced age, being in his fifties, he relies heavily on John to manage the inn's affairs. In fact, it is for this reason John had not, and still hasn't, joined the army to defeat the rebellion. Charles could not handle the inn without him.

It was Thursday around noon, and John was in the middle of the dinner business when he noticed the stranger who arrived at the inn this morning. John watched as he found a seat on one of the benches at a table. He hesitated drawing near to the stranger, but noticed he was looking for some help and had met his glance. He walked to the table.

"Sir, you look like you could use a serving of food. What would you fancy, beef or pork? We have a fresh batch of Hog Maw just coming out of the oven."

"Excuse me sir, but what is Hog Maw?"

"I can tell you aren't from around here, as I haven't seen you here in the inn before. Where do come from?"

"I was born and raised in Baltimore, but now travel mainly in the East selling my recipes for fixing the taste of liquor. Hog Maw sounds interesting. What is it?" Jones asked with a look of hunger.

"Should have known. Baltimore. I recognized your talk as a Marylander. Hog Maw is smoked sausage, boiled potatoes, apples, an onion, some celery, and spices all mixed and stuffed into a pig's stomach, cooked in boiling water and then baked. It is really satisfying and is one of our specialties here at the inn. How does it sound to you?"

"Isn't it a little early in the year for hog slaughtering?"

"My, you are astute," Will replied impressed by Jones' knowledge that hog slaughtering usually was done in the winter. He continued:

"Our butcher supplied us with what we need for the dish as we requested special."

"Interesting. Well, that sounds just the thing, and I would like it very much."

"That's fine. I'll bring you some directly. What kind of beverage to go with that?" Will asked.

"An ale would suit me."

"By the way, I am John Charles Will. My father is the proprietor of the inn," Will said while offering his hand.

The two men shook hands, and Jones said:

"I am Samuel Jones, but everyone calls me Jones, not Mr. Jones, but just plain Jones. Sir, may I call you John?"

"Indeed Jones. I'll have the ale directly, and your dinner here in front of you without delay."

Will returned in a minute with the ale and then left to get the dinner order. Jones took a drink of the ale and reflected. He was pleased. He now had a new friend in this town, and without much explanation as to the reason he was here and where he was from. Further, John Charles Will seemed intelligent, observant, and most probably would be a really good source of information about the town. Just what he had imagined, what better source than the Innkeeper? A few questions about the town are in order, and depending upon the answers, a look about the town, where young Will "suggests" he go.

Will returned with a hot plate of Hog Maw, a piece of corn meal bread, a fork, a knife, and a napkin. He set these in front of Jones, saying:

"Jones, I hope you take pleasure in this."

"John, I am sure I will. It smells wonderful."

"I'll be around should you desire something else."

Jones placed the napkin in his lap, picked up the fork and knife, and took a bite of the Hog Maw. He followed this with a drink of the ale, and thought as he chewed: "Very tasty. These farmers here in Pennsylvania really know how to grow food and these innkeepers sure know how to fix it into a marvelous meal. I must enjoy it, as it is part of the spoils of war, spoils for those who will soon be coming. They must know about this place."

After he finished, he decided it was time to go to work, to play his part as the salesman. Will came to the table to remove the plate and placed another ale in front of him saying:

"So, Jones how was it?"

"Quite enjoyable, I haven't had a meal such as this in awhile." He took another drink of ale and continued: "Say, I am only going to be in town for a few days and like I said earlier, I have for sale a few recipes to fix the taste of liquors. I think you might find these interesting, recipes to serve with this great food. What types of liquor do you have?"

"Whiskey, white brandy, and gin, and as you know, we have ales and lagers."

"White brandy, hmm. I may have a recipe that you would like. Do you have currants around here?"

"They grow all over Adams County, and we can get as many as we could use."

"Marvelous, then I have the recipe just for you. It's called Currant Champagne, and it turns brandy into a wine with a sweet and pleasant flavor. It would be ideal to serve with a meal such as the one I just finished. With this fixing, the inn should be able to make your stock of brandy last. Some of my associates have been able to make their supply last up to three times longer, and earn substantial profit by charging more per drink that the straight brandy."

"Jones, that sounds appealing. We here at the Inn are always looking for new recipes and new ways to satisfy our customers' appetites. Is this recipe difficult to make? Is it costly?"

"No, you probably have all the ingredients right here at the inn, except the currants. As for the price, well my friend, we can discuss this further. What would such a recipe be worth to you?"

Will was intrigued and thought this was something his father would be in favor of.

"This is very interesting to me, interesting indeed. Let me have a chance to talk with my father and then we can talk further. He will be here for the supper hours beginning at five o'clock. How about I talk it over with him and then we can have supper together, say seven o'clock?"

"That sounds fine. In the meantime, I would like to go around the town to see if I can offer my recipes to other businesses. But, I promise not to offer anyone the Currant Champagne. That one is strictly for the Globe Inn."

Will was impressed and said, "I can see you are a gentleman."

"I can see you are a man I can do business with. I have a few more recipes that can be made from the crops grown around here in the Littlestown, Hanover, and the Cumberland Valleys. May I inquire as to the condition of the yield of wheat, corn, oats, barley, rye and buckwheat, and how profitable the farms have been?"

"As far as I know, and my talks with the farmers around here, they all seem to have done well this past year. In fact, the prices we pay to buy some of these crops have dropped a little in the last year, even with the war needs. Father says this is because the yield was above normal. So to answer, there are plenty of crops to be purchased."

"That is wonderful for you and for the town. I imagine the banks, the goods stores, and the merchants have been making a good profit."

"That is true, true as I can see it, and true for the Globe Inn. Good crop means good business. That's the way it has always been around here," Will replied.

"And, true for a businessman like me. I think I would like to see this for myself. Where in this town do you suggest I go until supper? Where are the banks, the goods stores, and the merchants?" Jones asked.

"Which way did you enter the town?"

"I came from the west, rode through the town square, and directly to the inn."

"Well, the Adams County seat is here in Gettysburg and it is a thriving town with many banks, shops, and stores. We call the center of the town the Diamond. Four streets meet at the Diamond, Chambersburg from the west, where you came from, Carlisle from the north, Baltimore from the south, and York here in the east. Baltimore Street is where you want to go. On the way, just west of here on York Street, is the Gettysburg Bank, one of two banks in town. Among the stores, and just south of the Diamond, on the west side of Baltimore Street is J.L. Schick's Store. Further to the south on the same side of Baltimore is the Fahnestock Brothers Store. South of town, on Baltimore Street, are two tanneries owned by Mr. Rupp and Mr. Weinbrenner. Along the way to the tanneries, at Breckinridge Street,

**The Diamond
as is today.
(Faber)**

you can also find the butcher, Mr. James Pierce. But, for a merchant of recipes, you may want to visit the Eagle Hotel located west on Chambersburg. You must have seen it, the three-story Hotel on the north side of Chambersburg. Finally, I would visit the Washington Hotel, north on Carlisle Street at the railroad."

Jones was pleased with this information. There were two banks, many stores, and some local businesses, just the right information needed for his report, and all within a short ride. He could visit all without much effort. He finished his ale and said:

"I sure am obliged to you for this information. It sure will make it easier for me to find some business in this town. I think I will take a ride and see what I can see. As you said, shall we say seven o'clock here in the restaurant?"

"I will talk to father about your Currant Champagne, and then we can have supper together," Will said.

With that, Jones left the inn, got on his horse and rode west toward the Diamond and Baltimore Street.

CHAPTER 2

Jones rode the short ride to JL Schick's Store, which was located on the southwest corner of the Diamond. He tied his horse to the hitching post and went into the store. Schick's Store was a three story brick building with several windows on each floor.

"Afternoon, can I help you?" asked the man behind the counter.

"Perhaps you may. I am a traveling man of business and I have recipes to sell, which fix the taste of liquor. Might you point me in the direction of someone who would find this a suitable business venture?" Jones replied.

"Fixing the taste of liquor, you say? Have you tried the Globe Inn just yonder on York Street?" the clerk asked.

"Yes," Jones said. "I was looking for another place or two who might want to buy my recipes."

"Try the Eagle Hotel on Chambersburg Street and the Fahnestock Brothers Store further south on Baltimore Street. You should find some business there."

Jones thanked the clerk, and walked back to York Street and to the bank. He spied the bank from the outside for about an hour, walking along York Street and around the Diamond to be inconspicuous. He judged the bank to a successful concern, as he saw many townspeople going in and out, making deposits and withdrawals.

"If this is a good example of the banking business in this town, then cash will be no problem for the army when they get here. Indeed, this is a good town to visit and get resupplied on the way to the capitol in Harrisburg, as long as the supplies are plentiful," he thought.

So, satisfied of the money in the town, he thought he should next check the supply of flour, salt, sugar, and coffee, as well as shoes and hats. He took the short ride down Baltimore Street south to Middle Street to visit the Fahnestock Brothers Store. He arrived and gazed at the building.

The store was located on the northwest corner of the Baltimore Street/ Middle Street Intersection. It was a brick, three-story, warehouse type building with a slanted roof covering the northerly third of the building. On the east side, facing Baltimore Street, were three rows of windows, six windows on the first and second stories, and five on the top. Jones surmised the northern portion of the building was originally built as a house, or a smaller building, and later the southern two-thirds added to increase the storage area. The join line of the two was visible on the east side of the

Fahnestock Brothers Store as is today, northwest corner of Baltimore and Middle Streets. (Faber)

building and was accented by the different color of the bricks. The entrance was located on the north side of the building.

Jones hitched his horse on the east side of the building and proceeded to the entrance to the store, but hesitated as he caught a glimpse of a pretty young lady walking north on Baltimore Street. She approached the store and then the entrance. She was of average height, with brown hair, parted in the middle with the back of her hair braided and pinned up to the back of her head. She wore a brown, narrow, flat skirt, looped for walking, and a brown, high neckline shirt with a white collar, tightly pinned at the neck with a large brooch. Jones stepped aside to allow the lady to enter the store first, tipped his hat, and said:

"Afternoon, ma'am."

The young lady responded: "Good afternoon to you, sir," and then entered the store. From within the store, Jones heard a greeting:

"Ginnie, how nice to see you today. You sure are looking fine."

Jones entered and heard the conversation continue. The young lady replied back:

"Why thank you Matthew."

"Any news from Jack?" the man named Matthew asked.

"Not a word and I am a mite concerned."

"Well, I wouldn't fret as you know the mail always takes so long to get here from Virginia, particularly through the War Department, unless there is bad news. That seems to come quickly, so really no news is good news," Matthew Franklin said.

Matthew Franklin was just about 20 years of age, but looked older. He was dressed in a long sleeve shirt, trousers, and an apron.

"Well, I just get so worried about him. I haven't gotten a letter from him in over a month," Ginnie Wade added.

"Now, never you mind, he is just fine. We'd have heard something from the army by now if he was wounded," Franklin said, purposefully saying wounded, and not killed, so as not to worry Ginnie any further.

"Matthew, you are so strong and you are right; we would have heard if something terrible had happened to him. I just miss him so," Ginnie said dabbing her right eye with a handkerchief.

Jones sensed it a good time to strike up a conversation with the clerk to lighten the tense atmosphere. He tipped his hat and said to Franklin:

"Good afternoon, sir."

"Afternoon, may I help you?" he said.

"Perhaps you may. My name is Jones. I am a traveling man of business and I have recipes to sell, which fix the taste of liquor. Might you be interested?"

"Mr. Jones, I am Matthew Franklin and this young lady of virtue is my good friend Miss Ginnie Wade. What do you mean fix the taste of liquors?"

Jones bowed and said "Miss Wade, my pleasure again. Matthew, how do you do?"

"I am doing well, but I am not sure how I can help you."

"You asked about how my recipes can fix the taste of liquor, and that is a good question. I can sell you formulas to make the taste of liquor more pleasant, taste sweeter, add some fruit flavor, and become more appealing to more folks," Jones replied and looked at Ginnie to make sure she would be included in the conversation.

"Mr. Jones, I hope you are not implying that I would even think to touch a drink of liquor?" Ginnie responded and act insulted.

"Oh no, ma'am. I was merely wanting to include you in the conversation."

Franklin interjected: "I don't think we would be interested in…how did you say it, formulas. We don't sell much liquor here except to places that serve it, like the Globe Inn and the Eagle Hotel. Did you try there?"

"I have been to the Globe Inn and may be doing some business with them, and I plan on visiting the Eagle Hotel, but I am also looking for other folks to buy my recipes."

"Well, our store sells supplies and is a dry-goods store. You can buy sugar, flour, coffee, tea, salt, baking soda, soaps, sundries, candles, clothes, shoes, hats and just about anything you may need. We do sell liquor, but mainly to the hotels/taverns in town, like the Globe Inn. So, we really don't have any need for your formulas."

"Thank you kindly. Do you mind if I inquire how your business is faring, with the war and everything? Do you have any troubles with supplies? And, how about men's shoes?"

"No, Mr. Jones. We get a lot of our supplies right here in Gettysburg, including shoes so we have a lot of them, and those that we don't come from Philadelphia, Hanover, Baltimore, York, and as far away as New Jersey and New York. Our railroad carries much of the goods to town, and since its opening in '58, the time to get supplies has been greatly diminished. We always keep enough on-hand here at the store for at least a couple of months, in the event the war interrupts our orders."

Franklin was about to continue, as he was proud to talk about the store, when a young woman and a small boy with his dog entered the store.

"Good afternoon Matthew," the lady said, and: "Ginnie, how lovely to see you."

"Mrs. Buehler, afternoon to you. I see you brought Allie and Bruno with you today. Has Mr. Buehler gotten any news of the Rebels movements?"

"Not any different than what the *Sentinel* is printing, Matthew, and I am very concerned for Mr. Buehler if indeed they come to Gettysburg. I have heard the Rebels arrest the local politicians and anyone who works for the government as David does, and some have not returned home. At any rate, Allie and I came to get some flour, salt, butter, and some baking soda. Matthew can you help us with this?"

"Fannie, Allie sure is growing," Ginnie remarked as she reached down and tenderly squeezed the boy's cheek bringing a giggle from him, patted the dog on the head, and continued, "Whilst Matthew is getting your supplies, can I introduce you to Mr. Jones? By the way, Mr. Jones, do you have a first name?"

"Sam, Miss Wade. How do, Mrs. Buehler?"

"Fine, Mr. Jones."

"Why Mr. Jones, that too is my little brother's name."

Franklin gathered up Fannie's supplies and asked: "The usual amount I assume Mrs. Buehler?"

"That would be wonderful, Matthew."

Jones watched intently as he was always fascinated by how folks from smaller towns were so very kind to each other. Just then however, this all changed. Into the store walked a young man, in his twenties, tall about six feet, around 200 pounds, well muscled, dressed in shabby clothes, worn boots, and dirty. The atmosphere in the store instantly changed.

The man addressed Franklin saying, "Franklin, get me some flour, salt, and coffee, and put it on my account."

"Silas, you will have to wait until I am done with Mrs. Buehler."

Silas McGee was just getting off his shift at the Rupp Tannery south of the store on Baltimore Street. He was drunk and smelled of it, as his usual habit was to hit the whiskey before making it home. Occasionally, he would stop at Fahnestock's to get some supplies for his wife. Today, he had chosen to drink more whiskey than usual.

"I'm sure Mrs. Buehler won't mind, will you Fannie?" McGee slurred the words more than saying them, and emphasizing the word Fannie insultingly.

"Matthew, go ahead and take care of Mr. McGee," Fannie replied hoping he would go as soon as possible.

"You see Franklin, she doesn't mind. She's a refined lady. And, look who we have here, Miss Ginnie Wade. How are you?"

"Silas, you're drunk."

"Why Ginnie," Silas answered, annoyed at Ginnie's accusation, "maybe, but not too drunk to come over for a visit tonight. Folks say you like to have male callers in the evening, and I thought I could call too, so how about it?"

"Never, even if you were the last man in town! I don't like your tone or your suggestion I have improper visits. You know I am waiting for Jack's return."

McGee staggered over to Ginnie, grabbed her by the arm, saying "Awe Ginnie, I insist. I think I will come by tonight. I know Jack won't mind."

Ginnie tried to pull away: "You're hurting me. Let go of my arm."

McGee held tight to Ginnie, moved his face closer to her, and as she looked away, said more forcefully, "say, eight o'clock?"

Jones sized up McGee and quickly closed the gap between them.

"I think you should let the lady go."

McGee turned to look at Jones, then let go of Ginnie.

"Well, what do we have here, a short man with a big mouth. Maybe we should step outside and discuss your butting into other people's business, if you have the spine for it."

Jones said matter-of-factly, "Are you sure you are up to it? Whiskey can make a man, even a big man like you, think he is bigger than he really is."

Still slurring but clearly angered, McGee said: "Mister, I don't know you and you don't know me, but I am going to enjoy making sure you don't forget me. You first."

16

Jones turned and walked toward the entrance to the store. After taking two steps, he felt a push in his back, as McGee shoved him hard, but not enough for him to lose his balance. Jones turned and pivoted to his right around on his left leg and caught a glimpse of McGee's right-handed punch coming at him. Quickly he ducked the punch and then drove his left fist into McGee's ribs and followed by smashing his right fist into McGee's jaw. This left-right combination was too much for McGee and he crumpled to the floor.

Jones went to Ginnie: "Miss Wade, are you alright?"

"I'm okay, Mr. Jones, a little shook up, but fine thanks to you," Ginnie replied.

Jones then approached McGee, who wasn't knocked unconscious, but clearly dazed, and offered his hand saying, "McGee, are you alright?"

"Don't touch me."

McGee staggered to his feet, wiped the blood oozing from his mouth, and said to Jones: "This isn't over. I'll see you again. This is a small town." He then spit blood on the floor of the store and left.

CHAPTER 3

It took a couple minutes for things to settle after McGee's departure. Franklin finished Mrs. Buehler's order and she paid the bill. She thanked him and took Allie and Bruno home. Jones was still comforting Ginnie when a teenage girl and a younger boy entered the store.

The young boy said, "Hi sissy, I didn't know you'd be at the store this afternoon."

"Hi Sammy," Ginnie said affectionately. "Yes, I thought I would do a little shopping. How are you? Are the Pierce's treating you well?"

"Fine, just fine," Sam Wade replied, with a look toward the teenage girl he was with.

"That's fine, but you will let me know if they don't, you hear?" Ginnie replied in the part of an over-protective big sister. She didn't like Sam having to work and be boarded by the Pierces, and she didn't hesitate to show her displeasure, but she knew to make ends meet, it was necessary.

"I will," Sam responded again with a look toward his companion.

"Afternoon, Matilda," Ginnie said being much too formal on purpose.

"Afternoon, Ginnie. You sure are looking fine today," Tillie said to Ginnie. And, to the others: "Does anyone have any news of the Rebels?"

"Thank you, and no new information on the Rebel army," Ginnie replied.

Seeing the conversation with Ginnie wasn't going very far, Tillie turned to Franklin and said:

"Matthew, can I get three barrels of salt and a couple of pounds of flour and sugar?"

"Certainly. If young Sam can help us load the salt onto the wagon, we can have that delivered to your Papa's shop within the hour. In the meantime, let me get your flour and sugar. This is on your account, right?"

"That would be just fine, Matthew."

Ginnie looked at Jones and said with pride toward her brother:

"Mr. Jones, this is my younger brother I told you about. You know, the one I said shared your name?"

"Mr. Sam, it is indeed a pleasure," he said offering his hand. The boy took it and shook it vigorously.

Franklin left the counter and went into the back of the store to arrange for the salt to be loaded onto one of the store's wagons. With a quick hug and goodbye to his sister, Sam followed.

Jones was left in the company of the two young women. He could tell there was some sort of dislike between them, so he decided he should introduce himself to the younger girl to break the awkward silence that was growing.

Tipping his hat, he said: "Good afternoon, ma'am. I am Samuel Jones, a traveling man of business."

"Matilda Pierce, but people call me Tillie. Nice to meet you Mr. Jones," Tillie said extending her hand.

Jones politely shook Tillie's hand and replied: "The pleasure is mine, ma'am."

"Mr. Jones, you are a traveling man. Where do you hail from?"

"Originally from Baltimore, but I now travel all over the east selling my recipes."

"Baltimore and the east. How exciting. Have you been to New York and Boston?" Tillie asked clearly more interested in where Jones had been than what his business was. "I have always wanted to go there, but maybe someday…" Tillie said with a faraway look in her eyes.

"Yes, many times to each," Jones lied.

As Tillie was about to continue her questions of Jones, Franklin reappeared from the back and said:

"The salt is being loaded. My hired hand will deliver it shortly, and here is your flour and sugar."

"Thank you Matthew. Mr. Jones I hope you enjoy your stay here in Gettysburg."

She turned to leave when into the store walked an elderly man and his elderly wife.

"Good afternoon Constable Burns, and to you Mrs. Burns," Tillie greeted them.

Jones heard the man being referred to as constable and he instantly become alert to the dangers of what he was doing. He momentarily cursed at himself, as he was becoming too comfortable, too arrogant. But, the actor in him took over, and he immediately relaxed and began again playing the part. He looked over the older couple.

John L. Burns was a former constable of the town, but had lost the most recent election for the post. Despite that, he still felt a man of authority in town and readily expressed it. He was 69 years old, a couple of inches over five feet tall, clean shaven, graying hair, thinning in the front and longer in the back. He dressed in a white collared shirt, waist coat, and a brown coat, matching pants, and brown leather boots, with a top hat. Jones instantly determined he was a staunch man because of the non-existent smile and the way he pursed his lips. Barbara Burns was in her early sixties, slightly shorter than her husband, not quite five feet tall. She wore an ankle length blue skirt, with a white, floral pattern lined vertically, with a matching bodice and white collar. She also had a red coat and black bonnet. Her outfit was completed with white gloves. She seemed friendlier as she smiled brightly to Tillie's greeting.

"Not much good about it. The Rebels are coming and what am I doing, shopping for a dress!" Burns replied.

"Good afternoon Tillie. Don't mind Mr. Burns. He is in his usual merriment."

Tillie said: "I must be on my way. Papa is waiting for me, so I should get back. Good health to you both."

Burns mumbled something not quite audible, while Mrs. Burns said: "And to you Tillie. Please give our greeting to your family, too."

Tillie left the store, and the attention of Burns shifted to Ginnie and Jones, as Ginnie greeted the Burns politely: "Afternoon Mr. and Mrs. Burns."

"Ginnie, how nice to see you today. You are looking very well, and such a pretty dress you are wearing," Mrs. Burns replied.

"I know why you are so contented; your kind is coming and maybe, to here…" Burns said looking at Ginnie pointedly. "That would please you and your Rebel kin."

Ginnie didn't reply, as she was hurt by the accusation of her being a Southern sympathizer. This was not the first time, and each and every time she heard this, she felt humiliated and angry. Her father was from the South, but her loyalties remained firmly with the Union.

Mrs. Burns saw the hurt in Ginnie and soothed saying: "Ginnie, don't you never mind about him," emphasizing "him" sarcastically and pointing to Burns. And to Burns, she said: "Why don't you keep silent?"

Burns replied: "Woman, I'll say what I want." He then turned his interest to Jones saying: "Who might you be?"

"Allow me to introduce myself. My name is Samuel Jones, a traveling man of business. Afternoon ma'am," Jones bowed.

"Afternoon Mr. Jones," Mrs. Burns greeted him warmly.

"A traveling man of business? You mean a spy. What is your business here?" Burns grumbled.

"I sell recipes for fixing the taste of liquor, and I am traveling for a fortnight trying to earn a wage for my family."

"Sounds like a spy to me. Fixing the taste of liquor, just what we need 'round here more reasons for harlotous living," Burns replied showing his temperance attitude, and then continued:

"You ain't from around here. Where are you from?"

"Originally from Baltimore, but shortly after the outbreak of the war, my wife and I decided to move us and the youngens north. We didn't like the politics in Baltimore and were thoroughly ashamed of how President Lincoln was treated on his first trip to Washington in '61. Didn't think we wanted the little ones growing up there." Jones embellished his story. He used it in Chambersburg and it worked well there. He continued:

"After that, we moved to a small farm just outside of Philadelphia, to a town called Howellville, in Delaware County. Perhaps you heard of it?" Jones intentionally ended with a question to shift the burden of explanation to Burns.

Burns didn't bite, saying: "Howellville, never heard of it. Where did you say it is?"

"'Bout a short day's ride west of the city, so if we need to get there, it is no bother. I ain't much of a farmer, I soon found out. But, I can make a living selling goods to others. Although it ain't a prosperous calling, it is what I must do to feed the family. So, that is my charge, and here I am to do it." Jones changed his language pose to more of a county type talk with the words "ain't" and "bout" for affect, hoping to appeal to Burns as a small towner.

"Well sir, I am one of the constables of this town, and as constable, it is my duty to protect this town and its citizens from Rebs and I aim to do it by jailing anyone I may suspect has any dealings with those Southern traitors."

"A fine calling it is, sir. You needn't worry about me. I love this country and would gladly be of service to you in this work, should you find the need of my assistance. Gettysburg is such a thriving and splendid town. Nice people and good commerce. Why, just earlier today I visited the town center and saw such activity as I have never seen before in a town this size. Yes sir, I would be more than proud to assist you, should you need my help, in protecting such a fine town and fine people," Jones countered with his offer of service, and as smoothly delivered as if it were indeed the truth. However, the old man was rather shrewd and continued his interrogation of the stranger.

"If you love this country so much, why aren't you in the army defending it?" Burns emphasized "defending." "That's where I'd be if I were younger. What are you, some sort of chicken-hearted sissy?"

"No sir," Jones said respectfully and continued: "It's the youngens. Me and my wife, we ain't got no living kin, and we just moved to Delaware County just last year, so I cannot abandon them and their welfare. I

21

must take care of them, first," Jones said with sadness in his voice and his manner.

Tired of this type of interrogation, Mrs. Burns chimed in saying:

"Burns, enough of this constable stuff. You aren't even the constable anymore, so leave the man be. We came here to see my dress and that is what we will do. Matthew, has my dress come in from Philadelphia?"

Burns scoffed at his wife: "Old woman, tend to your dress so we can go back home." And, to Jones:

"Mr. Jones, I'll be watching you and your business extra careful. Where are you staying in town?"

"Why the Globe Inn, where I already may have some business dealings with Mr. John Will."

Franklin ignored the rest of the conversation between the two men and replied to Mrs. Burns: "Yes, yes it has, it came in just yesterday."

"Wonderful. May I have a look?"

Franklin gestured for Mrs. Burns to follow him as he went to the back of the store and the two left the room. Jones smiled at Burns, but he just glared back at him.

"I have a right mind to lock you up right now. The Rebs are coming and I need to make sure I take care of strangers like you before they can do any harm."

Jones realized Burns may not be satisfied with his answers, but was comforted by the fact he had his .44 caliber derringer, he got from Booth, in his coat pocket should he need to use it to get away. He smiled at Burns and said:

"Mr. Burns, I certainly am not the type of man you need be concerned with; just a simple farmer turned peddler."

"We shall see Mr. Jones, we shall see."

CHAPTER 4

Ginnie was listening to this whole exchange silently. She liked the stranger, but Mr. Burns was more than she could take today, so she decided it was time for her to return home. Indeed it was almost time for her mother and her to pay a visit to her sister Georgia. She excused herself by saying:

"Beg your pardon, but I must be going. It is almost time for my mother, Mrs. Comfort, and I to visit Georgia to tend to her as she is with child and is due in only a couple of weeks. Mr. Jones, it was very much a pleasure meeting you, and I hope you have success with your business whilst here in Gettysburg," the latter sentence delivered with a sarcastic look to Burns. She continued her sarcasm by saying:

"Always nice to see you Mr. Burns."

Jones offered his hand to Ginnie saying: "The pleasure was all mine Miss Wade, and I hope to see you around the town as I plan on staying a couple of days."

Ginnie shook his hand and replied: "If our paths cross that would be just fine. And, thank you again for your assistance with that, that ugly man."

Before she could leave the store, an elderly woman entered. Jones watched Ginnie's expression change immediately. She stopped short of the door and gave way to the woman. She then addressed her in a formal, but not at all warm, manner.

"Good afternoon, Mrs. Skelly."

"To you Ginnie," the woman said with more than a hint of sarcasm in her voice. She purposefully didn't stop her pace into the store and quickly, and deliberately, turned her attention to Franklin, who had just returned from the back with Mrs. Burns.

"Matthew, a pound of sugar and flour, if you please."

Franklin instantly provided attention and said:

"Yes, Mrs. Skelly, right away."

She then turned to Burns and Mrs. Burns and said:

"John, Barbara."

Barbara nodded and Burns replied: "Mrs. Skelly."

Jones noticed a dislike of this woman from both the Burnses and Ginnie. Ginnie then said to Mrs. Skelly:

"Have you heard from Jack, Mrs. Skelly, and would you mind if I came by later for a cup of tea?"

"No, I haven't heard from Jack. And, not today. Maybe some other time."

This was all the attention Mrs. Skelly would afford Ginnie and so she turned to go, clearly hurt by Jack's mother's cold and heartless demeanour toward her-again. She knew this came from her jealousy of Ginnie's relationship with her boy Jack. And, she knew Mrs. Skelly was most likely responsible for the rumors of her having improper visitors. But, the harder she tried to get close to the woman, the further she was pushed away. This frustrated her to no end. Therefore, today she had no choice but to go, and so she then left the store.

Jones decided it was time for him to go, but before he could execute his departure, Mrs. Burns chimed in, saying:

"Matthew, thank you. But, if you could arrange to return it and get one just like it a little larger, that would be just fine." She continued by turning to Burns:

"Burns, let's go home where maybe you can learn to mind your manners, especially to visitors to our fine town."

Burns growled and turned to follow his wife out of the store, with one more penetrating look to Jones.

Jones tipped his hat and said: "Afternoon ma'am, Constable."

As he watched the Burns leave, he noticed the couple hesitate at the door as two young women and an older black woman were attempting to enter. The young women entered, but the black woman waited for the Burns to exit before coming into the store. Jones heard Mrs. Burns greet the ladies saying:

"Afternoon Sallie, Annie, and to you Old Liz. Excuse us, but we must be on our way."

"Have a nice afternoon Mr. and Mrs. Burns," Elizabeth Salome Myers said.

"Yes, please do," said Annie Myers.

"Miss Burns and Constabull. You dun hev wunderfil dey," Elizabeth Butler replied.

Then Elizabeth Salome Myers and Annie Myers entered the store, shortly followed by Elizabeth Butler. Jones noticed the three women with interest. Elizabeth Salome Myers looked twenty years old, more or less, with dark hair and brown eyes. She was a little over five feet tall, slender and well dressed, similar to Ginnie Wade's attire. Annie Myers looked in her late twenties, and was dressed almost the same as Salome Myers, the only difference was Annie wore a gray dress, while Salome wore a red dress. Elizabeth Butler was a black woman in her early fifties, or so, and was dressed in an older, floor length, brown dress with long sleeves rolled up to her mid forearm, and a white, soiled head-wrap.

"Afternoon Matthew. I trust all is well with you," Elizabeth Salome Myers addressed

Franklin, as she browsed around the store.

"Hello, Matthew," Annie Myers added.

"And to you, ladies. What can I help you with today?"

"I've come for some supplies for Mamma and Papa," Salome Myers replied.

"Ladies, may I introduce you to a new friend of mine?" Matthew asked gesturing to Jones.

"I suppose. I did notice a visitor was among our midst," Annie replied, while Salome Myers said nothing and stared shyly at Jones.

"Miss Elizabeth Salome (Sallie) Myers and Mrs. Annie Myers, may I present Mr. Samuel Jones, a traveling man of business."

Jones again bowed and tipped his hat saying simply: "Ladies."

Elizabeth Butler politely interrupted the conversation, saying: "Mathue, I's in a pow'rfil herry. I has gots lots of werk todey n dun haf to git to duing it. Kin I git sum soap and two breshes witout much buther to ya?"

Franklin looked at Elizabeth Butler with an annoyed look and replied:

"Now Old Liz, you know I cannot help you until all the others have been taken care of first. You will just have to wait until I am done with Sallie and Annie."

"I's do, bit I gots so much werk to git dun fore dey's end."

"Well Old Liz, you know I have to finish with the white folks first, and then I will tend to you."

Sallie replied: "Matthew, it's fine with us to mind Liz first, as we are not in that much of a hurry."

"I'd like to Sallie, but you know I have to follow what the bosses say and that is all white folks must be helped before any colored folks."

Jones watched Liz and admired the way she accepted being placed behind the white women with a certain dignity he hadn't seen in many colored folks. He surmised she was a strong woman, and thought: "But, she would have to be, right? After all, she was a free, colored woman living in the North." He hadn't met many free, colored people. He looked her over again, this time with a sense of esteem. He also had a feeling of regret, for his side was fighting to keep control over these people. Nevertheless, slave labor was essential to life blood of the Southern economy. He knew his country depended upon it. He thought: "So be it."

"Now Sallie, what can I get you?"

"Well Matthew, the usual I guess, a couple of pounds of flour, sugar, some peach jam, and peach butter."

"I'll have that in an instant."

Franklin disappeared into the back of the store. Sallie and Annie followed leaving Jones with the black woman.

"Ma'am I couldn't help but to hear you have a lot of work to do yet today. What kind of work do you do?"

Liz looked at Jones with a curious look, wondering what a white stranger was doing being friendly to a colored woman. She replied:

"Sur, I's a wesh'r womun. I wesh fokes clothes, dri 'em, fold 'em, n bring 'em to dey howse."

"Interesting, how long have you been living in Gettysburg?"

"Fur a bout fife year. Me n my man Sam'l dun fount a gud spot her n Gittysburg. He werk for Mr. Will n the Globe en."

"How pleasant. I am a traveling man of business and am staying at the Globe. I have a meeting with Mr. John Charles Will for supper. I will ask about Samuel and maybe I can meet him."

"That be wundrfil, Misser Jones. You dun see Sam'l, you tell 'em Old Liz spects 'im hum fore tin clock tonight."

"I'll do that ma'am."

Just then Franklin returned from the back and said:

"Sallie, on your account as usual? And Old Liz, here are your soap and brushes."

Sallie replied: "Matthew, that would be grand."

Old Liz paid silver for the brushes and the soap and left the store saying:

"I's gotta get to wesh'n."

Sallie and Annie also left the store and on her way out, Sallie paused and turned to Jones, offered him her hand and said:

"Pleasure to meet with you Mr. Jones. I wish you much luck in your business here in our town."

Jones shook her hand politely, saying:

"Likewise ma'am, and I do appreciate your kind words."

And, with that Sallie and Annie left the store, whispering as they went, presumably about the stranger who had come to their town.

CHAPTER 5

As Sallie and Annie left the store, Jones could hear two wagons pull up on Baltimore Street and some voices outside the store. A couple of moments later, three men entered.

Franklin spoke first: "Good day Reverend Sherfy, Mr. Rose, and Mr. Ogden."

Sherfy replied before the others: "And to you, Matthew. We've come for supplies, and have already spoken to your hired hands in the back of the store." Turning to Jones: "Is this another one of your hands? Ah, but it cannot be as his clothes are not those of a working man," he said answering his own question.

Reverend Sherfy was Reverend of the Gettysburg German Baptist Church, was fifty years old, of average height, graying hair, his cheeks clean shaven, but with a long beard along his jaw line, which ran from temple to temple. He wore a light colored, long sleeve shirt, brown trousers and brown leather boots. John Rose was slightly older, also with graying hair and a full beard that hung a couple of inches below his chin. He had deep set eyes and a large nose. He wore a dark shirt and gray trousers, with black leather boots. Francis Ogden was younger, in his early thirties Jones surmised, dark hair, slightly shorter than both Rose and Sherfy, but more muscular. Jones could see he was used to hard labor on a farm. He wore a light shirt, braces supporting brown trousers, and brown leather boots.

"No sir, this here is Mr. Samuel Jones, a traveling man of business." Then turning to Jones, Franklin continued the introductions:

"Mr. Jones this here is Reverend Joseph Sherfy," then gesturing to the other men: "And, Mr. John Rose, and Mr. Francis Ogden. Mr. Rose and Mr. Ogden live on a farm a couple of miles south of town. Reverend Sherfy also lives on a farm a couple of miles south of town and grows the most splendid peaches you have ever tasted in your life. In fact, we sell Sherfy fresh peaches, canned peaches, dried peaches, peach jam, and peach butter. Over here, have a taste," Franklin said and took Jones over to the shelf where the Sherfy canned peaches were displayed, opened a jar used for offering samples, took a fork, poked a peach and offer it to Jones.

Jones took a bite, and then with a smile exclaimed: "That is simply wonderful. I do not believe I have ever tasted a peach like this. How sweet, and the texture…it just melts in your mouth."

Franklin, pleased with Jones's response, turned to Sherfy and said: "Reverend, maybe we found another procurer of your fine peaches. Did you bring some more jars of canned peaches and some peach jam?"

"Your hired hands are unloading them this very moment. Here is a listing of what we brought," Sherfy said handing the list to Franklin.

"Grand. Let's see left over from last year's crop, ten cases of canned peaches, ten jars of peach butter, and fifty jars of peach jam. That's just what we needed, as you can see here, we were running low. So, 120 jars of canned peaches at ten cents each for $12; ten jars of peach butter at 25 cents a jar for $2.50; and 50 jars of jam at ten cents each for five dollars. So, added altogether, it comes to $19.50. What would you like for this amount?"

Sherfy said as he looked at his written list: "Well, that's just what we figured. We'll need three barrels of sugar, three barrels of flour, one barrel of onions, a barrel of salt, a barrel each of corn and potatoes, a couple of jars of tea, some soap, a jar of nails, some candles, some shoe laces, and several jars of apple butter. Here, it may be easier to just go from this here list," he replied as he handed Franklin the list.

"Yes, that will be much easier. Mr. Rose and Mr. Ogden, do you also have a list?"

"No, as usual, we are together."

"Splendid. I will return in a few moments after I arrange for your supplies to be loaded onto your wagons."

Franklin disappeared to the back of the store, where he could be heard giving instructions to the hired hands.

Jones said to Sherfy, "Your peaches are really tasty. How do you do it?"

"Well, Mr. Jones, is that right?"

"Yes."

"Well, Mr. Jones, my father Jacob Sherfy moved into this area in around 1790, and worked on the local farms until he saved enough money to buy his own in 1805. He planted the peach trees and worked the land to make the soils rich for the trees. He learned from his mistakes and his successes until he made the conditions right for the trees. He taught me everything I know, and that is simply to work and nurture the soil, with just the right amount of watering too. I combined this knowledge and consulted with Professor Jacobs, who helped refine the process, and the result was very pleasing."

"It sure works."

"Mr. Jones, I have an orchard just south of town and would be glad to show you, if it peaks your interest?"

"It does, but I am only in town a few days. Perhaps next time I am here?"

"Suit yourself. What kind of business do you do?"

Jones, embarrassed to be talking about liquor to a reverend, replied sheepishly: "Reverend, I sell recipes for fixing the taste of liquor."

"Oh," the reverend responded, but didn't say anything else.

Franklin returned from the back of the store in time to renew the now awkward conversation, saying:

"Reverend, we have just about all of your supplies loaded. So, let me see about your total. Three barrels of sugar at four dollars a barrel for $12; three barrels of flour at three dollars a barrel, for nine dollars; one barrel of onions for two dollars; one barrel of salt for two dollars; one barrel of corn and one barrel of potatoes at two dollars each for four dollars; six jars of tea for three dollars; five bars of soap for fifty cents; one jar of nails for twenty five cents; twenty candles for fifty cents; a dozen shoe laces for one dollar; and six jars of apple butter for six dollars. Hm, the total is $40.25, and with the $19.50 we owe you, your total is $20.75."

"That sounds about right, Matthew."

The Reverend paid Franklin, and then said to Jones: "Pleasure to make your acquaintance Mr. Jones. Although I really don't approve of what you are selling, I do wish you success. And, if you are still interested, I would be glad to show you my trees, and Mrs. Sherfy makes the best peach pie in all of Adams County. It goes perfect with a cup of tea."

The two men shook hands, as did Jones with Rose and with Ogden. Jones said: "I am much obliged by your invitation Reverend, and will be looking forward to a piece of that pie and a cup of tea."

Jones realized it was time for him to go, for he had another stop to make before his supper appointment. He turned to Franklin and said:

"Quite an interesting town you have here, and many interesting folks living in it. I guess I will be on my way."

"Yes we do, and in your short time in the store, you have met a good portion."

Jones looked at his watch, almost half past 5 o'clock. He left the store thinking he could get to the Eagle Hotel and spend some time there before his supper meeting with Will. He said to himself: "Positively, I have met some colorful people so far today," and indeed he had.

Jones got on his horse and rode north on Baltimore Street back toward the Diamond. He was in good spirits and being such, he failed to notice McGee had returned to the store and now watched Jones ride off. McGee had listened from outside the store as Burns interrogated Jones and found of particular interest Jones was staying at the Globe Inn. He watched Jones riding north toward the town center, and smiled as he thought tonight would be a perfect night for a visit.

CHAPTER 6

Jones rode north on Baltimore Street and quickly reached the Diamond. He steered his horse west onto Chambersburg Street. He rode the short distance to Tate's Eagle Hotel, located at the next major north-south thoroughfare, Washington Street. The hotel was on the northeast corner of the intersection of Washington and Chambersburg Streets. It was a grand hotel, three stories tall, taking up the whole corner of intersection along both streets, adorned in white with the lettering "EAGLE HOTEL" in bright, capital letters between the second and third stories. It had seven windows, each ornamented with brightly colored shutters, across the second and third stories facing Chambersburg Street; those on the second story also functioned as doors, opening to a wrought-iron railing protecting a balcony. The hotel had an "A" shaped roof, slanting to and from Chambersburg Street, and chimneys on both the east and west sides of the building. The entrance was located on the southwest corner of the building.

Jones rode past the hotel, turned the corner north onto Washington Street, got off his horse, and handed the horse over to the boy waiting. He walked back around to Chambersburg Street and entered the hotel. The inside of the hotel was dark, and so Jones hesitated a moment until his eyes got used to the dim lighting. Once his vision cleared, he saw the first floor contained the hotel lobby straight ahead from the entrance, and the restaurant/tavern, located on his left. He made his way to the restaurant on the west side of the building and entered into a large room containing many long tables with adjoining bench seating, located on the left side of the room. It also had smaller, round tables, located on the right side. Each of the round tables, which were closer to the kitchen, had nice linen table cloths. The kitchen was located off the dining room, to the right. Straight ahead was a long bar, about half the length of the room. "That's what I am looking for," he thought, and he made his way over.

"Good afternoon," he said to the man behind the bar. The man was tall, probably in his sixties, mustached, with no beard, mostly bald, with graying hair on the sides of his head. He was a little overweight, but seemed full of energy.

"And to you. What can I get you?"

"How about an ale?"

"I'll have it right up."

The bartender returned shortly and placed the ale in front of Jones, saying: "That will be five cents."

Jones reached into his waist coat and produced five Indian Head Cent pieces and handed them to the bartender.

The bartender looked at the coins and Jones, saying: "Interesting. We don't get many of these types of coins here. I thought so, but now I know for sure, you must be from out of town." Extending his hand he continued: "My name is Tate, John L. Tate. I am the proprietor of this here grand hotel, The Eagle."

Jones took his hand and shook it saying: "My name is Samuel Jones, and you are right that I am a newcomer to the town, as I am a traveling man of business. I sell recipes for fixing the taste of liquor."

"In your travels, have you heard much of the coming of the Rebels? Folks round here are mighty concerned they are coming this way."

"Not any more than can be found in the newspapers, I'm afraid, so I cannot be of much help to answer you."

"Well, at any rate, Mr. Jones, tell me what you mean by fixing the taste of liquor."

"Mr. Tate, I can sell you formulas to make the taste of liquor more pleasant, taste sweeter, add some fruit flavor, and become more appealing to more folks. And, it should be able to make your stock of liquor last. Some of my associates have been able to make their supply last up to three times longer, and earn substantial profit by charging more per drink than the straight liquor."

"Do you have an example of this Mr. Jones?"

"Please call me just Jones. Certainly. Say for example I could give you a very simple recipe for adding a citrus flavor to whiskey, called a whiskey sour, that will not only make it taste better, but will make your stock of whiskey last much longer. And, you will be able to charge your customers more than double the price of a regular whiskey. How much might that be worth to you?"

"Jones, I would be very interested and might be inclined to pay up to $20, if I like the taste and I have sole rights to it here in Gettysburg."

"You sir, have a deal. How about if I write up the recipe and deliver it to you tomorrow over dinner?"

"The next ale is on the house. What time should I expect you and the recipe tomorrow?"

"I shall be here at noon o'clock. Do you mind if I ask you how your business is going? It suits me to make sure there are lots of customers that may enjoy the types of drinks you can make with my recipes. How are you suited with supplies, like flour, sugar, salt, meat, coffee, and tea?"

"It is the hotel's way of doing business that we keep ample supply of all of those in the event the war may put an interruption to our ability to get them. We keep a couple of month's worth at the least, particularly flour, salt, sugar, and salted meat, so you see we have plenty of stock for our customers, and yours."

Jones thanked Tate for the second ale, picked it up and walked around the restaurant. At one of the round tables, he noticed a nice looking couple eating supper. The man looked in his late thirties, with thinning brown hair, long in the back. He had a full beard, which extended a couple of inches below his chin, and was slightly gray. Jones noticed one of his eyes was not moving with the other, so he surmised it might be a glass eye. He was dressed in a blue long sleeved shirt. The lady was about thirty, was dressed elegantly, wearing a blue, narrow, flat skirt, looped for walking, and a blue, high neckline shirt with a white collar, tightly pinned at the neck with a large brooch.

He walked over to the table, which was covered with an elegant white cloth, removed his hat, and said:

"Evening ma'am, sir, I am new to town and wonder if I could join you for pleasant conversation whilst I finish my ale?"

The lady looked up at him while the man stated in a thick Irish accent:

"Certainly; my wife and I always enjoy good conversation, particularly with someone not from around here. Please sit."

Jones extended his hand, saying: "That would be mighty kind of you. My name is Samuel Jones, and I am a traveling man of business."

"Mr. Jones, this lovely lady is Mrs. Sallie Broadhead and I am her husband, Joseph."

Jones shook Joseph's hand and then Sallie's next, and sat down next to Broadhead, across the table from the lady.

"Mr. Jones, what brings you to our fair town?" Broadhead asked.

"Well, I sell recipes to fix the taste of liquor and am here to earn a wage for my family."

Sallie asked with friendly curiosity: "How interesting. Where do you come from and how many children do you have?"

"Mrs. Broadhead…"

"Please, Mr. Jones, call me Sallie, and Mr. Broadhead, Joseph."

"That sounds fair, but only if you call me Jones."

"Do you mind me calling you Samuel? It would be so much more comfortable for me," Sallie asked.

"Sallie, since you have invited me to your table, how can I resist?"

"Good Samuel, now tell us of your family."

Jones thought this lady was really charming, and usually he is the one who can be the charmer, so she must be an extraordinary person. However, it was again time to play his part, so he began to get into the part of the family man.

"I have been married to my Jenny for over ten years now, and we live in the Howellville township, west of Philadelphia. Jenny and I have three little children, William is seven, James is five, and little Jenny is three. They are the light of our world and it is so hard for me to be away from them, but I must, as I am not a farmer."

"How charming Samuel, they just sound grand. You must be very proud."

"That I am, full of pride. Do you mind if I asked about your family?"

Sallie responded: "We have our Mary, she is four years old, and really a treat. She is staying with our neighbor Mrs. Gilbert while Joseph and I have a supper for just ourselves. Joseph operates the town railroad and is gone a good period of time, like you, but not as long, so we like to take supper occasionally, just the two of us."

Jones heard Broadhead worked for the railroad and he couldn't believe his luck. He had found another great source of information about the town, and it essentially just came to him. He said:

"That sounds fine. It is important to spend some time together without the children," Jones said as he remembered his mother and father doing the same when he was a child. He continued to Joseph:

"So, Joseph, you work for the railroad. That must be really interesting work?"

"It is. I'm in charge of the baggage and supplies, and make the run daily. The line runs between Gettysburg and Hanover. It is mainly for transporting goods and supplies in and out of Gettysburg, as most supplies are transported by rail. It is just much faster than by wagon."

"I can imagine. How often to you make runs to Hanover?"

"Just about every day, save Saturday and Sunday. The railroad only runs on those days in rare occasions."

Before he could continue his questions, Tate came to the table and asked about dessert for the Broadheads. Sallie ordered for both saying:

"Joseph and I would like two helpings of Peach Jam Pudding. We hear Mr. Sherfy's trees are producing sweet peaches this year, and so the pudding must be delightful."

"Coming right up, Sallie. Jones, is there anything I can get you?"

"No, thank you, I am fine. I have an appointment for supper at seven o'clock, so I will be on my way in a short while."

Jones then continued his questions about the railroad, as Tate brought the Jam Pudding, saying:

"Do you have a lot of trips where you are gone for several days at a time? It must be hard on Sallie and little Mary. I know it is hard on Jenny and the little ones when I am away."

Sallie answered: "Not very often, Samuel. But, when he is gone, it is so hard on Mary. She is so close to Joseph."

She then took a bite of the Jam Pudding, and said:

"Umm. This is so good, right Joseph? Samuel, do you want some of mine. I don't think I can eat it all."

"I am fine Sallie, but thank you just the same." Changing the subject, and wanting to know how dangerous Burns was to him while he was in town, Jones said:

"I was at that large store, south of here down on Baltimore Street, Fahnestock's I think, today and met an interesting, but strange old fellow named Burns. Do you know him?"

"We certainly do. He and his wife live just down the street from us. He is strange, as you say, but his wife is a real nice lady," Sallie said.

"Is he a constable of this town?"

"No, he hasn't been for the last year or so, but he still thinks he is, and acts like it, too," Joseph replied.

"Yes, I got a hankering of that from him today. He couldn't stop with the questions, mainly about why I came to town. I didn't really get much hospitality from him."

"That's our Mr. Burns. He's suspicious of strangers and grouchy to the folks that live here. A fine combination, wouldn't you say?" Sallie asked.

"Well, does he actually arrest people?"

"He did when he was a constable, but not lately that we know of. So, you are safe," Sallie teased.

"That's good to know, thanks."

Jones finished his ale, looked at his watch, and seeing it was just before seven o'clock, rose from his chair, thanked the Broadheads for their company and excused himself, bowing to Sallie and saying:

"Ma'am, Joseph, I did really enjoy your company. I will be here a couple of days and hope to see you again."

"That would be wonderful, Samuel," Sallie said. And, Joseph replied:

"Good evening, Jones."

Jones turned to Tate and said:

"See you tomorrow at noon o'clock with the recipe."

"I'll be here, Jones. Good evening," Tate replied.

Jones left the hotel, mounted his horse, and rode off to his meeting with Will at the Globe Inn.

CHAPTER 7

BURNS

JOHN L. BURNS and his wife, after leaving Fahnestock's, walked north on Baltimore Street toward home. Mrs. Burns was in bright spirits, mainly due to her pleased nature because of her dress. She liked the pattern and the colors, a red dress with similar floral patterns to the one she was wearing, and so she remarked to Burns:

"I really like the dress and am so looking forward to when it finally arrives. It is even more than I imagined," she said with a smile and excitement in her voice.

"Humff; a traveling man of business, indeed. He's a traitorous, rebel spy, that's what he is."

"Are you still fretting over that nice young man, Mr. Jones? I rather liked him."

"Do you understand the Rebels are coming? Of that there is no doubt; only when. He's a spy, and I aim to prove it. No one can come into my Borough to bring it harm."

"Mr. Burns, you are not a constable in this Borough anymore, so stop acting like it."

"Old woman, I'll act as I see fit and nothing you can say about it can change me or what I do."

Mrs. Burns, knowing how this type of conversation goes with Burns and that she can never dissuade him from what he would do when he gets like this, no matter how fool hearted, said, more to end the topic than anything else:

"Go on, make a fool of yourself, like you always do. See what you can do about a nice young man trying to earn a living to take care of his youngens."

Burns mumbled something under his breath that Mrs. Burns chose to ignore. They reached the Diamond and Mrs. Burns said:

"Let's cross and walk on the north side. You know how I just love to walk by the Eagle."

They crossed the street and turned west on Chambersburg Street. They walked silently together. Soon, they approached Washington Street, and Mrs. Burns glanced at the Eagle Hotel. It was just after five o'clock in the afternoon, and the sun was still quite high. The hotel looked majestic with the sun's rays bouncing off the brightly painted hotel walls and the glistening windows. They crossed Washington Street, and then heard a familiar voice and greeting from a man and woman approaching:

"Good evening, Mr. and Mrs. Burns," Sallie Broadhead said.

"Sallie, how nice to see you. You sure are looking fine this evening. And, Joseph you look downright handsome," Mrs. Burns replied.

"Why, thank you love," Joseph Broadhead said and continued: "Evening, John."

"Joseph," Burns grunted more than spoke, not bothering to give Broadhead a full measure of his attention.

Mrs. Burns continued: "Where are you going dressed so fine?"

"We are taking supper at the Eagle Hotel this evening. It is our night out," Sallie said.

"How wonderful. I hope you have a fine supper together. How's Mary getting along? She is such a nice little girl. You two should be very proud."

"How nice of you to say. She is fine and is spending some time with Mrs. Gilbert this evening."

Burns, tired of this idle chatter, began to walk on. Mrs. Burns looked annoyingly at him as he was leaving and realized she must end the conversation politely, so she said:

"Well, we must be going. Enjoy your evening and that you are still young enough to enjoy time together," she said with a stab at Burns, which he ignored by not stopping or even slowing his pace.

"Thank you and good evening," Sallie replied, and she and Broadhead walked on.

The Burnses walked west to Franklin Street, crossed Chambersburg Street to the south side, passed the Slentz' house, and continued to their house near the Chambersburg Pike. They turned south along the alley next to their house, and then climbed the steps to their second story entrance to the house.

The Burns' house faced Chambersburg Street and was a two-story, white dwelling with, east to west, three windows on the first floor, adjacent to a double door storage area. The second story had three windows, matching those on the first floor, next to the porch area, which served as the landing for the stairs descending down to ground, next to the alley west of the house. The second story was completed with another window off the kitchen. It had an "A" framed roof with two chimneys, one each on the west and east sides of the house, the westerly chimney off of the kitchen and the easterly one off of the parlor/living room.

They entered the house and Mrs. Burns removed her bonnet and coat and hung them in the hallway leading to the kitchen. Burns did the same with his hat and coat and, without a word to his wife, walked past the kitchen to his right and turned toward the parlor area on the east side of the house. He found his usual chair in the parlor and sat contemplating what he should do about the suspicious stranger. He reflected on the conversation he had with Jones at the store. A traveling man of business, yet he sells, what did he say, "recipes to fix the taste of liquor"? Shouldn't a peddler peddle items of use to sell folks, tools, or the like? He puzzled on this for awhile and then he heard Mrs. Burns summon him for supper.

"Not now, woman, I'm busy," he replied to her.

Mrs. Burns answered in an annoyed tone and referenced her name for him when she was so:

"John Burns, supper is ready, and you will come at once to eat it! She paused and then continued:

"Besides, Martha is off with the baby and I should like to have some company!" referring to their adopted daughter, Martha Gilbert, and her baby girl.

Burns reluctantly got out of his chair and made his way to the kitchen table, where a plate of boiled beef was set for him. He approached the basin stand silently and washed his hands in the basin, dried them with a towel and sat at table. Mrs. Burns sat down and passed him a plate of corn meal bread.

Burns, still thinking of Jones, said:

"Why would a real peddler offer recipes and not goods...?" His expression was that of not requesting an answer from her, but rather more like talking aloud. She answered anyway:

"Why can you not let the poor fellow be?"

"Woman, how many times must I tell you it is my responsibility to know what he is doing in our town?" emphasizing the word "know."

"You won't be satisfied until you have him thrown in jail, will you?"

"If that is where he belongs, then the sooner I get him there the better, and that sooner means tonight. I am going out right after supper."

"You'd be better served to get a good rest this evening. Martha's got schooling tomorrow so we shall be caring for the baby," Mrs. Burns said.

"That is fine for *you*," again emphasizing a word, this time "you." He continued: "Looking after babies is for women. I shall be busy with your Mr. Jones."

They finished supper and Burns announced he would be leaving for the evening. He put on his coat and hat and then, as Mrs. Burns cleared the table, went to his study to fetch his Paterson Colt No. 5 revolver he purchased when he was first elected constable of Gettysburg in '53. His Colt was a .36 caliber, six-shot pistol with a four-inch barrel and a folding trigger. He loaded the gun and placed it in his right coat pocket. He then left the house without so much as a word to his wife. He descended down the stairs, walked down the alley and then east on Chambersburg Street toward town.

Burns decided to cross Chambersburg Street to the walk along the north side, so he crossed at Franklin, essentially retracing his and his wife's path earlier. And, like earlier, he noticed the Broadheads, but this time they were exiting the Eagle Hotel making their way home. They saw him and Sallie again greeted him warmly:

"Mr. Burns, a pleasure again to see you. Say, we met this nice young man at supper, who said he met you earlier today, a Mr. Samuel Jones."

"Jones, you say…?," and he immediately took interest in talking with them. He continued: "I think he is a spy. What was he doing at the Eagle?"

"Huh, a spy, really? Are you sure? He just seems like such a nice man and he has such a nice family waiting for him back in Philadelphia," Sallie said.

Broadhead chimed in saying: "John, you must be mistaken. He's no spy, but just a man looking to make a little money."

Burns ignored Broadhead and concentrated on Sallie. He said to her: "What was he doing there?"

"Well, he had a talk with Mr. Tate at the bar, shook hands and then came over to our table wanting conversation whilst he finished his ale."

"Could you hear what they were talking about?"

"Well, you will have to ask Mr. Tate, and we were not prying, but I thought I overheard Mr. Jones talking about some type of drink mixture. Mr. Tate was very interested and it seemed like they struck a deal on it."

"Yes, yes, the liquor mixture. Did they talk about anything else? Something unusual you might remember?"

"Well, now that you put it that way, there was something a little strange. I think I overheard Jones asking about how much supplies the hotel kept."

"*Supplies*, are you sure?"

"Well I can't say for positive, but that's what I thought I heard. He sure was curious about Joseph working for the railroad."

"Is he still there?"

"No, he left just before us, about a quarter of an hour ago."

"Did he say where he was going?"

"Joseph, did you hear him say, because I cannot recall him doing so?"

"Love, no he didn't. John, we just enjoyed his visit and didn't really think anything suspicious about him."

"Well, it's a good thing I am. You folks should be more aware of strangers. Them Rebs are coming and they may already be here. It would do us a lot of good if you folks could understand that like I do," Burns said in his usual, sarcastic way. He concluded saying:

"I must be on my way." He left the Broadheads without even a thank you or goodbye.

After leaving the Broadheads behind, Burns decided he will visit the Eagle and Tate. He became excited due to his quest and because of this, his heart beat and his walking pace quickened. He thought to himself: "I knew he was a spy, after all why would a traveling peddler be concerned about supplies at the Eagle, unless he was a forager for the Rebel army? I need to talk to Tate, and then George Swope from the Bank of Gettysburg. Yes, that's right, Jones said he had been to the bank earlier today, but Swope wouldn't be right."

He thought for a moment, and then remembered T. Duncan Carson worked in the bank, and would be one to a talk to, and he lived between the bank and the Globe Inn. He continued his thought pattern: "I'll go back down to the Fahnestock's, no to Franklin's house."

He formulated in his mind his path, first to the Eagle to talk to Tate, then to Franklin's house, then back up Baltimore Street to York Street to Carson's house, then to the Globe Inn and confront Jones.

He looked at his watch. It was half past seven o'clock. The sun had not yet disappeared under South Mountain to the west as he approached the hotel. He crossed Washington Street and entered the hotel. As it was still a semblance of daylight outside, he had to wait for his eyes to adjust to the dark inside. Once his eyes adjusted to the lamp-lit interior, he made his way over to the tavern and to the bar. Tate greeted him, while serving an ale to another customer:

"Evening, John. Didn't think I'd see you in here, and with the way you feel about the drink, you usually don't enter the tavern area."

"Not here for pleasure, Tate, for answers to some questions."

"Must be important for you to take company with the drunken heathens," Tate replied poking fun at him and his devoted belief in temperance.

"That it is Tate, but never mind that. You had a customer by the name of Jones earlier this evening, is that the truth?"

"Why yes. A Mr. Samuel Jones. I am purchasing a drink recipe from him, not that it would interest you. Just what is your concern with him?"

"I think he is a traitorous, Rebel spy. You know the Rebels are coming and they are sending men like Jones on ahead."

"You must be daft. That man a spy? He's no more a spy than I am."

"Of that, Tate, we shall see. Were the Broadheads here for supper this evening?"

"Sure were. They ate a great meal and enjoyed themselves. Say, they took dessert with your Mr. Jones and spent about a half hour visiting with him at their table."

Tate was called to the other side of the bar, saying:

"Excuse me. Let me take care of this and I'll return shortly."

Burns thought to himself: "How come these people can't see what I see? Too wrapped up in making money, probably. And, too many false alarms about the Rebels coming, so now they don't believe it at all." Tate returned, and Burns said:

"Sallie Broadhead said Jones had a long talk with you, even asked about the stock of supplies at the hotel."

"Yes he did. I thought it a little strange, but he wanted to make sure the hotel had a lot of customers for the drink he was selling me."

"Why would he concern himself with that if he already sold you the mix?"

"I guess he wants to make a name for himself so he could sell me another."

"Maybe he wants to make sure there are ample supplies for the invading Rebel army when they get here?"

It hit Tate just then that the old fool Burns might just be right. Tate had never taken Burns seriously before now, as not many of the townsfolk had. He had been at times the target of many jokes and pranks, some of which Tate had been a party to. He thought: "Could he be right about Jones?" Seeing the look on Tate's face and getting no response, Burns continued:

"I aim to arrest him. When did he leave and do you know where he went?"

"About a half hour ago and no, he didn't say where he was going. A spy, do you really think so?"

"Yep, I'll find him and when I do, I aim to throw him in jail where he belongs!"

And with that, Burns left the tavern and the hotel.

Burns made his way down Washington Street and turned east onto West Middle Street. The sun dipped below South Mountain and dusk began when he arrived at Franklin's house. He debated knocking as it was half past eight in the evening, but this was too important a pursuit to worry about disturbing him, and this type of worry wasn't common to him anyway. He walked up the stairs to Franklin's house and knocked on the door loudly. After about a minute, Franklin opened the door, and said with a surprised tone:

"Mr. Burns, I didn't think it would be you. Why are you here at this time of the evening?"

"Franklin, I have some questions for you."

"Really, at this time of night? What could be so important it cannot wait until tomorrow?"

"I need to know about that Mr. Jones. I think he is a spy, like I said today at the store. Did he ask you a lot of questions, maybe about supplies?"

"Mr. Burns, Jones is just a nice man who is visiting. He cannot be a spy, he even defended Ginnie Wade's honor against that rogue Silas McGee."

"Well, Franklin, did Jones ask about supplies within the store?"

"Yes, he did. He seemed most interested in the store's supplies, whether the war affected our ability to get them, and he even asked about men's shoes. I thought it queer he would ask about the shoes. I told him how we get our supplies mainly here in Gettysburg, and those we cannot get here, we get by the railroad from Philadelphia, Hanover, Baltimore, York, and as far away as New Jersey and New York, and that we always keep a couple of months at the store just in case of shipping problems caused the war."

"Franklin, did you ever think he may be foraging for the Rebel army, looking for towns with enough goods for an army the size of theirs' and that you gave him all the information he would need about our town? And, shoes. Wouldn't you think a large army would be in need of those?" He dropped his chin, shook his head and then said: "For God's sake man, if they weren't coming to Gettysburg before, they sure will be now. I've got to stop him before he leaves town and reports this information. I must throw him in jail where he belongs."

Franklin didn't know what to say. And, then he thought to himself: "Burns is an old fool, who thinks everyone is a spy or a criminal. What more does he have with his life to do?" He responded quickly:

"Mr. Burns, if everyone is a spy who comes from out of town, our jails would be full."

But, Burns was already down the steps, purposely too far away to hear or to care of what was said. Skelly closed the door.

Burns thought: "Supplies, shoes…now if he was interested in the town's cash, then I have him."

He made his way to Baltimore Street and north toward the Diamond. He crossed to the east side of Baltimore Street at the Diamond, and then crossed York Street to the north side of the street. The evening was in full and the street lamps were all lit. He passed the Tipton's Barber Shop, the Robert McCreary House, the bank, and then came to T. Duncan Carson's house. He climbed the stairs and knocked on the door to Carson's house. It was just before nine o'clock. Carson answered saying:

"Constable Burns, what a surprise. What brings you to my house to-night?" showing him legal respect, yet wondering if Burns was here for him, but knowing he hadn't done anything to warrant this visit.

"Carson, I have some questions for you." He continued saying: "Were you working at the bank today?"

"Yes, I was there during my normal hours, from 10am to 5pm."

"In the late forenoon or afternoon, did a well dressed man, a stranger to this town, come to the bank and ask any questions about the bank's business?"

"No, I didn't help anyone not from the town today. Why do you ask?"

"Never mind that. How about anyone strange hanging around the bank?"

"No, can't say I saw anyone hanging around outside, except our usual folks."

"Think, man. There must have been someone who you didn't recognize."

Carson thought for a moment, and then realized he did see a stranger a couple of times at the front of the bank, but never once did he enter. He said:

"Now that I think about it, I did see a man, well dressed as you say, about midday. He passed by the bank several times for what seemed at least an hour. I kept thinking he would come in, but he never did. I did see him talk to several customers as they left the bank."

"So, he never came in?"

"No, he didn't. But, he seemed interested, like he should have come in. As I said, I thought he would. But, when he didn't I dismissed it as someone who wasn't trusting of the bank, and nothing more. What is so interesting about this man?"

"He's a spy and I aim to arrest him."

"A spy, in our town?"

"Why do you people not think spies are nosing around Gettysburg? The Reb army is coming, and so their spies come first. It would do you good, and also the bank, to keep your eyes open and be mindful of strangers to our town."

And, with that comment, he left.

Burns walked on pavement toward the Globe Inn. As he approached, he looked up at the inn. It was a two-story building with a large, A-frame roof and chimneys on each the west and east ends of the building. The roof was supported by six columns across the front side, facing York Street. The entrance was located on the southwest side of the building, and the first floor had four windows east of the entrance. The second floor had five windows and a balcony with a railing across the full length of the inn. Burns entered the inn and went directly to the east side where the restaurant/tavern was, looking for John Charles Will. He entered the tavern area, and found Will serving customers some plates of supper. He hesitated momentarily, and then made his way over to Will.

"Will, do you have a couple of moments for some questions?" he asked.

"Why, Mr. Burns what is this all about?"

"I have some questions for you about someone staying at this inn."

"Well, give me a moment to finish up here and I will meet you over by the entrance."

Burns acknowledged Will's request and went over the entrance to wait for him. After a couple of minutes, Will came over. Burns said:

"Serving supper a little late this evening?"

"Mr. Burns, you know the Globe is always willing to serve our customers, no matter who or what time."

"Yes, I have heard that. Now, I want to ask you about a man named Jones. Is he staying here at the inn?"

"Yes he is. In fact I just finished having supper with the nice gentlemen about an hour ago. We have agreed to do some business. Why? What do you want to know of him?"

"I believe he is a spy…"

Will interrupted him before he could finish, saying:

"A spy? What kind of prank is this? I have heard your history with pranks in this town. But, what I heard is they were always played on you. Is it now your turn to play on others?"

"Good God, man. This is serious business. He has been going around town asking about supplies and spying on the bank."

"I know what he has been up to. I suggested places for him to go see. He is looking to establish a business here, and is curious about the town's wealth in both supplies and money, seeing if this would be a good place to visit on a regular basis."

"Don't you know the Rebel army is on their way and men like Jones will come first?"

"Sure, we have heard all about the Rebel army coming, for what now two years? How many times have the townsfolk been stirred up by rumors of the Rebs? I remember our town being alarmed last year when the Rebel cavalry was in Chambersburg, but they never made it past South Mountain and to Gettysburg. Don't you think you are obsessed with this idea of spies among us? This is not your first time with this accusation."

"Will, are you blind or just dumb? They are coming. Don't you read the news?"

"Plenty, but I have more important business and that is making sure the Globe is taken care of. If not, don't you think I would be in the army?"

"I don't know about you, but I would if I was younger, I would already be in the army fighting those traitors, whether or not I needed to take care of the Globe Inn's business."

"Mr. Burns, with all due respect sir, I am not you. Now what else can I answer for you? I must get back to my paying customers."

"Is he still here?"

"Yes, he is. But, you will not disturb him tonight. He is our guest and he has come to get a nice meal and a rest. He has had his meal, and now he will get his rest. If you want to talk with him, you will do it in the morning, so come back then."

"You will not allow me to talk with him tonight?"

"That is right. As I said, he is our guest, and I will not have him disturbed by your wild ideas of him being a spy."

"Alright, but make no mistake about it, I will be back in the morning. And, if I lose him, I will hold you responsible."

"Fine, and when you come tomorrow, bring an appetite for dinner, as I would at least like you to pay for a meal here for my trouble and for that of my guest."

"Never mind that Will, just make sure he is here tomorrow for me, as you can count on me being here."

And with that, Burns left the inn for home. He would be back in the morning. Of that he was sure of. He walked the long walk past the Diamond and along Chambersburg Street to his house. He thought to himself: "Jones, tomorrow you will be in jail. It would have been tonight if not for that dumb John Charles Will."

CHAPTER 8

WILL

JOHN CHARLES WILL was setting up for the supper hours, straightening the long tables and the benches, making sure the table clothes for the individual tables looked neat and clean, and adding napkins and silverware where appropriate. It was five o'clock and he was hard at this work, when his father came into the restaurant area and greeted him warmly:

"John, the restaurant looks real good. I think we are ready for our guests for supper. How's the food coming along?"

"Father, yes we are. As usual, this being Thursday, we are serving generous portions of Pork Cutlets. We also have another batch of Hog Maw; Boiled Beef; and Veal and Ham Pie available for those who want something else. The Onion Soup is just about ready, and the Jam Pudding will be ready in an hour or so."

"You always have things under control. I don't know why I bother to ask, so I'll be getting to the bar and making it ready."

Charles Will was in his fifties, of average height, with a full head of hair, graying at the temples. He wore a long sleeve white shirt buttoned up to the neck, with a Baker City red waist coat, adorned with two rows of vertical buttons, black trousers, and matching black boots. Charles made his way over to the bar, and John followed. John decided now was the best time to talk to him about purchasing the liquor recipe from Jones, so he started by saying:

"Father, we have a guest staying here at the inn who is a traveling man of business. I had a conversation with him during dinner here, and he has offered to sell us a recipe for a liquor drink, that can make brandy taste like champagne."

"Really, tell me more about it."

"Well, the man's name is Samuel Jones, and he is from Baltimore. He told me that we could mix our white brandy with currants, and some other common ingredients we have here, and make a drink called Currant Champagne."

Charles seemed interested, and didn't reply, allowing John to continue.

"Jones also said this recipe could make our supply of white brandy last two, maybe even three times as long, and with the taste of this champagne, we could charge more per drink, raising our profits maybe by three times."

"That is very appealing. Did he say how much he wants for the recipe? And, will he provide a sample so we can taste it?"

"Father, these are to be discussed as I am having supper with him at seven o'clock here."

"John, have you thought of the price you want to pay for it?"

"That I have, and I am thinking $15, but no more than $20."

"That's a large investment. Do you know how long it would be to make it back?"

"The way I figure it, given at least a doubling of our supply of brandy, and maybe charging two pennies more for a drink, we should be able to clear about thirty cents per night extra at the supper hour, so it should be between one and two months at the most, and then beyond that, it would be pure profit. So, what do you think?"

"Two months, huh? I leave this up to you, and whatever you decide, I will support your decision."

"I'll work the details out with Jones at supper."

"That sounds fine. Make sure you introduce him to me, as I would like to meet him."

At a couple of minutes after seven o'clock, Jones walked into the restaurant, and greeted Will warmly:

"John, good evening. Are you ready for our supper together to discuss Currant Champagne?"

"Yes, but before we sit, I want you to meet my father."

They walked over to the bar, and while Charles was serving a drink to a customer, John called to him, saying:

"Father, I would like you to meet Mr. Samuel Jones."

Charles Will came over to the end of the bar where Jones and Will were, extended his hand to Jones and said:

"I'm Charles Will. Mr. Jones, John has told me about you, and your recipe. I am pleased to meet you."

Jones shook Charles hand and said:

"Likewise, sir. And, I am looking forward to a nice meal, and a successful business venture, with John, here," as he gestured toward young Will.

"Mr. Jones, where are you from, and have you heard much news about the Rebel army?"

"Baltimore, sir. And, no I haven't any news of the Rebels, not more than can be read in the newspapers, I am afraid."

"Well, folks around here get mighty alarmed when they hear the Rebels are coming. We have heard it so many times before, but I don't think it is true.

Our boys will never let them get into Pennsylvania. Well, never mind that. What is important, here, is we continue our business and make this inn the most appealing place for visitors, like yourself, coming to Gettysburg," he said gesturing his hand across his body to signify the whole room.

"You and your son, John sure have made it that way for me. I couldn't ask for any more hospitality than I have been shown."

"Glad to hear it. Well, I don't want to take any more of your time as you and John have business to discuss. Please let us know if there is anything you require to make your stay here at the inn more pleasant. All you have to do is ask."

And with that, Charles Will made his way to the other end of the bar to serve the other customers. Will led Jones to the table, set off on its own, which was used for special customers, or in this case, a place to talk business.

"Here's our table. Have a seat and make yourself comfortable."

Jones sat in one of the chairs, removed his hat and placed it on the chair next to his. Will sat in the opposite chair, and said:

"Let's order some supper first, and then we can talk business. We have more Hog Maw, like you had for dinner today; Boiled Beef; Veal and Ham Pie; or our specialty for today, Pork Cutlets. We flour and bread the cutlets and then cook them in hot lard. It is really delicious, and we serve them with corn-meal bread. We can start off the meal with Onion Soup, and complete it with Peach Jam Pudding."

"The cutlets would be wonderful, in fact the whole meal sounds grand."

"And, an ale? I'll bring it right over?"

"Ideal."

Will disappeared into the kitchen for a moment, and then went to the bar to get two ales. He returned to the table and set one in front of Jones and the other where he was sitting.

"So, how was the rest of your day looking around our fine town?"

"Very informative. I went down to Fahnestock's and met some very interesting people. I did the same at the Eagle before returning to the inn."

He took a drink of his ale, and continued:

"At Fahnestock's, I had to take care of a bothersome oaf named McGee who was badgering a young lady by the name of Wade."

"McGee, huh, that would be Silas. He is an overgrown child, a bully, and a drunk. I trust you weren't hurt?"

"Naw, he was nothing I couldn't handle, and did so. I have had much worse encounters on the docks in Baltimore. He was not much of a concern. I also met a former constable named Burns, who had a lot of questions for me."

"Aw, our Mr. Burns. He is a grouchy old man who sees the worst in most people, particularly of anyone who has a drink of liquor, as he is firmly against it."

"Well, then let me propose a toast to him."

Jones raised his mug and said:

"Here's to Mr. Burns. May he one day find the healing powers of the drink. But, for him not too much."

Will laughed, raised his mug, clicked it against Jones' and drank. As they placed their mugs back on the table, the server brought over two bowls of Onion Soup, and placed them in front of the men.

"Umm, that sure smells good," Jones offered.

"Just one of our specialties here at the inn. I hope you enjoy it as much as I do."

Jones unfolded his napkin, placed it on his lap, and continued:

"Shall we talk about the Currant Champagne? Have you had a chance to think about it? I assume from your father's discussion, you have talked to him about it?"

"I have talked with Father, and he will support whatever decision I make about it. And, I have thought about it and am willing to offer you $15 for it."

"John, you are to the point, and I like that about you. Usually, I would want to get $20 for it, and am selling Mr. Tate at the Eagle a recipe for $20, but because I like you, and your inn here, I will accept your price."

Will was pleased he got the price he wanted and without having to haggle with Jones. He smiled and said:

"Now, let me make a toast. Here's to the Globe Inn's new drink, Currant Champagne."

The two men clicked mugs again and drank.

"Now, let's talk of the details of our arrangement. I want to sample the drink, prior to the completion of our transaction. Can you make a batch?"

"I can indeed. I will draw up a bill of sale tonight, which we can sign tomorrow, and as a part of the bill, I will make a small batch, bottle it, and then let it mix together for a couple of days, whilst I move on to another town. I will return to open and sample the mixture, and do all prior to payment of the $15. I will need you, however to procure the supplies, including the currants. I will make a list of the ingredients I need and will give it to you with the bill tomorrow. How does that sound?"

"Fine, when tomorrow can you provide these to me?"

"In the morning. I will get it written up tonight."

"Deal," Will said and offered his hand to show his acceptance. Jones shook his hand with a nod. Just then, the plates of Pork Cutlets, and a basket of warm bread, arrived and were placed on the table. Jones remarked:

"You folks sure know how to cook up a great meal."

"Enjoy, and if you would like more, just ask," Will said as he passed the bread to Jones.

"Thank you. Say, I also met this very dignified and interesting colored woman by the name of Elizabeth Butler at Fahnestock's today. She told me her husband Samuel works for you here at the inn? If so, can I meet him?"

"Yes, he does. Just a moment."

Will got up from the table and went into the kitchen. He returned a minute later, followed by a large, colored man.

"Samuel, this here is Mr. Jones. He met Liz today and wanted to make your acquaintance."

Samuel Butler was in his fifties, looked just shy of six feet tall, had broad shoulders, and was bald. He was wearing a white long-sleeved shirt, blue trousers held up by black braces, and had black boots. He also wore a white apron, which he used to dry his hands before offering to shake Jones' hand.

"Samuel here is a wagon maker by trade, but to earn extra money, he helps us out here at the inn," Will added.

"Misser Jones, I's pleezed to meet ya."

"Likewise, Samuel. Liz told me to tell you be home by ten."

"Well sur, I's gots to do my werk fore I's go."

"I'm sure that is the case. Your wife is a remarkable woman, Samuel."

"Yes, sur, Ol' Liz, she a fine womun. Well, I's gots to git back to werk. Sure nice to meet ya, Misser Jones, yes sur."

"And you, Samuel."

With that, Samuel went back to the kitchen and Will returned to his seat. After they finished their meal, the dessert arrived, and Jones noted:

"The Broadheads had Peach Jam Pudding at the Eagle, and it looked good there, but not like this."

After taking a bite of the pudding, he remarked in confirmation:

"Not like this, indeed."

The two men finished their meal, and as they sat back, a man approached the table. It was McGee, who went over and stood right next to Jones, looking down on him and saying:

"Well, now Mr. Jones, we meet again," McGee said, again slurring his words and swaying, as he was even drunker than earlier today, having spent the day in a bottle.

Will answered quickly:

"McGee, we will not have any trouble in our restaurant or our inn. So, I will kindly ask you to leave."

"Oh, no trouble, Will. I just wanted to be friendly to our guest in town," he said as he leaned on Jones.

Jones was about to rise when Will put his hand across the table on his arm as if to say, he will handle McGee and to stay seated. Jones understood. Will continued, but softened his language:

"Silas, why don't you go home to your wife and leave Mr. Jones be? I'm sure she is worried about where you are."

"In due time, Will. I just wanted Mr. Jones to know we still have some unfinished business, and to remind him I will be looking to collect on the debt he owes me."

Seeing reasoning with this drunken fool wasn't getting anywhere, Will delivered an ultimatum to him, saying:

"Silas, don't misunderstand me. There will be no trouble in my inn, and if you don't leave straight away, I will have you thrown out."

McGee looked over at Will and Will met his gaze. McGee then retreated, saying:

"Okay, Will. I'm leaving, but just so you will know, I aim to collect that debt you owe me, Mr. Jones, before you leave town."

And with that, he turned for the exit, walked out, swaying, and the tipping his hat to folks as he left.

Jones, then looking at his watch and it being after eight o'clock, said to Will:

"Thanks for the help with that idiot, although I am not used to having others fight for me. Also, thanks for the meal. Now, I must retire to my room and get writing that bill and the ingredients list. If you can make sure I am not disturbed, I know I can have it done by the morning."

"You can count on that. I'll personally make sure you are not disturbed in any way, and I look forward to meeting you in the morning to complete our agreement. Shall we say nine o'clock?"

"Fine, in the morning then?"

Jones shook Will's hand once more, rose from his chair, placed his hat upon his head and left the restaurant for his room. Will watched him leave, very pleased with the deal he struck with Jones. Now, if he would just be able to deliver.

A little after nine o'clock, Will was serving late supper to some guests, when John L. Burns approached him in the restaurant. Will had a rather heated discussion with Burns about Jones, which ended with Will dismissing Burns without letting him talk to Jones, but Burns promised to return in the morning. Will decided he should warn Jones about Burns' impending visit in the morning. He climbed the stairs to the second floor and went down the hall to Jones' room. He listened at the door and hearing a noise of movement inside, he knocked on the door. Jones opened the door, slightly, and said:

"Oh, John. I was just working on the bill. Is there something wrong? Did you change your mind?"

"No, no. I wanted to warn you about Mr. Burns. He stopped by the inn tonight and just left. He wanted to talk to you. He thinks you might be a spy. I didn't let him come up, but I cannot stop him from coming by tomorrow, and he will be here in the morning, the stubborn cuss."

"Can he arrest me?"

"He can, but I know the constables won't let him unless he has something more than suspicion. He wouldn't, would he?"

Jones thought he was done for the day playing his part, but clearly he wasn't. He had to get rid of Will, so he could finish his report for General Early. So, again into the traveling man act, and he said:

"I'm just what I said I am, a traveling man of business. Tomorrow, I will answer any questions Mr. Burns wants to ask."

"That's good. I just felt it my duty to let you know he was coming in the morning."

"Thanks again. Now, if I can get back to drawing up that bill and the ingredients list."

"Certainly, good night Jones."

"And, you the same John," Jones said as he closed the door.

For the first time, Will had a slight suspicion about Jones, as he thought it strange that Jones only opened the door ever so slightly, and didn't invite him in, as the conversation took place in the hallway. But, then he thought: "That Burns…now he has me suspicious."

After Will left, Jones began to panic a little. His day was too public as he now has two enemies in town, and after only the first day. He said silently so only he could hear: "Nicely done Jones; maybe you aren't as good as you think you are."

As he thought this, he also knew he must leave the town before sunup, as Burns could be here first thing in the morning. And McGee, who knows when he will show up to cause trouble? He decided to head to York right away instead of waiting until Sunday. But, first he must finish his report to Early, and this may take some time, so he must get to it.

Jones wrote a long report detailing his visit to the stores, the bank, and the Eagle Hotel, as well as the inn, including how friendly and hospitable the inn was. He concluded his report by recommending the army indeed visit Gettysburg, and even included a shopping list for Early. The list included:

> 7000 lbs. of Bacon.
> 1200 lbs. of Sugar.
> 1000 lbs. of Salt.
> 600 lbs. of Coffee.
> 60 barrels of Flour.
> 10 barrels of Onions.
> 10 barrels of Whiskey.
> 1000 pairs of Shoes.
> 500 hats.
> Or, $5000.

It was about two o'clock in the morning, when he put the finishing touch on his report, folded the papers carefully and put it into his saddle-bag. He also put two envelopes on the desk, one addressed to "John Charles Will," and the other to "John L. Tate." The inn was quiet at that time of night, but just then he heard a sound coming from the hall. He pulled his derringer from his coat, and approached the door, listening intently. He thought: "It couldn't be Burns, but was it McGee?"

He listened for a moment, barely breathing. He heard what he thought were footsteps in the hall, but then there were no sounds. He decided to listen near the partition separating his room from the one next to his to see if that was the source of the noise. He moved to the partition and listened. A couple of minutes of silence produced no new sounds, so he put his gun back into his coat, blew out the desk lamp, and retired for a few hours of sleep, before he would leave prior to the sun rising.

Will retired about eleven o'clock. His room was right next to Jones', and was separated by a partition, which had a slight tear, wide enough for Will to look in on Jones. Curiosity got the better of him, and seeing the light from the desk lamp shining through the tear, he walked silently over and peeked through. He saw Jones sitting at the desk, working hard at writing the bill. Good, he thought, he will be able to deliver. Being tired, Will decided it was time for him to turn in. He turned down the wall lamp, and went to bed.

Something woke him about two o'clock, and he looked over at the partition. Seeing the lamp light still coming through, he knew Jones was still working. He went over for another peek, and then heard a noise from the hall. He looked over at the door, and then back through the tear, just in time to see Jones pull a pistol from his coat pocket and walk silently to the back of his room door. He thought: "Why would Jones have a gun?"

He continued to look through the tear, when he thought he saw Jones look over toward the partition and him. He looked away, and then silently moved away from the partition. Just in time, as he heard Jones come over to it. Will was barely breathing as he stood silently. A minute passed, and Will began to sweat. Then, another. Had he moved or was he still there? Finally, he heard Jones move away from the partition and over to the bed. He did the same as quietly as possible, removing the covers and slipping inside, where he decided he should stay until morning.

Jones awoke just before five o'clock in the morning. Good, it was still dark, he thought. He gathered his saddlebag, put on his boots, his coat and hat, and quietly opened his room door. Silently, he went down the stairs, opened the door, and exited the inn. It was a good thing for him he paid attention, when he came back from his visit of the town and just before supper with Will, to where his horse was being boarded, and he knew he could get in to the stable and escape fairly quietly. He turned east on York Street and then north into the alley leading to the stable. He was about half way down the alley, when McGee appeared from the shadows, blocking the alley and brandishing a long knife in his right hand.

"Well now, Jones, leaving town so soon? I knew you were a coward."

"McGee, let me pass. I don't want to fight you. I have an appointment I need to get to early this morning."

"You sure do, and it is with me."

"No, it is with someone else. Now, I must pass."

"Not without me getting a pound of your flesh you owe me," he said while patting the blade of the knife into his left palm.

Jones thought, this is not good. A fight will likely wake up everyone around here and they would see he was leaving, and they would find his report to Early. He would be arrested and held in jail to wait being charged as a spy. Damn McGee. Think man, what to do? He decided he had to fight, and to dispose of him as quickly, and quietly, as possible. He took steps toward McGee and analyzed whether he was still drunk. Seeing that he was, he formulated a plan. If he could get on top of him before he could jab with the knife, he could get it from him and then turn the tables on him. He would not make any more noise than necessary and counted on McGee to do the same, as being beaten twice in one day would be not something McGee would want to the townsfolk to know. For comfort, he felt his right pocket, knowing the derringer was there should he need it. He needed a diversion, and so he decided to play along with McGee, saying as he moved closer:

"McGee, I really wanted to apologize for today. I shouldn't have gotten involved. And, besides, Miss Wade told me after you left I shouldn't have, as she secretly wants you to visit her."

McGee was taken by surprise, and said:

"She did? "

"Yes, she said she gets so lonely with Jack being away at the war," Jones said as he came even closer, close enough now to smell his foul breath.

"I knew it. I knew she wanted my company."

Jones now knew he was close enough to make his move. He extended his hand, saying:

"Do you accept my apology? Let's shake on it."

As he was finishing his sentence, he lunged at McGee with both hands. His left hand grabbed McGee's right wrist, momentarily holding off the knife. With his right hand, he punched McGee square in the throat, and then followed with a crushing blow to his temple. McGee lost his balance and fell backwards into the dirt. Jones still held his right wrist as he went down, shoving McGee down with his left arm. Once he was down, Jones pounced on him and with both hands jerked the knife from his grip. He grabbed the knife and whipped it around to McGee's throat. This all happened in a blur to McGee, and as he lay on the ground, he couldn't breathe because of the blow to his throat. He was unaware of the knife to his throat until Jones leaned close to him and said:

"I thank you for the knife, McGee. I want you to remember that it is I who could cut you like the pig you are, but I'll not tonight, as I am in a generous mood, and I have an urgent appointment to get to. Just so you will know, that lady, Miss Wade, thinks you are pig also, and didn't say what I told you, as it was a well placed lie."

He continued saying:

"Should you follow me, or in any way try to stop me, I will kill you."

He then reached into his pocket and removed the derringer, and holding it to McGee's temple, said:

"I'm pretty handy with this, and am a very good shot, so if you want to see your wife ever again, you will lay here quietly until after you hear me ride off."

McGee could only manage a nod, not able to talk and barely able to breathe. He was afraid for his life, and still groggy from the blows he absorbed. Jones quickly got up, retrieved his saddlebag and sprinted to the stable. He found his horse, saddled it up, climbed aboard and rode up the alley toward York Street. He saw McGee still lying on the ground, grasping for breath, and he kicked the horse, and so it galloped faster, right at McGee. Reaching McGee, who was groveling on the ground in fear, the horse jumped over him, close enough that the shoe from the lead hoof clipped McGee in the head. Jones and the horse then turned east on York Street and toward the edge of town.

In less than a minute, Jones left Gettysburg behind in a cloud of dust.

CHAPTER 9

WILL

JOHN CHARLES WILL awoke on Friday morning the 5th of June very anxious. He spent a restless night where he witnessed his prospective business partner, Samuel Jones, pull a gun in response to noises in the hallway outside the door of his room. He saw this very clearly through a tear in the partition separating Jones' room with his. Will also thought Jones saw him spying as Jones made his way to the partition to investigate. Will had stayed very quiet. Satisfied, Jones went to bed and Will quietly did the same.

It was about eight o'clock in the morning when Will got out of bed. He made his way silently over to the partition and looked into Jones' room. Jones wasn't there. Will, wondering if Jones would be downstairs in the inn, maybe having breakfast, dressed and left his room, went down the stairs and into the restaurant/tavern. He looked at the few customers sitting at the long tables, but Jones was not among them. He then went back to his room to dress for working at the restaurant.

Will was serving customers shortly before nine o'clock when he saw John L. Burns enter the restaurant. Burns made his way over and said:

"Will, I am here to question Jones, as I said I would night last."

"Mr. Burns, I haven't seen Jones this morning. He must be about the town."

"Are you sure he hasn't left? Did he check out of the inn?"

"Not that I know of."

Burns was getting very irritated and said, "Will, is he still here or not?"

Will matched the intensity of the moment, saying: "How should I know? I am not his keeper."

"Good Lord man, can't you look in his room? If he is still here, he should have left some of his affects."

"I will not, without his permission, so we will have to wait until he returns."

"If you don't have the spine for it, and are a sissy, I'll do it."

Will's anger started to boil in him, but then he wondered why he was protecting Jones. He thought: "Maybe this old fool is right to question Jones, after all what was he doing with a pistol? And, he sure looked like he knew how to use it. Still, insults by this old man were not to be tolerated."

"Burns, I will not be called a sissy by you, and would take delight in throwing you out of here. But, if you can act more gentlemanly, I will show you his room."

"Lead the way."

Will led Burns out of the restaurant, up the stairs and then to Jones' door. Will knocked loudly and said:

"Mr. Jones, are you awake? Are you in there?"

They waited for about a minute, and with no answer, Burns said:

"Open the door, Will."

Will produced a master key and opened the door. Burns pushed past him, entering the room first. Will entered after and looked around the room. The bed was not made, and there was no sign of any of Jones' belongings. Will made his way to the desk where Jones was working last night and found two envelops, one addressed to Will and one addressed to John L. Tate. Will picked up the envelop address to him, opened it and read aloud:

"Dear John,

Sorry, I had to leave town in a haste, but it was necessary. Thanks for your hospitality. I consider you a friend. Here is the recipe for Currant Champagne. For 30 Gallons:

> *150 pounds of Currants.*
> *75 pounds of Sugar.*
> *3 pints of White Brandy.*
> *28 gallons of Water.*

Mash the fruit to break each berry and then add a portion of the water. Strain over a grain sieve. Concurrently, add the sugar to the brandy in a large tub. Once all of the sugar has dissolved, add the strained berries and the remainder of the water. Stir the mixture to add air. After one hour, bottle the mixture and then let it continue to mix for about two weeks, before serving.

John, I hope this will bring the inn much profit. As for the $15 debt you owe me, well I'll be back in town soon enough to collect. Can you do me a service and give the other letter to Mr. John L. Tate? Thank you kindly.

Your Friend, Samuel Jones"

"Will, you idiot. I told you he was a spy, and now he has gotten away, and it's your fault. I could have arrested him last night. Do you know what you have done? The Rebs for sure will be here in Gettysburg. He even says so. A friend to the Rebs and to a traitor, that's what you are."

"Burns, I have had enough of you. Please leave, *now*."

"Glad to get out of this traitorous place," he said and stormed out of the room.

Will wondered indeed what he had done befriending this man. Had he endangered the town? Would the Rebels indeed come and destroy the town? The inn?

"I must have a talk with father this afternoon when he gets here," he thought, and then he put Jones' letter to Tate in his pocket and left the room.

Charles Will came into the restaurant at his usual five o'clock time. Will asked:

"Father, can I talk to you for a moment?"

"Of course, what's on your mind?"

"Well, evening last, I introduced you to Mr. Jones. We had supper together, and made a deal for the inn to purchase one of his recipes."

"Yes, yes, you told me that. Is there something wrong?"

"I don't really know. He left town in a haste early this morning, but left me a letter and in it was the recipe."

"Did you pay him?"

"No. We agreed he would mix a batch before I pay him, and that's just it, he left without making the sample. Burns thinks he left because he is a spy and needed to get out of town before he was caught. Burns blames me for not letting him arrest Jones last night whilst he was still here."

"Never you mind that old fool. Maybe Jones just needed to go. People have all sorts of reasons for doing things that we cannot understand until they do some explaining. If we owe him a debt for the recipe, he'll come back eventually to collect and then you can find out what really happened to him.

"Father, what if he actually is a spy? Should we think about moving some of our supplies out of town to keep them out of Rebel hands should they come here?"

"You may have a point, son, but that is a big expense and if we put them on the train, it may be more storage that we would need. Why don't you go over to the Eagle and see if Tate would like to share a car with us."

"I'll go over there after the supper hours and discuss it with him this very night."

"That's the stuff. Now, let's get ready for our guests."

Once the supper time was over, Will decided to deliver Jones' letter to Tate. He told Samuel Butler he would be gone for about an hour and set off to the Eagle Hotel. He continued to be bothered by the incidents concerning Jones as he was walking along York Street and then through the Diamond. But, then it occurred to him it was his business to be friendly to strangers, after all he ran an inn, where the majority of the business comes from strangers and visitors to the town. He thought: "I wouldn't be a very good innkeeper if I wasn't hospitable." This thought calmed him some.

He entered the Eagle Hotel just before nine o'clock, went over to the registration desk and asked if Tate was about the hotel. He was told Tate was in the tavern, and that he was welcome to go on back to see him. Will entered the restaurant and made his way to the bar where Tate was serving customers.

"Mr. Tate, can I speak with you privately for a moment?"

"Is that you John Will? Why certainly, let's go over to my table."

Tate came around the bar and gestured they should sit at the nearest table and Will obliged sitting at the chair on the other side of the table. Tate sat across from him and said:

"What do you think of the new lounge? It's not quite done, but it will be in a couple of weeks. You know, we are also putting oil lamps in every room, like the Globe has."

"Looks great, so far. I have something for you from a friend of ours. A letter."

"A letter? From whom?"

"Samuel Jones. He was staying at the inn and left either last night or early this morning. I found this letter at his desk. It is addressed to you."

"Awe, Mr. Jones. I was expecting him here at noon o'clock to complete our business and he never showed. I wonder if his letter explains why he didn't come? Do you know for sure he has left town?"

"Yes, he also left me a letter and in it he explained it was necessary for him to leave town unexpectedly."

Will handed Tate the letter. Tate thanked him and put on his glasses to read it. He read it silently:

"Dear Mr. Tate,

Sorry, I won't be making our noon o'clock appointment today, but I had to leave town. It was necessary. Still, I feel I owe you for your kindness and so here is the recipe for a Whiskey Sour:

Whiskey Sour

1- 1/2 to 2 oz. bourbon or rye (depending upon desired strength).

1/2 oz. fresh-squeezed lemon or lime juice.

1/2 oz. simple syrup (1:1).
dash of bitters.
1/2 tsp. very fresh egg white (optional).
cherry or lemon or lime garnish.
Shake all ingredients. If using egg white, shake until a froth forms, about 1 to 2 minutes and then serve.
Mr. Tate, I hope this will bring the Eagle Hotel much profit. As for the $20 debt you owe me, well I'll be back in town soon enough to collect.
Your Friend, Samuel Jones"

Tate folded the letter, placed it back into the envelope, and into his pocket. He thought for a moment and said:

"Interesting fellow that Mr. Jones. Why would he leave town before completing a business transaction, and give his part of it away without payment?"

"He did the very same to me. He gave me a drink recipe and said he would be back to collect the debt for it. Burns thinks he is a spy."

"He and I had that very same, shall we say, disagreement last night. But, maybe the old fool got this one right. It sure would explain why he had to skedaddle out of town."

"Yes, it would. He wanted to arrest Jones last night at the inn, but I stopped him. I now wonder if that was not wise."

"John, I would have done the very same thing. If Jones was my guest, I would not have let that peculiar, odd man harass him."

"That's good to know. I somehow feel, and this is from listening to that old gentleman, I have betrayed the town and the town's folk."

"Don't be daft. He'll probably turn up back in town in a month or two looking for his money. Think of it this way, we each have a recipe we can use to make more profit on our liquor sales, and have permission to use it without paying one cent out of our pockets. I say Mr. Jones, wherever you are, thanks for the recipes."

"Mr. Tate, you have a unique way of thinking about things; one that puts my mind at ease. Thanks. Just the same, in the small chance he is a spy, father and I think it wise we move some of our supplies out of town. He wanted me to discuss this with you to see if you would like to share in this transaction."

"John, you may be right. For once, old Burns may have done us a good turn with this spy hunt of his. Let me think on it and I will come to the inn to discuss it further, if indeed it makes sense to me."

Will rose from the table and offered his hand. The two men shook hands and then Will turned to leave, but when he was just about out of the restaurant, he turned back to Tate, saying with a smirk:

"Mr. Tate, should any of your customers prefer a quiet, little inn to a loud, large hotel, send 'em my way."

"And the same to you, John."

Will was further put at ease with the help of his father's words, thinking both he and Tate must be right: "After all, who should he believe, father and Mr. Tate, or Burns?" He decided the answer was obvious, and he should fret on the matter no more. Besides, he thought: "The Rebels won't get too far even if they decide to come north. Our army will stop them."

If only he knew about the unstoppable gale building into a hurricane and approaching from the South.

Part 2

The Invaders Cometh This Way

In early June 1863, the Confederate Army of Northern Virginia was on the move north toward Maryland and ultimately Pennsylvania. On June 5th, Lee's Army began crossing the Rappahannock River and did this by heading westerly from Fredericksburg, located in central Virginia, toward the planned gathering point at Culpeper, about 25 miles west of Fredericksburg.

On June 9th, the Confederate cavalry clashed with the Union cavalry at Brandy Station near Culpeper. This battle between the two cavalries was, until 1865, the greatest fight between the two mounted forces, but was relatively a standstill in its result. Even though the battle was by all practical purposes a draw, it failed to stop, or even stall, the Rebel momentum north.

After Brandy Station, the Rebel army continued its advance northwesterly, through the Blue Ridge Mountains at Chester Gap, across the Shenandoah River, into the Shenandoah Valley, and northerly to Winchester, Virginia, where a Union stronghold waited. In May 1862, General Stonewall Jackson and the Army of Northern Virginia defeated the Union defenses at Winchester by attacking from the west. Between June 12th and the 15th, 1863, the Rebel army engaged the Union defenses at Winchester, and this encounter was named the Second Battle of Winchester. The main Union garrison consisted of a trio of forts-the West Fort, the Main Fort, and the Star Fort. The West Fort guarded the west approach to the town, the Main Fort guarded the town proper, and the Star Fort guarded the north and east approach. At stake in this battle was the Union army's last opportunity to stop the Rebel move into the North, since the main body of the army was slow in reacting to the Rebel initiative north and were still in central Virginia, somewhere north of Fredericksburg.

At the Battle of Winchester, the Confederate strategy was simple: attack from the west as it had in the 1862 victory. In a brilliant move, led by General Jubal Early, the Rebel army's main force maneuvered around to the high ground west of the town, undetected by the Federal forces, and positioned their artillery where it could pound the West Fort from both the northwest and the southwest. The West Fort was caught in a cross-fire. When the fort's defenses were in shambles from the shelling, a Louisiana Brigade, known as the Louisiana Tigers, attacked and captured it. Once the West Fort was occupied by the Rebels, they turned the fort's own artillery against the remaining two forts, maneuvered their forces to surround them, and sent the Federals into retreat, where they were routed. The battle was decided. The Rebel *army, including the Stonewall Brigade of Virginia, smashed the Union defenses, captured the forts, and sent what remained of the Union army at Winchester into retreat.*

The battle included two separate occasions where the Stonewall Brigade, specifically the 2nd Virginia Infantry Regiment, clashed with the 87th Pennsylvania Volunteer Infantry. In these clashes, one man from Gettysburg, fighting for the Confederacy, fought against his brother and his childhood friends.

At the completion of the battle, the Rebel army resumed their march north, without any opposition to stop them from invading Northern soil.

CHAPTER 10

CULP

JOHN WESLEY CULP awoke on Tuesday morning the 9th of June just after daybreak to the sound and feel of his close friend William Arthur shaking him.

"Wes, wake up. Wake up. We're a movin' out this mornin'."

Culp opened one eye and rolled over, facing away from him. Undaunted, Arthur decided Benjamin S. Pendleton was an easier mark. He moved over to where Pendleton was sleeping, shook him saying with a thick southern accent:

"B.S., get up. We're a movin' out. Goin' up noath to whup 'em Yanks."

Pendleton groaned, also turned over, and said, too with an accent although not a pronounced as Arthur's:

"Shut up, William, and let us get a little more sleep. That can wait awhile."

Culp grabbed his blanket and threw it at Arthur, playfully saying:

"Be still, you jackass, and go get us some coffee. And, gimme back my blanket."

Arthur threw the blanket back to Culp and said:

"Coffee, humph, get up and get ya own. I'll see y'all by the fia when ya decide to get ya lazy beehine's up."

Culp grabbed his blanket, covered back up, and remarked in finality, but still in play:

"We'll see your loud ass by the fire soon enough. Now get out and give us some quiet."

John Wesley (Wes) Culp was a private in the Army of Northern Virginia. He enlisted into the 2nd Virginia Regiment in April of 1861 along with his two best friends, William Arthur and Benjamin S. (B.S.) Pendleton, in Harper's Ferry, Virginia. The 2nd was attached to the famous Stonewall Brigade. Culp was a short man, standing just over five feet, was 24 years old, had brown hair, relatively long as it covered his ears, a long beard that hugged his jaw line, and brown eyes. He had a big smile, was confident in himself, and was an individualist, as he showed by enlisting in the Confederate Army, yet his birthplace and his home until five years ago was Gettysburg, Pennsylvania. Born in the North frequently got him called "Yank" by his comrades in the regiment, which irritated him, depending upon if it was a friend or a foe addressing him as such.

Five minutes or so passed, and then Culp rolled back over and said to Pendleton:

"B.S., we better start rousting. Are you up for some coffee?"

"S'pose. Sounds like we in fo some maaching today. Ya up fo it?"

"Yeah, I think my foot is pretty much healed. Besides, do we have a choice?"

"Nah, but them Yankees need a good whuppin'. Say, why don't ya take a kerchief, cut it up and stuff it in that hole in ya boot? That might give ya foot a little more shieldin'."

"Sounds like a good idea. Let me have your kerchief," Culp said teasing Pendleton.

"Use ya own, and let's get some of that black stuff. What did ya call it?"

"Coffee."

"That's what they a calling it these days…?"

Culp just smiled at Pendleton and the two friends dressed quickly and left their tent to find their buddy Arthur.

They found Arthur by the nearest campfire drinking coffee from his tin cup, engaged in conversation with another soldier, whose back was to them. As they drew nearer, they could distinguish the soldier's voice. It was Charles Milton. Milton was not friendly or polite to any of the three friends. In fact, Culp viewed him more of an enemy than the Yankees. Milton was much taller than Culp, around five feet, nine inches tall, and outweighed him by a good fifty pounds. He was obnoxious and was not shy at constantly reminding everyone who would listen, Culp was from the North and not a "true man of Virginia." Culp would like to make Milton know what a man of Pennsylvania was capable of, but the Army of Northern Virginia did not permit fighting within the ranks unless given permission by the colonel of the regiment, and thus far Colonel John Q. A. Nadenbousch had not done so. Culp had tried.

The two friends approached the fire and Culp greeted Arthur, ignoring Milton:

"There you are William. Where did you get the coffee?"

"The wagun yonder," Arthur replied pointing to a wagon about twenty yards from where they were. He continued:

"Grab sum and then come on back."

Milton chimed in saying:

"Mornin', Yank."

Culp and Pendleton ignored Milton and walked to the wagon.

"Ya know Wes, ignoring him just a stirs him up."

"Yeah, I'm counting on it."

They got their coffee and returned to the fire in about five minutes. As they approached, they overheard Arthur saying:

"I heard we a marching toward Sperryville today. It's about twenty miles distint."

Culp approached and said to Arthur:

"Sperryville? Is that it? There aren't any Yanks in Sperryville."

"Well ya outta kno, Yank," Milton challenged again.

"Maybe. But, better than that, I can read a map, you big, jackass."

Milton reddened a little, as he didn't like being taunted about his inability to read. He started to walk away, and then turned back to Culp and said:

"Don't turn ya back on me in a battle, Yank. Ya might find a bullet in it."

"Really, you dumb oaf? You better watch yours, as there are three chances for a bullet in yours."

Milton walked off and Arthur said:

"Wes, ya shouldn't push him so hard. I think he is dangaous."

"So are we, three Rebs no one wants to mess with. Forget him. Now, what were you saying about Sperryville?"

The three finished their coffee, had a quick breakfast of bacon fat and hard bread, and then returned to their tent to pack up and prepare for the day's march. Sergeant Dan Sheetz had come by and ordered them ready to march by ten o'clock. It was just before ten when they fell in line awaiting the order to march. It was a sunny day in central Virginia and the temperature was headed into the eighties, so it would be a warm march.

When the order to march was given, the regiment started heading northwest on the road leading to Sperryville. Sperryville was a town nestled on the eastern foothill of the Blue Ridge Mountains. It took about an hour for the 2nd Virginia to gain a rhythm for the day's march, and the three marched side by side in a column of fours. Pendleton was located on the left side of the three and said to Culp, who was next to him:

"Did ya try the kerchief in ya boot?"

"Yeah, it seems to be working. Thanks for the thought. I don't know why I didn't think of it."

"Simple, ya not as smart as me."

"Sure, clerk," Culp said, referring to Pendleton's occupation as a bank clerk before the army.

Culp reflected on thinking of Pendleton as a bank clerk and it reminded him of Shepherdstown, back in late '58. Then, his memory got the best of him, as it did frequently on long marches. It helped pass the time for him, and his active mind, during the boredom of marching. He recalled a time in the summer in 1858, before he moved to Shepherdstown, when he and his friends met on his cousin's hill, near his father's farm, in Gettysburg. It was a bright, warm, sunny day, followed by a beautiful sunset over South Mountain. He was joined by Jack and Daniel Skelly; Billy Holtzworth; Annie, his older sister; Annie's friend Sallie Myers; and Ginnie Wade. Jack and Daniel bought some fresh pork cutlets from the butcher, Mr. James Pierce. The girls brought potatoes, bread, butter, jam, and peaches. Aw, how the fresh bread smelled. He could smell it as if he had a slice in his hand. Billy had built the fire, and with his memory he could smell it too, and even see the smoke rising from the burning wood. And, then the pork began to sizzle. His mouth watered from the memory of the fresh pork cooking. He remembered how great the meal was, and after they finished eating, he remembered how they sat around the fire and just talked until it was time for the ladies to return home. "What were we talking about?" he thought, and then he remembered.

"Because of the tension between the North and the South, do you think it will in due course lead to war?" Annie asked.

"Nah," Billy said as he produced a bottle of whiskey from his coat.

"Billy Holtzworth! Is that liquor you have there?" Ginnie asked.

"Well, it ain't water. Anyone care for a sip?"

Culp remembered saying: "Surely, pass it over when you're done."

"Why, Wesley Culp, what on ever do you think you are doing? What would Papa and Mama say?" Annie asked.

"I reckon Mama wouldn't be pleased, but Papa would, if they were still alive."

Culp remembers taking a sip and the passing the bottle to Jack. Jack took the bottle and said:

"War with the South may be coming, indeed. I've heard tell that the divide between us is growing larger as the country moves west, and that a compromise may not be possible this time. Did any of you read that article in the Sentinel about the fella from Illinois…what's his name? Yeah, Abraham Lincoln. Anyway, Lincoln said in a debate, something like: '… a house divided upon itself cannot stand.'"

"What does that mean, Jack, a house divided against itself?" Annie asked.

"It means slavery. One part of the country, in this case the house, allows it while the other part doesn't. The house is divided."

Pleased with himself on the explanation, Jack raised the bottle to his mouth and then looked over at Ginnie, whose admiring look while he was talking turned into a disappointed look. Jack saw it and then decided not to drink, instead handing the bottle back, saying:

"I shouldn't. Here, Wes."

Daniel Skelly said:

"Hey Wes, what about me?"

The bottle was given to Daniel and he took a big gulp before Jack could object.

As Daniel began coughing, Jack scolded him:

"Daniel, what is mother going to say? You are too young for liquor!"

"So you say, big brother."

Culp remembered fondly as Daniel continued coughing.

"Wes, let me have a sip," Annie said.

"Billy, should I?"

"I don't see no harm. Let her have one. It's about time."

Annie took a small sip and she too coughed. It was a funny sight, seeing both choking like that. He smiled at this memory.

"That makes me feel warm all over," Annie said.

"If it does turn into war, will you go?" Ginnie asked looking at Jack.

"Of course I will, Ginnie. I have to protect our country."

"So will I, Billy echoed after taking another sip of the whiskey and handing Wes the bottle. He remembered taking a sip and saying:

"So will I."

"Then it's a pact. We're all goin', right?" Billy asked.

"It's a pact," both he and Jack replied.

His mind returned to the present and he said to himself: "A pact; we all went alright; them in the Union army and me in the Confederate Army. Never mind that, Wes. It's best not to talk of that." His mind returned to the fond memory he was having.

"If the trouble is all about slavery, why can't the South just let them go? We have free coloreds in our town and it's no bother to us," Sallie said.

"Sallie, it's just not as easy as all that. They depend upon slaves to pick their cotton," Culp remembered saying.

Annie interjected saying:

"What makes them different from us? We have fruit needing picking, but we don't have slaves picking it!"

"Annie, that's just the law down there and it may take a war to change it," Jack said.

"Well, I pray to the Lord it doesn't happen. I don't want to see any of you boys going," Ginnie said, and then she turned to Jack and gave him a deep gaze into his eyes. He remembered seeing Jack blush a little, turn away, and then look back with a shy smile. Jack was sweet on Ginnie!

Billy took another sip and continued:

"Even if it does, we will whip them boys from the South. Ginnie, your Pa's from the South. Do you think we can whip them good and fast?"

"Billy, just cause Papa grew up down South, doesn't mean I know any more about them than you."

Culp remembered saying:

"Easy, Ginnie. Billy didn't mean no harm."

"I sure didn't. Wes, have another," Billy said as he handed the bottle to Culp.

He remembered the evening ending with Jack and Daniel taking the ladies home, and he and Billy finishing the whiskey, talking for hours by the fire.

While he was still reflecting, he heard the sergeant order the men to halt and take a rest for about ten minutes, which instantly brought him to the present. After the brief rest, the order was given to march again, and the three friends fell back in line and continued the march. They reached the place to camp for the night, which was about half way to Sperryville from Culpeper, around five o'clock in the afternoon. Campfires were built and then food began to be cooked. The three friends set up their place to spend the night, went to the wagon, grabbed some biscuits, coffee, and some bacon, and then they made their way to the nearest fire.

"Wes, whea were ya today during the march?" Arthur asked as he was used to Culp drifting off during the marches.

"I was remembering a picnic a few years ago with Billy Holtzworth and Jack Skelly on my cousin's hill in Gettysburg."

"Holtzworth and Skelly. Aren't they the ones you told us are in the 87th Pennsylvania?" Pendleton inquired.

"Yeah. At the picnic, we all made a pact to enlist together if war came. Funny, huh?"

"Do ya think we will face 'em on this campaign?" Pendleton asked.

"I hope not. My brother William is in that unit, too."

"What will ya do if ya do see him?"

"B.S., I don't know. I hope I never have to find out."

CHAPTER 11

CULP

JOHN WESLEY CULP started his day early on Thursday, June 11th, as the men were awakened around four o'clock in the morning. A late sleeper, he waited until the very last minute, so he had to rush. He quickly packed up his blanket, knapsack, rifle, cartridge box, and the rest of his belongings, found the food wagon in the dark, ate a biscuit for breakfast, drank a cup of coffee, and joined the rest of his men in line for the day's march. It was a cool morning, but Culp could tell it was going to be another warm day, and he hoped a long march was not in order.

"Where are we headed today? Anyone know?" he asked.

"Word tell is we a headed fo Winchesta, about 45 miles distant," Pendleton replied.

"Great, they wake us up in the middle of the night and make us march all day long. And then tomorrow, we'll do it all over again."

"What's the matter, Yank, too soft to make a long day's march?"

Culp turned around to see Milton lined up directly behind him. He thought this will be a long day. Then he thought, "I'll have some fun. Let the games begin." He turned to face Milton.

"Morning, Milton," he said politely hoping to bait him into more.

"Yeah, yeah Yank, on to Winchesta. Ain't that closa to ya countra? Maybe, soon we can see some of dem pritty girls from Pennsylvania. Don't ya haff some kinfolk up thea?"

"Maybe, Chuck. But, none of them would give a big, ugly, smelly guy like you a second look," he said knowing Milton didn't like being called Chuck, and he said it with carefully placed sarcasm.

"Yyyyank, soon I's going to make ya pppay," Milton said with his voice stuttering and cracking.

"Chuck, I live for that day, and it will be me who makes you pay."

"I could crush ya like the little weasel ya a, Yank."

"Really, a big, slow, lump of coal like you? You wouldn't even know what hit you. You'll just be flat on your back, bleeding, looking up at me."

Milton closed quickly and grabbed Culp's coat with his left fist. Culp cocked his right fist, just as the sergeant arrived.

"Ya men thea, get back in line now," Sergeant Sheetz yelled. And then: "Let's get going, we haff a long maach ahead of us. Now maach."

"Wes, soona or lata, ya're going to have fight that guy," Arthur said.

"The sooner, the better. That guy needs a lesson, and I aim to be the one to give it to him."

"I hope ya know what ya doing."

"Believe me, I do," Culp said as they began to march.

The sun rose a little after six o'clock and the day began to warm. The dust from the marching horses and men began to rise, sticking to the men's uniforms, getting into their hair, and creeping into everyone's nostrils and mouths. The men were in a good rhythm and, because of this, they were making a good pace. They passed a plantation off to the left of the road, and Culp looked at the rich house, with the white columns and the porch on the front of the house. Out front, he saw a nice carriage. He marveled at the bright colors. It had black roof and red sides, with white lining, and black wheels, with a black horse strapped to it. The carriage stirred his memory and he reflected on working for Mr. Hoffman at Hoffman's Wagon Maker Shop. He was a harness maker, and a good one, and he also sewed upholstery. His mind then drifted to the time in 1858 where he had to decide on whether to move to Shepherdstown, Virginia, or stay at home in Gettysburg. Mr. Hoffman had decided to move his business to Virginia, and wanted to take as many of his employees as would go. Culp had a tough decision to make and remembered discussing it with his sister Annie.

"Annie, I don't know what I should do. I really like what I am doing at Hoffman's and I make a good wage, but move to Sheperdstown? It has to be some 50 miles distant from here. I've never been that far from home."

"Wes, we will never see you. Stay home here. You know we need your help here at the farm," Annie said.

"Annie, you know I don't take to farming. I'm a builder. Besides, William is not going."

"Yes, thank the Lord your brother isn't leaving us."

"I know you don't want me to go. But, I think I have to. I like my work and I like working for Mr. Hoffman. He is fair and has offered to give a bonus to come with him. Twenty dollars; that's one month's salary, and I could use this to set up a place to live. It could be exciting and adventurous."

"It seems as though you have made your mind up already. Wes, do you really have to go?" Annie asked, and she began to cry.

Culp remembered this with a very sad heart. He also thought how much his life had changed because of this one decision, and how much his missed home. He wondered if where the army was headed would eventually lead to home. Home to Gettysburg.

A little after eight o'clock in the morning, the 2nd Virginia passed through a small town of Woodwin, Virginia. Young ladies lined the road and handed out flowers, handkerchiefs, pieces of bread, water, hugs, and greetings. As they marched, they heard a band playing music and singing. As they moved closer, they could make out the rallying song of the South, *The Bonnie Blue Flag*. Culp strained to hear.

"Hurrah! Hurrah!
For Southern Rights, Hurrah!
Hurrah for the Bonnie Blue Flag
That bears a Single Star!"

Sergeant Sheetz had stopped his march waiting for half of the brigade to pass so he was within earshot of all:

"Men of the Stonewall Brigade, look sharp. Left, right, left, right, left, Hurrah fo Dixie!"

This was their usual call when marching to *The Bonnie Blue Flag*, to shout aloud and in unison "Hurrah fo Dixie" after the words "For Southern Rights, Hurrah," and so the men marched smartly and yelled as one: "Hurrah fo Dixie." After they passed the band and were just about out of range to hear the music, Pendleton said:

"That was the Noath Caaolina Baass Band, and they played oua song. That song always gives me a chillin' to the bone."

"And, me. It sure does make marchin' easia," Arthur exclaimed.

Milton was overhearing the conversation and decided it was time again to engage Culp.

"What about ya, Yank? Does it make ya blue belly all waam and fuzzy?"

Culp was about to answer, but then he reflected on how he chose to enlist in the Army of Northern Virginia. He thought back to when he first met Pendleton and Arthur and how this indeed led to his enlistment. When was that, he thought, "Yes, back in October of '58." He walked into the bank and behind the counter was Pendleton.

"Good aftanoon, sur. What can I help ya with?"

"My name is Wes Culp, and I am new in this town. I came to see if I could open an account."

The two men shook hands and Pendleton said:

"Pleased to meet ya, Wes. I am Benjamin S. Pendleton. Those I allow, call me B.S. Ya can call me Ben, for now. Welcome to Shephadstown. Are ya stayin' hea long?"

Pendleton was around twenty years old, just about the same age as Culp, was five feet six inches tall, dark hair, brown eyes, and a warm smile. Culp instantly knew he would like him.

"Thanks, and yes. My employer just moved his wagon making business here from Gettysburg, Pennsylvania. It's called Hoffman's Wagon Making Shop."

"That's grand. A wagon makin' business is just what this town needs."

"Well, I know my employer hopes so."

"Ya know, since ya are new in town, I haff an idea fo ya as to how ya can get to know folks round hea. All those young gentlemen who want to get to know the ladies aroun hea join the local militia, the Hamtaamck Guards. I too am a memba."

"That sounds appealing. What do I have to do?"

"Why don't ya come to a meetin' with me on Tuesday evenin'?"

"Should I meet you here?"

"How about we meet at the tavern tonight and we can discuss it over an ale?"

Culp remembered then Catherine came into the bank. Miss Catherine Butler. The minute his eyes caught sight of her, he knew. He knew that she was the one. His heart always felt so warm when he thought of the first moment he saw her. He continued with his pleasant memory.

"Good afternoo B.S.," she said.

"And to ya, Miss Catherine. What can I do ya today?"

Catherine noticed Culp, smiled, but then quickly, and shyly, looked away. Catherine Butler was eighteen years old, making her a year younger than Culp, was about five feet tall, about the same height as Culp, long blonde hair, deep blue eyes, and a very bright smile. She wore a light blue bonnet, a dark blue long dress with a white collar, tightly pinned at the neck with a large brooch.

"Why, I would like make a quick deposit," Catherine said with a fairly thick southern accent.

Culp just had to find out who this was, so he said to Pendleton:

"Ben, I don't mean to bother your business with this fine lady, but would you indulge me and introduce me to her?"

"Why ceatainly. Miss Catherine Butler, this hea is Mr. Wes Culp. He's newly arrived in Shephadstown from Gettysbuag, Pennsylvania."

Culp bowed, saying:

"How do, ma'am?"

Catherine offered her hand and said: "Mista Culp, I do just fine."

Culp shook her hand gently and said:

"That ma'am I can see. Please don't let me interrupt your business here. But, being new to this town, just had to meet you. I hope you don't mind?"

"Mista Culp, I don't mind indeed. I am, hoaeva vea busy this day. So, if it's no botha, I will be on my way. Good afternoo."

Pendleton accepted Catherine's deposit and wrote her a receipt while she was talking to Culp. He handed the receipt to her and then she left. After she was gone, Culp said:

"Ben, that's the most beautiful woman I have ever seen. Tell me is she promised to anyone?"

"No, not at the moment. She has just become eighteen yeas of age, and ha fatha is mighty patective of her, being of ol' English stock. So, ya may haff a little of a haad time if ya haff ya eyes on hea, paaticularly since ya ain't from aroun hea,"

"We shall see. Does she know you are a member of the militia"?

"She sua does. She is vea much a supporta, and she is vea involved with the politics of the day."

"Well, then you can count me in. The Hamtramck Guards. I like the sound of that."

Culp continued with this memory, and recalled meeting Pendleton at the tavern that night. He went in and noticed Pendleton at the bar talking to another young man. Pendleton saw him, smiled and waved him over. The bar was relatively long and bellied up to it were a lot of patrons, so squeezing in was somewhat of a chore. The tavern was dark and was being lit by oil lamps at each end of the bar and at all the round tables between the entrance and the bar. Culp hesitated until his eyes got used to the lighting and then made his way over to Pendleton.

"Wes, this hea is William Arthua. William hea is also a memba of the Hamtaamck Guards, but just 'cause we let him. Just joshin'. He's my best friend. Bill, this is Wes Culp. He's the one I haff been tellin' ya moved hea recently from Pennsylvania. What town was that ya said, Wes?"

"Gettysburg. My employer moved his wagon making business here, and I had no real ties at home, so I came along."

The two men shook hands while Arthur said:

"Welcome to oua litta town. Let's get ya an ale." He turned to the bartender and said:

"Baatenda, get my new friend hea an ale if ya please." Then turning back to Culp, he continued:

"B.S. says ya want to join oua militia group?"

Culp remembered just then, the man next to Arthur took a drink from his glass and as he was setting it down, his friend slapped him on the back, which caused him to spill it all over Arthur. Arthur shook his shirt sleeve and then looked at the man, who paid no attention. Arthur said to him:

"Excuse me, sur, but ya seemed to haff spilled on my shurt."

The man looked older than the three, maybe in his thirties, wore a dirty, torn shirt, dirty trousers and worn out boots. He smelled like a farm animal, and he himself was soiled, even his raggedy hair.

The man still paid no attention; Culp surmised because he had had a few too many, so Arthur said it again, only louder this time. The tone in Arthur's voice got the attention of the man next to him who had created the spill, and he said to his companion sarcastically:

"Hey, Ed, ya friend hea thinks ya spilled on his shirt."

The man named Ed turned to Arthur, but addressed his friend:

"Really now, Maatin? And, what is he going to do about it?"

"I dunno, Ed," the man named Martin, who looked and smelled like his friend, said and then turned to Arthur and continued:

"So, friend what are ya gonna do about it?"

Pendleton noticed the two were together and that Arthur needing backing. He said to both:

"No harm done, friends. How about we buy ya'all a drink."

The man named Martin replied, turning to the man next him:

"Hey, Harry. Lookey what we haff hea, a couple of young, fresh 'uns. And they'a buying."

The third man turned toward Pendleton and said:

"As much as I'd like to oblige, I'd much ratha dirty 'em up a bit. What ya say, Ed?"

The third man was a little taller than the other two, at about five feet nine inches tall. He too was dirty from head to toe and smelled it.

"Yeah, they look too pritty and need some mudding up. What say we meet ya in the alley, friends?"

Culp remembered saying: "three to two, not real fair odds, would you say, fellows? How about I come along, too?"

The man named Harry said:

"Sua, little man. Ya come and play with the big boys."

The six men left the tavern and went out to the alley located on the east side of the building. As they were walking along, Pendleton said:

"Wes, ya don't haff to come. It's not ya fight."

"If it's your fight, then it is my fight, B.S.," purposely saying Pendleton's nickname. He continued:

"Besides, I have taken to the big one. What's his name…Harry?"

The men went into the alley, lined up and faced each other. Then, the man named Harry said:

"Which one of ya wants it fiast?"

Culp remembered saying:

"That would be me. Would I be getting it from you?"

"Baash, I like that. And, I am going to enjoy shovin' ya face in the diat."

Harry clenched his right fist and swung at Culp's head. Being shorter by a head, Culp instantly and easily ducked the punch. He took a side step to his right and jabbed his right fist up hard into the man's nose, exploding it in blood. He followed with a left upper cut to his chin and the man staggered back and fell. Culp was on him instantly, and punched him twice more in the face, with one left and one right. Culp remembered getting off the man and turning to see if his new friends needed any help. He saw the man named Ed approach Arthur and throw a wild right punch, which Arthur almost ducked, but caught on the top of his head. Arthur staggered back, but instantly caught his balance and as the man threw another punch with his left hand, Arthur blocked it with his right arm and then dug his left fist in the other man's right eye and nose. This punch too caused the nose to also explode in blood. The man staggered and Arthur followed with a perfectly placed right to the chin. The man crumpled and fell.

The third man was startled to see his two comrades cut down so easily by the young men, and his hesitation was enough for Pendleton to make his move. Pendleton closed on the man named Martin and punched him with a quick combination of a right and a left, both connecting with the man's chin. He too staggered and went down.

Pendleton and Arthur were done with their foes and they looked over at Culp, who was smiling and rubbing his knuckles. Culp remembered saying:

"Well boys, that was nice work. How about a drink?"

Arthur said to Pendleton:

"B.S., it looks like we haff dun found ouaselves a thiad, don't ya think?"

"We sure haff."

Culp remembered the two slapping him on the back and leading him back into the tavern to celebrate their new found friendship.

He was brought back to the present with the order to halt and to take break for some food and some rest. It was about noon. The sun was high in sky and the heat was stifling. The three friends found themselves a little shade from a tree by the side of the road, and shared their tree with about twenty of their company. Arthur stuck up the conversation first, saying:

"Whew, it sua is a hot one today."

"Not as hot as we a goin' to make it fo them Yankees once we find 'em. Wes, think they know we all a comin'?" Pendleton asked.

"Probably not. We've just been moving for a week, now. But, they know we have left Fredericksburg, so they gotta be itchin' to find out where we are."

"I heard tell that oua cavalry skirmished with theas at Brandy Station Tuesday last. That had to give 'em an inklin' we a moving noath," Arthur said.

"Yeah, but whea and how fa noath?" Pendleton asked.

"We shall see. It may be as far north as we can until they stop us," Culp said.

"Oa, get destaoyed a tryin'," Arthur said with a finality to his voice.

CHAPTER 12

CULP

JOHN WESLEY CULP and his friends began marching again bright and early on Friday, June 12th, north toward Winchester. The ground changed from farm lands with sparse trees, to mountainous terrain containing a thick forest. They were approaching Chester Gap, a pass through the Blue Ridge Mountains. The road climbed slightly as they were traversing the pass, which made marching a little more difficult. However, as they climbed, the road afforded more shade from the trees and the air was cooler, and this made it easier to catch a deep breath, which was a pleasant change from the heat of the valley. The three friends breathed the air in deeply.

"Mount'n aia always smells so good," Arthur said.

"Yeah, like the smell of a woman, fresh from a wash in the crick, all powdaed and pafumed. Delicious," Pendleton replied.

Culp thought of Catherine. How sweet she smelled, not just after a wash, but all the time. He had been courting her for about four years now, and would marry her if only he could get her father's blessing. He had asked twice, but to no avail. The first time was in the spring of '60, after he courted her for a year. He could remember the response as if it were yesterday:

"My daughta will not be marrain' no Yankee, paaticularly one who has no real stake in the woald," the old man said emphatically.

Culp knew himself well and knew he would never give up, and told Mr. Butler so:

"Sir, I love your daughter, and will not stop trying to get you to accept me for her husband."

And so, he tried again, that fall, but the response was the same:

"My daughta ain't marraing a Yankee, paaticularly if that Lincoln fella becomes President."

Culp remembered his walks with Catherine and her staunch support of the Southern cause, particularly as the Butler family was originally from Richmond.

"Wes, I know ya are a Noatherna, but I feel ya see oua position, too. We jus want to left be. To pasue oua way of life, but it doesn't seem like those in the Noath are gonna let us."

"Catherine, my love, it's because the South has slaves, and some in the North will never let that be."

"Well, we haff slaves, and ya seen 'em. Do we treat 'em so bad?"

"No, you don't. But, I've heard tell most are treated badly. Besides, they aren't free. Some folks in the North want them all freed."

"I do declaa, that would ruin us. Who would tend oua fields? Oua houses? We just must haff oua slaves. It's just natural, fo us and fo them."

"Some folks don't see it that way."

"What about ya?"

"Catherine, I just don't know. It seems immoral to me for a human being to be owned by another human being."

"Well now, that's just it, silla. Like I said, it's the natural way."

"We may never agree on this. All I know is I love you and want you to be my wife in the worst way."

"Papa may neva agree if ya continue thinking in ya Noathern ways. Paaticularly if that awful man Lincoln is elected President. That just might be the final straw."

"I sure hope not."

His attention came to the present as he thought her recent letters told of the old man softening his position, particularly because of the success of the army and his brigade. She wrote of her father's pride in him because he was a member of the infamous Stonewall Brigade. He had hoped for this result, but so far it hadn't been enough to get the full blessing. Culp remembered his talks with her, particularly that one April evening in '61, as Virginia had succeeded from the Union a day earlier, about the possibility of his enlistment, since Pendleton and Arthur were joining up, and were leaving the next day.

"Wes, that would be so grand, and Papa would be so proud. He might even, finally, give us his blessin'."

"Catherine, I would be turning my back on my family, my friends, and my home."

"Wes, ya home is hea now, and so is oua future, *togetha*. We could run the plantation togetha. Ya know, Papa will be looking to give it to his kin, his grandsons."

"This is just not leaving home. This is making war on them, helping to defeat them, maybe even killing them."

"Wes, I love ya, and I want to marry ya, but until Papa approves, I cannot."

"I must think this over a spell. Let's not talk of it until tomorrow."

Culp remembered having a terrible night's sleep that night, knowing this is the decision of his life. If he enlisted in the Virginia Army, as the rest of his friends from the Hamtramck Guards were going to do, he would be hated at home, branded a traitor. He would never be allowed to come home. Yet, he loved Catherine more than anyone, and deeply desired to be her husband. Butler stood in the way, and maybe, just maybe, enlisting would be enough for his blessing. He thought of Pendleton's and Arthur's insistence on joining the army and their urging him to do the same. What if he did? Would he see some of his friends from home on the battlefield? Have to kill them? What about his family? What if he had to shoot at them? But, what if he saw Pendleton and/or Arthur on the battlefield? Could he kill them? They were leaving in the morning, and either he goes or he stays. And, if he stays, how can he face Catherine, and her father?

He didn't have an answer to any of these questions until the sun came up. Then, just as the dawn signified a new day, and yesterday was gone forever, he understood his way. Here, this place in Virginia, and Catherine, was *his new day*, and Gettysburg was his yesterday. He would enlist.

Culp remembered he felt peace with his decision, and at the same time, excitement. He quickly dressed and ran over to Catherine's plantation outside of town. He had to hurry, as Pendleton and Arthur were leaving before noon. He knocked on the Butler house door, and asked to see Miss Catherine. The door was shut and he waited on the porch for her. After about five minutes, Catherine opened the door, and said:

"Why, Wes. Ya hea so eaaly."

"That I am, my love. I wanted you to be the first to know my decision. I'm going to enlist with B.S and Bill."

Culp remembered it took a moment for her to understand, but then it hit her, and she smiled so brightly. She thrust herself into his arms and hugged him with all her might. She then pulled away slightly, a tear in her eye, looked at him and kissed his lips ever so gently. He was so pleasantly surprised, as she never allowed this before. She then pulled away and said:

"Oh, Wes, I am so happy. I love ya so much."

"We haven't much time. Do you have an hour to walk with me?"

"Just give me a few moments to get prasentable."

Culp remembered their walk, how beautiful she looked and how happy she was.

"I don't care what your father says, I want to marry you, so will you?"

"Oh, yes, I will. When ya come back, Papa will give us his blessin'. I promise. And, when ya come back, we can marra and haff a wondaful life togetha."

Culp remembered walking her home, kissing her deeply, and pledging his love to her as he waved goodbye. With tears in her eyes, she said goodbye and pledged she would wait for as long as it took for him to return. He then rushed to meet Pendleton and Arthur at the bank, and the three friends left to war together.

Culp was still thinking of this critical moment in his life, when the sergeant gave the order to halt, saying:

"Men, we will camp hea fo the night and await fuather ordas, so spread out and find a place to set up ya camp."

Culp had not noticed they had passed into the Shenandoah Valley and had marched north all afternoon, and into the early evening. They had been marching on the Fort Royal Pike up to a small town named Cedarville, located south of the town of Winchester. Here is where the 2nd Virginia would spend the night awaiting what action the next days would present.

CHAPTER 13

SKELLY

JOHNSTON (JACK) HASTINGS SKELLY, JR. was in an outfit with approximately 400 men from his unit, the 87th Pennsylvania, with 200 men from the 13th Pennsylvania Cavalry, and with Battery L of the 5th U.S. Artillery. Corporal Skelly and the men from his unit were deployed along either side of Valley Pike, the western pike leading north to the town of Winchester, Virginia. They were deployed awaiting the advance of the Army of Northern Virginia. Intelligence and scouting had given the Union garrison at Winchester advance notice the Rebels were headed straight toward them and so the 87th Pennsylvania was sent south along the Valley Pike to give them a proper reception.

Jack Skelly was 22 years old, of average height, about five feet six inches tall, medium build, light brown hair, usually parted on the right side of his head, which was trimmed just above his ears, light brown eyes, and a thin mustache extending just to the corners of his mouth. He had enlisted, just after the beginning of hostilities with the Southern states at Fort Sumter, in April, 1861. He and his close friends Billy Holtzworth and William T. Ziegler enlisted together. They were originally assigned to the 2nd Pennsylvania with whom they fought in the first battle of Bull Run in July 1861. Later, many men in the 2nd Pennsylvania enlisted in a new regiment, which became the 87th Pennsylvania Volunteer Infantry, and so when their enlistment expired, Skelly and his friends decided to re-enlist into the 87th.

It was around noon and the sun was making this a very warm day. Sergeant Holtzworth and Corporal Skelly lined their men on both sides of the road, facing south and awaiting the arrival of the Rebels. They waited behind a small, rock property wall, which concealed their presence. Just behind the line, and unseen behind lumps of hay, were the artillery pieces. The cavalry was stationed on either side of the road, hidden within the trees. The plan was to lure the Rebels into an ambush by showing themselves to the enemy and then retreating, hoping they would follow into the concealed infantry and artillery. Colonel John W. Schall of the 87th was in command.

"Sergeant Holtzworth, take twenty men up the road and wait for the Rebel advance. Once you see them, fire and then get back here as quick as you can," Colonel Schall ordered.

"Yes sir," Holtzworth replied, and then continued:

"Corporal Skelly, pick twenty men and let's get up that road."

"You twenty, let's get ready to move."

Holtzworth, Skelly, and the twenty men quickly made their way up the road about 1000 yards, between two curves in the road, and then re-deployed, ten each on either side of the road.

"Men, lay low, load your weapons and then stand and fire in unison, on my signal only. Once we are done firing, retreat back to our position with the rest of the men as fast as you can. Wait for my signal," Holtzworth ordered.

"Billy, here we go. Are you ready?" Skelly asked.

"Ready as I'll ever be. Make sure you keep your head low and run as fast as you can back to position, okay?"

"You do the same."

The men waited for nearly an hour and then a dust cloud preceded the sounds of marching horses and men, which reached their hearing.

"Steady men. Let's let them get a little closer," Holtzworth ordered.

Another couple of minutes passed, and for Skelly it seemed like a lifetime. Sweat was rolling down his face and he could feel it rolling down his back inside his uniform. Finally, around the bend in the road came the enemy column. They were marching four abreast in their butternut uniforms and with their shouldered rifles glistening in the sun. Skelly judged they were about 300 hundred yards away, while the advance skirmishers were within 200. Skelly looked over at Holtzworth, who nodded in return. Holtzworth aimed his rifle at the nearest enemy soldier and gave the order:

"Fire!"

All at once, the men stood up, and discharged their weapons. Then, they turned and ran back up the road, not noticing that very few shots made their mark. The Confederate infantry immediately halted and confusion spread among the men. By the time order was restored, the Federals were down the road, around the bend, and out of sight.

Skelly and the men got back to their positions behind the wall in less than three minutes, where they waited for the impending approach of the Rebels. Hopefully, they had taken the bait and were carelessly on their way. He didn't have long to wait. Within five minutes, the dust cloud and the sound of the marching men signaled the Rebels were just about within range. Holtzworth used his spyglass and said to Skelly:

"Make sure the men know to let them get closer this time, and don't fire until I give the word."

Skelly went down the line and passed the word to wait for Holtzworth's order to fire. He returned to his position, lying in wait next to his friend

George Prowell, when Prowell looked back and noticed in a house adjacent to road in their rear, ladies waving in the upstairs window. He said:

"Jack, look, they're waving at us."

Skelly noticed the women were looking over their heads, feverously waving, and banging on the pane of glass. He looked at them and then at the approaching Rebels, and judged they were trying to warn the Rebels of the trap.

"My God, they are trying to warn the Rebs."

"Are you sure?" Prowell asked.

"Look, they are not looking at us, but over us to them," Skelly said, pointing to the approaching Confederates.

"Awe, Jack, don't worry. They can't hear them, and they are too far away to see them. Even if they do, like us, they would think they are waving to them."

The suspense of the pending battle was overwhelming. Although Skelly had been in battles before, the intense anticipation of the first shot always turned his stomach. His hands on his rifle were slipping his grip as he was sweating profusely. He looked as the Rebs cautiously approached, skirmishers leading the way. He could see the enemy looking intently to find where the first band had disappeared to. Holtzworth turned to him, after seemingly getting the word from Colonel Schall, and nodded. He then said again:

"Fire!"

All at once, the Federals fired their rifles and then artillery men cleared the hay from in front of their cannons and these too fired. This time the Rebels were not caught off guard like before and they quickly got out of column and formed a line of battle, doing so by seeking any kind of shelter available, behind the rocks and trees near the road. As they were alerted by the Federals first shots earlier, they had loaded their rifles and so returned fire in a short minute.

Skelly fired his rifle, then bit open his powder, poured it into the barrel, loaded his shot, used his ramrod to jam the bullet to the end of the barrel, and fired again. He had several targets to shoot at, but noticed a Reb relatively exposed behind a tree, firing in his direction. He decided to concentrate on this target. His next shot hit the trunk of the tree and splintered bark at his foe. He noticed the soldier loading his rifle and looking in his direction, as he judged where the shot had come from. He reloaded and watched as his foe came partially from behind the tree to aim his shot. Skelly pulled the trigger and watched as the bullet hit his target in the throat. The force of the impact knocked the soldier clear off his feet, and as Skelly continued to watch him, his feet wiggled, and jerked, and then stopped.

The battle lasted less than half an hour, with not much damage inflicted on the Rebels, and none on the Yankees. The Rebels, seeing the strength of the Federal position, chose to retire and await reinforcements before returning. As they retreated, a yell came up from the Federals. Skelly joined in. "So, this is what it feels like to actually drive them from the field," he thought. But, then he thought of the boy he killed, and his enthusiasm was tempered somewhat.

It was about ten o'clock in the evening when Skelly and his comrades returned to Winchester. The men were tired from the long march they just completed from Middletown, about 14 miles distant, but they were also very excited about the way they handled the Confederates in the skirmish. Skelly and Holtzworth made their way to the Taylor Hotel tavern to have a celebration prior to turning in and awaiting the arrival of the Confederates, who most assuredly were on their way. They entered into the tavern and were greeted by the bartender in a most unfriendly manner. Several of their unit were already doing a little celebrating of their own.

"Jack, Billy come on over and let us get you a drink for your success today," William T. Ziegler said, and then to the bartender, he continued:

"Bartender, an ale for the boys in blue here."

Without a word of acknowledgement and a snarl of a look, the bartender turned and filled two glasses with ale and shoved them over to Ziegler.

"What's the matter with him?" Skelly asked as he pointed to the bartender with his glass and took a well deserved sip.

"Words out in the town about how you boys gave the Rebs a licking today at Middletown, and the local folks here aren't too happy with your success. They think the Rebs are on their way to liberate the town. They don't know old Milroy. He ain't about to let go of this here spot without a good fight. Ain't that right, Charlie?" he finished by directing his conversation to the unfriendly bartender.

Ziegler was referring to Major General Robert H. Milroy, who had been in command of the garrison, and the town of Winchester, for about the last six months. Milroy had not been popular with the townfolk. In fact, he was viewed more as a tyrant than anything else.

The bartender gave Ziegler another look of disgust and said:

"Soon, vea soon we will be rid of that intoleaable excuse fo a commanda, and a man. Today won't stop oua aamy from a comin' and when they do, reckonin' will begin, and with that Milroy fiast."

"Pretty damn strong words there, Charlie," Holtzworth replied.

"Pritty strong aamy we haff sageant, and they a comin'.."

"Well bring 'em on, I say, and we'll give 'em the same they got today at Middletown," Skelly added.

He then raised his glass and continued:

"Here's to the boys in the 87th Penn, who skunked them Rebs today."

The three friends drank, and Holtzworth said:

"There's more of that a coming for the Rebs when they show up here. Speaking of more, Charlie, get us three more of these here ales."

"Drink up boys, all ya want. Celebrate all ya want…," Charlie said as he placed the three new glasses of ale in front of them. He continucd:

"'Cause come the morrow, things a goin' be diffeaent hea."

CHAPTER 14

CULP

JOHN WESLEY CULP awoke early on Saturday morning, June 13th. He had a difficult night of sleep, which was unusual for him unless something was weighing on his mind. Today, he knew the brigade was going into action, and so he thought about that most of the night. He hadn't tasted battle since Chancellorsville in early May, so he was apprehensive. The next day's battle had been discussed most of the previous evening among the men around the fires. Winchester, about five miles distant, was a heavily fortified garrison. A local boy in the unit told of receiving a letter from his folks describing the town being guarded by three forts located north of the town proper. The men marveled at how such a letter could be received with this information, which told of the West Fort, appropriately named due to its proximity to the town, the Main Fort located north of the town, and the Star Fort located northeast of that. Each fort was strategically placed to guard the two roads heading north from the town, the Pughtown Road, which ran northwest from the town, and the Martinsburg road heading northeast to Martinsburg.

Culp was awake when Arthur, as his usual practice of rising early, and then returning to the tent to roust Culp and Pendleton, came in.

"Wes, ya awake?"

"Can't sleep; excited about what the day will bring. And, a little nervous."

"Awe, don't ya worra. We gonna whup those Fed'ral boys. Haffn't stopped us yet. B.S., ya awake?"

"Am now."

"Let's get some coffee and get a movin' around. Word is we a marching befo sun up," Arthur said.

"Why don't ya get us some and we will meet ya by the fire?" Pendleton asked.

"Today, in honor of oua great success a comin', I will oblige. Get up now and I'll haff the hot stuff waitin' fo y'all."

The men broke camp and were on the move north toward Winchester before the dawn. They marched on the Front Royal Road, forded a small creek named the Opequon Creek and continued north to another named Buffalo Lick. After fording Buffalo Lick Creek, the column was ordered to form a battle line and to press forward toward the high ground southeast of the town, near the intersection of Millwood Road and Front Royal Road. The Federal troops were stationed just beyond and northerly of a small creek named Abram's Creek. Among the Federal troops was the 87th Pennsylvania, which was not lost on the men from the 2nd Virginia.

"Boys, that's the 87th Pennsylvania right in front of us. Let's give it to 'em," Sergeant Sheetz said.

"Wes, ya hear that? The 87th Pennsylvania?" Pendleton asked.

"I heard B.S. Why did it have to be them?"

"Ya in the Army of Noathern Virginia, the Stonewall Brigade now. Jus' rememba that," Arthur added.

Unfortunately for Culp, Milton was within earshot and added:

"Yank, I'll be watching ya real careful like, and betta see ya firin' that thea rifle of yas, kin or no kin over yonda."

Culp was angered by Milton, more so than usual, as he was attempting to deal with actually going into battle against his childhood friends and maybe even his older brother. His anger got the best of him, and he shot back, finger pointing and fire in his eyes:

"Milton, when this battle is over, I am going to take care of you once and for all. If we survive, don't count on living much longer."

Milton was temporarily taken aback by Culp's intensity, but then composed himself and replied:

"I am gonna enjoy it, Yank."

The Confederates attacked around noon with a full measure of the Rebel Yell. Culp advanced and began firing his rifle at the Yankee forces, and while doing so, strained to see his targets before discharging his rifle. From this range, it was hard to make out any of the faces of the enemy, and the field had begun to fill with smoke from the shots. The Rebel's shot was fairly deadly, punching holes in the Federal line, and then the Yankees began to give ground. Culp raised his rifle to fire his next shot and then he looked harder at his next target, an officer giving orders, which stirred a familiar memory. He could see a familiar face, or what he thought was familiar. His vision was always good from a long distance. Could it be William? His finger began to squeeze the trigger, but the emotions of the moment overtook him. His vision blurred and the surroundings began to spin. He lowered his rifle, focused his eyesight on the ground, and wiped his brow with his sleeve. He then raised his rifle again. He focused on the officer again, and saw William again, who was firing his pistol at his general area. He hesitated, and then looked closer after the smoke had risen and broken up enough for him to see the Federals more clearly. It was

William alright, but now William was looking at him. At that moment, the recognition of the brothers was complete. William looked at him with a soft look of an older brother. But, that expression quickly changed to a look of rage. William loaded his pistol and then fired right at him. The bullet missed high, Culp judged. He raised his rifle, but hesitated again. He lowered his rifle, and looked over at William. Just then the Yankees gave ground and William looked as if he was ordering his men to retreat. He turned around with a scowl and then made off with the Federals. Culp raised his rifle and fired in a different direction, not that which William had occupied or where he was going. Culp was relieved the moment passed, but was stunned by the fact that William was actually over there. And, William clearly didn't have any reservations about killing him. This was not going to go away, not during this battle. The sins of joining the Rebel army were coming around, right at him in the form of his brother. And, payment for those sins maybe dying at the hands of his brother, or even worse, having to kill him.

"My God, what have I done?" he thought.

He was pulled back to the reality of the battle by Pendleton's urging him to come forward and join them. As the Yankees gave ground, the 2nd Virginia and the rest of the men advanced. As he advanced with the men, he regained his composure. He had to, otherwise he would be putting, not only himself, but his comrades in danger. They approached the high ground southeast of town, but then came under fire from the Union heavy artillery within Winchester, coming mainly from the Main Fort. The Rebel artillery was out of range, so the army needed to take cover. General Richard S. Ewell was with the 2nd Virginia, and was realistically too close to the front for someone of his rank.

"Men, take cova," Colonel Nadenbousch ordered.

"Bill, B.S., over there," Culp said while pointing to an empty spot behind the wall.

Culp, Pendleton, and Arthur heeded the order in a quick manner, and positioned themselves behind the wall. Culp looked at the men next to him and saw the colonel and the general. The rest of the men also took cover from a stone wall, but the artillery fire was accurate and one shell ripped into the wall, sending debris into the air and showering the men.

"Colonel, orda ya men to pull back," General Ewell said.

Culp looked over the wall and saw a depression in the ground beyond it.

"B.S., see that gully about ten yards in front. Wouldn't that be good cover?"

Pendleton looked and replied:

"Yeah, that would be betta than this hea wall."

"General, excuse me, sir, but there is a gully in front of the wall. Wouldn't that serve as better cover?" he asked, and then continued:

"Better than retreating."

Ewell looked over the wall and replied:

"Yes, I believe that area will do us betta. Colonel, orda ya men to advance to that position."

Ewell then turned to Culp:

"Private, what is ya name? I want to remember it."

"Private Wes Culp, sir."

"Private Culp, ya just continue to keep ya eyes open and ya head down."

"Yes, sir, I will."

The men moved forward to the depression in the ground and then waited for further orders. While the advance along the Front Royal Road was stalled, the Confederates attacked the Union Forces on the other road leading into town, the Valley Pike. Even though the firing was continuing on their unit, Culp could hear the firing intensify toward the west.

"B.S., we must be giving it to 'em out west."

"Yeah, listen to the guns. I hope they ain't pinned down like us."

"What do ya think they will haff us do?" Arthur asked.

"I imagine we sit still a spell until somethin' can be done about the aatillery fia reigning down on us," Pendleton said.

"Yeah, maybe that relief will come from the west," Culp added.

"It'd betta. I don't see much advantage to this ground. Say, Wes, I saw ya hesitate during oua exchange of fia right befo the Yankees retreated. That's not like ya. What happened?"

"B.S., I saw him. I saw my brother William."

"Ya sure? How could ya see him with all the smoke?"

"Yeah, we was pritty fa, Wes," Arthur said.

"I tell you, I saw him. And, he saw me. The look he gave me. I'll never forget it. And, he fired purposely right at me. He wants to kill me."

Culp hesitated and then continued:

But, I couldn't shoot *him*."

Neither Arthur nor Pendleton knew what to say to their friend, as they saw the emotion in his eyes. After a moment of silence, Pendleton said:

"Wes, I cannot begin to undastand what ya going through. But, the chances of ya seeing him, and him seeing ya, a not good."

"Who else might be out there, who else might I see?"

"It's best not to think that. They a the enemy of oua cause and they a hea to destroy oua way of life, capture oua towns, abuse oua women. Rememba what the Yankees did in Fredaricksburg?" Arthur said referring to the destruction the Federals brought to Fredericksburg when they occupied the town for a day during the battle in December of '62.

"You're right of course. It is just hard. Hard to see my brother shooting to kill me."

"Waa is hard. We've seen it, heck lived it, fo the past two years. Let's just pray to God it will be ova soon and we and oua families, all of them, savive it," Pendleton said.

"I know how hard it is. But, I will not kill my brother or any of my friends. I just cannot."

"Well, ya better hope ya don't see 'em again."

The regiment was indeed pinned down by the Union artillery the remainder of the day and through night. It rained hard that night and Culp and his friends spent a very wet night wondering what the next day would bring.

CHAPTER 15

SKELLY

JOHNSTON (JACK) HASTINGS SKELLY, JR. was awakened before dawn on Saturday morning June 13th, by his good friend Billy Holtzworth:

"Jack, get up. We need to get the men up. The Rebs are coming and we are ordered to march out of the town to meet them."

Skelly was sleeping soundly as a result of the celebration he, Holtzworth, and Ziegler had done last night. They were up until well after midnight toasting the Union victory at Middletown the previous day, so he was very foggy. He shook his head to rid it of the cobwebs and said:

"Billy, really this early?"

"Orders are for us to ready to move by six o'clock, and that's only thirty minutes. We are going to march out south of the town and form a skirmish line near Abram's Creek. Let's get 'em up."

"Yes, sir."

Skelly rousted his men and had them form up. Once they were in line, Holtzworth addressed them:

"Men of the 87th, we are moving out south of town to meet the Rebs. They are on the way as we stand here, so let's not let them get there before us. We will form a skirmish line this side of the small creek south of town, Abram's Creek. Alright, let's get going."

The 87th Pennsylvania, the 18th Connecticut, and the 5th Maryland, marched to the south side of the town and met the 12th Pennsylvania cavalry. As ordered, they set their line before nine o'clock, behind a stone wall, and then waited for the Confederates. Skelly, Holtzworth, and Ziegler were behind the wall together.

"Hey, Billy do you think they be coming with more strength than yesterday?" Skelly asked.

"Wouldn't be a surprised. It did look like that was an advance group yesterday. If they are truly coming this way, and they are, I think they will hit us much harder."

"I think so too. They are on a major offensive north, which may mean they will be going into Pennsylvania if we don't stop them here in Virginia, or in Maryland," Ziegler added.

"You really think so?" Skelly asked.

"I do, so we must stop them or the next fight might be on the home soil," Ziegler said.

"William is right. We need to make a good stand here or who's to stop them from going all the way into Pennsylvania, and maybe even Gettysburg? It's on the way to Harrisburg and Philadelphia from where we are right here," Holtzworth stated.

"On to Gettysburg? Bringing the war to our town and to our families and friends? I never have thought of that. We always have had distance between them and home," Skelly said.

"We have, except for Antietam. But, other than that, they have always been on the defensive. Not this time. They are coming and will not stop until we stop them. I, for one, would like to do that here in Virginia," Ziegler said.

"What if they get to Gettysburg? What if we can't stop them? I'm worried for mother and for Ginnie," Skelly added.

"Let's not worry about that now. Let's just stop them. And, stop them here and now," Holtzworth concluded.

It was just before noon when the Rebel army approached on the Front Royal Road. They marched across Buffalo Lick Creek and formed a skirmish line north of the creek. The Rebel infantry then advanced directly toward the Union line. Skelly recognized from their regimental flag it was the Stonewall Brigade.

"It's the Stonewall Brigade. Isn't that where Wes Culp is attached?" he asked.

"Yes. I wonder if William knows? Skelly, let's go talk to him," Holtzworth said.

They went down the line to where William Culp was positioned.

"Lieutenant Culp, may we have a word?" Skelly asked.

"What's on your mind Sergeant, Corporal?" Culp asked.

"Lieutenant, do you know that is the Stonewall Brigade out there?"

"Yes."

"Isn't Wes with them?"

"Yes."

Holtzworth looked at him as if to say: "Is that all you can say?"

"Men, what do you want me to say? That I know my brother is out there? He's not my brother. He lost that privilege when he joined the Rebel army. If I get a shot at him, I am going to shoot him right between his eyes and kill that traitorous bastard. Do you understand that?"

Skelly and Holtzworth looked at Culp with a shocked look and didn't respond. So Culp said:

"If that's all, then you men return to your posts. And, make sure your men are at attention. They are here and I want to stop them here, before they get into town."

"Yes, sir," they responded.

Skelly and Holtzworth saluted Culp. He returned the salute, and then they went back to their position. After getting back, Skelly said to Holtzworth:

"Billy, he's really, *really* upset at Wes."

"I know. It's got to be hard on him to think his brother is a traitor to his country. It must be hard on the whole family."

"You and I both know Wes from when we were young. He's not the type to make a brash decision like that. He must have had a really good reason."

"Maybe. But, if it were me, I wouldn't, couldn't have any reason. I could never turn my back on my country."

"Neither could I," Skelly said.

At that moment, the Rebels charged.

"They're coming and there's that damn yell," Ziegler exclaimed.

"Let's shut that yell up with lead," Skelly said in return.

"Here they come boys. Let's give it to 'em. Fire!" Holtzworth ordered.

All at once the Union forces fired a volley at the Confederates, who returned with a volley of their own, and the fight was on. The Union artillery opened fire on the Confederates from two locations behind the Federal lines. The Rebel artillery answered and soon silenced one of the Union batteries. Although the Federals fought valiantly, the pressure of the Rebel attack, and the accuracy of their artillery, shortly forced them to give ground.

"Boys, move back to the town. And, let's do this orderly. Corporal Skelly, lead the men back," Holtzworth ordered.

The Federals then retreated into Winchester and the Confederates began to follow. Once the Federals cleared the field, the Union heavy guns from the town and from the Main Fort opened up on the Rebel infantry, stopping their advance. The Federals made it safely into the town and then set up a defensive position. They barricaded Main Street, the road leading north/south in the middle of town, and then waited for the next Rebel advance, which would not come for the remainder of the day, due to the heavy shelling. Skelly, Ziegler, and Holtzworth took position up behind the barricades. William Culp was not far from them.

"Looks like our batteries are holding them," Skelly remarked.

"For now, it looks like a stand-off," Ziegler returned.

Holtzworth noticed Culp positioned about twenty feet from him, and said to Skelly:

"Let's go see how William is doing. He doesn't look quite right, not his normal self."

The two made their way to where Culp was, and Skelly said:

"Lieutenant, you alright?"

"Jack, Billy, I saw him."

"You saw Wes?"

"Yes, and he saw me. He hesitated, but I didn't. Once I recognized him, I took a shot right at him. Missed...," Culp said as his voice tailed off. But he continued:

"Then, we had to pull back."

"You shot at him, purposely?"

"Sure, he's a Reb isn't he?"

"William, he's your brother, and our friend," Holtzworth said.

"You be friends with him. As for me, like I said, he's no brother to me. He is the enemy of these United States. And, as with the rest of 'em...," he gestured swinging his arm in front of his body:

"...he deserves to die with the rebellion."

"William, I know it is hard to think of this, but..."

"Not hard for me. He's been dead to me ever since we received his letter he was joining up with them. Annie cried for days, so don't try to tell me he's my brother. Like I said, he's dead to me."

"Jack, let's get back."

And to Culp, Holtzworth said:

"Lieutenant, if you don't mind, we would like to go back?"

"Men, carry on."

"Keep your eyes open, Lieutenant."

"Will do. Extra special, as I am looking for someone in particular."

It rained very hard that night and so the order was given for the men to abandon the barricaded Main Street and find cover within the town. They fell back and spent the night inside the town's buildings and houses. The Confederates realized the barricade was abandoned, and so the advance skirmishers from the Maryland battalion entered the town and took cover in the buildings on the south edge of town, awaiting daylight, when they could surprise the Federals.

CHAPTER 16

SKELLY

JOHNSTON (JACK) HASTINGS SKELLY, JR. rose early on Sunday June 14th. He spent a restless night in a building, which served as dry goods store. Inside the store were about twenty of the men from the 87th. Holtzworth and Ziegler slept near Skelly, but they too didn't get more than an hour or two of rest. Skelly spoke first:

"Are you awake?"

"Yes, William, you?" asked Holtzworth.

"I really never got to sleep," Ziegler replied.

Skelly went to the window, moved the curtain, looked outside, and saw that the sky was clear and the sun was beginning to make its presence known.

"The rain has stopped and it looks like it is going to be a warm day."

"I need to find Lieutenant Culp, to see what our orders are. And, to get some coffee. Stay here until I return," Holtzworth said.

He moved toward the door, opened it and left the store. It wasn't more than a couple of seconds, when Skelly and Ziegler heard a rifle shot. They rushed to the door and saw Holtzworth running back to the door, holding his hat to his head as he ran. They quickly opened the door and Holtzworth rushed in, slamming the door behind him.

"They have positioned sharpshooters at the buildings on the south edge of town. I was lucky they missed. I was on my way over to the Taylor Hotel, when the first shot was fired. It hit one of our men right on the steps of the hotel. He might be dead. I made it back here as fast as I could."

Holtzworth was breathing heavily and then ordered:

"Men, we need to flush 'em out or we won't be able to repel the attack on the town. Load your weapons, and let's go get them Rebs."

The men loaded their rifles and all of them nodded they were ready. Holtzworth ordered:

"They're on the upper floors on both sides of the street. Open the door slowly, then quickly go out and form a line. Once there, give it to 'em. Corporal Skelly, pick six men to go out first. Three of you fire at the buildings on the other side of the street and three on this side."

"I want five volunteers," Skelly said.

"Corporal, I said six," Holtzworth reminded.

"I'm going too."

Once the five volunteers came forward, Skelly went over to the door, turned the knob and pushed it open slowly. Once it was all the way open, Skelly said:

"Men, let's go, *now*."

They rushed out into the street, formed a line and aimed their rifles. Single shots came at them from each side of the road. The shots all missed the six. Knowing where the shots came from, they aimed their rifles and all shot in unison. Skelly hesitated as the other shots were fired. He did this purposely while waiting for his target to show. He saw a ruffle of the curtain on the window and then a shadow. He fired. Five had missed, but Skelly's found its target. He saw clearly a figure in a butternut uniform fall.

"You got him, Corporal," one of the soldiers named Smith yelled.

Just then the other Rebel fired again, hit Smith in the lower leg. He fell. Skelly reacted quickly.

"You two help me get him back inside. The rest of you back in, now."

Skelly and his two companions brought the wounded soldier back into the store. One of the men then dressed his wound.

"Not bad, it's just a nick. You'll be alright."

Holtzworth slapped Skelly on the back, saying:

"Jack, great work. I'll see you get recognized for that."

"Never mind that, Billy. There's still one out there."

"Yeah. Let's get him. Jack, how about we go get him?"

Ziegler chimed in:

"Count me in too. I want a piece of that Reb."

"We'll need two others. Again, only volunteers," Holtzworth ordered and continued:

"We'll go out on the street and keep close to the building. Once we get there, we'll go in after him. Are you ready?"

Skelly opened the store door only partially, so as not to alert the Confederate they were coming. Quietly they made their way out of the store, hugged the buildings and approached the building the shooter was occupying. It looked like a boarding house. Ziegler was posted outside to make sure the rear was covered. Then, they descended the steps and quietly opened the door leading into the cellar of the building and entered. It was very dark, but when their eyes adjusted they saw the cellar was cluttered with barrels and crates. They cautiously went to the back of the room and began climbing the stairs leading to the first floor.

"Quietly boys, quietly. He's on the third floor," Skelly said.

They reached the first floor, and continued to the second. The second floor had a larger landing and a large window facing east. Just then they heard shots being fired and the window glass then shattered, right next to them. Two of the four men fell. Skelly and Holtzworth also then dropped.

"Jack, you hit?"

"No, you?"

"Alfred, Charles?"

"I'm hit in the arm," Alfred exclaimed.

"Me to, Sergeant," Charles added.

"We need to get out of here. Can you two follow us back out?"

"Yes," they both said.

The four men kept low as they passed the shattered window, crunching glass with their boots as they passed. They went down the stairs into the cellar and then back out the door where Ziegler was waiting.

"You guys alright?"

"Jamieson and Zimmerman are hit."

Jamieson was wounded worse than Zimmerman, and didn't respond very quickly. Zimmerman said:

"I'm alright, just a nick."

Holtzworth looked over to Jamieson and said:

"You, Alfred?"

"I don't know Sergeant. I think I'm hit pretty good," he said looking down at his right arm where his hand was covering it. Blood was oozing between his fingers. He continued:

"It hurts real bad."

"Jack, get his rifle and let's get back to the store. William, where did the shots come from?"

Ziegler pointed to the area outside of town, east of the town, saying:

"Over there. They had a pretty good look at you being up there."

"Okay. Let's get back to the store. One at a time. Count to three before you go and run like you're being chased, because you are by the next man. I'll go first. Jack you go last. Now, let's go."

They all made it safely back to store.

Once the excitement calmed down, Skelly realized how close it was for him to being killed without knowing where the shot was even coming from. He began to shake. He crossed his arms tightly and bent over. Holtzworth noticed and asked:

"Jack, what's wrong?"

"Billy, I don't know. I just got a real fright. We didn't even see 'em. We could be lying on that second floor amongst that broken glass, bleeding and dying."

"Jack, I know. But, we've been through worse. What's got you so scared?"

"I don't know. I'm not afraid to die. But, all of a sudden I'm afraid I'll never see Ginnie again."

"Don't talk like that. You'll be just fine."

"I can't shake it. I can't shake this feeling I won't see her again, and it's got me really scared."

"Jack, that's daft."

"No, it's real. I can't even remember what she looks like."

"Jack, you got to get ahold of yourself. This battle is just getting started and we have a lot of work to do. We have to stop the Rebs here and now, so they don't make it to Pennsylvania or Gettysburg."

Holtzworth then went to the back of the store and was gone for several minutes. When he returned, he had a bottle of whiskey.

"I found this in the back."

To the men tending Smith's, Jamieson's, and Zimmerman's wounds, he said:

"Soak the bandages in this and give 'em each a sip."

To the rest of the men, he said:

"Boys, this is the only one, so let's make sure everyone gets a taste. Skelly, you first after the wounded men."

The bottle still was over three quarters full, when it was brought to Skelly, who took a small sip making sure he left plenty for the rest of the men to get their share. Once the liquor made its way down into his stomach, he began to warm up and the shaking stopped.

"Better?" Holtzworth asked.

"Yes, thanks. I think I just realized how much I love her and want to be with her. Billy, I have to ask her to marry me. I have to write her and ask her…"

"Well, then do so. Why wait until after the war is over? We don't know if it will be anytime soon, so do it. It will maybe put your mind at ease."

"I think it will. I'll do it tonight."

"Why not do it now? We're not going anywhere anytime soon, so now's as good a time as any."

"You're right, of course. Thanks, I already feel more at ease."

"Jack, congratulations. She's a fine woman and will make a fine wife. We always knew you two would be together, didn't we William?"

"Sure did. Jack, I'm real happy for you," Ziegler added.

"I got to tell mother first. I better write her, too."

Skelly then commenced writing the two letters. Holtzworth looked at his friend as he was working on the letters and noted how much he was at peace, smiling intensely. He wished he could find that peace he saw. But, how could he in the middle of this struggle? Amongst this death and carnage? He looked over at Jamieson and Zimmerman, and then realized how close he was to the end of his life this day. A cold shiver overtook him.

Skelly finished his letters and then looked over at his friends. They were asleep. He decided he would get some rest too. He laid his head down on his blanket and closed his eyes. As he was beginning to fall asleep, he thought of Ginnie. Sweet, Ginnie. He imagined the time when she would receive his letter asking for her hand in marriage. He saw clearly how she would react; pressing the letter hard to her bosom, tears in her eyes. As he fell asleep, he heard her saying: "Oh, Jack, yes. Yes..."

The three friends, along with the rest of the men, were awakened in mid-afternoon by the sound of many guns out to the west of town. They all got to their feet immediately, and Ziegler said:

"Billy, ours or theirs?"

"Sound like theirs. And, a lot of 'em. Out to the west near the West Fort. Now those are ours."

"I thought the Rebs were out east?" Skelly said.

"So did I. Could they have made it to the west like they did last year? If so, we may be in trouble," Holtzworth added.

"What shall we do?" Ziegler inquired.

"I'll go find the lieutenant and see if we can get some orders as to what we are doing," Holtzworth said.

"What about our friend out there?" Skelly asked.

"I'll just have to take that chance. Care to give me some cover?"

"Sure thing."

The two men went outside and Skelly aimed his rifle at the boarding house. He fired his gun while Holtzworth sprinted across the street. No shots were fired in return, so Skelly returned to the store. Less than a half hour later, Holtzworth returned.

"Our friend is gone and it looks like the Rebs are preparing to attack the town from the east. We are ordered to man the barricade and hold Main Street at all costs. Men, let's pack up and get out to the barricade. Jamieson, Zimmerman, and Smith report over to the Taylor Hotel. They're setting up a field hospital there. Men, let's get out there, now."

The men moved to the barricade and awaited an attack from the east that never came. The shelling out west became heavier, particularly the Rebel artillery. All at once the shelling stopped and then came the sound of the Rebel Yell, signifying the Confederates were attacking the West Fort. Shortly, thereafter the shelling from the fort stopped.

"They've just taken the fort. Men, get ready for the assault," Holtzworth said.

The shelling commenced from the West Fort, but the shells were aimed at the town and at the Main Fort. Still the Confederates did not come from the east. After a couple hours, the shelling from the Main Fort began to subside, but that from the West Fort intensified. This continued until dark. Once darkness came, a courier came from General Milroy to Colonel Schall. Schall sent for all his captains and lieutenants and issued the orders from Milroy to retreat, to the west on the Martinsburg Road. The orders were to retreat to Harper's Ferry, and these came directly from the War Department in Washington. Lieutenant Culp was summoned to Colonel Schall's headquarters and was told to get the men ready to move before midnight. By the time the orders were issued, it was well after midnight. The night was dark and so the movement along the Martinsburg Road was slower than intended.

Skelly, Holtzworth, and Ziegler tried to rush the men along as they were leading the march.

"Men, steady pace now. We cannot afford to be caught, otherwise we'll be spending a lot of time in a Reb prison," Holtzworth said.

"Billy, do you think they are following?" Skelly asked.

"Nah, their probably happy they kicked us out. But, let's not wait around to find out. We got a late start to this march, so we need to make up time."

The 87th marched hard until just before dawn, when they reached Stephenson's Depot. They passed a bridge on the right of the road. Five minutes later, they heard a roar of gunfire to their rear.

JUNE 14-15, 1863 WINCHESTER, VIRGINIA

CHAPTER 17

CULP

JOHN WESLEY CULP and his friends awoke early on the morning of Sunday, June 14th in a trench located southeast of Winchester. They had spent a cold, wet night. The artillery fire had ceased as it began to rain the previous night, and had not resumed with the coming of the new day. The sun came up and began to warm the day, and as it got warmer the puddles of water began to steam as the water evaporated.

Their unit awaited orders, which were finally given around mid-morning. They were to advance northwesterly, engaging the enemy as the opportunity provides. Just like the previous afternoon, the heavy fighting and the real action was west of town. It was around four o'clock when the action out west really heated up. Culp and his comrades were holding their westerly facing line, just east of Winchester, when the Rebel artillery, two separate units, one each northwest and southwest of the West Fort, posted on a high ground, opened fire. The cross-fire from these artillery units soon overwhelmed the fort and Rebel infantry stormed in and captured it. Once this was accomplished, the fort's own guns were turned on the Main Fort and the Star Fort, joined by the artillery from the west of the forts. With the loss of the fort and the high ground for the artillery, the tide of the battle turned in favor of the Rebels. Around nine o'clock in the evening, the decision was made by General Milroy that defeat was inevitable, and the Yankees should retreat while the getting was still good. About the same time, the Stonewall Brigade was ordered to support the army's move east to cut off the retreating Federals.

Johnson's Division, of which the Stonewall Brigade was attached, moved east along the Berryville Pike, and then turned northerly to the Martinsburg Pike. But, it wasn't until eleven o'clock that the Stonewall Brigade was ordered to follow.

"Men, we haff the Yankees on the run and need to cut 'em off befo they can escape to Maatinsburg. Now, we a behind and will need to catch up. Let's get staated and stay together, in night maach foamation," Sergeant Sheetz ordered.

Culp was excited about the victory and about not having to engage the 87th during the day. His mood was much lighter, and so he exclaimed:

"Let's hurry boys. Let's get them before they get away."

Pendleton chimed in, saying:

"Boys, they a fo the takin.' Let's go."

They were marching hard and were within about a mile of their destination, Stephenson's Depot, just before dawn. The remainder of the division was ahead of them, and then Culp heard the sounds of a fierce battle being waged.

"Men, let's go on the double quick to get in thea," the sergeant ordered.

The men began the trot of the double quick and in less than an hour reached the Winchester and Potomac Railroad. They crossed over and reached Martinsburg Pike. Taking position on the Pike, Culp noticed the battle was decided won by the Rebels, and all around the Federals were fleeing in an unorganized manner.

"Let's gatha 'em up, boys," the sergeant ordered.

And so, Culp, Pendleton, Arthur, and the rest of the men closed on pockets of Union troops who had not made their escape. While he was ordering several Yankees to move out, Culp looked out further and saw another group of about five enemy men attempting to escape. He heard his comrades order them to halt. They were about 300 yards out, so he could only see them by the color of their uniforms. They ignored the order and continued to run, so one of the Rebels fired, knocking one of the Federals off of his feet. He fell and then Culp noticed two of his companions stop to help. The Rebels were quickly on this trio of Yankees and forced them to surrender. The wounded one looked pretty seriously hurt to Culp, as it took awhile for the other two to get him to his feet and then walk him back toward the rear. And, he was heavily leaning on his companions for support. Culp shook his head thinking it a waste to try to escape.

"Alright boys, hands up," Culp ordered a group. He and his friends led the group back to the rear area.

As they were doing this, a shot rang out from behind them. They turned to see a Rebel soldier stagger and then fall. Another shot was fired, and Culp saw one of the fallen man's companions shoot the Federal soldier. Culp rushed over to see if he could help the fallen Rebel. Two men were standing over him when he got there. He looked down and saw it was Milton. Milton was shot in the chest and blood was beginning to stain his uniform. Milton started gasping for breath and began coughing. Culp was startled to see his arch enemy stricken like this. Then, he experienced pity for Milton. He kneeled beside him and asked gently:

"Charles, you alright?"

"Is that ya, Yank?"

"Yeah, it's me. You look okay. Can I get you something?"

"I'm a gettin' thirsta," Milton replied as his breathing became shallower and more frequent.

"Hurry, get him some water from the creek," Culp told one of the onlookers.

Culp took out his handkerchief and wiped Milton's brow. The soldier returned with a cup of water and Culp pressed the cup to Milton's lips. As he drank, Culp said:

"Charles, we are going to have to get you to the rear. Do you think you can do it? We will carry you there."

"I can, but I'm startin' to feel cold."

Culp unbuttoned Milton's uniform and saw the hole in his chest, above his heart, running with dark red blood. He dipped his handkerchief in the cup of water and wiped the blood from the wound. He pressed the handkerchief tightly to the wound. Milton groaned.

"You hold this tight, and don't let it go," Culp said to the soldier who brought the water.

"You three, we need to get him to the rear and fast. Pick up his legs and his other arm. I'll take his left arm near the wound. Alright, one, two, three, lift."

They carried Milton over the railroad tracks and about another two hundred yards, where they came upon an ambulance transporting the wounded from the earlier battle. They gently placed Milton into the wagon. Culp looked at Milton. How pale he looked. He was about to say goodbye, when he noticed Milton had fainted. He leaned down to see if he was still breathing. He was. Then, the wagon took off toward where Culp figured the hospital was. He was very melancholy as he left to find his friends, as he had seen his enemy, or more so his former enemy, so helpless and dying.

Culp returned to his unit as the remainder of the Federal troops captured were deposited to a secure area being used to guard them. He was exhausted from the last three days of excitement, but was pleased as the Army of Northern Virginia was once again victorious over the Federal Army of the Potomac. Culp found Pendleton and Arthur sipping coffee and discussing the battle with soldiers around a campfire. It was about noon and the sun was high in the sky.

"Hey Wes, come on ova hea and haff some coffee. Ya hungry?" Pendleton asked.

"Really hungry. What have we got to eat?"

"They a cookin' us some poak and biscuits. Should be done in a few minutes. Smell that aroma. Good stuff," Arthur said.

"Wow, this battle sure turned quickly yesterday. I wasn't sure when we were in that trench, were you?" Culp asked.

"No. I heard tell that Gen'rl Early circled aroun to the west of Winchesta, set his aatillery and pounded the West Foat. He then maached his infantry aroun without them even knowin'. Then them Louisiana boys took the foat. After that, it was all ova," Arthur said.

"That must have been some move. Can you imagine the surprise of them Yankees when the Louisiana boys charged?" Culp asked.

"Those Louisiana Tigas are handful even when thea is no saprise. It musta been a route," Pendleton said.

The three friends grabbed some food, drank more coffee and then set their tent for the night. Each decided a rest for the afternoon was necessary. Much of the army did the same and the afternoon rest turned into a rest for the remainder of the day and night.

CHAPTER 18

CULP

JOHN WESLEY CULP had slept all afternoon the previous day, all night and most of the morning. The army was to move on to Winchester the next day, but were given this day to rest. Culp arose, leisurely made his way to the fire, drank a cup of coffee, ate some food, and went to find Pendleton and Arthur. He found his friends talking with some of the other members of the Stonewall Brigade.

"Well, nice to see ya alive this moaning. We weren't sure ya gonna make it afta hearing ya snoring," Pendleton said.

"Ya were like a rock thea, Wes," Arthur added.

"I did really need some rest."

"Wes, we heard some of the prisonas are from the 87th. We thought ya might want to make a visit."

"Indeed I do. Would you like to come along?"

Sure. We was hoping ya would invite us."

They made their way to the area of camp where the prisoners were being kept. They walked around the area for only a minute, when a voice cried out:

"John Wesley Culp."

Culp followed the sound of the voice and saw a familiar face emerge from the group of Union soldiers.

"Billy Holtzworth."

The two men approached each other and shook hands, but then Culp embraced Holtzworth and said:

"How are you? No wounds? Oh, forgive me. This is B.S. Pendleton and William Arthur. B.S. and Bill, this is Billy Holtzworth, one of my closest friends from home."

"How do Billy?" Pendleton said shaking his hand.

Arthur shook his hand too. Holtzworth cordially greeted them in return, but then turned to Culp and said:

"Wounds, no. But, Jack Skelly has got a nasty wound in his upper left arm. So far no one has looked at it."

"Billy, take me to him," Wes replied.

The three men followed Holtzworth to where Skelly was laying. As Culp approached, he heard Skelly groan in pain.

"Jack, I found Wes Culp."

Skelly turned and looked up at Culp.

"Wes, it's great to see you. How are you?"

"I'm fine, but how are you?"

"Not so good I'm afraid. I think I've lost a lot of blood and I think the bone is in pretty bad shape. There's a lot of pain. The doctors haven't been here. I think this here bandage should be changed. Holtzworth got me this stick to chew on, which helps some."

"Jack, if the doctors aren't coming to see you, then let's get you to them. B.S., can you see if we can find a doctor or an ambulance?"

"Of couase."

"Jack, this is B.S. Pendleton and William Arthur."

"Pleased to meet you. Wes it is so good to see you. I know a lot of folks back home would love to know you are alright," Skelly said wincing in pain.

"That's for sure. How long has it been?" Holtzworth asked.

"Late '58, so almost five years."

"My God, has it been that long? You really haven't changed much."

"Neither have you two. How are my sisters and William?"

"They are doing fine. William escaped and I assume is on his way back home. Oh, did you hear your sister Annie married Jefferson Myers?"

"Really? That's grand. I knew she was sweet on Sallie's brother, after all she spent a lot of time at the Myers and I knew it wasn't just because of Sallie."

"That's right, we kind of figured something like that would happen, too. Annie and Sallie were almost inseparable. Remember that picnic we had on your cousin's hill in summer of '58 just before you left?"

"Sure do. I just thought about it the other day and told B.S. and Bill about it. Bill, remember about the picnic and the whiskey? It was Billy's whiskey."

"I do, and was a hoping I'd get to meet 'im one day."

"Billy, remember Jack wouldn't have any because of Ginnie? How is she, by the way?"

"She's fine. I miss her so. I need to get back home to see if she's alright. Maybe this arm will get me home. Damn, it hurts," Skelly said.

"You get back home for good and Ginnie will be hitching you up," Holtzworth teased knowing about Jack's intentions.

"Yeah, that's the general idea."

Pendleton returned saying:

"Wes, he's gonna haff to go to the hospital set up in Winchesta. I arranged to haff a wagon take 'im right away. Let's get 'im ova to the supply tents and they will get 'im a wagon."

"B.S., that's wonderful, thanks," Culp said.

"Hey, a friend of ya's is a friend of mine."

"Billy, I wish I could get you out of this area, but I'm afraid I can't. We'll take him over and get him a ride to Winchester and then return later today to see how you are."

Culp then went over to Skelly and said:

"Jack, let me help you up."

Holtzworth and Culp helped Skelly to his feet, and then put Skelly's good arm around Culp's shoulder, and with Pendleton's support, walked Skelly to where they could put him in a wagon. It was already going to Winchester, so making room for Skelly was easily accommodated. Culp decided he should go along to make sure Skelly was treated more like a wounded soldier and not an enemy soldier.

Culp found a blanket and folded it into a pillow, and then placed it under Skelly's head saying:

"Jack, here, this should be more comfortable. We should be there in an hour or two, so try to rest."

"Wes, thanks. It's so good to see you."

"And you, my friend."

The wagon ride was a little less than two hours. Skelly slept the whole way. Once they arrived in Winchester, the driver drove immediately to the hospital, where two orderly soldiers came out to see Skelly. Seeing his arm, they took him immediately to the area where the doctors were treating the wounded soldiers, most were Confederates. Culp went with him and stayed until the doctor came over. The doctor unwrapped the bandage, looked at the wound, felt the bone area, as Jack let out a mild scream of pain.

"Is he with ya?" the doctor asked Culp.

"Yes."

"Well then ya can hear this. The arm has to come off right away. The bone is shattaed."

"No way it can be saved?" Skelly asked.

"None. And, we need to do it now. Can ya assist us?" the doctor asked Culp.

Culp had never done this before, and swallowed hard.

"Yes, what do you need me to do?"

The doctor ignored him and said to the orderlies:

"Take him to the sagery room and get him ready."

And, then to Culp:

"Come with me."

Culp followed the doctor into the surgery room. The doctor said to him:

"Ya are going to haff to help hold him. Thea is a lot of pain with this, so a friendly face is sometimes helpful. Ya will be that friendly face, understood?"

Culp gulped hard again and said:

"Whatever you need of me."

"Really, I just need ya to do ya best to keep him still and as calm as possible."

No sooner was this said, than the orderlies brought Skelly into the room. They removed his bandage and stripped him to the waist. They lifted him onto the table and then strapped his legs and his good arm.

"Private, ya hold his shoulda hea and put this in his mouth. Haff we got any whiskey? Private, give him this."

"Jack, here drink this."

Culp put the bottle of whiskey to Skelly's mouth and poured a little in. Skelly swallowed and then coughed.

"Another," the doctor said.

"One more, Jack."

Skelly drank and when he was finished, Culp said:

"Now what would Ginnie say?"

Skelly smiled at Culp, and didn't notice the doctor had begun to saw. It took a couple of seconds and then Skelly screamed in agony. The doctor continued to cut and said:

"Get that stick in his mouth."

The saw reached the bone and so the doctor adjusted it to above the bone and with a faster motion of the saw, the arm was removed just below the shoulder. A tourniquet was set and then bandages were wrapped around the stump that remained of Jack's arm. Culp kept the stick in Skelly's mouth and told him:

"Keep biting Jack, keep biting."

After a few long, agonizing moments, the pain was too much for Skelly to handle, and he then fainted. Culp removed the stick from his mouth as the doctor completed wrapping the wound tightly.

"Ya did well, Private. Ya friend is a tough customa. Usually, thea is much more screamin'. We'll take it from hea, and get him a bed. He should sleep for awhile and one of the girls will look after him, so ya can return to ya unit."

"Doc, we are coming to Winchester tomorrow, so I will come by and see him. Please take care of him. He is a good man."

110

"We'll do the best we can."

Culp left the hospital, deeply saddened to see his friend like that. It didn't help him as he thought one of his comrades had caused the wound. He thought: "I just wish this damned war would end. So many lives changed, ruined."

What he didn't know was soon how many lives would be ruined in the fields and hills he grew up and played in.

CHAPTER 19

CULP

JOHN WESLEY CULP and his unit broke camp around mid-morning on Wednesday, June 17th. They were heading for Winchester to re-goup as an army and prepare for the continued movement north. The Yankees were swept from Winchester and the Federal army garrison located there destroyed. So, now there was nothing to stop the Rebels from entering into Maryland and ultimately into Pennsylvania. Into Northern soil, a place the Confederate Army had not been. With this, came the chance for a victory and maybe a chance to end this war. The men knew this and so morale was extremely high.

Culp packed his belongings and met his friends by the campfire.

"Wes, I hear tell we headed fo Maryland. Today we go to Winchesta, and then Friday up to Maryland," Arthur said.

"And, after that, Pennsylvania. Who's to stop us? The Aamy of the Potomac is still south, too far away to even attempt it. Even, if they did, we'd whup 'em just like at Winchesta," Pendleton added.

"That was some fight at Winchester, wasn't it?" Culp offered.

"Whew, we sure did sho' 'em. We are the best fightin' aamy in the whole woald," Arthur added.

"I do believe ya are right, we are the best aamy in the woald, and we weren't even commanded this time by General Lee, so they didn't get oua best. Just wait to see what we will do up noath, when we are all togetha at full strength. I pity those folks up thea," Pendleton said.

"Hey Wes, ya ain't saying much. Ya alright this mornin'?"

"Fine. I am as excited as you all. But, I just wish it wasn't Pennsylvania we were headed. I'm going to go say goodbye to Billy Holtzworth."

Culp went to where the prisoners were being held. He found Holtzworth and then said:

"Billy, we are headed to Winchester today and then up north into Maryland on Friday. I guess I won't be seeing you for awhile."

"Yeah, word is we're headed to Richmond and a prison there."

"Billy, that's not such a good place. You got to take care of yourself. It's going be rough going."

"I know. It's not going to be no picnic on Culp's Hill, that's for sure."

Culp smiled and said:

"I sure do wish we could do it again, Billy."

"Yeah, me too. Except this time, you bring the liquor."

They both laughed and Culp embraced Holtzworth. He pulled away and grabbed him by the shoulders and said:

"Really, take care of yourself. I want to make sure you are going to be there when I bring the whiskey."

"I will and you too. Keep your head low. And, if you get to Gettysburg, tell everyone I am fine and will be home in no time."

They shook hands and Culp said:

"Billy, I will, I promise."

The army marched to Winchester and arrived in town around two o'clock in the afternoon. They set up camp and Culp decided it was time to see Skelly. He went to the hospital at the Taylor Hotel. Once there, he asked for Skelly and was shown the bed where he was resting. The hotel smelled of antiseptic, whiskey, and the sweet, sickening smell of rotting flesh. Culp momentarily held his handkerchief up to his mouth and nose. He could feel his stomach turning. But, he thought of Jack and how pitiful he looked when he left yesterday. He approached the bed where Jack was staying and gave himself a talking to make sure he was in good spirits. Jack needed that.

"Hey Jack, wake up."

Skelly was sleeping soundly, and then woke up. He looked awful to Culp; pale and sweaty. A young woman was wiping his forehead, when he stirred from Culp's greeting. He opened his eyes, saw Culp, and said weakly:

"Wes, is that you?"

"It's me, Jack. How are you doing?"

"I feel awful. The amount of pain is intolerable."

"You know the doc told me yesterday you are one tough piece of hide."

"Well, I don't feel so tough today. And my arm, what am I going to do with only one arm?"

"Jack, you're lucky. Once you get well, like we said yesterday, they'll probably send you home. Home to Gettysburg."

"You really think so?" Skelly said with a smile and then a wince at the pain.

"Sure do. Your war days are over."

"I sure would like to go home. I can see Ginnie. But, what's she going to say when she sees me like this?"

"Jack, she's daft about you, one arm or two."

"You know, I'm going to ask her to marry me when I get home. I even got a letter to her to ask. Also got one for mother, to let her know too."

"That's wonderful."

"It is in God's hands now if I can recover and get home to her."

"You'll be fine, it's just gonna take a spell."

Skelly coughed and then winced again at the pain.

"Wes, I sure am tired. Can you come back tomorrow?"

"I'm afraid I can't. We are moving out in about an hour. Up north."

"Your army sure whipped us and we were the only force to stop you from getting north. Are you going to Pennsylvania?"

"Dunno. All we know is we are headed into Maryland on Friday."

"Say Wes," Skelly said as he pointed to two letters and then continued: "I know I won't be able to post these letters for awhile and I sure would like Ginnie and mother to know real soon about the marriage proposal. Could you take 'em and if you get to Gettysburg, you can drop them off, or just post 'em at a post office?"

"Are you sure? We might not get to Gettysburg."

"That's okay, then just drop them off at a post office and they'll get there. Sure a lot sooner than if I hold onto them."

"I'll be honored to do so," he said and then stuffed them into his shirt.

Skelly coughed again and then turned his head away. Culp could see the tears in his eyes, partly from the pain in his body and partly from the pain in his heart, he surmised.

"I need to be on my way, Jack. Take good care and follow doc's orders."

"Wes, you too. And, thanks for the help you gave me. I will be forever grateful."

"You'd have done the same for me. After all, what are friends for?"

Culp leaned down and said goodbye, without words, with only a deep look into his friend's eyes. Skelly returned the look and then looked away, tears rolling down his cheeks. Culp needed to leave as tears were filling his eyes too. He turned away and patted his shirt where he stored Skelly's two letters. He would keep his promise to Jack, he thought. He just wondered if Jack would live to be able to come home to Gettysburg and marry Ginnie.

As he was leaving, he stopped one of the nurses and asked:

"Will you please write me a letter if his condition worsens?"

The nurse nodded and so Culp gave her his name and his unit and then left. And, then she said:

"Culp, huh? I heard not such good news about a friend of yas."

"Really, who?"

"A man named Milton, Charles Milton. He up and died this morning."

Culp was saddened by this news. He remembered how pitiful Milton looked as he was caring for him in the field two days ago. And, now he too was gone. So much death and destruction from this war. He left the hospital area in much despair.

As he was returning to his unit, he couldn't help but to sadly reflect on his friend Skelly. He also wondered what his reception would be if indeed the Army of the Northern Virginia invaded his home, where his family and friends were. The same family and friends he hadn't seen since '58. The same family and friends he turned his back on. The same family and friends who thought he was a traitor. He was going home, whether he wanted to or not.

Part 3

The Invaders Cannot Be Stopped

On June 15th a small band of Confederate cavalry crossed over into Pennsylvania and briefly occupied Chambersburg, a town just 25 miles west of Gettysburg. Along with harassing the citizens of Chambersburg, the Rebels engaging in rounding up free blacks, ultimately sending them back South and into slavery.

Also on June 15th, the reality of the Federal Army, in its present state, to not be able to stop the Rebel invasion of the North became clear to President Lincoln and spurred him into action. He put out a request for 100,000 men to be enlisted to meet the invasion, including some 50,000 from Pennsylvania. This call for troops was a failure, as less than 20,000 men answered the call, 8,000 from Pennsylvania and 12,000 from New York. But, these men were at best amateur, not well trained, and simply no match for the battle hardened veterans of the Rebel army.

General Joseph Hooker, General-Commanding of the Union army of the Potomac, began moving his forces northerly in mid-June, placing his army squarely between the Rebel forces and Washington and Baltimore. His movement, being slower than wanted combined with his lack of recent success, was enough to have him removed from command, and so Hooker was replaced in late June by General George Gordon Meade, a Pennsylvania man. Meade continued the move of his army north, tracking the Rebels and protecting the Union capitol.

On June 19th, the advance forces of the Rebel army, led by those of General Jubal Early and General Dick Ewell, crossed the Potomac into Maryland. On the 22nd, the main army crossed into Pennsylvania and entered Chambersburg, and on the 23rd fully occupied Chambersburg, and then the town became a staging point for the army.

Once in the North, and over a period of less than two weeks, the Confederates confiscated a great deal of supplies, paid as a "tribute" to the conquering army. During this time, the towns in Maryland and Pennsylvania paid tribute adding up to: 6700 barrels of flour; 7900 bushels of wheat; 5200 cattle; 1000 hogs; 2400 sheep; and 51,000 pounds of cured meat. As a result of this foraging and tribute collecting effort, the army didn't just survive in enemy country, it thrived. And, what was just a few short weeks before, an army living on just enough to subsist, became a well-fed fighting machine. But, supplies weren't the only things gathered by the Southern Army. As earlier in the month, people of color were rounded up and sent south back into slavery.

At around 3:00 in the afternoon on Friday the 26th, the first Confederates entered Gettysburg. These were the cavalry forces of the 35th

Battalion, Virginia Cavalry, later in the war popularly known as "the Comanches." They made a grand entrance into the town riding hard and fast, hooting, hollering, shouting for Jefferson Davis, and firing their pistols in the air, making quite a spectacle for the local folks. The Virginia horsemen were followed shortly thereafter by the infantry forces of Early, and these soldiers were described by the town folk as dirty, shoeless, and certainly less than human looking, rather more like animals. The front and back covers of this book illustrate this very same moment of the first Confederate occupation of Gettysburg.

Early's troops left Gettysburg the next morning, moving easterly toward York and then on to the Susquehanna River at Wrightsville, only to return on July 1st to join and support the Rebel's attempt to win this crucial battle and the war.

The citizens of Gettysburg, both black and white, experienced being occupied by the enemy forces for a day over that last weekend in June 1863, but that was nothing compared to what was coming.

CHAPTER 20

BROADHEAD

SARAH (SALLIE) M. BROADHEAD awoke early as her four year old daughter Mary came into her room she shared with her husband Joseph. Mary climbed into bed and snuggled up next to her. Sallie marveled at the girl as she loved her with all her heart. She said:

"My, you are certainly up early this morning, little one. Are you feeling well?"

"Yes, Mama. I had a bad dream and it scared me."

"What scared my precious little Mary?"

"Mama, I dreamed that dirty, bad men had come to our town, a whole lot of them. And, they were coming into our house."

"Oh, my sweet little Mary, now don't you fret. We are safe here in this house, and no one is here but your Papa and me."

Joseph was slowly waking up, but when he heard about Mary's dream, he was now at attention, and chimed in:

"Your Mama's right, little one. We won't let anyone come into our house and we sure won't let anyone scare our Mary. You will always be safe with us."

"Morning, Papa. I hope I didn't wake you. You need your rest for work."

"Morning, my little love. No, I need to rise now, so I am glad you were here to wake me. Do you feel better now about that dream?"

Mary smiled brightly at both her parents, saying:

"Yes, Papa."

"Since Papa is already up, let's hurry downstairs and see if we can cook us some breakfast. Now, you go back and get some warmer clothing on and we will whip some up."

Mary jumped out of the bed and ran to her room. Sallie got out of bed, went over to the window and pulled the curtain open. She guessed the time was around five o'clock in the morning, as the sun had not yet risen, but the eastern sky was glowing. She was disturbed about Mary and so she said to Joseph:

"No wonder she has dreams like that, with all the talk in the town of the Rebels coming. Joseph, how are we going to protect her? What if they do come?"

Broadhead house as is today. (Seamon)

"Sallie, now don't you fret neither, love. We gotta be strong, and particularly for Mary's sake. Let's just take it one day at a time and keep the house as we always have. Best for us and for Mary."

"Joseph, you're right. We must keep our house as happy and safe as we can for her. And, we have to not talk about the Rebels, at least in her hearing."

"Aye, for Mary."

Sallie left the bedroom, went down the stairs and into the kitchen, just as Mary came running in.

"Mama, what shall we make for Papa's breakfast?"

"Well, can you help with the biscuits and set the table? I'll put on the coffee and get the bacon and the eggs cooking. Wash up first."

"Yes, Mama."

Mary helped Sallie cook breakfast and when Joseph came down the stairs, they all sat down at table and ate bacon, eggs, and biscuits. After finishing the food, Joseph rose from the table saying:

"Mama, Mary that was wonderful. I must be getting off to work. The railroad waits."

Sallie saw her husband to the door, kissed him goodbye, and turned to Mary and said:

"Now young lady, you are up a little early for your age, so I want you to go back in your room and see if you can get a little more sleep. After you wake, we can go for a nice walk, maybe to the store, and visit Mrs. Burns."

"That sounds grand, Mama. Can I play with Ruthie for awhile and have her nap with me, too?" Mary asked referring to her little doll.

"Yes, sweetie, you make sure Ruthie gets her sleep, too."

Sallie cleaned up the breakfast dishes and went upstairs, tucked Mary in, and then went to her room to lay down for awhile. She lay down, but her mind raced with worry. She thought:

"The whole town was talking about the Rebels. What if they do come? What shall I do? How will I get through this? I must have a way to free myself of these worries, and still keep Mary sheltered from them. But, how? Maybe, I'll keep a diary. Yes, that might help."

This thought eased her mind a little and she finally fell asleep, but the anxiety and the worry was never far from her mind.

Sallie woke up around ten o'clock, got out of bed, dressed and went to wake Mary up. Mary woke with a slight whimper, but once her eyes were open, that warm smile returned to her face.

"Hi, Mama."

"Did you have a nice sleep?"

"Yes, Mama. What shall we do?"

"Well, let's get dressed and go for a walk out to Mr. McPherson's farm and see if we can feed some apples to the horses. Then we can go to the store and get you some peaches and a piece of hard candy. Would you like that?

"I sure would. Can Ruthie come along?"

"Why sure, you bring Ruthie, but make sure she is a good girl like you."

"I will, Mama."

After feeding and petting some of the horses on McPherson's farm, Sallie and Mary walked back to town along the Chambersburg Pike. They turned south on West Street where they met Mrs. Burns cleaning one of her carpets, hanging it over the railing and striking it with a broom, on her landing outside her front door.

"Good morning, Mrs. Burns," Sallie greeted.

Barbara Burns stopped her cleaning and said:

"Why, good morning Sallie. And, to you too, little Mary,"

"Thank you kindly, Mrs. Burns."

"Mary, would you like to come in and see the baby? Sallie, you look like you could use a cup of tea."

"That would be wonderful."

Sallie and Mary crossed West Street and mounted the stairs to the entrance to the Burn's home. Barbara opened the door to the house and the two women and the little girl entered. Once inside the house, they walked through the kitchen and into the living room area, where the Burns' adopted daughter, Martha Gilbert, was playing with her little daughter, Mary Jane. Mary Jane was about eight months old, but was already crawling, and so Martha made a funny sight, Sallie observed, following the fast little child around the living room.

Sallie remarked with a smile:

"Good morning, Martha. I see Mary Jane is a fast little one. I remember those days, not long ago."

"She certainly is, and a handful at that," Martha replied.

Martha Gilbert was 23 years old, was a little over five feet tall, had brown hair parted in the middle, shoulder length and curly in the back of her head. She had brown eyes, a slightly wider than average nose and a warm smile. She wore a multi-colored, with lots reds, browns and whites, multi-patterned blouse, commensurate with her outgoing personality, buttoned tightly around her neck and topped with a white, laced collar. Her long skirt was dark brown and was loped as if she would be doing a lot of walking, and she was doing so, chasing her daughter around the house. She wore no shoes.

She was born in December 1839, and was baptized in 1841 under the name of Martha "Gilbert." Her mother was named Mary Little, and her father was thought to be man named Henry Gilbert. They were unmarried at the time of her birth and remained that way, as her grandmother brought suit against Gilbert charging him with Fornication and Bastardy. The courts dismissed the charge, so Gilbert's paternal role in Martha's life remained unclear. Her mother spent most of her life in the Almshouse, a place for those folks who needed help, mostly mental help. So, little Martha was then adopted by the Burns' in the early 1840's. She loved her adopted mother, and felt the same about John Burns, and she loved showing it as she knew it made him feel uncomfortable, a fact she relished.

Little Mary Broadhead approached Mary Jane, leaned down to her and said:

"Hi, little Mary Jane. Would you like to see my little girl, Ruthie?"

The child stopped, sat with her behind down and reached for the doll. Mary handed it to her and the child took it and put it up to her mouth and hugged it.

"Martha, Sallie and I are having a cup of tea. Would you like one also?" Mrs. Burns asked Martha.

"That would be wonderful, mother."

As Mrs. Burns disappeared into the kitchen to fetch the tea, she passed Mr. Burns, who came into the living room.

"Father, good morning to you. How are you feeling today?" Martha asked.

"Tired," he remarked sharply.

"Well, a good, hot cup of tea will fix that. I'll tell mother, but in the meantime can you help Mrs. Broadhead and little Mary keep watch on Mary Jane, please?" knowing Burns was not fond of watching the baby.

Burns grunted. Mary came over to Burns, grabbed his pants leg and said:

"Morning, Mr. Burns."

Burns patted the little girl on the head and said, as politely as he could muster:

"And, to you. You too, Sallie."

He moved away and followed his daughter into the kitchen. Sallie could hear his voice in the kitchen saying:

"Two little ones in our house. Just what I need. I'll be taking my tea in the parlor."

"Father, now you shouldn't be so rude to our guests. Come join us in the living room," Martha said.

The two women reappeared with four cups of tea, and Burns in tow. Mary was playing with the baby and her doll, so after passing around the tea, Martha said:

"Sallie, have you heard any more news of the Rebels?"

"No. We heard there was a huge battle at a town named Winchester in Virginia, about 85 miles southwest of here, but we haven't heard what the outcome was."

"Do you think they will come to Gettysburg if we don't win that battle?"

Burns piped in using his civilized manners and voice, even though he was looking very uncomfortable being around the two children and the three women, but being on his best behavior for his daughter:

"Of course. This town is a growing concern, and it has nice roads to York, Carlisle, and Baltimore. They will come here."

"I hope you are wrong Mr. Burns, I really do," Sallie said.

"Us too," Martha said pointing her cup toward, and looking at, her mother.

Barbara Burns changed the subject saying:

"Where are you and Mary headed today?"

"Well we just made a visit to Mr. McPherson's horses. Mary fed them some apples, didn't you sweetheart…?"

The little child nodded and said in an excited voice:

"And, pet and scratched their noses, too."

"Now, we thought we might go down to Fahnestock's for some fresh peaches and a piece of hard candy."

"That sounds like fun, huh Mary? I love hard candy. Will you promise to bring me a piece, too?" Martha asked.

"If it's okay with Mama."

"Sure it is."

"Well then it is settled. Make sure you pick out the piece for me."

"I will, Aunt Martha," the child said and using her affectionate name for Martha.

"Thank you, sweetie."

It was after noon when Sallie and Mary left the Burns' house. Mrs. Burns offered them to stay for lunch, much to the chagrin of Mr. Burns, but Sallie politely declined, saying they wanted to get to the store and home in time for Mary's nap. They continued their journey south on West Street and then they turned east onto West Middle Street. After about 10 minutes, they turned north onto Baltimore Street. Fahnestock's was on the corner of Middle Street and Baltimore Street. They entered the store and were greeted warmly by Daniel Skelly:

"Afternoon, Mrs. Broadhead, and to you, Mary."

"And to you, Daniel."

"How can I help you?"

"Well, we came for some fresh peaches, some tea and some sugar, and some hard candy, for this young lady, here."

Skelly leaned down to Mary, touched her politely on the nose and said to her:

"I'm sure we can find some of that for you."

"Daniel, do you also have a diary book?"

"Yes, there are a couple on the counter over there," he said pointing to the front counter.

As Skelly went over to the shelf with the peaches, Professor Michael Jacobs entered the store and seeing Sallie and Mary, greeted them warmly:

"Well, Mrs. Broadhead, how nice to see you. And, is that Mary? My, she sure has grown."

"Nice to see you, Professor."

Professor Michael Jacobs was the professor of Mathematics, Chemistry, and Natural Philosophy at Pennsylvania College, in Gettysburg. He was 55 years old, was of average height, with light brown hair and light brown eyes. His hairline was receding, and his hair was cut just above his ears, which he parted on the left side of his head. He had ears that stuck out from his head more than average, a strong nose, and a beard on his cheeks, but was clean shaven above his mouth and his chin. He also had a warm smile.

"What brings you to our little corner of the town?"

"Mary and I wanted to get some of Mr. Sherfy's peaches and a piece or two of hard candy."

"That's wonderful. I think I will get some peaches too, now that you mentioned it. Ah, Daniel, how are you today?"

Skelly came over with a bunch of the peaches, and said to Jacobs:

"Very well, Professor, thank you."

Skelly turned to Mary and said:

"Follow me, young Mary, and we will get you some hard candy."

"I need to get a piece for Aunt Martha, too," Mary said with excitement as she followed Skelly.

When Mary was out of earshot, Sallie said:

"Professor, do you have any news of the Rebels? I heard there was a battle at a place called Winchester, Virginia."

"Yes, I'm afraid I do. I was just over at the telegraph office, and I heard the Rebels swept our forces from Winchester, including the 87th Pennsylvania, just this morning."

"Really," Sallie said putting her hand over her mouth. She continued:

"How awful. Do we know if the 87th lost a lot of men? What of our boys from Gettysburg?"

"No, but the news isn't good. There are reports the Rebels are headed toward the Potomac River and into Maryland, with very little opposition. The Governor has sent out a telegram warning of the Rebel invasion and directing the storekeepers to move their goods."

"Oh, Lord. Mr. Burns maybe right, they will head here."

"They could very well come to Gettysburg. After all, we are between them and Harrisburg and Philadelphia."

Skelly returned with Mary, and having overhead some of the conversation between Sallie and the Professor, his face had turned white with concern. He said quietly to Jacobs, so as not to alarm the child:

"I thought I heard you say the 87th was swept from the field in Winchester?"

"From what I heard. It doesn't sound good, Daniel."

"Any news about Jack?"

"None specific. I'm sorry, I wish I had more."

"I'll have to tell mother."

Just then Ginnie Wade, Sallie Myers, and Annie Myers entered the store. Ginnie said:

"Good afternoon, Daniel…"

She stopped short seeing the look of concern on Skelly's face.

"Daniel, what's wrong?"

"Nothing, Ginnie," Skelly replied.

Ginnie would not accept his answer and said in the soft voice, like a big sister to a little brother:

"Daniel, now you tell me what's got you troubled."

"Professor Jacobs says the telegraph reported the Rebs defeated our forces at Winchester, Virginia."

"What of the 87th?" Annie Myers asked.

Both women looked intently at Skelly, and then at the Professor, with Ginnie saying:

"Professor…?"

"The news is not specific about the 87th or any of our boys," he replied.

"Oh my Lord," Ginnie replied, her hand moving to her bosom across her heart. Annie looked at her friend, and made her way over to her.

"Now, Ginnie, I'm sure Jack is fine. And, I'm sure William is, too."

"Yes, I am too," Sallie added.

Skelly got a hold of himself, went over to Ginnie, hugged her and said:

"Ginnie, of course, Annie and Sallie are right. They are both fine."

He turned to Sallie and said:

"Let me pack up your diary book and your peaches and get you on your way."

While he was doing this, Mr. James Fahnestock, the owner of the store, came in with his ten-year old son, Gates. After greeting the ladies, Fahnestock turned to Skelly and said:

"Daniel, we must make arrangements to move our most valuable goods out of the store and to safety. Ah, Mrs. Broadhead. I will need to speak with your husband about shipping these goods to Hanover and then on to Philadelphia. Will he be at the depot first thing in the morning?"

"Yes, he gets there around six o'clock."

"That's fine. Will you tell him I will be calling on him at six to lease some space on his cars to move my best goods on to Philadelphia?"

"I will indeed, Mr. Fahnestock. Now if you beg my pardon, I have to get Mary home. Good afternoon, ladies. My thoughts and prayers are with you and Jack and William."

Sallie paid for the diary, the peaches, and the candy and she and Mary left the store, suddenly very saddened about the news of the battle at Winchester. She was also concerned. "Could the Rebels be on their way?" she thought. She suddenly grabbed Mary's hand and squeezed it tightly.

"Mama, are you alright?"

"Yes, but we must get you home. It is time for your nap."

While Mary was taking her nap, Sallie got out the diary book she bought, and began penning an entry. She wrote the date and her first entry, which contained her thoughts about the Governor's direction for the people to move the goods quickly, and about the news of the Rebels crossing the river and coming this way.

CHAPTER 21

BROADHEAD

SARAH (SALLIE) M. BROADHEAD was awakened just after midnight by Mary shaking her.

"Mama, I had that dream again, can I come in bed with you?"

Sallie became fully conscious and looked down at the concerned child's face and said:

"Climb on in here with me."

The child climbed in the bed. Sallie hugged her tightly, and began to stroke her hair. She then rocked her. This was very comforting to the girl and she began to calm down. Sallie sang her a lullaby softly, not to wake up Joseph. Soon, after about five minutes, the girl was settled, and so Sallie said:

"Are you alright now? Can you go back to sleep in your own bed?"

"I think so, Mama. But, I'm thirsty. Can I have a drink of water?"

"Certainly. You hop back into your bed and I will bring it right directly."

"Thank you, Mama."

The child went back to her room, and Sallie put on a robe. She went down stairs to get the water. As she was in the kitchen pouring a glass of water from the water pitcher, she suddenly heard a loud noise from outside. She ran over to the front door of her house, moved the curtain back and looked outside. Off in the distance, to the south, the dark sky was glowing. Her husband Joseph came down the stairs, followed by Mary, as they too were awakened by the noise.

"What's going on, love?"

"I don't know, but look at the sky over there," she said pointing to the south. She continued:

"Could it be a fire?"

"I dunno, love. I'll go outside and see. You stay here with Mary."

Joseph opened the door and went outside. He went down the steps and onto Chambersburg Street, where he met his neighbors Jacob and Elizabeth Gilbert. The Gilbert's lived two doors down the street from the Broadheads.

"Joseph, is that a fire?" Mrs. Gilbert asked.

"Looks like it, love."

Just then a group of people rushed by running toward the middle of town. One of men stopped, looked at Joseph and said:

"The Rebels are coming and they are burning as they go."

And with that, he was off. More groups of people passed and the panic was on. Another man stopped and said to Joseph:

"We're getting out of town. You should too, if you know what's good for you."

Joseph turned to look at Sallie. She opened the door, descended the steps with Mary in hand, and joined her husband and her neighbors in the street. She said:

"Joseph, do you think we should go?"

"I dunno, love," he said, and continued to Gilbert:

"What do you think?"

Before Gilbert could answer, John Burns, Barbara Burns, and Martha Gilbert, with baby Mary Jane, joined them.

"What's all the fuss about?" Burns asked.

"Mr. Burns, look over there. It looks like a fire. And, people are saying it's the Rebs."

"Well, Gilbert and Broadhead, let's go and see. Get your guns and I'll get my rifle."

"Oh no you won't, Old Man," Mrs. Burns said.

Burns looked at his wife with a stunned look. Then his face turned into a grimace.

"Woman, I will not stand by like some sissy, if those traitors are invading our town. I'm getting my gun and that will be last we speak of it," he said emphatically and stormed off toward his house.

Mrs. Burns was about to object, when Martha said:

"Mother, leave him be. You won't be able to talk him out of it."

"Martha, my dear, he is almost seventy years old. Don't you think his time has passed?"

"Mother, he doesn't, so it really doesn't matter what we think."

Burns returned about five minutes later, gun in hand, hat on his head, and a determined look on his face. He joined Broadhead and Gilbert, who have retrieved their pistols and were waiting for his return.

"Well, let's go see if the Rebels are comin' and if they are, let's see what we can do about it."

"Joseph, you're not going with him, are you?" Sallie asked.

"Love, it seems like I have very little choice in the matter. Besides, someone needs to go with him to keep him from getting into trouble. Jacob, that burden falls to you and me."

Gilbert nodded. Joseph turned to the women and said:

"Ladies, now please go back into the houses. If it is the Rebs, they will respect women and the property if you are inside. We'll return shortly."

"Joseph, please be careful," Sallie said.

"Father, you too. And, don't do anything brash," Martha scolded.

"Old Jacob, you come back to me safe," Mrs. Gilbert added.

Burns gave an affectionate stare at his wife, as much as he could muster, but said nothing. Neither did she. The three men started walking south on West Street. More people passed them heading north toward Chambersburg Street, including some colored folk. Joseph recognized Samuel and Liz Butler, and so he greeted them:

"Samuel, Old Liz, where are you going to go?"

"Why masser Joseph. We's headed fo the road to Chammersburg. We ain't waitin' fo no Rebel sulders to ketch us, no sur," Old Liz said.

"Is it a fire in the town?"

"It's a fire alrigh', but it ain't in town proper, no sur. Looks like toward Emisburg," Samuel replied while pointing off in the distance toward the glowing sky.

"Sam'l, yu stop yur yappin'. S'cuse masser Joseph, but we be on our way. No sulder going ketch us, no sur," Old Liz said as she grabbed her husband's arm and pulled him along the street.

"You two be careful, now," Broadhead said as they disappeared into the night.

They continued walking south until they got to the edge of the town at the intersection of West Street and West High Street. They turned east onto West High Street and continued the two block walk to Washington Street. They stopped and looked south into the distance and saw the sky continuing to glow from the fire. Just then Professor Jacobs and his eighteen year old son, Henry, approached them and said:

"Good evening, gentlemen. That's got to be some kind of fire. The sky is sure bright."

Broadhead smiled at Jacobs and replied:

"Evening, Professor, young Henry. Sure is. But, it doesn't look threatening to Gettysburg. Folks say it's the Rebs and they're burning as they come."

"Well, they ain't gonna be burning our town, without some spilled Rebel blood," Burns added with one shake of his rifle.

"Professor, you have a good view in that direction from your attic. Maybe we could have a look to see if any Rebs are coming?" asked Gilbert.

"Mr. Gilbert, gentlemen, that is a real good idea. I do have a great view to the south. Let's go have a look."

The five men walked north on Washington Street to Jacob's house. Upon reaching the two-story house, which was made of red brick, had red-painted doors, numerous windows on both floors, topped with an attic that had several windows so that the the house had a view in all directions. The men entered the house and made their way up the stairs to the attic. The elevated view provided by the attic gave a little better prospective of the fire, but more so, a relief to the men as they could see the fire was not anywhere close to the town, but looked like it was at Emmitsburg, ten miles distant to the southwest. Jacobs was the first to speak:

"It looks as though it is in Emmitsburg."

"Looks that way. It must be a big blaze to light the sky like that," Gilbert said.

"Any sight of the Rebs on the road?" Henry asked excitedly.

The men stared intently to the south, and saw nothing resembling any organized movement of men or horses. Burns spoke next:

"Nothing. Just some folks coming this a way to get out of town."

"I don't see nothing either, but we should stay a spell whilst we are here, just to make sure," Gilbert added.

Broadhead pointed southward and observed:

"Professor, I didn't realize you had such a grand view of the south end of town. Why you can see all the way down the Emmitsburg Pike to the west, Seminary and Cemetery Ridges and all the way to Round Top to the south, and Cemetery Hill and Culp's Hill to the east."

"Yes, you might say I have a good view of anything that happens here."

"We like to come up here during clear nights to see the stars and do it regularly," Henry said.

"All this talk about the view. You can stay a spell, but I'm bored and am going home to bed," Burns growled.

"Yes, Professor, it doesn't look like we are in danger from the Rebs to-night. We will be on our way. Thank you for obliging us," Broadhead said.

The three men left the house and walked home. Burns, clearly disappointed with the lack of action besides seeing a good view of the massive fire, sulked the whole walk home, and mumbled to himself, saying:

"No Rebs. I am beginning to think they won't be coming at all."

"Let's hope so," Joseph added even though Burns wasn't addressing him.

It was just after two o'clock in the morning when the men reached their houses, bid goodnight, and went inside. Sallie and Mary were waiting for Joseph in the kitchen. They ran to him as he closed the door behind him. Sallie hugged him and Mary hugged his leg.

130

"Joseph, thank God you are home."

"Now love, it's alright."

A moment passed as the three hugged each other. Sallie said:

"Would you like a cup of tea?"

And to Mary, she said:

"That's quite enough excitement for one night, young lady. It is time for you to go off to bed."

"Yes, my little pet. Let's get you tucked in nice and tight."

They followed Mary up the stairs and into her room and tucked her into her bed, and said their goodnights to her. The girl looked up at Joseph and said:

"Papa, could you tell me a story?"

"Why sure, little one."

Sallie went downstairs and waited for Joseph. He came down the stairs a couple of minutes later and said:

"Bit of excitement for one of her tender age. She is resting pretty soundly now."

Sallie poured Joseph a cup tea. He drank and said:

"It looks like the fire is in Emmitsburg. It sure is a big one, love."

"Any sign of the Rebel army?"

"None. But, the town is in a rage, even the colored folks are leaving."

"Do you think we should leave?"

"No. We must stay here and protect our property."

"Alright. We will stay."

Michael Jacobs house as is today located at Washington and Middle Streets. (Faber)

CHAPTER 22

CULP

JOHN WESLEY (WES) CULP and the rest of the Stonewall Brigade made Shepherdstown about six o'clock in the evening on Thursday, June 18th. They just completed the 35-mile march from Winchester in the last day and a half, with the majority, about 25 miles done today during a sixteen-hour march. Orders were the brigade, as a part of General "Allegheny" Johnson's division of the army, was to be in Shepherdstown by the 19th and be ready to cross the Potomac River and proceed into Sharpsburg, Maryland. Some of the men were excited and glad their orders were to get to Shepherdstown the night of the 18th, as many were going home, and maybe a night of home cooking would be enjoyed. As a reward for their recent success at Winchester, passes were distributed to the men for a night of homecoming. Culp was excited to see Catherine. He knew the news of the arrival of the brigade would precede them and so he hoped she would be there to greet him when the army arrived. She did not disappoint. As the army marched into Shepherdstown, there she was dressed up in a fine yellow-and-white dress, with a matching bonnet. She looked lovely to him. She was accompanied by her house mistress, Jessie, a fine looking colored woman in her thirties, Wes guessed as he got to know her during his courtship of Catherine.

"Wes, Wes, over here," Catherine said as she waved a handkerchief wildly at him.

Culp looked at her while he continued the march, and gave her the biggest smile he had planted on his face in months. He moved his gaze back to straight ahead as the army continued their march to the north side of the town to camp and prepare to cross the river in the morning. Within an hour, the army reached the place where they would camp for the night, he had unpacked his things, had helped Arthur and Pendleton set up their tent, and had obtained his pass for the night, good until after midnight when he was due back. He excitedly made his way back in town to look for Catherine. He found her waiting for him in her carriage with Jessie. He approached the carriage without her knowing and addressed her:

"Miss Butler, could you come out of that carriage and greet a man from the Stonewall Brigade?"

She opened the carriage door and held out her hand for his assistance to descend the stairs. He grabbed it eagerly and as she made it down to the last step, he pulled her into his arms. She jumped into them with a soft, but happy, yell. He twirled her around and then put her down. She said:

"My, oh my, Mr. Culp, ya sure a frisky this evenin'."

"Only because I have missed you so, so much and because you are so lovely."

She leaned in kissed him softly on the lips and he returned the kiss. She tasted so sweet to him. They parted and he grabbed her by the shoulders and said:

"It's been so long, let me take a good look at you. You haven't changed a bit. I have every inch of your face deeply engrained in my mind, so I would know."

"Neitha have ya, except ya beard is a little longa."

"I must trim it for you then."

"Fatha is waitin' for us at the plantation. He is lookin' forward to hearing about ya battle stories."

"Is he ready to give us his blessing?"

"I dunno, but mayba, mayba...Let's get goin'. I know he is anxious to see ya."

"Good evening, Jessie."

"Evening, Masser Wes."

Culp helped Catherine back into the carriage and followed her up and in. The driver slapped the reins and the horse began to pull the carriage. It took about ten minutes to get to the plantation, as the horse was not in a hurry and neither were Culp and Catherine. He didn't speak, but rather drank her looks in. When the carriage pulled up in front of the house, Culp opened the door, climbed out and helped both Catherine and Jessie out and down to the ground. On the porch, Butler waited, and paced impatiently. He was dressed in formal wear, a gray ditto suit, with the waist coat and trousers matching the coat. The outfit was complemented with a black bow tie, a white shirt under the waist coat, and a gray bowler hat on his head. He smiled as Culp turned to look at him and said:

"Wes, welcome home. It is good to see ya. Ya a lookin' fine."

"Thank you, Mr. Butler, and you are looking well yourself."

The two women and Culp climbed the stairs to the porch, and reaching the top, he held out his hand to Butler. Butler took it and shook it a few times up and down.

"Wes, come, come, let us have suppa, and ya can tell us of ya brigade's successes."

Catherine grabbed Culp by the arm and snuggled up next him:

"Father, not quite so fast. I want to have 'em for myself befo suppa."

"Well alright, then. You two sit out hea on the poach, whilst we get the table ready. Jessie, go in a make sua suppa is ready and the table is set."

"Yes, Masser."

Jessie went into the house and Butler followed. Culp and Catherine went over to the porch swing and sat, her hand in his.

"Oh, Wes, I have missed ya so."

"Catherine, you don't know how I have missed you. I think of you every day and dream of this moment."

"And I, darlin'. Ya, know we a fixin' to move back down to Richmond, due to the awful man, Mista Lincoln's proclamation of this new state of West Virginia being final on Saturday. We will be leavin' on Sunday to get out of hea, so ya coming now was perfect timin'."

She kissed him again, lightly, and they just held each other closely and swung back and forth on the swing. After about fifteen minutes, Jessie appeared saying:

"Miss Catherine, Masser Wes, suppa is ready."

They went into the house and sat at the table. Jessie brought in plates of boiled beef, a baked chicken, biscuits and butter, boiled potatoes and cabbage, cooked carrots, and cherries. After saying grace, Butler took a helping of beef, a leg from the chicken, some potatoes and vegetables. While he was fixing his plate, he began the conversation:

"Well, it is fittin' ya are hea to join us in one of ou last suppas hea, before we go back to Richmond on Sunday. We'll be givin' this plantation up, and movin' back to the other we have. I'm sure Catherine told ya all about it."

"Yes, sir. I only wish I could help you with the move. I know it is going to be hard."

"Wes, tell us of the battle down at Winchesta. We heard ya boys whipped them Yanks good."

Wes waited until Catherine began to fill her plate and then began filling his.

"Yes, sir. It was a tough fight and the Yankees were well fortified. They had three forts guarding the town. We attacked the east side of town last Saturday, made some good progress and took some good high ground, but they pinned down with their big guns. We waited the night out in a heavy rain. The next day, we again attacked the east side of the town, but much to our surprise, our attack was a diversion as General Early made a brilliant move around the Yankee defenses and attacked from west of town. It caught them completely by surprise."

He took a bite of the chicken and potatoes, and couldn't help but to enjoy the food.

"Jessie, this chicken and potatoes is wonderful," he said loud enough for her to hear from the kitchen.

"Why thank ya, Masser Wes," came from the kitchen.

"Yes, yes, tell us more of the battle," Butler said impatiently.

"Well, when General Early attacked he had the high ground to the west, and so our artillery pounded the western fort from two directions. We could hear the roar of the guns, although from east of town, we couldn't see much. And then, the next thing we heard was the yell of the boys from Louisiana. They charged the fort and took it in short time."

He paused again to take a bite of food, and then looked over at Butler, who was on the edge of his seat waiting for more. So, he continued:

"After taking the fort, we turned the Yankees own guns on 'em at the other two forts and with the high ground to the west, we were pounding them from three locations. It was just a matter of time, after that. Late on Sunday night, we got orders to pursue the retreating Yankees to Stephenson's Depot, and caught up with 'em right before dawn. After an intense battle for about an hour, they surrendered and we gathered 'em up. It was a total victory."

"How excitin'," Catherine said.

"Yes, yes, glorious. We have heard how them dirty Yankees treated the good folks in Winchesta and to route 'em and kick 'em out that way. My, my how glorious indeed. Ya and ya regiment should be real pleased."

"Yes, sir. We are very proud."

Catherine detected something in Culp's voice just then, and remarked:

"Wes, ya don't sound so proud. Anything the matta?"

"No, Catherine, no. Well, yes, there is."

"What is it?"

"During the battle on Saturday, the Yankees we were attacking were from the 87th Pennsylvania."

"So, what does that mean?"

"My brother and a couple of my closest friends are in that regiment. And, I saw him."

"Saw, who, silly?"

"My brother."

Catherine took her napkin and covered her mouth. There was silence for a moment and then Butler remarked:

"Ya saw ya brother on the field of battle?"

"I did indeed, sir. And, he saw me."

"Did ya fire at him?"

"No, I couldn't do it. He's still my brother, even though he is a Yankee. But, he doesn't feel the same about me. When he saw me, he took a shot right at me. Fortunately, he missed or I wouldn't be sitting here right now."

Catherine looked pale. For the first time, it dawned on her that he could have been killed. But worse, by his own flesh and blood.

"Wes, ya alright? That must have been a awful ordeal," she said.

"I'm alright. But, then when we were chasing 'em as they were retreating, I saw two of my closest friends. They were captured, and one was shot in the left arm. I helped him to a hospital, where they cut off his arm whilst I watched. Oh, Catherine, excuse me. I didn't want to say that, especially at table."

"That's alright, sweetie. It must have been purely awful, indeed."

Butler, wanting to change the subject back to the glory of the victory, said:

"So, now the boys are on the march north. Will you go into Maryland and ultimately Pennsylvania?"

"I dunno, sir. They don't tell us much. But, I expect so. With Winchester out of the way, there's nothing to stop us from going there."

"An invasion of the North. How glorious. A victory or two on thea soil, and this war might be ova."

"I hope so, sir."

"Well, I declare, I hope so, too. Ya have been gone from hea much too long."

"I feel the same way, Catherine. I am tired of being away from here and from you."

"Papa, is now a bad time to talk of the futua? I mean once, we defeat the Yankees and have oua independence?"

Butler grunted and shrugged, but didn't answer. So, Catherine continued:

"After the wa, Wes is coming home, and as we a going to Richmond, he may not be able to go back to the carriage maka shop. He could help us out on the plantation in Richmond...?"

She looked over at Wes and with her eyes indicated it was time. He got the hint and said:

"Sir, I know I have asked you before, twice as a matter of fact, but I think this time it is different. I love your daughter with all my heart and want to make her my wife. I ask you for your blessing. Will you give it?"

Both Catherine and Culp looked at him to await his answer. He then spoke.

"Wes, as ya know, Catherine is my only daughta, my only child. My wife died when she was born, so I have loved hea with all my heart, as she is the only kin I have. That's why we moved up here, the memories were too painful down thea. But, now we have to go back, because of that, that man, Lincoln.

At any rate, I have always wanted the best for hea. I have sent hea to finishin' school to be trained as a real lady. I have instructed hea on the matters of running the plantation. I have protected hea from several suitas whilst ya have been away at wa, because I thought it ungentlemanly to allow any otha man to court hea whilst ya are fightin' so valiantly for oua cause..."

He paused and took another bite of meat and potatoes, took a sip of wine, wiped his mouth with his napkin, and then continued:

"I have done a lot of thinkin' on this matta. Ya are a Northerna by birth. But, I do believe ya have earned the right to be a Southerna by ya service in this hea aamy. I have watched how Catherine has waited for news of ya and the brigade, and I have watched hea light up this last day knowin' ya would be coming home, even for this short visit. So, it is my conclusion, that she loves ya with all her heaat. Therefo, I have decided to grant my pamission, with one condition, though, and that is the weddin' will have to wait for the end of the wa. Understood?"

"Oh, Papa, really......? I am so happy."

She got out of her chair and ran over and hugged and kissed her father. Wes approached him also and when Catherine was done, he shook his hand vigorously.

"Thank you, thank you, sir. I won't let you down. I will take good care of her and will always make her happy."

"Ya betta. But, I know ya will. Anyone who has been that persistent deseaves to marra my little girl. And, I know she is happy with ya. Now, let's sit down and finish ou suppa. Then, we can celebrate ya engagement propaly with some fine wine."

They finished dinner and retired to the parlor to make plans for the wedding. Culp thought it the best meal and the best day of his life. Even though he would only be there until midnight, as he had to return to his unit, he wanted to make every moment last. They made merry until around ten o'clock, when the old man decided it was time for him to turn in. He said his goodbyes to Culp and said he will make sure the wedding would be a grand affair; a fitting way to celebrate the winning of the war.

Culp and Catherine again went outside to the porch swing. She lay her head on his shoulder and said:

"Oh Wes, I cannot believe what we have waited so long for is finally gonna happen. Mrs. Wesley Culp. I cannot wait. Whilst you are gone, I'll make all the wedding plans, so right when the wa is ova, ya can come home and we can get married right away."

"That sounds wonderful, sweetheart."

"We'll invite the whole family as we will be in Richmond and have a grand affair. Do ya think ya family would want to come?"

Wes turned solemn. He hadn't thought about that part of it. Would they come?

"I dunno, my love. Maybe my sisters Annie and Julia would come. I just dunno."

"Maybe, when ya are up noath, ya'll get a chance to see them?"

"Yeah, I'm sure they'll welcome me in this uniform."

"Well, if ya do see 'em, why don't you tell 'em? Let them decide to come down and see ya life hea in Virginia. The plantation in Richmond is so much bigga than this one hea. Ya going love it thea."

"I'll love it anywhere you are."

"I'll have it all ready for ya thea. Ya just win this wa and come home to me, ya promise?"

"I will, I promise."

"Wes, life will be so grand. I am so happy, I just can't stop saying it. I am…"

"And, I am too. We will have a long life together and we will make sure we have a big family, and give your father a lot of grandsons."

The hour stuck midnight and so he had to leave. He held her tightly, kissed her hard and said he would be back just as soon as the war ended, maybe in a matter of weeks. She smiled and said:

"Now, ya Mista Culp, ya keep ya head down and come home to me. I just don't know what I'd do if I lost ya."

"Don't you worry, my love. I will be home before you know it."

They stood and he kissed her one more time. They then parted and he held her hand as he pulled away from her, looking deeply into her eyes. He finally let go, walked down the stairs while facing her. When he got to the bottom, he ran right back up, kissed her one more time and relished the moment, as it would have to do for awhile. He turned and ran down the stairs and disappeared into the night.

CHAPTER 23

WADE

MARY VIRGINIA (GINNIE) WADE awoke on Friday morning, June 19th in a troubled and anxious state of mind. It had been four days since she heard the news from Professor Jacobs of the loss the Union army sustained in Winchester, Virginia, and she had yet to hear if Jack was all right, or where he might be. Nothing was known of William Culp either, her sister-in-law Annie's brother. She had not been sleeping well these past four nights as a feeling of dread had entered her heart and no matter how hard she tried, she couldn't cast it out. If only there would be some news. She heard today that some of the soldiers from the 87th, who escaped capture, would be arriving at Gettysburg. Hence, her anxious mood for the day, as she also heard neither Jack nor William would be among them.

She started her day with her devotions. She went over to the sitting area in the living room of the house, where she kept her Bible. Today she decided to concentrate on the 23rd Psalm, and so she sat, got comfortable, opened the Bible and read aloud:

"The Lord is my shepherd, I shall not want. He makes me lie down in green pastures, He leads me beside still waters. He restores my soul, He guides me in the paths of righteousness for His name's sake, though I walk through the valley of the shadow of death, I fear no evil for You are with me, Your rod and Your staff they comfort me. You prepare a table before me in the presence of my enemies, You have anointed my head with oil, my cup overflows. Surely goodness and grace will follow me all the days of my life, and I will dwell in the house of the LORD forever."

She closed the book and shut her eyes letting the psalm flow into and over her heart. It was the perfect message to strengthen her for what she may have to face today, bad news of Jack. But, she knew very well the Lord was with her, today and always, and because of that fact, she was not in fear of what was to come. She prayed for strength, and as always when she asked the Lord for strength, as she had done countless times in her twenty years of life, He had answered with a warm calmness descending over her heart and her being. She finished her prayers, returned the Bible to its usual place on the sitting table, and rose from the chair, ready to face what challenges and hardships the day would present.

It was about seven o'clock in the morning, so she knew it was time to cook breakfast for the boys. Her mother was tending to her sister Georgia, who was ready to give birth to her first child at any moment, at the McClellan house a couple of blocks away, so she was running the household. This included caring for her little brother, Harry, who was eight years old, and a boarder, six year old Isaac Brinkerhoff. Little Isaac was crippled. He was not able to walk on his own, and his mother worked out of Gettysburg during the week, so the Wades agreed to board him. Ginnie loved him like he was her own brother, as he was polite, kind, and caring to her in particular. They shared a special relationship, one he didn't have with any other person, save his mother. The boys got along very well, too, as Harry was of great help to Ginnie in caring for Isaac.

She went to the room where the boys slept, opened the curtains to let the sun's light in, and said:

"Boys, it is time to rise and meet the day."

Harry was the first to stir. He groaned and turned over in his bed so he faced the wall and not the window, saying:

"Sis, it's too early. How about another hour?"

Isaac chimed in and pleaded: "Yeah, Miss Ginnie, another hour?"

"As much as I would like to let you sleep in, the day's chores come a calling, so we must do our part."

"Awe, do we really have to?" Harry asked.

"Harry Marion…," she said, using his middle name for emphasis:

"It is time for you to get to doing your chores. You know Mama is away helping sister Georgia, so this house is left up to us to run. Now, you boys can have a few more minutes whilst I cook your breakfast. But, I expect you to be dressed, washed and ready for eating by the time I get it on the table."

Harry, now mostly wide awake, said to her with a smirk and a wink to Isaac as he was about to use his teasing name for her:

"Yes, Miss Ginnie."

Ginnie gave him a stern look, but then she softened her mood as she saw the boys giggle at Harry's tease of her. She rushed over to Harry, to his surprise, and tickled him in the ribs. He began to laugh, and when the tickling became too much for him to bear, he pleaded with an uncontrollable laugh:

"Ginnie, stop, stop!"

Isaac too was laughing, so Ginnie decided he needed tickling too, and was on him and doing so before he could prepare. After about ten seconds, he too was pleading for her to stop. She finished with him and said:

"Now that you two boys are sufficiently wakened, I can expect to see you in a few minutes at table?"

Both boys still laughing, said in unison:

"Yes, ma'am."

She carried Isaac to the kitchen table, where Harry was waiting. She cooked and served the boys a breakfast of eggs, warm biscuits, and fruit. She sat and ate with them. The boys ate heartily, and she said:

"There is much to do today, Harry. I want you to sweep the floors of the living room and kitchen, fetch water from the barrel outside, and fill the pitchers, and the washing area outside, bring wood into the kitchen, and make yours' and Issac's bed. When you complete all of those, you and Isaac can go outside and play. I need to go to the store this morning, so I expect you to keep an eye on Isaac whilst I am gone. If you need anything, you know to go to Mrs. Comfort's house."

"Okay," the boy said, and added:

"Will you bring us some candy from the store?"

"Yes, but only if you do all of your chores."

"I will. Can we, maybe later, walk down to Georgia's house to see Mama and Georgia?"

"Yes, that would be a good idea, but not until later in the afternoon. I have a lot of sewing to do. Isaac, I expect you will get your reading done this morning."

"Yes, Ginnie."

Ginnie worked as a seamstress in the house to help support the family. Her father was, more than ten years ago, committed to the Almshouse in town, a house for the poor and for the mentally insane or unstable. This left Ginnie's mother Mary, her sister Georgia, and Ginnie herself to support the family. Consequently, money was never plentiful in the Wade household.

They finished breakfast around eight o'clock, cleared the table, and then she returned Isaac to the bedroom, where he got busy with his reading. She set him up with an easy lesson, but one that would take him several hours to complete, gave him a chalkboard and some chalk for practicing his letters, and left him to his work. She next went to supervise Harry in his chores. Satisfied he was doing what he was told, she went to her room to dress for the trip to the store.

By ten o'clock, she entered Fahnestock's store. She was surprised to see so much activity there. Daniel Skelly was busy organizing the filling of wagons with merchandise from the store. He looked up pleasantly at Ginnie:

"Good morning. You are here early today," he said.

"Yes, I am anxious to see if there is any news. Have any of the boys from the 87th made it back to town?"

"Not that I have heard," Skelly said trying to be as calm as possible as he shared what he knew her feelings of concern for Jack were.

"Lots of fussing going on today at the store?"

"Yeah, Mr. Fahnestock wants to get most of his valuable goods on the train to Philadelphia. It is a lot of work, but it is coming along. Can I get you anything?"

"Well, maybe some salt and some flour."

"The usual amounts?"

"Yes, that would be grand."

As they were speaking, Fannie Buehler and her two youngest children Kate, twelve years old, and Allie, four years old, entered the store.

"Why, Daniel, there's lots of goings on here," Fannie observed.

"Yes, I was telling Ginnie, Mr. Fahnestock wants to move his valuables to Philadelphia by train."

"Good morning Mrs. Buehler," Ginnie greeted.

"And to you, Ginnie."

"Has your husband heard any news of the boys of the 87th?"

"I am afraid not. All we know is some of them are expected home today. We have heard news of the Rebels, though, and word is they are coming this way, expected to cross into Maryland today. With the loss at Winchester, we really have no one to stop them."

"Do you know how soon?" Ginnie asked.

"No, but it cannot be long. I am sending my Martha, Myra, Henry, and my mother back to her house in Elizabeth, New Jersey, on the morning train. If the Rebels do come, well you know, David will have to leave town as they could capture him and send him to a Southern prison. I will be left alone to care for the children. I just think it is better to send them to safety, those old enough to travel," she said with tears in her eyes.

"Yes, that is probably best," Ginnie said supportively, and continued:

"If you need any help, I mean the boys really enjoy the times Kate and Allie visit our house, so if you need us we will be there."

"That is very kind of you, Ginnie. May I ask you to watch Allie tomorrow morning when I put the other children on the train? Kate is old enough to go with me, but I think it would be better Allie doesn't go."

"We would be glad to have him. What time should I come get him in the morning?"

"The train leaves at eight o'clock, so if you could get him at seven, that would be wonderful."

"I'll be there a little before seven."

"Thank you, Ginnie. You don't know how much that would mean to me. It is going to be hard enough sending them off, and I think it would go better if I knew Allie was being cared for."

Sallie and Annie Myers entered the store, and greeted everyone with a good morning. They were closely followed by Professor Jacobs; Tillie Pierce; Mrs. Hettie Shriver and her two children, Sadie, who was eight years old, and Molly who was six; Reverend Sherfy and his wife Mary; and John Wentz. It was quite a gathering of town folk. All were concerned about news of the Rebel advance.

Mrs. Sherfy addressed everyone with a warm smile and a cheerful good morning. She was in her mid-fifties, of average height, light blue eyes, a strong nose, thin lips, and brown hair covered by a white bonnet, tied under her chin. She wore a black, long sleeved, full length dress, with a white collar tightly buttoned at the neck.

"The Reverend and I thought it necessary to come to town and see if there is any news of the Rebels," she said.

The Reverend removed his brimmed hat and bowed to the ladies, saying: "Good morning, ladies."

He turned to the men, saying: "And to you, gentlemen."

"We are here for that, too," Hettie added.

Hettie Shriver was twenty six-years old, was a little over five feet tall, had light brown hair, short and curly, blue-green eyes, slightly further apart than average, an average nose, and full lips. She wore a brown, long sleeved, full length dress, with a white collar tightly buttoned at the neck.

"I too, would like to know," John Wentz added.

Wentz was in his seventies, but looked older, as he was hunched over more than slightly. He was shorter than average, had white hair, much of it gone by now, a long white beard, blue eyes, bloodshot, and an average nose and mouth. He was dressed in a shabby, old white shirt, brown trousers held up by brown braces, and old brown boots.

Fannie addressed the group and said:

"At this point, we don't know much, except that our army was beaten at Winchester Sunday last, leaving only scattered forces between the Rebels and us here. David just heard from the telegraph operator they are crossing the river into Maryland today."

"Are you sure they are headed this way?" Mrs. Sherfy asked.

"It looks that way, but we don't know for sure. Either way, we need to be prepared if they do come. I am sending my three oldest children and my mother to her house in New Jersey on the morning train."

"We don't have anywhere to go, and I have two little children," Hettie said.

"Now, now, don't panic, Mrs. Shriver," Mary Sherfy said, as she went over to the children and patted them on the head, then continued:

"We mustn't alarm the little ones."

She leaned down to them and said:

"If it is alright with your Mama, would you like some candy?"

The children looked at their mother, who nodded in approval. Mary looked to Daniel and said:

"Can we get them a piece of candy each, Daniel?"

"Yes, Mrs. Sherfy. Follow me."

Mary and the two children left the room with Skelly. Then the Reverend spoke:

"We must calm down a little until we find out more news of where they are going and where our army is."

"Yes, the Reverend is right. We must try not to panic," Wentz added.

Tillie, seeing her neighbor Mrs. Shriver upset, went to her, hugged her, and said:

"Hettie, it will be alright."

"I know, I know. I just wish George were here to take care of us," she replied referring to her husband who was off fighting for the Union, and had been gone since August of 1861.

"Papa, Mama, and I will be here for you and the children," Tillie said reassuringly.

Annie Myers asked:

"Any news of the 87th?"

Just then, they could hear voices of a crowd gathering outside. They all went to the front door and out to the street. A crowd was gathered around a soldier. They joined the crowd to listen to the soldier, whom no one recognized as from Gettysburg, as he was saying:

"They licked us good at Winchester. We thought it was a fortress with our three forts, but last Sunday they flanked us without us knowing, and got the high ground out west. Then they pounded us with their artillery from two directions. Caught us in a cross fire. We didn't have a chance. After, the Louisiana boys attacked the West Fort and took it. They had that Rebel yell and we couldn't stop 'em. I was in the town holding the Stonewall Brigade off, but I still heard that yell. It was terrifying."

Someone in the crowd said:

"Then what happened?"

Others in the crowd scolded him for interrupting and urged the soldier to continue. He did:

"By Sunday afternoon, they turned our guns from West Fort on the other two forts and pounded away. By the evening it was clear we didn't have a chance, and so General Milroy ordered a retreat to Harper's Ferry. We got a late start getting out, I think, because the Rebels were waiting for us at dawn on Monday at Stephenson's Depot, west of the town. We attacked several times, but couldn't break through, and so once they counterattacked, we had had it, and they pretty much broke us up. I took off running as they were capturing us."

The crowd was stunned. It took a minute or two for anyone to say a word. Ginnie spoke:

"Did you see what happened to Corporal Jack Skelly?"

"No, but lots of us got away, some got captured. Some went to Harper's Ferry. I didn't see the corporal on Monday morning. He was fine on Sunday when we were getting ready to move out."

"What about Lieutenant William Culp?" Annie asked.

"I didn't see where the lieutenant was neither on Monday morning. But, he too was fine on Sunday."

Annie asked:

"What of the Stonewall Brigade. Were there many casualties?"

"No ma'am. We exchanged fire, mainly on Saturday. They swept us from our position, but there were not many casualties on either side."

Someone in the crowd said:

"Who cares about the traitorous Stonewall Brigade? What about our boys from the 87th?"

Annie knew why, as she was concerned about Wes also.

"Like I said, the 87th had very few casualties until Monday morning when the Rebs stopped our retreat. I don't know how many were killed, or wounded, or captured. All I know is the regiment was scattered like a flock of sheep."

Ginnie looked over to Sallie and Annie with a concerned look. They both came to her and Sallie said:

"I'm sure they are alright. He said a lot of them got away to Harper's Ferry. That must be where they are. Soon, we will hear, Ginnie."

"Yes, yes. I have prayed to God he will protect and deliver my Jack safely back home to me."

"I have prayed hard too, Ginnie," Sallie replied.

"I must get back to the boys," Ginnie said with tears in her eyes.

The three women hugged each other tightly.

Ginnie was back home around noon. She found both boys asleep in their beds napping, which to her was a pretty good idea, as the sewing work could wait. She undressed and then lay down on her bed. I must be strong and believe he got away, or at the very worst, captured, she thought. She fell asleep after a few minutes with tears rolling down her cheeks.

CHAPTER 24

BURNS

JOHN L. BURNS was anxious and excited Monday, June 22nd, as he just received word there was to be a meeting of the Gettysburg Zouaves, the local Gettysburg militia of which he was a member, at 2:00 p.m. The meeting was to discuss the town's situation with the Rebels being so close, rumored to be in Chambersburg, and what the Zouaves could do about it. Captain John Scott called the meeting and they were to gather at the court-house. Burns and Joseph Broadhead walked to the Diamond and turned south on Baltimore Street to the courthouse. They were early for the meeting, as Burns never liked to be late. He would say "I'd rather be a half hour early than a minute late." And, so there they were at half past one.

"John, I don't know why we're here so early."

"What difference does it make to you? You didn't go to work today anyway."

"Yes, but we are starting to prepare the house in the event the Rebels come."

"You should have come on your own. I didn't ask you to come with me."

Broadhead could see this was going nowhere, so he changed the subject.

"Do you really think the Rebels are in Chambersburg?"

"Yes. I've been telling everyone these past weeks they are coming. But, nobody would listen. And, now they are right across that mountain," Burns said pointing to the west at South Mountain.

"What can we do about it?'

"We can stop 'em. Why don't you just listen to what the captain has to say? After all, you joined the Zouaves. Did you think it was just for show, being a Zouave?"

"No, but what can we do against the whole Rebel army?"

"Bah, I'm tired of this conversation with you."

A few moments later, Captain John Scott stood up and called the meeting to order.

"Good afternoon. I called this meeting because of the reports the rebels are in Chambersburg and will soon be on their way here to Gettysburg. We are between them and York and further to Philadelphia. So, they will come. The question is what can we do about it?"

There was silence among the group. Then Burns said:

"We can march out Chambersburg Pike, hide among the trees and when they come, bushwhack 'em."

Scott thought for a moment and then said:

"Too dangerous. They would whip us and those not killed would be gathered up and hung."

A man named Johnston spoke:

"Well, if we can't stop 'em, maybe we slow 'em down? I mean our army has to be on its way, so if we can prevent them from an easy crossing of the mountains, or slow 'em up, maybe that would be of help and buy the time the army needs to get here?"

"That's good thinking, Johnston. Maybe if we can slow them a couple of days, or even one day, the army can get here in time to engage them out west before they get to Gettysburg," Scott replied, and continued:

"Alright, here's what we will do. I need some of you men to volunteer and we will go west on Chambersburg Pike, up to South Mountain, and construct barricades to block the road. We'll fall some trees and build some nice little dams for them to have to cross. Let's do this with a smaller party, say 10 to 20 men, in the event we have to get out quickly and also so they would know we aren't regular army, so no artillery would be engaged. At worse, they may fire at us."

"Captain, I still say we bushwhack 'em. But, if you want to cut trees, for the love of God, maybe, we can gather firewood for the winter early, too?"

The captain ignored Burns' sarcasm and waited for other opinions. After a quick discussion among them, they agreed to the plan, and 14 men volunteered. Burns was the first not wanting to miss this adventure:

"Count me in, captain, and also Broadhead, here."

"Very good. The rest of you, meet us at West and Chambersburg Streets at three o'clock. No guns. We want to be treated as civilians protecting their property and their town. Bring only axes, shovels, and saws."

At three o'clock Burns and Broadhead joined a group of twelve other men. They were also equipped with blankets, water, and provisions as it was expected this endeavor would take a couple of days, or so. They were careful not to be armed with firearms or pistols as they were ordered by Captain Scott. Burns was not happy about this:

"I should have brought my rifle. How am I to protect myself?"

Broadhead replied:

"John, we are to construct barricades to delay them, not try to shoot them. I just hope the army gets here soon."

They started their journey west along the Chambersburg Pike toward South Mountain, which was over ten miles away, more like 15. It took the rest of the day to get near the mountain. They camped for the night and were careful not to light campfires as not to alert the Rebels of their presence.

Burns didn't sleep well that night, but his spirit was high. This was an adventure to him, rather than the same old humdrum of everyday life. He was even pleasant to Broadhead, offering to share his dried beef. Broadhead declined politely and fell off to sleep.

The next morning, the Zouaves woke early, just after sun-up. They had a lot of work to do, so an early wake-up was the order. They sent four men out early to scout the area and select the best spots for the fallen timber damns. They were looking for areas of dense trees and brush right up next to the road, areas where the barricades would be most effective and not allow and easy by-pass route for the Rebel army. The men returned within a half an hour and told the captain the first spot was just about a half-mile ahead. Burns, Broadhead, and three other men volunteered to form the first group and so they set off with the scout team to build the first barricade.

The other five men also came along and would work on the first barricade until the second spot was located by the scouts. Scott proposed this as the strategy. Five men, which included Scott, would lead the scout team on ahead of the working crews. Five men would be assigned the first location, with assistance from the other five, working as a back-up crew, until the next location was chosen, then the second five would lead the construction of the second barricade. When the first barricade was completed, the first crew would join the second crew as the back-up crew for the construction of the second barricade. And, this would be the way it would go, staggered work crews, for the day in order to build as many barricades as quickly as possible. It was hard work falling the trees and carrying them to block the road. The back-up crews were needed to help carry the fallen logs into place, and then once done, they were sent forward, with the others applying earthen backfill to complete the works. The first barricade took about four hours to build. Burns was quickly exhausted and took several breaks to catch his breath. The sun was warm, which didn't make the work any easier.

"This is hard work. It better slow them down. That's all I can say," he said.

"Well, anything helps. If we can slow them down," Captain Scott replied.

"Do you really think the army can be here in time to stop them from getting to Gettysburg?" Broadhead asked.

"God help us if they aren't," Scott said, and continued:

"This one looks pretty good. Let's move to the next."

The next barricade was another half mile west on the pike. The first crew arrived just in time to help carry the timber in place. About a half an hour later, the scout team returned to escort Burns' crew to the third spot, and so off they went. It took them about a half an hour to get to the third spot. Once there, they commenced falling some trees. Within a few moments, the scout team returned in a sprint.

"Captain Scott, the Rebels spotted us and chased us. They should be right on our heels," one of them said.

"Are you sure?"

"Of course, their scouts saw us."

"Men, pack up and let's get out of here," Scott ordered.

"I'm not leaving until I see this myself," Burns replied.

"Burns, we need to leave now," Scott ordered a second time.

"Mr. Burns, let's go whilst we still can," Broadhead said.

Just then a shot rang out and clipped a branch off the tree directly above them, which fell on them. Burns was exposed in the front of the laid timber, when another shot was heard. Broadhead grabbed Burns and pulled him to the ground, just in time as the bullet whooshed over them.

"Let's get behind the timber," Broadhead said. He and Burns stayed low and quickly crawled over the stack of logs. Once on the other side, they regrouped with the other men and took off running back to safety along the pike.

A few minutes earlier, a half a dozen Confederate scouts were working their way easterly on Chambersburg Pike. Having just arrived from a morning march from Waynesboro, they were to set up camp west of Fayetteville like the rest of their regiment, but were instead ordered to scout the road to Gettysburg, on the east side of the crest of the mountain. Their orders were to scout the passage to identify any issues that might impede the army's progress toward Gettysburg in the next few days. They were also instructed to map out areas where the army could be ambushed by a small band of men from the Federal Army, or even the local militia. They were told to be cautious as the Confederates didn't know where the Union army was at present. They knew with a great deal of certainty they were a long way from Chambersburg and even Gettysburg. But about any local militia, they had no idea. Not that the local militia was a great deal of concern, but it could be a nuisance and could inflict some casualties given the right location and cover.

Although this assignment was important, it was also very tedious, so the men found ways to entertain themselves by pitching rocks and twigs at each other.

"Hey, careful that one could have taken my eye out," one said to the other after getting hit in the cheek with a small twig. The others laughed heartily and one said:

"Good aim. I can see the improvement in looks already."

They all laughed again and the soldier struck with the twig picked up another and threw it in response. It hit the first one in the leg and bounced off.

"Nice aim. I hope ya shoot better than ya throw," he said and stuck his tongue out.

They all had a good laugh. While they were still laughing, they heard a noise coming from around a bend in the road ahead.

"Shh," the corporal said with his index finger to his mouth. He continued:

"I thought I heaad movement up ahead."

They all stopped and raised their rifles. Around the bend came Scott's scouting party, led by John White Johnston.

"Ya men thea, halt and state ya business," the corporal said.

Johnston and the others froze. The corporal continued:

"Ya men, come ova hea and identify who ya is."

Johnston looked at the other three men with the pre-arranged signal, a quick nod of his head toward the road behind them, and with a move that surprised the Rebels, they pivoted and were off back toward Scott and the rest of the Zouaves. They were around the bend in the road before the Rebels could aim and take a shot.

"Let's go afta them. They could be spies and report ou progress over the mounten. But, be caaful, it could be a trap."

The soldiers spread out and advanced along the road at a rapid jog after the fleeing men. After about a minute, they looked ahead and saw some trees blocking the road and the men who fled earlier talking with more men. One of the Rebels took a shot at them to warn them to stay put. The shot traveled high. Another one aimed at an older man in front of the trees and he fired at his head. The shot missed as the old man's companion grabbed him and pulled him to the ground. The two men disappeared over the fallen trees in the road.

"Hold ya fia and take cova," the corporal ordered.

The soldiers spread out off the road and aimed their rifles ahead searching for targets. They saw a group of men running away down the road.

"Corporal, I have the ol' man in sight. Can I take 'im?"

"Nah, hold ya fire."

"But, sir, they seen us. Shouldn't we put a stop to 'em?"

"Let 'em go. We'll see 'em again. Besides, nothin' is moa joyful to my heaat than seeing Yankee folk runnin' like a big dawg is a chasin.'"

"Run, Yanks, run," another shouted.

"Now that we've been seen, let's head back to camp."

Burns and the others ran as fast as they could for about five minutes and getting about half to three quarters of a mile distance, Scott held up his hand and they stopped. All of the men were breathing heavily and were sweating profusely. Burns could not keep up with the younger men and so he was about a minute late arriving at where the others stopped.

Scott said: "Whew, that was close. Did you see them following us?"

"No, I looked back when we first took off and they weren't following," Johnston replied.

"Well, let's not wait to find out. Let's get back to Gettysburg double quick." And to Burns, Scott said:

"John, how are you doing? Can you make the trip with us?"

"Captain, you worry about them others. I don't need no fussing."

And, so they walked as fast as they could all day and reached Gettysburg at night fall.

Once they got back to Gettysburg, Burns, Broadhead, and the others went home to their wives and families. Burns tiredly climbed the stairs and entered in his house. It was about nine o'clock in the evening, so Mrs. Burns and Martha were awake, but the baby was sound asleep. Both women were taking tea in the kitchen when he entered the house.

"Oh, John you are home," Mrs. Burns said with a sigh of relief.

"Papa, you look terrible. Are you okay?" Martha asked.

"Hmmph, a long walk back. I'm sore and tired," he said as he took off and hung up his hat and coat.

"Oh dear, would you like some hot tea?"

"No, but what about some food? Is there anything to eat around here?"

"Yes, Papa. We have some biscuits and some soup. Would you like me to fix you some?"

"Yes, and some tea with it."

He washed his hands and face in the basin, dried them and hung the towel to dry. He sat down at the kitchen table, while Martha brought him a cup of tea. He took a sip and then Martha set a bowl of hot soup in front of him. He took a spoonful of the soup, swallowed and closed his eyes in reflection. The women were silent waiting for him to speak, and in a moment after more soup and tea, he obliged:

"They're on this side of South Mountain. Wouldn't be surprised if they are here tomorrow or the next."

Both women opened their mouths wide and took a gasp and put their hand to their mouths.

"John, what are we to do?" Mrs. Burns asked.

"Nothin', we will wait and see when they get here. I'm not leaving my house to them. I'll have you know that."

Martha asked: "You saw them?"

"Yes, and they took a couple of shots at us."

"My God, John, you're not hurt are you?"

"No, but could have been. One shot went right over my head. I'll tell you what...," he said as he squinted his eyes, and continued:

"I ain't never going without my gun for protection. Never. When they come here, I'll be ready and I'll make sure to show 'em how happy I is to see 'em."

"John L. Burns, you'll do no such thing. I'll not watch you get killed because you think you need to get back at them."

"Woman, you ain't gonna stop me. I'll protect my house, my family, and my town from those traitors as best I can."

"Papa, you can't do that. They'll kill you," Martha said and began to cry.

"Look at what you are doing to your daughter," Mrs. Burns said and then to her daughter:

"There, there, dear. You needn't get upset. Your father will do nothing of the kind."

"Woman, a man must protect what's his."

"Papa, but the whole Rebel army may be coming. They will shoot you dead for sure," Martha said and cried into her mother's shoulder. Burns pitied her, and so he said:

"Martha, don't cry. I won't do anything dim-witted. But, if our army gets here and there is a battle, and I can help, I will. And, I'll not hear anymore talk on it," he said with finality.

Martha came over to Burns, leaned down and hugged him by the neck. Mrs. Burns hugged Martha and Burns so the family was complete in each other's comfort. Martha was content to just stay in that position, but Mrs. Burns had worry in her mind, wondering just what her husband would do when the Rebels arrived, and whatever it was he would do, would it cost him his life?

CHAPTER 25

GENERAL JUBAL EARLY'S CAMP

General Jubal Early's Division of the main army had been marching north in Pennsylvania since crossing the Potomac the day before, stopping for the night at Waynesboro. This morning, the army marched from Waynesboro north to the Chambersburg Pike, which ran east/west between Chambersburg and Gettysburg. The road led east to Gettysburg. Early decided this would be a good location to camp, as they would then plan their excursion into Gettysburg. General Robert Rodes' Division had entered, and occupied, Chambersburg earlier that day, with plans to continue northeasterly to Harrisburg, so it was logical to head east to Gettysburg and eventually to York. Gettysburg would be where he could continue his gathering of tribute from the citizens of the Commonwealth of Pennsylvania.

"So, they know we are on the otha side of the mountain?" General Jubal Early asked his staff.

"Seems so, sur," Colonel John Warwick Daniel of his staff replied.

"Well, we will just have to pay 'em a visit, real soon, what ya say, Colonel?"

"Yes, sur, I think a visit is in orda. How 'bout this comin' Friday, sur?"

"Can ya get the arrangements made for it to happen? After all, the men just got settled and need a bit of rest, so waitin' until Friday is a good plan."

"Yes, sur, I'll start workin' on it right away."

A major came up to Colonel Daniel, saluted and said:

"Excuse me, Colonel, but thea is a civilian hea to see the gen'rul. He says he has important news and the gen'rul will want to hear it."

"Who is this civilian?"

"Sur, he says his name is Samuel Jones."

Early's ears perked when he heard the name Jones, and he said:

"Samuel Jones, huh? Aye was wondarin' when he would be back. Send him foaward."

Jones walked through the officers surrounding Early's tent and entered.

"General, it is indeed a pleasure seeing you again," Jones said.

"Well, Mr. Jones. How long has it been? Aye thought ya were lost, or worse, captured."

"It's been about a month, sur. I had a close call in Gettysburg a couple of weeks ago, but I managed. I have been to York and Harrisburg since, sur."

"It seems ya've been busy, Mr. Jones. Aye trust ya have some information for me from what ya learned in ya travels? Why don't ya sit down right hea and tell me all about it?"

Jones sat and began his report:

"Indeed I do, sur. It would seem the folks in Gettysburg are fairly wise to the presence of spies and the needs of an enemy army as it moves into their country. I spent a day there and was lucky to get out without being arrested. I made a survey of the supplies in the town, and found it plentiful. There are several well established hotels and inns, several banks, and some fine stores where foodstuffs and clothing can be, shall we say, acquired. I made a list of what I thought might be a fine, as you would say, tribute to our men."

Jones produced the list and handed it to General Early. Early read the list:

> 7000 lbs. of Bacon.
> 1200 lbs. of Sugar.
> 1000 lbs. of Salt.
> 600 lbs. of Coffee.
> 60 barrels of Flour.
> 10 barrels of Onions.
> 10 barrels of Whiskey.
> 1000 pairs of Shoes.
> 500 hats.
>
> Or $5000.

Jones continued:

"Like I said though, General, these Gettysburg folk, they aren't really the sharing type, so don't be surprised if ya may find they have moved a lot of these types of supplies out of town using the railroad. I met and talked with the engineer for the railroad, and he told me he runs back and forth to Hanover every day of the week, 'cept Saturday and Sunday. I overheard your men talking about how they encountered some of the townsfolk earlier today, so don't be surprised if when they get back to town, they don't start moving supplies, even tonight."

"Well, as long as we can get some supplies, we will be fine. We a taking what we need from the faams along the way, so where we get tribute isn't important, as long as we get it. Tell me of the town itself, besides the banks and the stores. Tell me about the hotels and the restaurants. Can we get a good meal in town?"

"Yes, sir. I met a man named John Will and his father, Charles Will. They own the Globe Inn in Gettysburg. I ate both dinner and supper there and the food was delicious. I had a dish they called Hog Maw for dinner and then Pork Cutlets for supper. Both of these meals were the best I had since I have been, shall we say, gathering information for you. And, the room I had was very large and comfortable. It was, all in all, a nice place. John and his father are really concerned about making sure their customers are happy there at the inn."

"How about the local militia?"

"Not much I could see, but I was only there one day. They do have a former constable, name of Burns, who was hot on my trail. An interesting fella, indeed. An old man, near seventy years old, but full of vinegar, still. Short for his size, but wears a tall hat, almost like a stovetop, like the one that Lincoln fancies."

One of the Early's staff overheard the description of Burns and said:

"General, that sounds like one of the men our scouts ran into earlier today. They were cutting trees and buildin' a barricade across the road."

Jones inquired: "Are you sure?"

"Sounds like 'im. I'll have the private come over and describe him to ya."

While the private was sent for, Jones continued his report:

"There are six major roads leading in and out of the town. The road you are here on approaches the town from the northwest. The other roads are the Emmitsburg Road, which approaches from the southwest, the Baltimore Pike, approaching from the southeast, York Pike, approaching from the east, the Harrisburg Road, approaching from the northeast, and the Carlisle Road approaching from the north. The railroad is located on the north side of town, and runs easterly toward York and ends at Hanover. They are building a cut westerly of the town to extend the railroad toward Chambersburg. The south side of the town has two tanneries. And, there are lots of shoes, as these are made in the town proper. Hmm, what else can I tell? Oh yes, there is a lot of liquor, in fact I sold two liquor recipes there, one to John Will at the Globe Inn, and one to the proprietor of the Eagle Hotel. I didn't collect the money, yet, but it was good cover. I was a traveling man of business, selling recipes to fix the taste of liquor."

Early laughed at Jones' ingenuity of his cover, saying:

"Did ya really sell recipes? They any good?"

"Sure. One is called Currant Champagne and the other is a Whiskey Sour. These are real recipes I learned from a bartender when I was in the theatre. I wonder if they have used them yet? Anyway, this bartender was an expert in making up recipes like these, and the theatre made a nice profit in liquor sales."

"Well, Mr. Jones, Aye can see how ya able to fit into a town," he said with another laugh and continued:

"Liquor recipes, indeed. Brilliant."

While they were still amused by Jones' cover story, a private approached the general's tent. He saluted Colonel Daniel and was escorted to the general. He stopped, saluted Early and said:

"Private Mason, sur, ya sent fo me?"

"Yes, private. Aye am to undastand one of the fellas ya ran into on the road earlia today was an eldaly gentleman, about sebenty?"

"Well sur, he looked like he could have been that old."

"Can ya describe him to us?"

"Yes, sur. He was short, no more than five feet tall, no beaad, and wore an old brown coat, matching pants, and brown leather boots, and a silla looking black top hat, with a light brown ribbon. I had him in my sights and could have taken him, but the corporal ordaed me not ta shoot."

Jones laughed heartily and said: "That's ol' Burns. I told ya he was full of vinegar. What a daft old man, cutting trees to block our army. One thing I knew about him, he ain't yella, he has got guts."

"Well, Mr. Jones, Aye would like to meet Mista Burns. We are going to ya Gettysburg on Friday. Aye want ya to accompany me as my guide, show me around this town ya fancy, and introduce me to the, shall we say, intaesting folk who live thea."

"General, it will be my pleasure. And, we might spend a good Friday evening enjoyin' a portion of Hog Maw and Currant Champagne at the Globe."

"We may indeed. Well, I have to get back to my staff, so y'll excuse me."

Jones got up the leave as Early turned to Colonel Daniel and said:

"Colonel, make sure ya pay Mista Jones a hundred dollas in silva and a hundred dollas in Confedaate script."

"That's very generous of you General."

"It's worth it to me just to hea ya stories and Aye am looking foaward to ou visit. Afta Gettysburg, Aye will look foaward to ya report on Yoak, but rememba ya already been paid, so don't go expectin' more. Good day, Mista Jones."

After Jones got paid, he made his way over to a wagon and asked for a cup of coffee. He took a drink and realized how army coffee really didn't compare to the coffee in the towns of Pennsylvania. Yes, he was looking forward to returning to Gettysburg and seeing the people he met three weeks ago. But he wondered, would they be glad to see him?

JUNE 24, 1863 GETTYSBURG, PENNSYLVANIA

CHAPTER 26

BUTLER

After the members of the 87th Pennsylvania returned from the Battle of Winchester, the fire at Emmitsburg, and the return of the Zouaves from their unsuccessful excursion to block the Chambersburg Pike, the town's people understandably became more anxious and agitated. Any news, rumor or else, was treated as essential knowledge everyone wanted to know, and so the bearer of the news attracted great crowds. Everyone wanted to hear the latest about the Rebels movements and whereabouts. They knew they were coming, but from where and when became the constant questions asked. No group of people suffered the news more than the 300, or so, free black folks who lived within and around Gettysburg, as they were being made aware of the Confederate Army's practice of gathering up colored people and returning them south to be sold as slaves. To them, no thought could be more terrifying than that of losing their freedom, and for some, losing it again.

ELIZABETH (OLD LIZ) BUTLER and her husband Samuel spent much of the day Wednesday June 24th discussing what to do now that the Rebels were certainly coming to Gettysburg. By around three o'clock in the afternoon, they decided what to do, or at least who to ask.

"Sam'l, what's we gunna du? We can't be ketched and throwed back to slavry. An, what of the yungens?," Old Liz said.

"Nos we wont. But, what's to du? Where kin we goest?"

"Dunno. If we leaves our home, we neva git it back that's sure, landlord say so, so's if we to leave, it would be fo good."

"Loost everyting we's werked so hard for? You's washin' and scrubbin' ya fingas to the bone, an me's brakin' my back at the inn? An, yungens schoolin."

"Yes, I hear tell frum folks in town Confedrates are winnin' the war. So, heres mite be southren when the war's ov'r anyhow."

"Mite be so, but Masser Will says we ain't lickt yet, no sur."

"Ya wonting to stay, dat's what ya sayin?"

"Mite."

"Maybe we oughtst to go ov'r ta see Isaak and Esther? Sees what dey's a doin?"

158

"Real fine idea. Sees if dey kin tell us."

They went over to Isaac and Esther Moses' house, who lived further south on Washington Street. Isaac and Esther were in their seventies and had lived in Gettysburg much longer that the Butlers. They were the unofficial elders of the colored community, as they were the people who were solicited for advice whenever a crisis occurred in town. This was indeed was a crisis. Rumors persisted among the black folks that they were also in charge of the local underground railroad station at the old Dobbin house on the Emmitsburg Road. Some knew this to be true, and the Butlers were among this small group. The Moses lived in a small one bedroom house near the intersection of Washington Street and the Emmitsburg Road, not far from where the Butlers lived, and not far from the old Dobbin's house. As the Butlers climbed the stairs to the porch of the Moses' house, the door was opened enthusiastically by Isaac, who greeted them warmly:

"Samuel, Ol Liz, mitey fine of ya to pay us ol folk a visit. Esther, the Butlers have cum a callin."

Moses was about five feet four inches tall, had an average build, thinning gray short hair, a full gray beard which he trimmed to be more like stubble on his face, brown eyes, a larger than average nose and a warm smile. He was wearing a white long sleeved shirt and black trousers, held up by braces, and black leather shoes. He gestured for the Butlers to come into the house, and so they entered where they were greeted just as warmly by Esther:

"Liz, Samuel, how nice ya to cum by."

Esther was shorter than her husband by a couple of inches, was slightly plump, had short hair only slightly above her scalp, accentuating her round face on which were her brown eyes, her petite nose, full lips and bright white teeth, which shown prominently when she smiled, as she did most often. She wore a full length dress, white with pink mixed in for a pattern, tied around her waist by a white apron, and brown shoes.

The house was relatively dark, so Samuel and Liz's eyes needed a moment to adjust. Once their eyesight cleared, they noticed the small living room and behind it, the small kitchen, from which the smell of baking bread pleasantly filled the house. Esther continued:

"Why don't ya sit and I bring ya sum tea and sum bread?"

"Be real fine, Esther," Samuel replied.

"Ya sit rite dere on dat dere sofa," Isaac said and noticed Samuel and Liz were not their usual jovial selves, so he asked:

"I's gathrin dis ain't no social visit, now is it? What's trubblin' yous?"

Old Liz spoke saying:

"No, Isaac, it taint. Me's and Sam'l here are talkin of leaving Gettysburg, with dem Rebels so close and surely cumin'. We must fend fo our chillen."

Esther overhead this and stopped what she was doing then returned to the living room.

"Now, Liz, you a leavin'?"

"Talkst bout it. We don't want to be ketched and sint back to slavry. No ma'am."

Isaac asked: "Where ya go?"

"We dunno. Got no kin, so's we's on our own. Hoped ya had some place ya could tell us," Samuel said.

Isaac replied: "Well now, we kin get ya to sum places further north, and maybe up to Canada. Sur ya wantst to goes?"

"Not sure. Old Liz, here, she wantst to goes. I dinkst we's werked so hard and makest us a fine home we's dontst wanta loose. If we's does go, landlord say he's rentin' to other folks right way."

"You's folks owns you's house, like us folks."

"Dat's right, but we's bought with de standin' landlord still owes de house."

Liz replied: "Now Sam'l, yous knowst I don't fancy goin'. But, back to slavry neither. An, our chillen, dey never be slaves, no sur. Isaac, Esther, whats ya gonna du?"

"Liz, we's too ol' to be goingst anywheres. Sides, dem Confederates ain't gonna be bothrin' us. Taint much value to us. Who would want a pair of ol' broke down folks like us?"

Samuel asked: "If you's a staying, thinks we too?"

"I kinst say fo sure. You's gotsta make that choice fo youself's. We kin getst ya north if ya want."

Esther asked: "Liz, Samuel, ya thinks careful on dis. If ya goes, ya kint cum back, dat's sure. Has ya dought of just hidin'?"

"If we's a staying and dem Southerners take the town ov'r, how longst can we hide frum 'em? Dey ketch us soon fo sur," Liz said.

"Maybe de Northren army whips 'em and den dey leave back south wherest dey belong? If ya's goes, ya loos ya home fo nothin'. Tuff to decide," Isaac added.

Liz said: "We's know. If we's do stay, kin ya hide us?"

"Yes, we kin put ya's in the ol' hidin' place at the ol' Dobbin House. De Zieglers, dey stillst lets us use dats place whenst we askt."

Esther had gone to the kitchen a moment before and now returned with a tray filled with cups of tea, slices of bread, and peach jam. She set the tray down on the living room table, and offered a cup to Liz, then to Samuel, and finally to Isaac. She spread some jam on the bread and handed each a piece. The Butlers both thanked her. Liz took a bite of the bread and a sip of tea, and said:

"Dat be fine, we hide in dat slavin' hidin' place if we needs. Sam'l, we needs to decide."

"Ol' Liz, we do. Isaac, thanks fo the offa of de hidin' place. We's a knew ya'd have some good doughts, that's fo sure."

The four friends finished their tea and bread and then the Butlers left to go back home. When they returned home, Liz went to the kitchen to fix her husband a quick supper, as he was to be at work at the inn by five o'clock. She poured two bowls of soup she had warming in the oven, fixed a plate of biscuits and then they sat at table to eat.

"Isaac, he's gots a fine idea hidin' at the ol' Dobbin house. We's do and we's kin stay."

"But, Sam'l whats if dem Southerners dey stay? We's kint hide fo'ever."

"Wheres we go? This the onlyest home we's know now. I don't wants to go to Canada."

"Sam'l, I's want to stay, but being ketched and takin' south to slavery agin, it's too much a chance. An, the chillen. I's want to go away. I's dink we's must."

Butler thought for a moment, took another bite of his soup and said:

"Thenst we go. If ya wants to go, we go. I let Masser Will know night."

"We's have much to do, but we's kin do it. Today is Wensday. We goes on Satrday. Kin ya make sur Masser Will pays ya full by then?"

"He will. He's fair man. Always been."

"I go tell Isaac and Esther whilest ya werking night, see if dey get us maps where to go."

Butler finished his soup, kissed his wife and left the house to walk to the inn and his work. Liz cleaned up the supper dishes and walked back over to the Moses' house. She knocked and Isaac again answered, saying:

"Liz, I didn't 'pect ya back so soon."

"Isaac, me an' Ol' Sam'l, we's decided. We's gonna go. Too much a chance stayin'. We's a wanting to go on Satrday. Canst ya make us a map where to go?"

"I's sure sorry you's a going. Are ya's sure?"

"We's are."

"Then, I's make you's maps and give ya de names of some folks who kinst help ya goes as far as you's want, even into Canada."

"Isaac, thanks. Kinst we cum over Friday to gets it?"

"I's have it ready, fo sure."

"Thanks. I's gotst to be going. So's much to do. Night."

Esther joined her husband at the door as Liz left. The Moses waved goodbye with heavy hearts. Isaac said to his wife:

"No peace fo us coloreds frum those devils down south, no sur, not even ups here in Gettysburg. Lord help us if dey come and dey stay."

CHAPTER 27

BROADHEAD

SARAH (SALLIE) M. BROADHEAD stood on the porch of her house, took a sip of tea and stared out the Chambersburg Pike toward South Mountain. She remembered last night when she and Joseph looked in the very same direction and saw the Rebel campfires on this side of the mountain, near Cashtown, only about ten miles away. It was almost ten o'clock in the morning. The sun had risen a few hours earlier and so the day was beginning to warm; a stark change from the rainy weather that was last night. She had awakened just before sun up, made breakfast for Joseph, packed his dinner, and got him off to work. Because the Confederates were so close, Joseph had very little time to waste, as he had another trainload of supplies leaving Gettysburg for Hanover, and ultimately on to Philadelphia. He was gone in a matter of minutes after they rose from bed.

She woke Mary up. They ate together, and after clearing the dishes, they went for a walk into town, mainly to get Mary out of the house. They didn't stray far. After they returned, Mary set off to her room to play with Ruthie, her doll. Satisfied she would be occupied for awhile, Sallie poured herself a cup of tea, and went out to the front of her house, where she waited; waited for any signs the Southerners were coming. She didn't have to wait long.

The 26th Pennsylvania Volunteer Militia had arrived just about an hour earlier, and were now gathering in the town. The 26th departed Harrisburg on Wednesday by train for Gettysburg, but had hit a cow about ten miles east of town, resulting in the derailment of the train. They camped at that location Wednesday night, and all day Thursday, waiting for the tracks to be repaired so they could resume their journey to Gettysburg. When they arrived, the townspeople were overjoyed and they welcomed them with cheers and shouts.

Sallie saw Mrs. Gilbert come out of her house to see what the noise and commotion was all about.

"Good Morning Mrs. Gilbert," she said.

"And, to you Sallie. What's the fussing about?" she asked as she began walking to the Broadhead house.

"I don't know, but it looks as though our militia has arrived in town. Maybe we should go see for ourselves."

"Thank the Lord. That sounds like a wonderful idea. Shall we bring Mary along? By the way, where is the little darling?"

"Inside playing with her dolly. I'll get her and then we can go see our boys."

After about a minute or two, Sallie returned with Mary in hand. Mrs. Gilbert said:

"Good morning, my little pet."

"And to you Mrs. Gilbert," the child said sweetly.

Mrs. Gilbert bent down so her face was close to the girl's and said:

"Do you want to go see the army men?"

"I sure do. Do you think one of them will carry me on his shoulder?"

"Maybe, sweetheart, maybe," Mrs. Gilbert said and noticed the smile on Mary's precious little face as she said this.

The two older women and the child walked down the street toward the Diamond. They could see the blue clad soldiers mingling with the townsfolk ahead. As they arrived, they saw an officer addressing the crowd in front of the Eagle Hotel. They approached and listened:

"...my name is Colonel Jennings, and we are the 26th Pennsylvania Militia, just arrived about an hour ago. We are here to protect this here town and all of you townfolk from the Rebs. We are ordered to encamp just west of the town and to engage and stop the enemy if they are a headed to town. We know they are close, but do not fear, we shall do our duty and protect you from them."

He finished speaking and the crowd gave him a grand applause, along with chants of "hurrah." Sallie noticed Sallie Myers and Annie Myers in the crowd, and so she, Mrs. Gilbert, and Mary made their way through the crowd over to them.

"Sallie, Annie, how nice to see you," Sallie Broadhead said.

"Mrs. Broadhead, good morning," they both said. Sallie Myers turned to Mary and said:

"To you, too Mary," as she reached down and patted the child on the head.

"Miss Sallie, how come you have the same name as my mommy?"

Sallie Myers laughed and said:

"Well, little one, I guess it's cause it's a good name, just like yours'."

Before anyone could speak further, the militia band struck up a chorus of *Always Stand on the Union Side*, originally dedicated to Governor Curtin of Pennsylvania, and they all sang along:

> *"Always stand on the Union side,*
> *And battle for the right.*

With conscience clear, we'll laugh at fear
In the midst of the boldest fight.

Always stand on the Union side,
'Tis better, as you see,
Heav'n will crown our gallant arms,
With Union victory!
If you would have your children learn,
To speak with holy pride,
Of this their dear beloved land!
Stand on the Union side!

Always stand on the Union side,
And battle for the right.
With conscience clear, we'll laugh at fear
In the midst of the boldest fight."

When the music and the singing stopped, Sallie Broadhead turned to Mrs. Gilbert and said:

"My, my, that is such a wonderful song."

"Yes, it truly is."

"And the soldiers who sang, they look so grand in their blue uniforms," Sallie Myers replied.

"They do. I do say, I haven't felt safe from those Southern traitors for quite some time, being so close. Our boys will whip them all the way back to Virginia where they belong," Annie added.

The soldiers began to form up to march and the crowd moved out of the way, gathering on the pavement of both sides of the street to see them off. The four women and the little girl joined, making their way over to the north side of street, just west of the Eagle Hotel. The drumbeat began and then the colonel ordered:

"Move out men."

And, so they did. They went right past the group and Sallie looked down at Mary, whose eyes were as big as saucers. Mary gripped her hand tightly, waved at the soldiers, and said goodbye softly enough that only her mother could hear. Sallie was very proud of her daughter and she leaned down and hugged her very tightly, saying:

"Mary, I love you with all my heart. You are my precious, precious little girl."

"Me too, Mama," the child replied.

After the remainder of the militia passed by, the crowd began to disperse, and so too did the women and the little girl.

"Goodbye, Mrs. Broadhead, Mary, and Mrs. Gilbert," Sallie Myers and Annie Myers said.

And then, they were gone. Sallie Broadhead led Mary and Mrs. Gilbert toward home. She said to Mrs. Gilbert:

"Do you really think those boys can stop the Rebels before they come to town? After all, our army couldn't in Winchester, and these boys look awful young and green."

"We must hope so, as they are our last hope. Where in the Lord's name is our army? They should be here protecting us, not those boys."

"Yes, but if these boys don't stop them, they could be here today. Tomorrow for sure."

Sallie got home, fed Mary a light dinner, and put her down for a nap. She was very worried about the militia and this caused her to be tired too. So, she lay down next to Mary, hugged her, and prayed to God to spare the men, and Gettysburg, from the Rebels. She soon fell asleep.

She was suddenly awakened by the sound of rifle fire west of town. Her mind was foggy as she had been fast asleep before the new sounds, and so it took her a moment to register the sounds as gunfire. It was about half past one o'clock. She woke Mary up and took her by the hand hurriedly down the stairs and to the front door. The gunfire sounds became louder and more frequent. She opened the door and went out to the street, looking west. Mr. and Mrs. Gilbert joined her, as did Mrs. Burns and Martha, holding Mary Jane, who was whimpering as if she also was napping. John Burns was the last to join the group, and when he did, he remarked:

"Give it 'em boys."

No one in the group spoke. They just looked west hoping for the best. Soon, maybe after ten minutes or so, the gunfire stopped. Burns said in response:

"Maybe them Rebs got the lead they deserve?"

Mr. Gilbert added:

"God willing."

"Yes, God willing," Sallie said.

They waited in silence for several minutes and then Burns said:

"No use waitin' out here. We'll know soon enough. Either they stopped 'em, or they didn't and if not, we find out soon enough."

He left and went back into his house. The others did the same and went back to their own houses. As they approached their homes, Mrs. Gilbert said:

"Sallie, can we come to your house for a cup of tea?"

"Yes, I think a cup of tea would do us all good. Mary, do you think Ruthie would like to join us?"

"Yes, Mama. What were those loud noises?"

"Mary, those were the sounds of men shooting their guns. You have seen your Papa do that, haven't you?" Mrs. Gilbert ask her.

"Yes, I have seen Papa. But, these were so much louder."

"Well, sweetie, there were a lot of men shooting their guns."

The little girl pondered this just for a moment, shrugged her shoulders, and said:

"Mama, can I have a biscuit and jam with my tea?"

Sallie, momentarily forgetting her concern about the Rebels, said:

"Yes, of course."

They made their way into the Broadhead house, and sat at the kitchen table. The little girl then set Ruthie up in a chair too. Sallie poured tea for the adults and spread some peach jam on a biscuit for Mary. She gobbled up the biscuit and pretended to drink tea with her doll. Sallie turned to Mr. Gilbert and said:

"How long do you think we will have to wait, Jacob?"

"Those shots were close, and it didn't last long, so one side had to move off. If it was ours, we should expect visitors soon."

"How soon?"

"Really, Sallie, hours, maybe sooner."

Mary finished her pretend tea, and she asked her mother:

"Mama, may I be excused from the table?"

"Yes, but go straight to your room. I want to know where you are at a moment's notice."

"I will, Mama."

The three adults drank their tea in silence, not knowing what to say to calm their nerves. Mrs. Gilbert broke the silence and said:

"This certainly is fine tea."

Before Sallie could answer, she heard the sound of wagons, and lots of them, coming in from the west. They all went to the front door and out to the front of the house. In the street, wagons were passing with great rapidity. One of the wagons slowed at the sight of the three adults staring with a shocked look, and stopped in front of the house. The driver wiped his face with the back of his glove, looked over at them and said:

"They licked us, killed some, captured most. What's left of us is in full retreat heading northeast of town. You better get prepared for the Rebels, 'cause if they come this way, nothing can stop 'em now."

And with that, he slapped his horse with the reins, and was off.

"My God," Sallie said with her hand to her mouth, and continued:

"It's really happening. They are going to be here."

After Sallie's words sunk in, they decided it would be best to go into their houses and wait to see if the Confederates indeed would show up. The Gilberts went off to their house and Sallie went to her's to look for Mary, so she could make sure she was safe.

"Mary, little Mary. Where are you child?"

"Up here Mama, in my room. Ruthie's here too."

"Can you come down, please, and bring Ruthie along?"

"If you say so, Mama."

Mary heard her daughter talking to her doll saying:

"Now Ruthie, we must go downstairs as Mama says so. She must really need us. Come along now."

A moment later, the child showed up with doll in hand. Sallie leaned down so she was face to face with the little girl.

"Mary, I really need to tell you something important, so I need you to listen. You too, Ruthie. In a little while, some soldiers will be coming to town, but these men are different from the ones we saw in town this morning. They are, how shall I say, not from around here, but from far away. And, they don't consider us friendly. I don't want you to be scared, but under no circumstances are you to leave this house unless you are with me. Don't open the door and don't go near the windows, until they leave. Do you understand?"

"How long will they stay here, Mama?"

"I don't know, but if we don't cause them trouble, maybe they will leave soon."

"Why are they here, Mama?"

"They are just visiting our town, to rest up for where they are going next, and to eat some supper."

"Shall we invite some to eat supper with us?"

"No, they are not our friends."

"Maybe they could be if we asked them to?"

"Sweet Mary, how can I make you understand? Let's try this, they are from places south of here and are mad at the people here."

"Why, what did we do to them?"

Sallie was running out of ways to tell her about the soldiers being the enemy without saying it. She knew Mary was bright even for her age, and being so she always told the child everything truthfully. But, now she was being backed into a corner by the girl.

"Well, do you remember that one time Papa and I had a disagreement and were mad at each other for a spell?"

"Yes, I do. You and Papa were mad for a whole year," the child said over exaggerating the way children did.

"Well, not a year, but only a couple of days. But, it is like that. They are mad at us and we are mad at them. Do you understand?"

"Yes. But, maybe they can stop being mad after a couple of days just like you and Papa?"

It seemed the little girl was satisfied and what was left was to just close out the conversation and so Sallie said, gently squeezing the child's nose:

"Maybe, maybe. But, until then, we are just to stay in our house. I want you to go back up to your room, close the door and try to get a nap. You didn't get enough sleep in your nap earlier. Okay?"

"I will, Mama."

Off she went, Ruthie in hand, saying:

"It is time for our nap, Ruthie. Mama noticed you are tired, so we must put you down for a rest."

Sallie marveled at the child and her questions, how smart she was. "Out of the mouths of babes," she said quietly, and thought: "how simply they view the world? Invite them in for dinner and maybe they wouldn't be mad anymore. If only it was that simple?"

Then, she thought of it differently: "Maybe the Southerners were not to be so feared of? After all they are people, too. Americans, even. Maybe the best way to act is not in fear, but rather indifference to whether they are here or not? They will be here, whether we like it or not, and there is nothing that can be done about it."

These thoughts eased her mind, but only a little. The enemy was near and whatever calm it brought her to think of them as people, Americans, could not erase the apprehension and sheer terror of what they might do once they got to town. Would the house be robbed? Would they damage and wreck the house? Would they want to stay in it? Her mind continued to race with these thoughts, when she heard a gunshot from outside. She knew instinctively who fired the shot and her stomach turned.

She made her way over to the front door, peeled the curtain back, and looked out. She heard them coming and she heard horses, lots of them. And, then she saw them as three horses went by the house at full gallop. One of men shot his rifle in the air, and all of them were yelling like wild animals. They were clad in the butternut uniform of the Rebs and their hair was flying from the wind caused by the speed of the horses. The first three rode past the house and then more and more rode by, shooting their guns and yelling just a fiercely and loud as the first three. The horses kicked up a lot of dust from the road, but even so, Sallie decided to open her door and stand just outside to watch them go by. Confederate cavalry, she surmised correctly. She looked over and saw the Gilberts open their door and look out just as she had. They looked over at her and she returned their blank stare, not knowing how to react. More and more cavalrymen went by yelling and screaming, saying:

"Hurrah for Jeff Davis. Hurrah for the Confederacy."

Sallie just watched them and then she thought of Mary. Quickly she went into the house, climbed the stairs and was in her room.

"Mary, are you alright?"

"Yes, Mama, is that the soldiers from far away?"

Sallie nodded and said:

"I am going to close your door again. You stay in this room until I get back. And, stay away from the window. Understand?"

"I will Mama."

She went back down the stairs. All the while, more cavalrymen were entering the town. The noise and the dust were becoming unbearable, but she decided she must watch, so she went back out the front door. After a few minutes the last of the horses passed, and one stopped in front of Sallie's house. He removed his hat, bowed ever so slightly and spoke with what seemed to Sallie a very thick southern accent:

"Afternoon, ma'am. We from da great state of Virginy, and have cum in da name of Jeff Davis and the Cunfedracy. Cum to pay y'all a visit."

Sallie hesitated and then decided to cautiously talk to the soldier:

"You are the cavalry. Is the infantry also coming?"

"Yes, ma'am. They's aint fa hind. Should be here in a spell, yes, ma'am. Are der any Yank sulders in town?"

"None that I know of."

"Well ma'am, if dey is, we find 'em."

And with that, he placed his hat on his head and rode off. She looked east along the road toward the center of town and watched as the cavalrymen rode off in two directions once they got to the Diamond, going east on York Street and south on Baltimore Street. As she was looking, the Gilberts came over, and Mrs. Gilbert said:

"They frightened me half to death, with all that yelling and shooting. What shall we do?"

Sallie replied: "That last one said the infantry isn't far behind them, so we should go into our houses and lock the doors, otherwise they might come in and take what they want."

"Yes, let's secure our houses before the army gets here," Mr. Gilbert said. Again, they went into their houses, shut and locked their doors. Sallie went upstairs and knocked on Mary's door.

"Is that you Mama?"

"It is. I am coming in, so we can watch the soldiers from your window."

"Didn't you say to stay away from the window?"

"I did. But, it will be alright if we do it together."

"I wish Papa was here."

"Me too, sweetie, me too. But, he will be alright. Remember, he works for the mighty railroad and the railroad will take good care of him," she said covering her thoughts of worry as to what would happen to Joseph when the army arrives and they take over the town proper. How he would get home safely concerned her deeply, but she didn't let on about this to the child.

Just then, they looked out the window to see the infantry units arriving. They were marching on the Chambersburg Pike and right past Sallie's house, following the movement of the cavalry earlier. The dust from the cavalry horses settled and so there was a clear view of the men. Mary was the first to speak:

"Mama, they sure are dirty looking. Not like the soldiers from this morning with their shiny, blue uniforms. "

"Indeed they are."

"Mama, look, look at those men," she pointed and continued:

"They have no shoes. And, those over there with their funny hats with furry tails."

They continued to watch the Rebel army for a few minutes and saw all sorts of men, tall, short, raggety uniforms, but most were outfitted with the southern gray, with some having uniforms more tattered than the rest. Then, came the officers riding on their horses. Mary asked:

"Mama, who are those men on horseback?"

"Those are the officers, ah, the leaders," she corrected making it more understanding to the little girl.

"They sure are dressed better than the walking soldiers."

"Yes, they are."

"Mama, look over there at that man," she pointed again to the group of officers, and continued:

"He's dressed, not like the rest, but the way Papa does when you go out for supper."

Sallie looked at the only man dressed in civilian clothes, outfitted with a black bow tie, a white shirt under the waist coat, black trousers, and a black bowler hat that fit snugly on his head. The man was tall and had shoulder length blonde hair flowing out from under his bowler. She continued to look at the man for about a minute as his horse made its way to right in front of their house. The man stopped his horse as the other officers had already done so. The officer to his left turned to the man and asked him a question, Sallie surmised, because the man took off his hat, ran his fingers through his hair, and pointed toward the Diamond as he answered. There was something very familiar about him, she thought. And, then she took a deep breath and put her hand to her mouth. It was Jones.

CHAPTER **28**

WILL

JOHN CHARLES WILL was serving his customers at the bar of the Globe Inn. It was around two o'clock in the afternoon, and Will was tending the bar and cleaning up after the dinner crowd cleared out. He looked up from wiping down the bar because of the noise created by a man running into the inn shouting:

"They're here, they're *here*! The dirty Rebel cavalry is riding into town right now."

Will looked at the man who was breathing heavily and said:

"Are you sure? We have had so many false sightings these last days that I don't believe anyone, *anymore*," emphasizing the last word.

"Well believe this. I saw 'em myself. The first group came through and pursued our boys retreating down Baltimore Street. But more are coming, and I am sure they will be passing this way any moment."

As he finished speaking, Will heard the sounds of many horses outside. He made his way around the bar, out of the restaurant area, through the inn, and outside. He stood in front of the door and under the balcony for the second floor of the inn, which provided shading from the sun. Because he had come from the dark inn to the shaded area below the balcony, it took a few seconds for his eyes to adjust to the bright, sunlit day. His ears could hear the cavalry going by, with the noises made by the hooves of the horses. His eyes adjusted, and he watched them go easterly along York Street. He looked beyond those, westerly to the Diamond, where he saw horsemen riding around the town square. He decided he needed a closer look, so he walked to the town center. It took only a moment or two, and when he got there, he noticed an officer on horseback giving orders to the cavalrymen:

"Ya men, ya folla them Yanks to the noath along this road," he said pointing to Carlisle Road. He continued:

"And ya men, ya go out that road," he pointed to York Street, where Will had come from the inn. His next order was:

"Ya men, ya go south along that road," pointing to Baltimore Street. He finished with:

"Ya's don't let any of them blue bellies get away, ya hear?"

At once the men rode hard off in the directions they were ordered. He observed the officer as more and more cavalry rode into the town. The officer noticed him and rode over:

"Ya, sir, we a hea and we a hea to stay. The aamy is right 'hind us. Do ya know whea the Globe Inn is? We comin' for a visit."

My God, Will thought, why would he be asking for his inn. He decided it was better to answer the question truthfully than maybe suffer the consequences of a lie. Besides, it would only be a matter of minutes before the inn would be found anyway.

"Yes, sir, I do. You see, I, with my father, am the proprietor of that inn."

"Kindly point it out, sir. The general, he'd like to know when he gets hea."

"It's just down that street and on the left," Will said pointing to York Street.

"Ya said, ya's the proprieta? Well, ya goest and set up fo the general as he will be along within the awa."

When he finished speaking, they heard a shot in the distance down Baltimore Street. In a couple of minutes, one of the Rebel cavalrymen rode up and addressed the officer:

"Colonel, sur. We chased three of the Yank militia cavalry. One wouldn't surrenda, so we had to shoot 'im. The othas escaped as they had a lead. Otha than those, the town is clear to the south."

"Well done, Maja."

Will asked: "You shot one of the militia boys? Was he killed?"

"Yes, sur, he was. Had to shoot 'im. We couldn't let 'im escape."

"Are you bringing in the body into to town? Some of those boys in that unit are from here, so if he is, I'm sure his kin would like to know."

"Sorra, sur, but iffen ya need to know who that dead boy is, ya gonna haff to do it yaself" , the officer said. He continued:

"Now, ya go an prepare the inn for the general."

"Not until I see the boy you killed."

"As ya wish, but if the general arrives and the inn is not ready, y'all is responsible."

Will lead a crowd to the area where the dead militia man was left, down south on Baltimore Street. Once they arrived where the body was, Will said:

"Does anyone know this poor soul?"

A middle-aged woman answered, with a shaken voice, clearly upset:

"I am from Barlow, and yes I know, knew, him. He is George Washington Sandoe. He lives, lived, there with his wife Diana. We must let her know. She was so upset when he volunteered for the militia."

She bent down and stoked the dead man's hair and said:

"Oh Lordy, he was so young."

Will bent down and helped the woman up. He turned to the crowd and asked:

"Can anyone help move the body from the street and take it to his home in Barlow. Can someone do that?"

A man by the name of Peter McAllister spoke up:

"I'll take him home to Barlow."

Will thanked McAllister and walked back to the Diamond. Not long after, the army began arriving in the town square. Will stayed long enough to see the group of officers ride in a short time after the army. He was just about to go, when he noticed the general and his staff, and a tall man in civilian clothes. He looked closer at the man and recognized him. It was Samuel Jones.

Jones had not seen Will yet. He was talking to the general and pointing in the direction of the inn. Will was disgusted. So Jones was a spy after all, and that old fool Burns was right. He turned and walked back toward the inn. On his way he came upon his father, who had begun walking toward the Diamond. His father greeted him:

"John, are you alright?"

"I am. You know who I just saw with the Rebel army? Jones, that's who. Do you remember him from a couple of weeks ago?"

"The fella who left town suddenly, but gave us that currant liquor recipe?"

"That's him. He is a spy after all. How could I have been so stupid?"

"Son, you weren't being stupid. You were just being friendly to an out-of-towner. That is your job, our job, as owners of an inn."

"Father, it doesn't make me feel less guilty. I gave him all the information about the town and now he has brought the Reb army to our home."

"John, an enterprising man like Jones would have found out all the things you told him on his own. You didn't tell him any secrets, just gave him the layout of the town."

"I could have let Burns arrest him."

"That old, daft man? Who in this town believes anything he says?"

"That maybe so, but what are the townsfolk going to say when they find out? Father, the colonel from the cavalry asked about the Globe by name. He must have gotten this from Jones."

"They'll say what they are gonna say, and who cares? You did nothing an innkeeper would not have done with one of his customers. These are different times, that's for sure. But, we still have to make a living, John.

Now, I don't want you to fret about it anymore. You say they asked for the inn specifically?"

"The colonel did, and said I should get the inn ready as the general will be paying us a visit this afternoon."

"Well, I don't see we have much choice here do we? They'll come with or without our permission and whether we want them or not. So, let's go back and tidy the place up a bit and wait for them to come. I don't want to hear any more about you feeling guilty you befriended a business partner."

"You mean a spy?"

"I mean a business partner. He gave you that recipe didn't he? And, how is it selling?"

"Well, the customers, they like it, particularly with supper."

"You see, a *business partner*."

They walked off toward the inn to prepare for the coming of the Rebel General, his staff, and Jones.

About a half an hour later, General Early and his staff arrived at the Globe. They tied their horses up to the railing in front of the inn and came in. Will could hear their conversation outside before they entered:

"So, this is the famous Globe Inn ya talked so much about?"

"Yes, sir it is. Let me take you in and introduce you to the fine gentlemen who own the place."

Will heard Jones' compliment toward he and his father and remembered how he liked Jones from the very start of meeting him. This memory calmed him a little and prepared him for facing the man he thought was his friend, or as his father said, business partner, who was in reality the enemy.

The Confederates entered the inn, led by Jones, who saw and greeted Will:

Jones offered out his hand: "John, how nice to see you again."

"Mr. Jones," Will responded not taking Jones' hand.

"John, this here is General Jubal A. Early of the Army of Northern Virginia."

"General."

Charles Will noticed the conversation from across the entrance to the inn, and how awkward it was, so he crossed the room and said:

"Good afternoon, General."

"Good aftanoon, sir," Early said and offered Charles Will his hand.

Charles shook his hand and said:

"I understand you asked specifically about our inn and wanted to come by for a visit?"

"Aye did indeed, sir. Aye have heard so much about this place from my friend here, Mista Jones, Aye just had to come by and see it for myself. Mista Jones here says the food at the inn is second to none. He even remembers a dish called hog's somethin' or otha. What was it, Jones?"

"It was Hog Maw, and it was delicious."

"Hog Maw. Would ya happen to have some? Aye am powerfully hungry, and could use a bit of food. We will pay for it, of course."

Father looked over at son and asked:

"John, have we still got some Hog Maw, or are we cooking some up for the supper crowd?"

"Father...?"

"You heard me, son. Are we making any Hog Maw?"

"Well, yes, it is on the menu for supper. It isn't ready yet."

"Why don't you go see how soon some can be ready?"

Young Will left without another word to the kitchen to check on how the supper preparations were coming and if there was some Hog Maw being readied.

"You'll have to excuse my son. He would like to be off fighting against you fellas, but I just cannot spare him from the family business here. Besides, I kinda like him, and it would break my heart if anything ever happened to him."

Early raised his hand and said:

"Ya needent talk any more of it. We are the invadas to ya fine town hea, and we expect a certain amount of grief. But, let me tell ya something about oua visit hea. It is to be short as we will be moving on in a day or so..."

Will returned in time to hear the rest of what General Early was saying:

"...as Aye said, Aye have heaad so much about this fine town from Mista Jones hea, Aye had to come for a look myself. Mista Jones has visited several towns fo me in the last few weeks, and by fa his most interestin' report has been on this town. He was genuinely impressed with Gettysburg and the people who live hea, particularly with ya son, Mista Will. And, as Aye have listened, Aye knew it would be best for me to come and act like a visita and not a conquera. Therefoa, treat me as such and Aye will ensua the aamy treats this town as such. Thanks to Mista Jones."

Will looked over at Jones and saw the friend he had gotten to know. Even though he was the enemy, he was a friend. He just hoped that delicate balance could be maintained. He said:

"Father, we can have some Hog Maw ready to serve in an hour."

"That will be fine, John. In the meantime, why don't we go into the restaurant and sit down. Would you fellas like an ale, or some liquor?"

"That would be fine," Early said.

"John, draw up five ales for our guests here and I'll get them seated at one of our tables."

As they walked into the restaurant, several customers chose to leave. Charles showed them to the prime table, which Jones remembered being the one he sat with Will to discuss the Currant Champagne recipe. He said:

"John, isn't this the same table where we discussed the Currant Champagne?"

"Yes, Jones it is."

"Did you get that recipe I left for you? And, did you give it a try?"

"We did and it is selling, particularly during the supper hours."

Jones smiled and said: "Glad to hear it. You know, you still owe me that fifteen dollars, don't forget."

"It seems, Mr. Jones, you already got paid for your visit here, and I imagine it was a lot more than fifteen dollars."

Jones still sensed the hostility toward him from Will, so he went over to the bar to help him with the ales.

"John, let me help you with those."

Then he said quietly:

"I know you are not happy with me, as I was not quite what I said I was. But, I hope you understand that, like you, I have a job to do."

"Jones, I understand, and the job you do is to be my enemy."

"That maybe true, but only until this damn war is over. Then I hope to be your friend, as I still hope to be now."

"We shall see. We shall see."

The two men brought over the ales and served it to Early, his staff, and Jones. Early took a sip and said:

"This is fine ale. It really is. Aye'd like to propose a toast, if Aye may...?"

He raised his glass and said:

"To the Globe Inn and to Hog Maw. May it be every bit as good as Mista Jones says."

The Southerners drank their first ale and ordered another. Half way through the second ale, the food was ready and so Will brought out the plates. They ate their food without much discussion, and when they were finished, Early spoke:

"Mista Will, that was one of the best meals Aye have ever had the pleasure of. So delightful. Mista Jones, ya was right."

"Yes, John, just as I remembered."

"Now, Aye have some business to attend to, and Aye hope ya do not mind me excusing myself for awhile? Ya see when Aye got into town, Aye delivaed a message for the mayor and Aye am expectin' an answa. Aye beggin' your pardon. Colonel Daniel, will ya please square up with Mista Will for the fine food and the ales?"

"Yes, sir."

Daniel reached into his saddle bag and produced Confederate script and said:

"Now, how much?"

Charles Will said:

"Let's see, ten ales at eight cents apiece, for eighty cents, and five meals at fifty cents each for two dollars and fifty cents, so the total is three dollars and thirty cents."

Daniel handed Charles Will four Confederate dollars, saying: "Will this do?"

Charles Will saw that the money was Confederate dollars and said:

"General, you mentioned we should treat you as visitors and not invaders. So with that in mind, I want good money I can use around here, not that Confederate money."

Early hesitated for a moment and then said to Daniel:

"Colonel, pay him with Union greenbacks."

Then to Charles Will, he said:

"Aye trust that is acceptable to ya, sir?"

"Yes, General, that will be fine."

"And, Colonel, make sure ya give him a little moa for his trouble."

Colonel Daniel gave Will four dollars and then the Confederates left. John Will turned to his father and said:

"Father, that was a little more than we usually charge for the meal and the ales, wasn't it?"

"Yes, we may treat them as visitors, but they are still here when we don't want them here, and they are still the enemy. So, they shall pay a little more for that priviledge."

As the Confederates left and mounted their horses, Jones failed to notice across York Street, a man watching from the pavement in front of the Tyson Brother's Photo Gallery. It was Silas McGee.

CHAPTER 29

BURNS

JOHN L. BURNS heard the horses from his parlor. He was resting after coming back into his house when the battle out west between the Union militia and the Confederates died down, and so the noises made by the galloping horses stirred him awake. He got up, went to the kitchen and outside the front door onto his landing for his stairs leading into the house. He watched as the Rebel cavalry went by and into the town. The dust stirred up from the horses even reached him on the upstairs landing, and he coughed and waved his hands in front of his face.

Irritated, he said to no one but himself: "Traitorous Rebels."

When all of the cavalry had gone by, he decided he would need to go into town to see if there was anything he could do to help the town. So he went back into the house and discussed this with his wife:

"Old woman, they are here. They are finally here, just like I said they would be. Would anyone listen? This town is full of stupid people. They won't know what to do with the Rebs. I am going to go into the town to see what I can do."

"Why do you need to go to town? Don't you think it would be better to stay here and protect us and the house?"

"Them Rebs won't bother you as long as you keep the door closed and locked."

"How do you know? You have an old woman, a daughter, and a grand-daughter needing protection and you are going to go to town where the Rebels are? And, no telling what they are doing and what kind of damage?"

"I ain't a sitting here like an old woman. The enemy is in our town and I aim to see what they are doing and what I can do to help."

"You go ahead, but if anything happens to us it will be 'cause of you. If anything happens to that little girl, you may as well not come back!"

"Awe, I've had enough of this. Goodbye. Keep the door closed and locked until I get back."

With that, he left and slammed the door behind him. He descended down the stairs and began to walk toward the town, still upset with his wife, and so he didn't notice the approaching Confederates, but he could see the cavalry riding around the Diamond, yelling and shooting their guns in the air. He heard noises behind him on the Chambersburg Pike. He stopped before crossing Franklin Street and looked back along the Pike, and saw them. The Rebel army was marching in strict formation and the point of the infantry was passing his house. He hurriedly crossed the Chambersburg Street and waited. As the Rebels began to pass where he was, he noticed how dirty they were, how tattered their uniforms were, and how a great many of them had no shoes at all. He thought, "How could this army be winning this war? How could the Union not be up to the task of whipping these grubby animals?" He decided he needed to get into town, to see what could be done, and so he continued walking along the side of the street keeping pace with the Rebs.

When he got to town, he settled on the northwest corner of the Diamond near Boyer's Grocery Store and waited. Soon, he noticed a group of officers ride by. He also noticed a tall man dressed in civilian clothes riding with them. The man looked familiar to him. He saw one of the officers address him and the man answered and pointed toward York Street. He looked at the man more intensely. Jones. It's that man Jones he should have arrested weeks ago. *He is a spy.* Before he could stop himself he yelled:

"Joooones."

Jones stopped talking to the officer and looked over in his direction to see who called his name. Their eyes met, and Jones smiled. Jones tapped the officer on the shoulder and pointed at him. Both Jones and the officer reined their horses over to where he was standing. Jones tipped his hat, and said:

"Well, if it isn't my old friend Mr. John L. Burns. General, this is the fellow I was telling you about who was chasing me a couple of weeks ago. Almost caught me, too. Mr. Burns, this is General Jubal A. Early of the Army of Northern Virginia."

"Mista Burns, it is indeed an hona to meet ya. Mista Jones hea has told me all about ya and ya adventuas. Why, just the otha day, Aye was informed ya were up on South Mountain building blockades."

Burns was surprised to say the least, and didn't know quite what to say. Jones noticed and couldn't resist:

"Why Mr. Burns. This is the first time I've seen you without nothing to say."

"Mista Burns, ya shouldn't be so modest. Ya a vera perceptive man and if ya succeeded in putting Mr. Jones hea in jail, we wouldn't have nea the infoamation about this hea town as we now do. But, then again, without the propa infoamation, we may have had to fia the town."

Burns forced the words out: "Fire the town?

"Well, we don't need to do that drastic measura now, not with Mista Jones' infoamation."

The general continued:

"Aye do admia a man such as ya-self, one with a lot of courage. Aye am so glad oua scouts decided not to shoot ya as ya ran away from the barricades the otha day. Aye understood one of the boys had ya dead to right, but was ordaed not to fia."

Burns still didn't know quite what to say. But, his courage returned and he said:

"Just doin' my duty General. I was the constable of this town and so I need to protect these people."

Early laughed and said:

"Well, Mista Burns ya certainly are eveaything Aye thought and moa. Aye told Mista Jones Aye would take a likening to this town and Aye do, starting with y'all. Good day, and Aye hope to see more of ya whilst we are hea."

"Mr. Burns, good day. I too hope to see you more whilst here," Jones echoed.

With that they turned their horses around and walked back to join the troops. Jones said:

"General, fire the town?"

"General Lee strictly prohibited that type of behavya on this campaign. We won't be treatin' them like they treated ouas in Fredericksburg when they sacked the town. But, it was entataining to see his reaction. Aye ratha relished it."

Burns didn't quite know what to do, so he decided he would pay a visit to his part time employer Mr. David Kendlehart, who was President of the Borough Council of Gettysburg. Burns had done all sorts of jobs for Mr. Kendlehart including official deliveries; town collections; and investigations that included reports, important because they represented, as Kendlehart would say, an "independent point of view." He knew Kendlehart would be busy now that the Rebel army was in the town, and so he wondered if his services would be needed in any way. He walked east and crossed Carlisle Street, turned south and crossed York Street. Everywhere there were Confederates. Three soldiers saw him and decided to approach. One soldier addressed him saying:

"Ol' man. How many Yank soldyurs a hidin' in this hea town?"

Burns huffed and said:

"None that I know of. Search for yourself."

The soldier decided his response was disrespectful, so he engaged his other comrades saying:

182

"Well, lookey hea, boys, we gots ouselves a sassy, little ole Yank."

His comrade said:

"Hey Yank what's the matta? Don't ya like us being hea in ya town?"

The other added:

"Now, where y'all live? I think we might pay a visit to ya house this evenin'. Have ouaselves a little suppa. What do ya say?"

Burns stopped walking and looked at the three soldiers. Dirty, young men, dressed like animals and smelling similarly. His temper began to grow, and so he responded:

"I don't like your traitorous army here in my town. And, I don't like you. A couple of fresh faced boys, that's all you are. Big army *boys*. When our army arrives, and they will, we'll see how brave you are."

The first soldier decided he heard enough from Burns, so he shoved him, but not hard enough to knock him down. But, he fell back against the David Wills' house. The three closed in on him. Just then, an officer yelled:

"Ya men, ya leave that man be, *now*. We a ordaed to treat these people with respect and ya shall follo that orda. Ya hea?"

The three soldiers backed away from Burns and disappeared down York Street. Burns brushed himself off, gave a quick look of thanks to the officer, and continued to walk down to Kendlehart's house. He arrived and knocked on the door. Kendlehart answered:

"Oh John, it's you. Come on it. I need your help."

Burns entered the house and followed Kendlehart into the parlor room where other members of the Borough Council were gathered. After greetings were exchanged, Kendlehart said:

"John, General Early has sent us a letter demanding what he calls "tribute." He wants supplies: food, whiskey, clothing, or money. As insulting as that is, and knowing we wouldn't pay it, the real problem is most of these types of supplies have been sent to Philadelphia, so we can't raise it even if they tried to force us to. And, the Council has no authority to borrow the money in the name of the town. We are trying to decide who should deliver a response letter to him with the bad news."

"If you are looking for a volunteer, you have one," Burns said.

"Real fine, John. Why don't you sit whilst I write the response letter?"

It took about ten minutes for Kendlehart to finish and then he folded it and handed it to Burns saying:

"John, good luck. He may not like the answer, so be careful. Also, tell him his army is free to search the stores and take whatever he wants."

"Mr. Council President, I will deliver it and explain why we cannot give in to his demands."

And with that, Burns left the house and walked toward the Diamond, where he hoped he would find Early. As he reached the Diamond, he looked over and saw the officer who assisted him earlier with the three Rebel soldiers. Burns addressed him:

"Do you know where I can find General Early?"

"Right now, I do believe he is havin' an early suppa at the Globe Inn. What's ya business with the general?"

"I have a message for him from the Borough Council President."

"Well, ya Borough Council President will just haff to wait till he finishes his suppa. Once he comes out, I'll let him know ya have a letta for him."

"I will wait for him right here."

Burns didn't have to wait long, no more than ten minutes, for Early and Jones to accompany the officer over to receive the Council's letter. Early said:

"Well, Mista Burns, Aye didn't expect to see ya again so soon. The maja hea tells me ya have a letta from the Council?"

"I do, General. I was instructed by Mr. David Kendlehart, President of the Council for the Borough of Gettysburg to give you personally the response letter about the tribute you requested."

Burns handed Early the letter. Early unfolded it and read. His pleasant smile faded, and he turned to Jones and the major, saying:

"It appeas we are a little late in gettin' hea. This hea letta says all the provisions have been moved out of the town, and furtha the Council has no authority to borra any money."

Jones spoke: "That's disappointin'. There are a few stores we can search, if you would like me to show the way?"

"Mr. Kendlehart said you can take what you want from the shelves, but you ain't gonna find much," Burns added.

"We might just need to do that. In the meantime, what am Aye to do as a propa response to this letta? I cannot just let the town not pay a tribute to our fine aamy, now can Aye?"

Early rubbed his chin and said:

"Well, if they cannot pay us, then Aye do believe someone should, and as Aye see it, Mista Burns hea is representing the town, so it may as well be him. Maja, arrest Mista Burns hea and put him in the town jail for a spell. Mista Burns, like Aye said, Aye like ya, but the town must pay this aamy a tribute, and if they cannot, well then ya must be jailed."

Burns looked shocked and irritated:

"By what authority do you have to jail me, General?"

"Simple, Mista Burns, by the authaity that comes with us being hea. That's all the *authaity* Aye need."

Early turned to the major and said:

"Maja, make sure he is comfoatable and gets everything he needs, and then let 'im go once we a movin' out."

"Yes, sur."

And with that, Burns was led off to jail.

CHAPTER 30

BUTLER

ELIZABETH (OLD LIZ) BUTLER was awakened from her nap around three o'clock in the afternoon. She had been busy all day making preparations for her and her husband Samuel to leave town and travel north, maybe all the way into Canada. They planned on leaving the next day. Just the previous night, she finished all of the laundry orders and today she was packing all of the items they could carry with them. They had no wagon, nor did they even have a horse, so what little they could bring would have to be carried. She was also selling all their belongings they could not bring and arranged for some folks to come over after supper to take a look and to make offers on what they wanted to buy from her. It was this sorting of their belongings that kept her busy this day. She was satisfied with her progress, and so a nap was in order. Samuel was also sleeping, as this night would be his last working at the Globe Inn, and with their journey beginning the next day, he too needed the extra rest.

She was awakened by a furious knock on the front door, followed by a desperate voice saying:

"Liz, Liz yous jus gotta anser."

She made her way to the front door as the knocking continued, louder and louder. She opened the door to find Esther Moses.

"Esther, why whatever do you mean?"

"Liz, Liz, it's dem Confedrats. Dey here. Dey here."

"Dem Confedrats here in Gettysburg?"

"Yes, yes, you mus hurry to our house. You be safer dere."

Butler understood the urgency of the request as the Moses' house had more opportunities to hide than their house did. So, she ran off to the bedroom to get Samuel and the children up and out of the house.

"Sam'l, Sam'l, Confedrats here. Hurry, hurry, we must go to Moses house to hide."

Samuel said: "Confedrats here?"

"Yes, yes. Now git youself movin'. We go now."

She ran into the bedroom where the children slept. They had two teen-age boys. She woke them up and told them to get ready to leave the house right away.

At that moment they heard horses riding by on Washington Street, coming from the north. It was too late for Esther to come into the house and as she watched them go by, she clearly saw one Rebel rider notice her. He continued to stare at her as he rode by, even straining his neck. This frightened her very much, so she went into the house quickly.

"Liz, oh Liz, one dem Confedrats, he saw me."

"Lets git to yours house, right quick. Sam'l, we go *now*."

The five ran as quickly as they could the couple of blocks to the Moses' house. Isaac ushered them in and slammed the door. When they got in, his wife said:

"Isaac, one dem saw me."

Isaac went over and hugged his wife comforting her.

"Now, Esther, don't you fret none. We's be alright. Dey won't be a bothering us none."

He moved away and grabbed her on the shoulders and looked deep into her eyes. Then he laughed and said:

"Leastwise, not us. We's too old. Dey know even if dey ketched us, we's not able to travel good back to de South. Now Liz and Samuel, and specially de boys, dat's diffrent. We must hid dem."

"We's must. Dey take 'em sure."

"Liz, Samuel no time to git to the old Dobbin House, so's we's hid you here. Let's git you down to de cellar and in dat secrat room ours."

Isaac lit a lantern and they all went down the stairs and into the cellar. Isaac led the way to the corner. He set the lantern down and moved some old crates away from the wall revealing a small, metal door, with a handle recessed into the door. Isaac lifted the handle and pulled the door open. It creaked as it opened as it was a heavy door. When it was fully opened, it revealed a small room. They were greeted with a musty, pungent smell that stung their noses slightly. They waited until the air cleared from the room and the smell to dissipate, and then Isaac picked up the lantern, bent down and went in. First, Esther followed and then Liz, then the two boys, and finally Samuel. The room was about six feet deep and about four feet wide, just barely enough room for the six. The ceiling was low, about five feet, so Samuel and Isaac and the boys could not stand fully. The floor was only dirt. In the back corner was a crate and a couple of old, dusty blankets.

"Not much to speak of, but a good hidin' place, dat's sure," Isaac said, and continued:

"You's stay here while. Keep dis lantern and some of dese here matches. Try to not keep it lit to awfully long, lest you run outta oil. Esther and me, we's bring you food and water and a bucket for goin' in. We's let you know when safe to come out."

"Sure obliged, Isaac," Samuel said.

Liz asked: "How long we's need to be here?"

"No tellin'. Maybes not too long. I's close the door and then pile up the crates, so's if dey cum, dey won't want to move 'em and you be safe. And, yous listen tight now, hear? If there's a Confedrat a lookin', I'll make sure I's warns you nice and loud."

"Oh thank you, Isaac, thank you."

With that, the Moses's left and closed the door behind them. Liz and Samuel heard the crates being put up against the door and then nothing. They were alone.

"Sam'l, what's we do now?"

"Old Liz, we waits like Isaac said. We waits."

Isaac and Esther went upstairs and to the front door. Isaac opened the door and looked out. At first they saw nothing, just a normal day outside. He left the door open as he normally did on a hot day. They went back into the living room and decided to have a cup of tea. Esther heated the water on the stove and then brought Isaac and herself a cup. They sipped their tea quietly. Esther began to knit. All seemed quiet, but a little too quiet.

Isaac took another sip of his tea, and before he could put his cup down, he heard voices outside. He strained to hear, and then heard:

"How many live hea?"

A young woman responded:

"Twos, nothin' but an old man and woman."

Isaac felt the chills go up his spine. He looked over at Esther who had a terrified look on her face. He nodded his head quickly as if to say "still, quiet." He sat motionless as he heard footsteps on the steps leading to their house. Then, a footstep on the porch. Then, a knock on the door, which was open. He froze.

"I know ya in thea, so may as well show yaselves, or we'll haff to come in afta ya," came a voice from the porch.

Isaac didn't respond immediately. He didn't know the best way of answering the voice. After what seemed like minutes, but was in reality only about ten seconds, a head appeared peeking into the house and then took one step into the house. The man was dressed in the butternut of the Confederate Army. He said:

"Awe, thea ya is. Now, why didn't ya respond to my callin'?"

He completely entered the house. Isaac, still frightened, did not move. But, his courage returned and he got up and said:

"We's surprised dat's all. Cum right in. Can we's git yas some tea?"

"That be right fine."

The soldier came further into the house and sat down on the couch. He said to his comrades outside:

"Hey, John, hey Jeffason, I'll be having a cup of tea with this darkie old couple. Shall I bring y'all a cup?

"Amos, that would warm my heaat like nothin' otha. Ya bring it right out, as we don't wanta lose our possessions out hea."

Isaac said: "Esther, git our guests some tea."

"Esther, is it?" The soldier named Amos hesitated until she nodded and continued:

"That would be mighty kind of ya."

Esther disappeared in the kitchen, and then returned with three cups of tea. She handed them to Amos, who got up to take them, and then she sat without a word.

"Thank ya kindly ma'am."

Amos went out to give the tea to his comrades and Isaac followed him out to the porch. Once he got to the porch, he gasped as he saw the three soldiers had rounded up five of the colored citizens of Gettysburg, three women and two men. He knew them all. Their ages ranged from the mid-teens to about thirty. They all had their hands tied in front of them and their heads down. They looked up at Isaac with a most pitiful look. One of women spoke, with tears in her eyes, and said "Isaac…?"

The soldiers named John and Jefferson were guarding them with their muskets. They took the cups from Amos and they all drank the tea heartily. When he was finished, Amos turned to Isaac and said:

"Old man, any moa daakies in that thea house of ya's?"

Isaac was still in shock seeing his neighbors being held by the Rebel soldiers. He didn't respond, so Amos repeated his question with some irritation and a louder voice:

"I said a thea any more daakies in that house?"

"No sur, no sur. We's, my wife and I, we's live alone."

"Ya don't mind if I take a look around, now do ya?"

Without waiting, Amos climbed the stairs and walked past Isaac and back into the house. Isaac turned around and followed him in.

"Now, let's see. Take me around this hea house and show me evaything."

Isaac showed the soldier the kitchen, their bedroom, and the parlor area. Amos inquired: "How bout the cellar?"

Esther gave her husband a worried look that the soldier didn't see, as he was busy looking down the steps and into the dark downstairs room.

"There's nothin' down there cept some ol crates and a couple of broke chairs."

"Let's have a look at 'em. Ya first."

"Esther, no need you cum. Stays here."

He gave her a confident look and lit a lantern and led the soldier down the stairs. The light showed an empty room, except for the items Isaac described.

He said again, a little louder so the Butlers could be warned:

"You's see, just like I's said, aint nothin' down here cept some ol crates and a couple of broke chairs."

Inside the secret room, Liz and Samuel and the boys started to sweat profusely, as they knew from Isaac's signal, there was a Confederate soldier searching the cellar. They quickly blew out the lantern and held each other as tightly as they could.

"Sam'l, we's going back to slavin, that's sure," she whispered.

"Old Liz, you's hush now. Be real still."

The soldier walked around the room and approached the crates. Isaac's heart stopped beating as the soldier looked into the top crate. He paused and reached into it. He pulled out an old book. It was the *Book of Psalms*. He held it up and said:

"Ya read, ol man?"

"Yes, sur. Taught me self once I's free and cum north."

"A darkie who can read. Ain't seen many of them."

He put the book back in the crate and turned to leave. He walked across the floor to the stairs, but then stopped. He turned around and looked back at the crates one more time, and without a word went back over to them. He bent down to the floor right next to the crates and hesitated. He reached out as if to move the crates. Isaac felt a chill even though a bead of sweat rolled down his face. The soldier picked up something, looked at it and walked over to Isaac.

"Found this hea coin. I'll be keeping it for my troubles. Now, let's get out of this hot cellar."

They climbed the stairs and the soldier walked over to the door. He pivoted and said:

"Ya two are lucky ya olda, or ya be comin' with us and soon headed back south. Well, anyway much obliged for the tea."

With that he left and so did his comrades with their prisoners. Isaac sat down in the living room and a tear rolled down his cheek mixing with his sweat. He prayed silently saying "Lord, please protect them."

CHAPTER 31

WADE

VIRGINIA (GINNIE) WADE heard her newborn baby nephew cry for the first time around two-thirty in the afternoon. She was assisting her mother and Mrs. Maria Comfort in the delivery. Mrs. Comfort was a good friend of both Ginnie's and Georgia's. She lived just a short distance up Baltimore Street from Georgia. She was 48 years old, and was in practicality like a second mother to both the women. Maria cut the cord and took the baby to be cleaned up. She brought it to Ginnie, who had fresh towels and some warm water for cleaning. She and Maria cleaned the fragile little one up while her mother tended to her sister Georgia.

"Georgia, it's a beautiful little boy. You and John should be so proud," Ginnie said.

"He's a fine, strong boy, Georgia," Maria added.

Georgia smiled but didn't say anything as she was too tired from the birth to muster the energy. But, Ginnie was just too excited to not continue, so she said:

"A little boy. Do you have any idea what you will call him?"

Georgia looked at Ginnie and decided the moment was too important not to talk about, she could rest fully later.

"No, not yet. Lewis and I will pick a nice name. I must send him a letter at once. Mother will you help me with it?"

"Yes, Georgia, I will. Now, I want you to rest."

"Not until I get to hold my little boy."

Ginnie finished cleaning the baby, which was not pleasing to the young one as he continued to cry, and then she wrapped it up in a nice little blanket and brought it to Georgia. She handed him over to her saying:

"Here you are, mother. Your first, of hopefully, many strong and healthy children."

Georgia took the baby and snuggled it up next to her. She got eye contact with him and he stopped crying instantly.

"There, there, little one, Mama's here."

The three women watched in joy as baby and mother shared their first moment together.

Ginnie said: "Well mother, Mrs. Comfort, I must get back to Harry and Isaac. I'll come back later and bring the boys to see the baby."

She walked toward home and had just crossed Baltimore Street at Breckinridge Street when she noticed wagons coming from town at a pell-mell pace. She stopped to see what was going on as they all went by. It was the militia who left town earlier to engage the Rebel army northwest of town. She couldn't speak with them, so she could only watch. She decided she would go to the Pierce house and see if they knew. Besides, it would give her a good reason to see her brother, Sam. She approached the house, climbed the steps and knocked on the door. Tillie Pierce answered. She looked very ruffled and was out of breath. Her hair was uncombed and her dress looked dusty. She said between gulps of air to catch her breath:

"Ginnie, how nice to see you. Please come in."

"Matilda, thank you," Ginnie said courteously enough but with the same disdain she held for the family because her brother Sam was a boarder at the Pierce house, a fact that offended her deeply, although she knew the necessity of it. Sam simply had to work to help her family survive.

Ginnie went into the house and noticed the Pierces busy making plans. Tillie's father James was talking to her brother Sam, saying:

"Now Sam, we mustn't let the Rebels get that horse. She is too valuable to our family and my butchering," he said and continued:

"We'll saddle her up and then you ride it south of town on Baltimore Pike for a spell, maybe an hour or so, until you feel you and the animal are safe."

James Pierce was 55 years old, was about five feet five inches tall, with graying hair, mostly gone with the exception of around his head just above his ears. He wore glasses, had a large nose and a small mouth. He was plump in stature, but not overly as he was a hard working man. He

Tillie Pierce House as is today, located on Baltimore Street near Breckinridge Street.
(Faber)

was a very successful butcher, for he and his son James Jr. (Jay Shaw Pierce, who was assigned to Company K of the First Pennsylvania Reserves and away from town at this time) were one of only five butchers within Gettysburg. He was dressed today in working clothes, which included a white apron, tied tightly around his waist, and stained with blood. There were hand prints of blood on the bottom of the apron, made from when he wiped his hands. Pierce's wife Margaret was 54 years old, was about five feet tall, also slightly plump, with graying hair pulled up and pinned in the back, a warm, round face containing small features. Today, she was wearing a modest blue dress and black shoes.

Ginnie listened intently, and decided she had to speak. So she said:

"Mr. and Mrs. Pierce, what is going on? Why do you need to get your horse out of town?"

Pierce liked Ginnie even though he knew she held his family in contempt. He replied:

"Oh, Ginnie, good afternoon. Haven't you heard? The Rebels are coming, the whole army, and they will be here in a matter of minutes. They will take every horse they can get their hands on and we can't afford to lose ours."

"The Rebel army is coming? Is it true?"

"Yes, our militia engaged them earlier and were routed. Did you see their wagons go by just a few minutes ago?"

"I did, that's why I came over, to see what was going on."

"Well, the Rebels are coming and we have no means of stopping them."

Pierce turned back to Sam, and said:

"Now, you are clear on what needs to be done Sam?"

"Yes, sir I am," the boy said.

"Excuse me Mr. Pierce, but isn't that a little dangerous for a young boy?"

Sam was the first to speak:

"Sis, I can handle it. I'm old enough."

Pierce said:

"Ginnie, your concern is natural. But, Sam can do it. He is a brave and smart young man. Besides, there is no other who can handle it. I need everyone to stay here and protect our property from the Rebs. You should do the same with your house."

"Oh, Lord. Georgia just had her baby, and Mama is needed at her house. I will be all alone with the boys."

"Ginnie, now don't you fret. Go to your house and lock the doors. They won't bother you if you stay inside. If you need us, we will be here for you."

As they finished speaking, they heard horses go by outside on Baltimore Street. They went to the front door and saw three militia riding by followed closely by Confederate cavalry.

"My God, they are here," Pierce said.

Pierce, followed closely by Margaret, Sam, Tillie, and Ginnie, went outside, down the stairs and out into the street. They all watched as one of the Confederates yelled for the militiamen to stop. They watched as one of the Union men halted his horse and took off running in the fields off the road. The other two kept on going. Again, the Confederate yelled for dismounted rider to stop. But, he kept running, and so the Rebel raised his rifle and shot the man. Ginnie watched in horror as she saw the man fall. She covered her mouth with her hand. Tillie Pierce was shocked as well. No one knew what to say.

"They killed him. Shot him in the back," Margaret said, with her voice shaking.

"Papa, they just shot him," Tillie said.

"Yes…, they did," he said with a strange calmness, but more out of shock. But then, he came back to his senses and realized he had to the get his wife and these young people back into the house:

"Alright, alright, let's just calm down. Everyone back in the house."

They obeyed his direction. The women were still shaken, so Pierce said:

"We must not think of that now. We must do what we must to protect ourselves and our property. Ginnie, you go on home like I said. Those little boys need you home, and make sure you lock the doors. Sam, get ready to ride on out of here."

"Sammy, now you take care and if they tell you to stop, you do so, hear?" she said.

"I will, sis, I will."

She hugged him tightly and said:

"I love you, little Sammy."

And with that, she rushed out of the house and toward home.

She arrived a few minutes later, entered the house and closed and locked the door. She assumed both boys were in their room doing their lessons. She called out to them:

"Harry, Isaac, where are you boys?"

Harry replied: "In here. Did Georgia have the baby?"

She went upstairs to the room and said:

"Yes, but never mind that. The Rebel army is coming to Gettysburg, and this time it is real. We must stay in the house, with the doors locked."

The house where Ginnie Wade lived during the battle, as is, located on Breckinridge Street. (Faber)

"Ginnie, are you sure this time?"

"I am. Did you hear that shot a few minutes ago?"

Both boys nodded with a look of concern now firmly planted on their faces. She continued:

"Well, the Rebel cavalry shot and killed one of our militiamen. I saw it happen, and it was just plain awful. That poor boy. I wonder who he was?"

After Ginnie Wade left the Pierce house, Tillie helped Sam prepare for the journey. She packed him some food, consisting of fruit, bread and some dried meat, and put it in a saddlebag. She also packed a blanket in the event he had to spend the night outside. Once the saddlebag was filled with these provisions, she and Sam went out to the back of the house where the horse was corralled. Mr. Pierce just finished saddling the gray horse up and so Tillie handed him the saddlebag and he slung it across the horse's back. He said:

"Sam, are you ready?"

"Yes, sir I am."

"Alright, off you go and ride fast."

Tillie went around to the front of the horse and stroked her nose and gave her a cube of sugar. The horse ate the sugar and responded like she always did with Tillie, very pleased to be getting Tillie's attention. Tillie hugged her neck and said:

"Now, don't you be afraid. Sam will take good care of you until you can come home."

Sam got up on the horse, pulled on the reins and guided the horse out of the corral. Once he was out, he waved, gave the horse a kick and was off. He steered the horse toward Baltimore Street and turned south headed out of town. He was gone no more than a minute when he heard horses behind him in pursuit. He turned his head around and noticed Confederate cavalry gaining on him. He kicked the horse again to go faster, but was no match for his pursuers and they gained on him quickly. He tried as best he could to get away, but was soon overtaken. One of the Rebels motioned for him to stop by giving a thumbs down sign. Sam pulled the reins on the horse and it came to a stop.

"Wherea ya goin' in such hurra?"

Sam said: "Leavin' town."

"Ya wea leavin'. Now, yas comin' with us back ta town."

They turned around and escorted Sam back into town. In a few minutes, they were by the Pierce's house. Tillie was sweeping the porch of their house when they went by, as she was told by her father to do something to take her mind off that awful thought of the militiaman being shot in the back. She saw Sam was captured, and so she immediately went inside to get her father and mother. A moment later, Pierce and his wife came out of the house and onto the porch. They looked north and saw their gray horse, with Sam on it, being walked toward the Diamond.

"They have our little horse and Sam," Tillie moaned.

"They do. We were too late. We must try to get her back. Tillie, go over to Ginnie's house and tell her they have Sam. We must try to get him back, too. Please, be careful. Do not attract attention to yourself and if any of 'em ask what you are doing, just say you are going to visit a friend."

"Yes, Papa."

Within about five minutes, Tillie arrived at the Wade house. She knocked on the door.

"They're here, Ginnie, they're here. Are you gonna answer it?" little Harry in a panicked voice asked his sister.

"I must, but I will not let anyone come into the house," she said.

She slowly walked down the stairs, half hoping whomever was at the door would go if it remained unanswered. Her hopes were dashed as she heard a second set of knocks, louder than the first. She got to the door and could see a young woman through the curtain. It was Tillie Pierce. She quickly opened the door.

"Ginnie, they captured Sam and our horse. Taken them to town. Can you come back to the house quick?"

She yelled back up the stairs to the boys:

"Boys, I have to go. You two stay in your room and Harry, come down and lock the down behind me."

The boy ran down the stairs.

"Now lock this behind me and don't let anyone in until I return, hear? I should be back directly."

The two women walked back to the Pierce house and as they approached, Ginnie could hear Tillie's mother talking to a Confederate, trying to convince him to release the horse back to the Pierces. She overheard her say she had no concern for the boy just the horse.

Ginnie was shocked at hearing such disdain for Sam's safety, and so she said in response, in a tone that all who were near could hear, she would hold the Pierce family responsible if any harm came to Sam.

Tillie and her mother were surprised at this proclamation, which could be viewed as a threat. But, they said nothing in return, as they knew Ginnie would be upset the Rebels had captured her younger brother.

"I need to get mother," Ginnie stated emphatically and in finality.

With that, she stormed off past the Pierces' house and down Baltimore Street, to Georgia's house where her mother was. She arrived at the McClellan house about five minutes later, and addressed her mother:

"Mother, the Rebels are here in town and they took Sam."

Ginnie's mother was Mary Ann Wade. She was 43 years old, had graying dark hair, parted in the middle, pinned up on the sides of her head, slightly above her ears, which were a little lower on her head than average, a strong forehead, dark eyes, and thin lips. She had unusually long fingers. Today, she was wearing a black dress with a white collar. It was her favorite outfit, and she wore it often.

"What? How did that happen?"

"Those Pierces. They wanted to save their horse from the Southerners and so they had Sam ride it out Baltimore Pike. Their cavalry must have caught up with him and took him," she said still in an anger.

"Ginnie, Ginnie, calm down now. We don't want to disturb Georgia and the baby. We just got the baby to sleep. Now, we shall go to town and see about Sam. Maria, can you tend to Georgia and the little one whilst we are gone?"

"Of course. Go, go and get your Sam back."

Ginnie and her mother left the McClellan house and walked north to the center of town. Mary knew she had to calm Ginnie, so she said:

"Are you calmer now?"

"Mother, I just don't know why we have Sam with those Pierces. They don't take proper care of him. And, to think they are more concerned about their horse than our Sam!"

"Now, Ginnie, you know that's not true. They love our Sam. Besides, you know they need that horse to make deliveries."

"I know, mother. I just don't like him having to live with them."

"Ginnie, it is necessary. We have to have him work and be boarded by the Pierces for the extra help it provides. Without that, we couldn't make it and have enough to eat. You must remember they are doing us a great favor with Sam."

Ginnie knew she was right but didn't want to admit it. It was better in her mind to have someone to blame for her brother needing to live away from home, and the Pierces always seemed to fit the bill. They walked silently until they got to the Diamond about ten minutes later. Once there, Mary asked to see the general in charge. She was told he was tending some business in front of the first house on the south side of York Street.

"Oh, you mean the Wills' house?" she asked pointing in the direction of the house.

"He is the one with the beard and the fancy hat," the soldier said pointing to Early.

Without a word of thanks, the women rushed over to where Early, a soldier, and another man were talking with a civilian.

"Mother, he is talking to Mr. Burns. *See...?*"

"Indeed he is. I wonder what old Burns is in need of?"

At that time, as they approached, they saw the soldier wrap a rope around Burns' wrists and lead him away.

"Mother, they arrested him. I wonder what he could have said to make them arrest him?"

"With him, no telling."

They approached and addressed the general.

"General, may we have a word?"

Early turned to the ladies, removed his hat, bowed slightly and said:

"Ladies, certainly, how can Aye be of service?"

Just then, Jones recognized Ginnie, and said:

"Why Miss Wade, it is a pleasure to see you again."

Ginnie hadn't noticed Jones before, but looked closer at him now because of the greeting. She recognized him and smiled.

"Why, Mr. Jones. How nice to see you again."

Then she looked puzzled and continued:

"What are you doing here and with the General?"

"First things first. General Early, this here is Miss Ginnie Wade, a lady of fine substance here in Gettysburg."

"Miss Wade, it is my hona to make ya acquaintance," Early said and bowed deeply.

Jones continued: "Miss Wade, who is the lovely, young woman with you?"

Mary blushed and smiled shyly to the compliment.

"This here is my mother, Mrs. Mary Ann Wade."

"Mrs. Wade," Jones said and offered his hand. Once his hand was taken, he kissed hers. Mary blushed even further.

"Mrs. Wade," Early said and he bowed again.

"Mother, Mr. Jones here defended my honor a few weeks ago against that oaf, Silas McGee."

"Well, Mista Jones, ya didn't include that detail in ya report," Early said.

"General, I didn't think much of it at the time. I did what any man would have done when a lady is being threatened," Jones replied. He turned back to Ginnie:

"Now, what was it you asked? Awe, yes, what am I doing here? Well, let's just say I am performing a duty on behalf of the Army of Northern Virginia."

"You mean you were spying on us before?"

"You could look at it that way, but I prefer it as gathering necessary information."

Early decided he had more pressing duties to attend to, so he said:

"Ladies, Aye am afraid Aye have much to do, so Aye do believe this was not a social call?"

Mary said: "Your men took my son about a half-hour ago. He is only twelve years old, and we wondered if you could release him to us?"

"Why, certainly. Aye am sure it was just a misunderstandin'. Lieutenant, please look into this and retrieve the boy to his motha. Now, if ya describe him to the Lieutenant, he will fetch the boy in a jiffy."

After receiving Sam's description and finding out where he was captured, the lieutenant went off to find the boy. In the meantime, Jones continued his pleasantry with the ladies.

"Ginnie, you are looking fine, today."

"Thank you, Mr. Jones."

"I do apologize we could not have met in more favorable circumstances."

"Mr. Jones, always the gentleman. Mother would offer to make you supper, if times were different."

"And, if they were, I would gladly accept that fine offer."

Within a few minutes, the lieutenant returned with Sam in tow.

"Hea is the boy, General."

"Mrs. Wade, hea he is. My sincerest apologies for the misunderstandin.'"

"Thank you, General."

"My pleasua. And, do let us know if we can be of any furtha service to y'all."

With that the ladies and Sam left. Mary said to her son:

"Sam, did they hurt you?"

"No, Mother, it was a grand adventure."

CHAPTER 32

WILL

JOHN CHARLES WILL was awakened by a knock on his door. He had just gotten to sleep not more than an hour ago after a long night of dealing with Rebel soldiers in search of whiskey, and so he was groggy. He hoped by ignoring the door, his would be visitor would go away, but no such luck for him as he heard a second three taps. He looked at his watch. Five-thirty. Who would be disturbing him so early? He got out of bed, put his trousers on and went to the door to answer it. He opened the door to see Jones.

"John, please pardon the interruption at this tender hour, but I had to come and say goodbye, given that during our last encounter I didn't have the time to do so."

"Leaving again so soon? How unlike you," Will said sarcastically.

"Now I know you are still a little upset, but I was a hoping a little time would help that. You see in my business you have to make friends, but then you may not see these friends for awhile."

"You mean you have to pretend to be a friend and use them for whatever information you can gather to help the enemy. That doesn't sound so friendly to me."

"John, it was nothing personal. You see I just help the army with places to go and supplies to gather. I guess you could call me, how does the army refer to it, a forager. And, as a forager, I don't influence the outcome of the war. I just help the army endure the hardships a little better."

"If you prefer to think of it that way, that's up to you. But, you cannot convince me you are not a spy. A forager is just a nice way of saying a spy, and spies get hung, so it is not such a harmless job after all, now is it?"

"S'pose not. But, I was hoping we could still be friends. The war could go either way, even though for the time being the Confederacy is winning. I had hoped that after the war, we could become friends. I like this town a whole lot and would be obliged to visit it and do business here. You see, I really do sell recipes that fix the taste of liquor. Your Currant Champagne is proof of that."

"I don't know, Jones. The folks around here may have a long memory as to how the Rebels knew so much of the town. Long enough to hold a grudge, no matter the outcome of the war, but particularly if our side wins."

"I do know that, and so as many friends as I could have here would only help."

"Them same folks may take a dim view of anyone who is a friend to the enemy."

"Indeed they might, but a friend such as yourself, a true friend, might also make enough of a difference that it really wouldn't matter."

"Why are you so interested in, shall we say, making peace with the town?"

"I truly like it here. It is a fine town, some place where a man could settle down, after all this ugly war business is over."

"Settle down? Really?"

"Why not? I've been to Chambersburg out west, and Hanover and York out east. This town has the most qualities of being a home, not just a town, of all of 'em."

Will didn't know what to say, so Jones continued:

"Well anyway, the army is moving out this morning, partly upon my urging, but mostly to get to the next town before the supplies can be moved out. The general, although he didn't so much as say it, was very impressed with the preparedness of this town and the lack of supplies here when he arrived. He is hoping other towns will not be as prepared."

"Well, we weren't so ready here at the inn. Late last night, some of the soldiers knocked on the door, after we closed up, and demanded whiskey. We had to give them three barrels."

"Really, did you happen to get their names and ranks? I will tell the general and he will compensate you. How much was the loss?"

"About sixty dollars."

"I will notify the general immediately. I do hope he can do so before we move out."

"So, I guess this is goodbye, Jones?"

"It is. But, as I was saying, I am hoping to return in better times."

He put out his hand. Will hesitated and then grasp it and shook it.

"John, I knew you couldn't stay too mad at me. We two are alike, just on different sides, that's all."

"Jones, take care of yourself. A man in your business can make a lot of enemies. And, not the kind who are so forgiving as I am."

"You take care too."

With that, Jones turned around and was gone down the stairs and out of the inn. It occurred to Will that he never wondered how he got into the inn this morning. But, considering the things Jones had done, getting into a locked inn must have been simple for him. He wondered if the inn door was locked behind him, and so he went down the stairs and turned the door handle to the outside. It was locked. He thought: "No surprise here, Jones is very thorough." He heard Jones' horse riding away from the inn, and thought he better go back to bed as he would have to open the inn in a few hours.

Jones left the inn, admired the stillness of the morning and his conversation with Will. He said silently so as to not disturb those sleeping who were within earshot: "Yes, after the war, I will definitely return to Gettysburg, and if I earn enough money, buy a place and settle here."

He climbed onto his horse, and became a perfect target for McGee who had him in the sight of this rifle.

Chapter 33

BROADHEAD

SARAH (SALLIE) M. BROADHEAD was awakened around one o'clock in the morning by her husband Joseph, as he was home at last.

"Oh, sweetie, you're home at last, and safe," she said as she hugged him tightly.

"I am, love, and am really tired. I've been walking since nine o'clock yesterday, all the way from Harrisburg."

"You must be famished. Can I make you something?"

"No, love. All is want is to lay here with you."

So, she snuggled up next to him, and they fell asleep. They awoke around ten o'clock in the morning as little Mary came into their room.

"Oh Papa, you are here. I am so glad. Mama was so worried. When did you get home?"

"Last night, real late, my little one. I really missed you. Did you miss me?"

"Of course. Did you bring me anything?"

"Not this time. Just myself. Will that do?"

"Oh yes, Papa," she said as she put her arms around his neck.

Sallie said: "You slept in late this morning. Are you feeling alright?"

"Yes, Mama, just tired this morning, I guess."

"That's good to hear. Shall we get some breakfast, you two?"

"Yes, let's go, Mama. Papa, will you carry me?"

"You know I will, little love. Climb on."

They went downstairs and Sallie fixed a late breakfast of biscuits, bacon, and hard boiled eggs. While they were eating, Sallie asked:

"We heard the Rebels burned some of the railroad cars and the bridge over Rock Creek?"

"Yes, love, they did, last Saturday. I barely escaped, but then they caught me. Once they determined I wasn't a threat to them and that the railroad would be down for a spell because of the bridge, they paroled me and told me to go to Harrisburg. So, I did."

"Is the railroad running anytime soon?"

"No, love, it will be down for a spell whilst we get the engineers to rebuild the bridge. That is if our Southern friends find someplace else to fight."

They finished the late breakfast and then sent Mary to her room to play with Ruthie. Satisfied she was entertained for awhile, they took tea outside in front of their house. Sallie was strangely calm, a calm that came from having her fears for her husband's life relieved. To her, it seemed the tension from the last few days, beginning with when the Rebels occupied the town last Friday and ending with Joseph coming home early this morning, was finally relieved. She took a sip of her tea and looked out toward South Mountain. She saw a glimmer of the sun reflecting off a field-glass lens, and the fears of the last couple of days instantly returned. She said to her husband in a fearful voice:

"Joseph, look out the Pike. Is that the Rebels?"

Joseph tried to remain calm. The last few days had hardened him. Being captured and held by the Confederates had given him a sense of courage he hadn't felt before, certainly not in his everyday life working at the railroad. And, so he said in as calm a voice as he could muster:

"It is indeed, love."

"What are they doing? Will they come to town?"

"Looks like they are scouting the town for our men, love."

"Do you think they will occupy the town again?"

"Might, love."

Just then, two Union cavalrymen rode up from the Diamond. By their uniforms, the Broadheads noted they were a captain and a lieutenant. They stopped to address Joseph and Sallie. The captain said in a pleasant voice with a thick Irish accent to match Joseph's:

"Morning ma'ma, sir. You might want to return to go inside, as the Rebs are right over that hill. No telling when they may come this way."

Sallie was both surprised and relieved. She didn't notice the activity in the Diamond when they first came out of their house. But, now she took a quick glance, and seeing the cavalrymen riding around, gave her a sense of safety. She thought: "Good, at least the army is finally here."

"Good morning, Captain. What outfit are you from and when did you get to town? By the way, thank God you are here," Sallie said.

"Ma'am, Captain Myles Keogh with the First Division, Cavalry Corps, Army of the Potomac, General John Buford commanding. We just arrived in town this mornin', and are here to see what the Rebels are up to, and to protect this town."

"An Irishman, like myself. Welcome to our little town, Captain."

"Thank you, sir. General Buford is setting up headquarters at the Hotel just down the street. I believe it is called the Eagle?"

"Yes."

"General Buford has sent me to find out who owns that building to the south and west, with the cupola, and to ask permission to use it as an observation tower," Keogh said pointing to the building on the Seminary campus.

"That is the dormitory of the Lutheran Theological Seminary. The First Professor of the Seminary is Pastor Samuel Simon Schmucker. He has a house quite near the dorm building. I'm sure he would grant you permission," Sallie replied.

"Thank you kindly, ma'am," Keogh said, tipping his hat and was about to ride off toward the seminary.

At that moment, Burns came out of his house and over to the cavalrymen.

"Good afternoon, gentlemen. My name is Burns. What outfit are you with?"

"And, to you sir. As I mentioned to this fine lady and gentleman, I am Captain Myles Keogh with the First Division, Cavalry Corps, Army of the Potomac, General John Buford commanding.

"Buford, huh. And, cavalry you said? Where is the army? Are they far?"

"Well, sir, let's just say the whole army is in the area, just not up yet."

"Are they on their way?"

"Not yet. We don't know what strength the Reb Army is and where they are going to strike. Until then, we will continue to wait on him to make the next move."

"Do you think it will be here?"

"Good possibility, that's why we are here.

"Well, you can tell the general if it is here, I will fetch my rifle and join in. Gettysburg can help in its defense and I aim to do so!"

Keogh looked at Burns and guessed he was in his late sixties or early seventies. He didn't want to be impolite, so he said nothing in return about Burn's declaration. Instead he said:

"Now if you will pardon me, I have to be on my way."

"Certainly, Captain. Please do thank the general for being here. We feel much safer with you boys in town," Sallie said.

And with that, Keogh again tipped his hat and he and his companion rode off toward the Seminary.

"Joseph, there's going to be a battle here, isn't there?"

"Love, might be. Let's get back in the house and prepare for it."

"I'll be preparing too…cleaning my gun and rounding up all the balls I can find," Burns said.

They all went back into their respective houses. The Broadheads went inside and began discussing what they would do if indeed a battle was waged and their house was caught in it.

"Love, we will need to get little Mary to safety. Yet, we must remain to protect our property."

"Look outside, it seems our neighbors are leaving," she said pointing out their bedroom window.

"Still, love, we must stay or there is no telling what will happen to our house. We have worked too hard to let it get destroyed. I'll stay and you get Mary up town to the Gautz' place on Carlisle."

"Yes, that would be safer as it is further away from the battle, and they have a cellar."

They looked outside in time to see the cavalry going by on Chambersburg Street toward the Pike. It took about a half hour for the 2,700 mounted men to pass their house. They marveled at the crisp formation. At the end of the precession, came the horse artillery. It was a grand sight indeed.

"My, my they sure look like a fine group of fighting men," Sallie noted.

"Yes they do. I wonder if they can hold off the Rebs?"

CHAPTER 34

JACOBS

PROFESSOR MICHAEL JACOBS at the same time was in his attic surveying the scene unfolding along the Chambersburg Pike, just west of town. He looked through his telescope and scanned the horizon in that direction seeing Union cavalry traveling out on the Chambersburg Pike about a mile and a half from the town limits, and then most deploying on McPherson's farm, while the remainder deployed along Mummasburg Road.

Jacobs' son Henry came up to the attic. Jacobs was still looking through the telescope, and said:

"Henry, good of you to come up. This is a splendid view of the army's deployment out on McPherson's Farm. Care to have a look?"

"Can I?"

"Sure. Here you go," Jacobs said and he moved so his son could look through the telescope.

Henry looked through the telescope and rotated south to north looking over the whole of McPherson's Farm. Just then a group of riders rode off the roadway and onto the farmland. The group looked like officers. Henry remarked while moving out of position so Jacobs could look through the telescope and pointing:

"Father, look over there, those riders, may they be the commanders of the cavalry?"

Jacobs looked through the telescope and replied:

"Sure looks as though they are."

Jacobs saw the officers looking at a map and then pointing to some positions both north and south of the road.

"They are moving the men around. Take a look."

"Yes, they are," Henry said in a more excited tone. He continued:

"Father, do you think there will be a battle?"

"Yes, I do, probably tomorrow. Look further out on the pike. If you look close, you may see the Rebels moving around near Cashtown. It's far, but maybe you can just make them out. Earlier this morning they were all the way down to Seminary Hill, but moved off once they saw our cavalry in town."

"I do see some movement out there, but we are too far to see who or what clearly. If there is a battle, we really have a good view of it from our attic."

"That we do, my boy. And, I plan on being here the watching the whole thing."

"Father, do you mind if I join you? I really would like to watch it. I have never seen a battle before."

"I really haven't either, but I get the feeling it is not as grand or glorious as the books and the newspapers make it out."

"How do you mean?"

"I mean it will probably be very horrible, men getting shot and killed everywhere. But, you and I need to watch it as the fate of the war may depend upon our forces holding this place and sending the Rebels back to Virginia where they belong."

"Do you think it is that serious that the whole war could depend upon this one battle?"

"I do. This war was supposed to be over in 90 days. Do you remember when the army and the government was saying so back in '61? Two years and almost three months later and we are no closer to ending it, or winning it, but the Rebels are. How else can we explain why the war has come to Pennsylvania and our town?"

"Do you think we can whip 'em?"

"It all depends on how fast the whole army can get here. At any rate, tomorrow when we come up here remember what you see, as it may be important to the history of our country."

"I will, Father."

Henry went back to looking through the telescope and suddenly turned to Jacobs and said:

"Father, the officers are riding over toward our house. Take a look."

Jacobs looked through the telescope and focused on the group of riders approaching the house. It was indeed the officers.

"Henry, let's go downstairs and out the back of the house to see if they are coming to talk with us."

They went down the attic stairs to the second floor and to the back door of the house, out the door and down the stairs to the landing. They were facing west as the officers came up to them. The officers pulled the reins on their horses stopping them about ten feet from Jacobs and his son. Two of the riders dismounted and came over to them. One of them saluted and said:

"Good day, sir. I'm Captain Myles Keogh and this here is General John Buford. Might we bother you for some information?"

"General, Captain, I would be honored to help in anyway," Jacobs said and continued:

"Pardon me, this here is my son Henry, and I am Professor Michael Jacobs of Pennsylvania College."

Buford stepped forward, removed his cavalry hat with his left hand and extended out his right hand, saying:

"Professor, it is my honor to meet you and your son."

Buford shook hands with both father and son, and Keogh did the same.

Jacobs noticed they both looked like a real cavalry man. Buford was of average height and stature, in his late thirties Jacobs guessed, had a full head of light brown hair, parted on the left side of his head, ears slightly away from his head, light blue eyes, a full mustache that extended well beyond the corners of his mouth. He was dressed in a traditional cavalry uniform, with a white shirt under a blue cavalry coat that had two columns of buttons lined up just outside his ears when buttoned fully, and a patch on both shoulders with a single star. He had blue regulation trousers and shiny black boots. Keogh was in his early twenties, was also of average height, but was rather skinny in stature, had short dark hair, trimmed above his ears and parted on the right side of his head. He had brown eyes and a thin mustache, with a thin goatee trimmed to line up below the center of his mouth. He too was dressed in the traditional cavalry uniform.

Buford continued: "Professor, we have received permission to climb up in the cupola over on the Seminary and wonder if you would join us in the morning. I would be grateful if you could offer some advice as to the ground and how best we can position our men?"

"General, as I said before, I would be honored to help in any way you would need."

"Then it is settled. Can you meet us there at first light?"

"General, I will be there."

"Much obliged, Professor. See you in the morning."

Buford saluted and then turned, mounted his horse and then rode back to where his troops were. Keogh followed closely behind. Father and son returned to the attic and stayed up there the rest of the afternoon. Jacobs surveyed and studied the ground so he could be ready for when Buford would ask of it in the morning. At around five o'clock, they retired back to the house, to plan the next day's viewing of the pending battle, both from the cupola and from their attic, and how they would need to take good notes to document what would be happening.

Part 4

The Evil of War Has Come to Our Town

Between July 1st and July 3rd, 1863, a great battle was waged in and around the little Borough of Gettysburg, Pennsylvania. At stake was in all likelihood the outcome of the war. The battle was the culmination of General Robert E. Lee's plan, and the purpose for the Army of Northern Virginia's invasion of the North. Lee could see the tide of the war turning, even though his Army had not been defeated in the field. In other places, such as Mississippi and Tennessee, the armies of the Confederacy were taking a beating; a beating he eventually knew might spread up from there to his army. After all, his war supplies were dwindling as Richmond could not meet his needs, particularly with men. Simply, the Confederacy was running out of able bodied men to fight this war. His equipment, particularly his cannon, were inferior to that of the Union and that fact was beginning to take its toll on the battlefield. He also knew that no amount of courting the British would make them enter the war, leastwise while the outcome was in doubt, and maybe never, as he doubted they would support the Confederate government who made the institution of slavery protected under the law.

So, here his army was, in Pennsylvania looking for a good place to lure the Federals into a great battle to destroy the Army of the Potomac. After which, he would march his army directly to Washington and demand peace and an end to the war. He had discussed this with President Jefferson Davis, and they had agreed a letter for President Abraham Lincoln should be prepared asking for terms of peace. This letter was to arrive on Lincoln's desk just after this great battle, and Lee had planned on being in Washington shortly after its arrival to seek the answer in person.

His army had been in Pennsylvania for almost two weeks and during that time had been spread out west of the Blue Ridge Mountains. The eyes of his army, his main cavalry force, led by General James E. B. Stuart, had been gone for a couple of days and their whereabouts were unknown. This left the Confederates, in effect, blind to the Union army's movements and indeed their location.

The Army of the Potomac was led by newly installed General George Meade, a Pennsylvania man. Meade was cautious by nature, but was a fighting man. And, he had the loyalty of most, if not all, of the staff generals. His nature led him to move his army north from Virginia in pursuit of the Confederate Army carefully, and somewhat slowly. This was understandable given this was his first few days on the job.

Lee understood this and so his confusion as to location of the Union army was greatly enhanced. So, as the calendar neared July 1863, he continued his strategy of spreading the army out to cover as much area as possible, while still affording him the opportunity of bringing the three corps of the army together quickly when the need arose.

On July 1st, Lee was headquartered at Chambersburg, about twenty five miles west of Gettysburg; the First Corps, under command of General James Longstreet, was located west of South Mountain, between Cashtown and Chambersburg about twenty miles west of Gettysburg; the Second Corps, under the command of Richard Ewell, was located at Heidlersburg, Pennsylvania about ten miles northeast of Gettysburg; and the Third Corps, under the command of Ambrose Powell (A.P.) Hill, was located between Cashtown and Gettysburg, less than ten miles from Gettysburg.

The Federal Corps on July 1st were spread out as well. In Uniontown, Maryland, about twenty miles southeast of Gettysburg, Meade located his headquarters, and this also was the location of the Second Corps under the command of General Winfield Scott Hancock. The Sixth Corps, under the command of General John Sedgwick, was located in Manchester, Maryland, about 28 miles southeast of Gettysburg. The Fifth Corps, under the command of General George Sykes, was located in Union Mills, Maryland, about 17 miles from Gettysburg. The Third Corps, under command of General Dan Sickles, was located between Taneytown and Emmitsburg, Maryland, about 16 miles southeast of Gettysburg. The Twelfth Corps, under the command of General Henry Slocum, was located between Littlestown, Pennsylvania and Two Taverns, Pennsylvania, about eight miles southeast of Gettysburg. The Eleventh Corps, under the command of General Oliver Howard, was located between Emmitsburg, Maryland and Gettysburg, about eight miles south of Gettysburg. And, to complete the Army of the Potomac, the First Corps, under the command of General John Reynolds, was located about five miles south of Gettysburg.

The previous day, June 30th, two brigades of General John Buford's cavalry, consisting of about 2,700 men, had arrived in Gettysburg and set up defenses for what Buford expected to be an attack from the Confederates the next day.

That attack came at about half past nine in the morning of July 1st. General Henry Heth, of A.P. Hill's Corps, was ordered to reconnoiter the town of Gettysburg and it was just north west of the town where he encountered Buford's cavalry. The Federals pushed the Confederate advance back, but knew they could not hold long. Buford had already sent word to Reynolds asking for his assistance to hold the town, but more importantly the high ground southeast of the town, and hoped this help would arrive in a timely manner. Before eleven o'clock, the First Corps of the Union army arrived and added about eight thousand infantry men to the defense. For

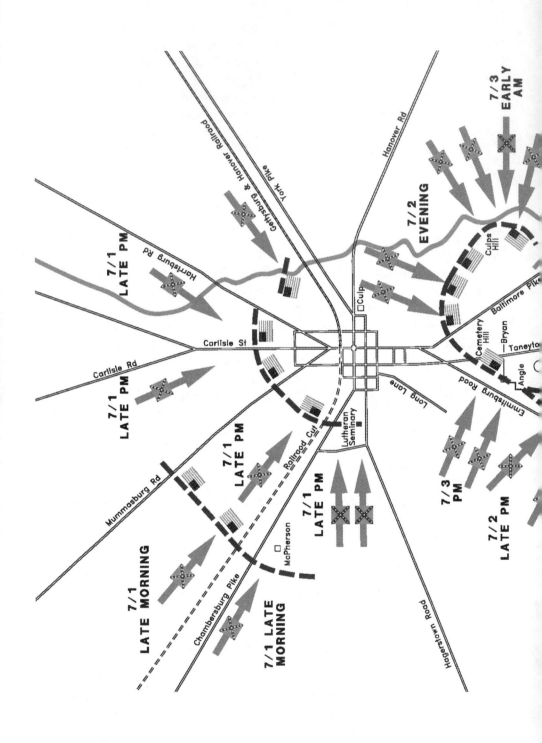

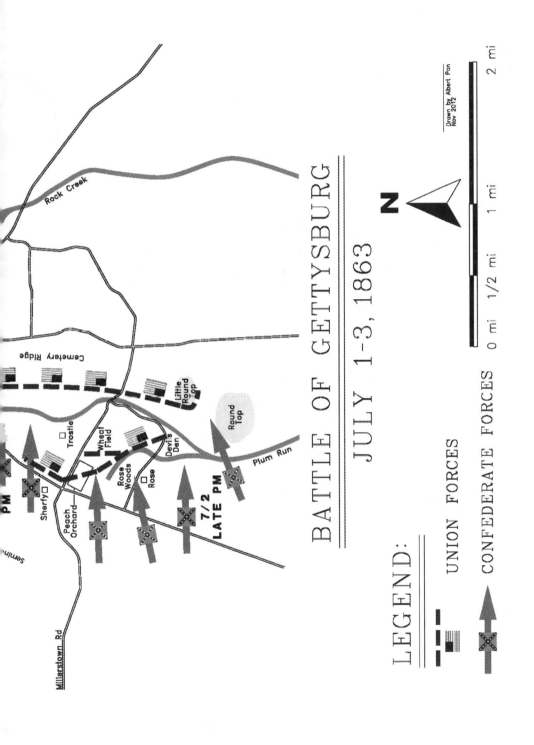

BATTLE OF GETTYSBURG

JULY 1-3, 1863

LEGEND:

UNION FORCES

CONFEDERATE FORCES

Drawn by Albert Pun
Nov 2012

0 mi   1/2 mi   1 mi   2 mi

N

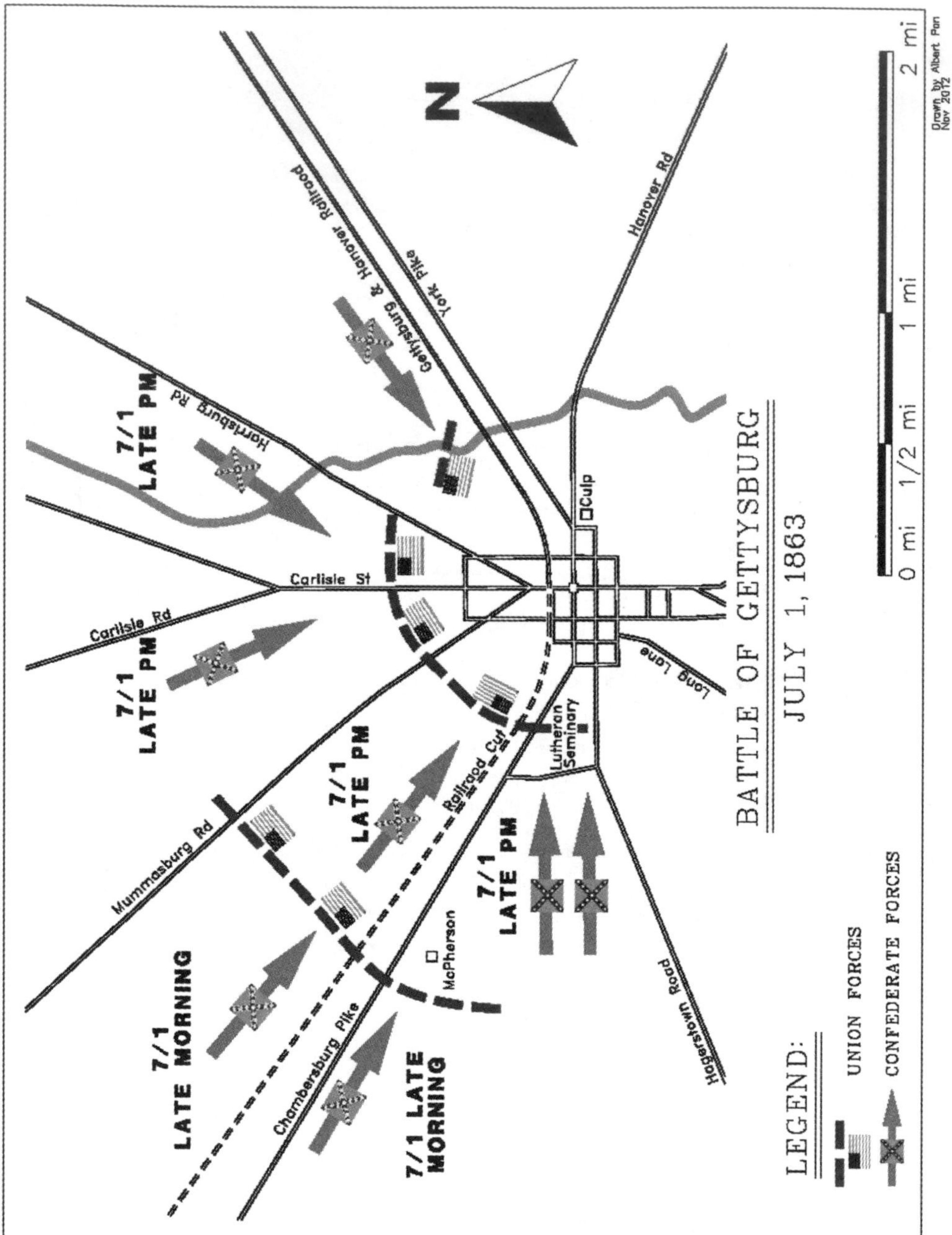

BATTLE OF GETTYSBURG

JULY 1, 1863

LEGEND:

UNION FORCES

CONFEDERATE FORCES

Drawn by Albert Pan
Nov 2012

0 mi   1/2 mi   1 mi   2 mi

7/1 LATE PM

7/1 LATE PM

7/1 LATE PM

7/1 LATE PM

7/1 LATE PM

7/1 LATE MORNING

7/1 LATE MORNING

York Pike

Gettysburg & Hanover Railroad

Harrisburg Rd

Hanover Rd

Carlisle St

Carlisle Rd

Mummasburg Rd

Chambersburg Pike

Railroad Cut

Lutheran Seminary

Long Lane

Hagerstown Road

Culp

McPherson

N

the Rebels, Heth was joined by the forces of General William Dorsey Pender and the total force was about twenty thousand. The two sides slugged it out, with the Confederates not able to get an advantage.

As news of the battle reached Lee, he was not pleased Heth had gone beyond his authority to continue the engagement and not pulled his forces back westerly of the town to await orders to engage fully. However, after surveying the ground, at and around Gettysburg, Lee decided this was a suitable place for the battle. He ordered Ewell to bring his Corps from the northeast and Longstreet from the west.

Reynolds, of the Union First Corps, was killed in action before eleven o'clock, leaving command of the field to Howard, who promptly dispatched forces of his Eleventh Corps, under General Francis Barlow and General Carl Schurz, north of the town to check Ewell's advance, being carried out by General Robert Rodes and later aided by General Jubal Early. The fighting continued until mid-afternoon when the Rebels gained the advantage and drove the Union forces into the town, and then out of the town by early evening. The Federals took position south and east of the town on Cemetery Ridge and Culp's Hill. The Confederates, satisfied of the day's progress, did not press the advantage, even though Lee ordered Ewell to take Culp's Hill, southeast of town, in his words "if practicable." Ewell judged it not and therefore the hill remained in Union hands.

This proved to be a costly mistake for the Confederates, as Culp's Hill became the anchor of the Union right and a stronghold where their line could be formed. During the night of the 1st, the Union forces occupied Culp's Hill with the Twelfth Corps, under Slocum, and built trenches and barricades, known as breastworks, to enforce their position. Also, the Second Corps, under Hancock, along with the Fifth Corps, under Sykes, and Third Corps, under Sickles, arrived and with the First and Eleventh Corps, formed the Union line running west from Culp's Hill and then south along Cemetery Ridge down to a hill known as Round Top. The line formed a fish hook, with the barb at Culp's Hill.

On the morning of the 2nd, Lee had decided to attack the Union lines to his extreme left and his extreme right. He dispatched Longstreet's Corps, led by General John Hood and General Lafayette McLaws, to attack the right, and Early's forces to attack the left. This attack was to be coordinated so as the Union forces would be spread thin and therefore reinforcing any weaknesses in the lines would be difficult. In the meantime, Sickles decided his position could be improved by coming down the mountain to the areas at the foothill. He positioned his forces within places that would become well known as the "Peach Orchard," the "Wheat Field," "Devil's

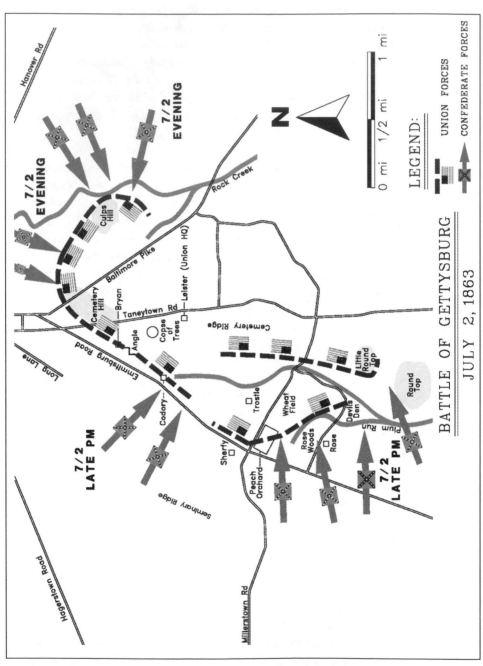

BATTLE OF GETTYSBURG

JULY 2, 1863

LEGEND:

UNION FORCES

CONFEDERATE FORCES

0 mi   1/2 mi   1 mi

Drawn by Albert Pan
Nov 2012

Den" and "Slaughterhouse Pen." This was a major mistake, as it broke the Union line and created a gap, which the Rebels soon exploited.

It took most of the morning and until four o'clock in the afternoon for Hood and McLaws to be in position to attack the Union left, and attack they did in what was some of the fiercest fighting of the war. The Wheatfield exchanged sides numerous times, and became the bloodiest ground, inch for inch, of the war. Likewise for the Peach Orchard, Devil's Den, and Slaughterhouse Pen, as the Rebels took advantage of the gap in the Union line created by Sickles. These places exchanged hands numerous times as each side would counterattack upon losing the ground. But, at the end of the day's engagement, the Union lines held. Early attacked the Union right at Culp's Hill at early evening and gained some ground, but not the objective of taking the hill. And, so the day ended with the Union lines intact, despite their heavy losses, and the Confederates with but a little gain in exchange for their massive casualties.

Lee had decided, correctly, the action of the 3rd of July would decide the battle, and maybe the war. He had his army here in Pennsylvania, and would not retreat, even withstanding the urging of Longstreet to pull out, move to the right around the Union lines, and deploy the troops between the Union forces and Washington. Lee would not entertain this change in strategy. He needed to strike a definitive blow and break the Union line. He decided an assault in the middle of the line was the best course of action, and so he ordered approximately fifteen thousand men to attack the Union middle. He also ordered Early to resume his action at Culp's Hill on the Union right. The attack in the middle would be led by General George Pickett and two other division commanders, all under Longstreet's leadership, and would become known as "Pickett's Charge." The charge would be preceded by a massive artillery barrage, led by Colonel Porter Alexander, to smash the Union center so the infantry could break through. Opposing the Confederate artillery would be a stout force of Union artillery.

The day began at Culp's Hill at around four-thirty in the morning. For six hours of bloody fighting, the two sides fought over possession of the hill, yet at the end of the fighting, the hill remained in Union hands.

Just after one o'clock in the afternoon, around 150 Rebel guns opened fire on the Union positions. This was quickly answered by about the same amount of Union guns, and so the two sides exchanged fire for a little less than an hour and a half. The Confederate guns were overshooting the Union lines and did not accomplish their objective to at least weaken the line. In addition, the Confederate guns and shells were less reliable result-

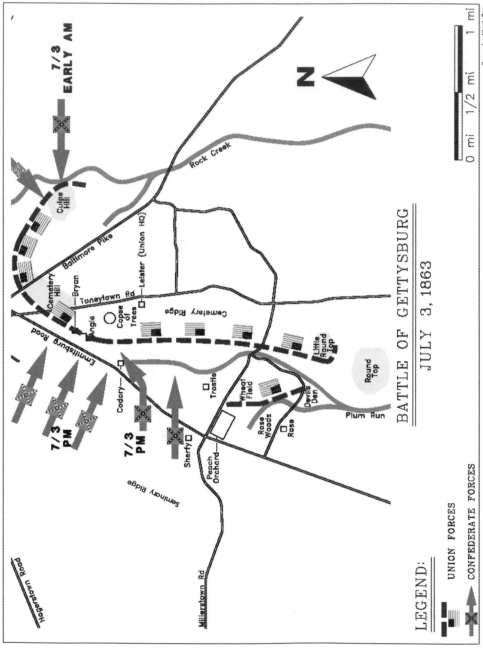

BATTLE OF GETTYSBURG
JULY 3, 1863

LEGEND:

UNION FORCES

CONFEDERATE FORCES

0 mi   1/2 mi   1 mi

Drawn by Albert Pan
Nov 2012

220

ing in many shots hitting the ground not far in front of the cannons. Because of this, the Rebel troops were positioned behind the cannons and therefore had a longer distance to travel to the Union line, while the Union cannons, not suffering from this dilemma, were placed behind their lines.

The distance to travel for the Confederacy attack was more than a mile over an open field that sloped up, and afforded no cover for the men. Also, the men had to cross Emmitsburg Road, which was lined by a post and rail fence, needing to either be scaled or torn down.

Around two-thirty in the afternoon, the Confederates under Pickett's command, and led by General Lewis Armistead, General James Kemper, General Richard Garnett, General Johnston Pettigrew, and General Isaac Trimble moved out from under the trees of Seminary Ridge. The line was about one mile long. The objective of the Confederate troops was a clump of trees known as the "Copse" and a turn in a small stone wall known as the "Angle." Upon getting a hand gesture from Longstreet, Pickett ordered the line forward to attack. The Union artillery opened up on them creating large gaps in the lines, which were quickly filled. Then, the Union troops opened up with massive barrages of devastating rifle fire. The Confederates suffered substantial casualties and at the Emmitsburg Road fence were stalled, causing opportunities for the Union forces to inflict heavy damage. Only a few troops made it to the Angle, and these were under the command of Armistead, but no reinforcements arrived, and those that scaled the wall were quickly killed or captured. A general retreat ensued and those Rebels who were able, made it back to their line escaping the fire of the Union cannons.

Lee assumed full responsibility for the failure of the attack and met the men personally as they retreated back to their line, apologizing as they went by. He came upon Pickett and ordered him to reform his Division to prepare for a possible Union counterattack, at which Pickett responded that he had no Division.

And, so the great Battle of Gettysburg was concluded. 170,000 men had participated, 95,000 from the Union and 75,000 from the Confederacy. Of these, 51,000 were killed, wounded, or captured, including 28,000 Confederates and 23,000 Federals.

The little town of Gettysburg, and its 2400 citizens, were left with the remnants of this great battle as the armies left in the next few days after the battle had ended: the dead, both men and horses; the wounded; the colossal property damage; and what would come later, the diseases resulting from the decaying bodies of the dead and wounded.

The First Day

CHAPTER 35

BURNS

JOHN L. BURNS was awake just before sunrise on Wednesday the first of July. He had not slept well this night as he was anxious for the upcoming battle of the day, and was determined to join in the fighting and do his duty to protect his town, his family, and his property. He stayed up late last night melting two of the Burns' pewter plates to shape balls to shoot with his old Enfield rifle. He spent some time, upon awakening, to clean his rifle and then he cleansed himself, washing and shaving and combing his hair. He dressed himself from toe to head in black boots, black pants and waist coat, a white shirt, buttoned tight around his neck, a blue coat with brass buttons, the coat he had not garnished for years, but had a fondness for as he purchased it long ago to dress as a gentleman. The outfit was completed by a black top hat and a light brown ribbon circled between the brim and the stove part of the hat. When he finished dressing and was satisfied at his appearance, he went into the kitchen to wait for the time to pass. He was fidgety and somewhat nervous, but very excited as he had not been involved in a fight since the United States war with Mexico in 1847. There he enlisted to fight, but saw no action. He had, since then, regretted he had not seen actual combat, but instead spent his time in camp in Cumberland County. He was reflecting on this when his wife, Barbara, came into the kitchen.

"What are you dressed up for Burns? You've even clean shaven."

"Old woman, there is going to be a fight. Right out there…," he paused as he pointed west of his house at McPherson's farm, and continued:

"I aim to join and do my part."

"You old fool. Don't you think it would be better to stay here and protect us and the house? And, how are you gonna fight? You are almost seventy years old, and those Reb boys are *real* soldiers. Besides, if they catch you fighting, won't they hang you?"

"I ain't worried about that none. If the Rebs want to take this town, they are gonna get the best this old body can give 'em."

"You will not be leavin' this house. We have family, Martha and the baby, needing your protection."

"Like I told you the other day, I ain't a sitting here like an old woman. The enemy is here and I aim to do something."

"Where did that get you? In jail, that's where."

"Old woman, don't you remind me of that."

Barbara looked at Burns and saw that determined look in his eyes and in his demeanor and knew arguing with him was pointless. She relented saying:

"Then, like I told you, you go ahead, but if anything happens to us it will be 'cause of you. If anything happens to that little girl, you may as well not come back! And, if anything happens to you, don't expect us to come get you, either!"

"I've had enough of this. I am going outside to see what is going on. Goodbye. Keep the door closed and locked until I come back for my rifle."

It was after eight o'clock when he left and slammed the door behind him. The day promised to be a warm one, however the deep blue sky was scattered with clouds. Still upset with his wife, he descended down the stairs and decided to walk west on Chambersburg Pike toward the battle lines. He observed a lot of activity going on in the field, as the Union forces were being moved around, both in the fields of the farm and also within a forest of trees on the south side of the farm. He continued to walk westerly, but decided he shouldn't get that close to the Union line in the event the Rebels opened up with their artillery. He looked around for a good, but safe, location to watch the action. He gazed south and on seeing the Lutheran Seminary Building, he decided that was the place. He made his way over to the Seminary and as he approached, he looked up to the cupola and noticed several uniformed officers and a civilian spying the field with glasses. He recognized one as the captain he met the day before. The captain was talking with another officer he didn't recognize, but the civilian looked familiar to him. He looked closer and saw Professor Michael Jacobs. Jacobs was using field glasses and was talking with both officers, pointing toward the field. After a minute, the captain called over the other army officer, explained an order, and then dispatched him. After another minute that officer ran out of the building, down the stairs, mounted his horse and was off to the front of the lines.

After about an hour or so, Burns looked out west on the Chambersburg Pike and saw a column of the Rebel army approaching. He wondered when the shooting would begin. It didn't take long for the action to start, which began when the Union dismounted cavalry opened fire on the approaching Confederates. The Confederates broke their marching column, busted through the post and railing fences on either side of the road and began to set their lines. Burns noticed the Rebel force was significant. After exchanging fire for awhile, the Union artillery began firing. The Rebel artillery was brought up and it too joined the fight. Burns watched the action for around a half an hour, noting that neither side was getting the upper hand. But, it seemed to him the Confederates were bringing more and more men into the fight, and it may only be a matter of time before the Union lines would break. Just then, he noticed a group of officers riding up to the seminary. Burns also noticed the officers in the cupola had seen them too, and then left their observation post to greet them. He was curious of the identity of the new officers and so he walked over to the front of the seminary building just as the officers from the cupola came downstairs to greet the newly arriving officers. After seeing them exchange salutes, Burns decided to move closer so he could hear what they were saying, as the sounds of the battle had made it increasing difficult to hear just about anything.

"General Reynolds. How good it is to see you and you are just in time. My boys are holding, but I fear not much longer."

General John F. Reynolds was tall, about six feet in height, in his early forties Burns surmised, with a strong build, had light brown hair, parted on the left side of his head, slightly graying, a full beard, neatly trimmed, an average nose, brown eyes, with semi-dark circles under them, particularly his left eye, giving the appearance he was tired, and was tanned, giving the look he was more of an outdoorsman than not.

"General Buford. I came as quick as I could this morning. The First Corps is just south of town right now, and I will get them to the fight directly as soon as I can get them through the town. What's the situation?"

"Henry Heth's Division, with approximately ten thousand men, has come up the road here west of town. I dismounted about three thousand of my men and deployed them in position to resist his movement into town. The rest of my group remain on horseback and are supporting our efforts. We assume the rest of A.P. Hill's Corps is behind Heth. Our scouts have further said Dick Ewell's Corps is coming in from the northeast and Pete Longstreet's Corps is about 10-15 miles west of here"

"John, you have done well. Is this good ground to make a fight?"

"Yes, General it is. But, my real concern is to not let them get that ground southeast of town. If they do, there will be a lot of blood spilled dislodging them from it, if we ever could."

"I did notice that ground and it is worth holding, in the very least. But, let's see if we can keep them from the town in the meantime. Is there someone around here who can show me the best route through town for my men to get here double quick?"

Upon hearing this, Burns stepped forward and addressed the officers: "Pardon me, General, but I can show you the quickest route to here." Reynolds asked: "What is your name, sir?"

"Burns. John L. Burns, sir. I used to be constable of this Borough of Gettysburg."

"Mr. Burns, I am General John F. Reynolds, a Commander of the Union First and Eleventh Corps of the Army of the Potomac, and this fine gentleman is General John Buford, Commander of the First Union Cavalry Division."

Reynolds extended his hand and Burns shook it with vigor. He shook Buford's hand.

"Sure pleased to meet you generals. We are certainly happy to have you here."

"Well, we are glad to be here. Now, let's get my Corps up to the front where we can do some good. How might we do this Mr. Burns?"

"General, there is a road just east of here and it runs north/south. It is West Street. West Street will take you to the south side of town, where it will end at High Street. You take High Street easterly a spell until you come to Washington Street. Washington Street will take you south, where you can meet the Emmitsburg Road. If you bring your troops the opposite direction I just told you, they will get here in the least time."

"Mr. Burns, it would be of help for you to show me in person."

"General, I would be obliged to help in any way I can."

"Very well, should we be on our way?"

"General, I will be on foot, as I don't have a horse."

"John, can you manage a horse for Mr. Burns. I'm sure he will return it promptly, am I correct Mr. Burns?"

"You are indeed, General."

"Then, let's be on our way. Our boys are dying out there, so we need to help them, now."

"Captain, please outfit Mr. Burns with a horse and have someone accompany him and the general out of town," Buford ordered Keogh.

Keogh called over one of Buford's couriers and ordered him to bring Burns a horse and escort General Reynolds out of town. Burns accompanied the courier and Reynolds' staff to Emmitsburg Road. At that point, Reynolds' staff separated from them and proceeded to the troops to get them up to the fight as soon as possible.

"Mr. Burns, I am certainly grateful for the directions. You have done your country a great service today."

"Thank you, General," Burns said and saluted.

226

Reynolds returned the salute and turned his horse to get back with his staff to hurry the First Corps into battle.

"Mr. Burns, we should be getting back to General Buford," the courier said.

"Yes, of course. General Reynolds is sure a fine gentleman and officer."

"Yes, sir, I suppose he is."

Within five minutes, Burns was back at the seminary, had dismounted the horse and had returned to his position he was in before he volunteered his assistance to Reynolds. The fighting continued, and he noticed the Rebels were beginning to push the Union left. Burns thought: "Hope General Reynolds can get here in time."

About ten minutes later, Burns heard the sounds of an army on West Street. He changed his position to be south of the seminary, and noticed the First Corps marching in the fields leading from the Emmitsburg Pike. They turned west, passed the seminary, and proceeded to the field to join the heavy fighting. Burns saw Reynolds leading what he judged to be a division of men and then saw Reynolds giving orders to another officer, and soon the First Corps was deployed in the field. Buford, who was in the cupola when the troops arrived, came down to confer with Reynolds. Again, Burns made sure he was in earshot of their conversation.

"John, your troops have done magnificently. Order them to fall back whilst we take over the field, to remount and then support our flanks," Reynolds directed.

"Yes, sir, thank you, sir."

And to Keogh, Buford said:

"Captain, slowly pull our boys out and then have them support the First Corps."

"Yes, sir."

Burns watched as the First Corps took over the fighting. He judged it to be just before eleven. He located and watched General Reynolds as he rode out to the area where the trees were between the Rebels and the Union troops. He continued to watch Reynolds, and then he saw something that horrified him. Reynolds body contorted and then fell; shot clean out of his saddle. At once, Reynolds' staff dismounted and surrounded him. Shortly thereafter, one of the officers remounted his horse and headed off toward the rear, toward where he was standing at the seminary. Buford had seen this too, and motioned to that officer to ride toward him. The officer did as directed, coming to where Buford and his staff were, dismounted quickly, saluted, and said:

"General Buford, General Reynolds has been shot. He's dead, sir."

"Are you sure Captain?"

"Yes, he was gone when we got to him."

"Is General Doubleday aware of this?" Buford asked referring to Reynolds' next in command of the First Corps.

"We have sent a courier to inform him, General."

"Very well. Please arrange to bring General Reynolds' body to the seminary here."

"Yes, sir," the Captain said and was off.

Burns was stunned. This nice young general, who he had gladly helped just within the last half hour, was killed right in front of his eyes. He felt sorrow for the loss of the general and then rage toward the traitors who shot him. He thought: "I will make those traitorous bastards pay, that's for sure, if it is the last thing I do."

Burns left the seminary area and immediately walked home to get his rifle and ammunition. He arrived a couple of minutes later, opened the door and saw Martha holding and comforting the baby, who was crying rather loudly, and Barbara at the kitchen table. Barbara said with a concerned voice:

"John, you are home. The noises are just awful. They are scaring the baby. Can you see what is happening? Are our boys holding them off?"

"They killed him," Burns replied, with a faraway look in his eyes.

Barbara looked puzzled, and said:

"Who? Killed who?"

"General Reynolds, that's who."

"Who?"

"General Reynolds. I helped him bring his corps through town. He was a gentleman, that he was. I saw him fall from his saddle, just a few minutes ago."

"You're not still planning on joining in, are you?"

"I wasn't sure until I saw him killed. I am going to make those dirty Rebels pay. Where's my gun?"

"Where you left it," Barbara replied knowing she could not say anything to change his mind.

"Papa...," Martha said before her mother's look stopped her mid-sentence.

Burns went into the parlor, retrieved his gun and his ammunition and left the house. He walked deliberately toward the field. Before he left his property, he noticed Joseph Broadhead.

"John, where are you going with your rifle?"

"I'm going to fight the dirty Rebs. Get your gun and come with me."

"I have my gun, but no bullets."

"Well, get your gun. I'm sure we can find some ammunition once we get to the front."

"John, I am not a soldier and would not stand a chance fighting against the Rebel army."

"Well, if you don't come with me, you are a chicken-hearted, sissy, and a damn coward."

"I don't appreciate being called a coward."

"Well, that's what you are. Good day," Burns said and walked away.

One of the neighbors overheard the conversation and decided to engage Burns. It was Miss Mary Slentz, who lived with her father and mother next door and wasn't fond of Burns at all. She said:

"Mr. Burns, how dare you call Mr. Broadhead a coward? You should be ashamed. You are insane if you think you are going to join that there battle. You should be at home protecting your kin."

"Miss Slentz, I am going to fight the Rebs and try to protect this town, you included. So, I advise you to return to your house."

"You have always been insane, Mr. Burns, and this idea of yours is the worst you have ever had. Leaving an old woman, a young woman, and a little baby to fend for themselves whilst there is a battled raging all around us is just plain crazy."

"Never you mind, Miss Slentz. Please attend to your own business, and go back inside."

Burns arrived on the field at about noon. He passed the seminary and walked up the road to close to the front lines, looking for the first officer he could find to place him among the men. He found the man he thought could help and walked right over to him.

"Excuse me, sir, but I would like to join the fight. Where can I be placed?"

The man looked over at Burns and said:

"Old man, this is no joke. These boys are good shooters and you're liable to get yourself killed."

"Major, it is major isn't it?"

The major nodded and said:

"Major Chamberlin."

"Major Chamberlin, I am a former constable of this town, and I am here to fight the traitorous Rebels. I want to kill me some Rebs. So, can I fight with your regiment?"

"Sir, let me take you to the colonel."

They walked over to the colonel, who was busy watching the movement of the enemy as he noticed the Confederates bringing more men into the battle to reinforce the Rebel left.

"Colonel, this here citizen, constable, would like to help us fight."

Colonel Wister looked at Burns and said:

"Sir, I really don't have time for this. The Rebels are gaining an advantage on our right and are readying for an attack. Can you go back home before you get hurt?"

"No, Colonel, I will not. And, I respectfully request you post me to fight the Rebs."

"Alright, you can fight. Take position over to the left into the woods, as it will be safer."

"Thank you, Colonel."

Burns headed over to the left as the colonel directed. On his way, he stopped by a wood pile, he recognized as Herbst's Woodlot. He came upon men who were preparing for the next attack, as there was currently a lull in the shooting. He made sure he was covered by the woodpile. He asked the nearest man who was in charge. He was pointed to a captain.

"Sir, I have been directed to report here to fight."

"Who sent you over here, old man?"

"A major, back behind yonder," Burns said pointing to the location where he had a conversation with Chamberlin.

"Well, sir this here is the 7th Wisconsin Brigade, the Iron Brigade. Perhaps you have heard of us?"

"No, sir, but I cannot think of any better outfit to join here in the field."

"So, you want to fight?"

"Yes, sir I do, and I could use a musket."

"Well then you shall fight with us. The captain instructed a lieutenant to get a rifle, and so the lieutenant outfitted Burns with a rifle taken from one of the fallen men, and gave him some cartridges, which he put in his pocket.

"I assume you can shoot, but can you load this?" the lieutenant asked.

When told he could not, the lieutenant showed him how by loading it for him.

"Sir, what is your name and why are you here?"

"My name is Burns, and I am a former constable of this town. We have been waiting a long spell for these Rebel traitors to show up. They did, last Friday, took over the town and threw me in jail. I thought it was a good idea to pay 'em back for that night I spent in jail."

The lieutenant laughed and said:

"Old man, you got mettle, that's for sure. My name is Lieutenant Rood. Are you sure this is what you want to do? It is likely you will be killed."

"Tut," Burns said as an expression of his frustration, and continued:

"I am not new to this, and if you don't let me fight, I will do it without you."

Just then, one of the soldiers said:

"Lieutenant, you're not gonna let the old man fight, are you? Look at his coat. He looks like Uncle Sam."

A couple of soldiers laughed and then said:

"He does. How fitting as it almost the 4th of July."

The group all laughed and then the lieutenant laid into them.

"You men, you keep your mouths shut and pay attention to the Rebs. They are coming shortly, that's for sure. Besides, this man probably has more mettle than all of you together. Do you think you would be here if you were his age?"

And to Burns, he said:

"You win, Mr. Burns. But, to prevent you from being taken as a bushwhacker, I must swear you in."

The lieutenant gave him an oath, which Burns gladly gave. He felt like a real soldier with his rifle and his oath. He passed a long the line of men and found a tree to use as shelter. Other soldiers looked at the old man who came to fight with them today with wonder and awe. One remarked:

The Iron Brigade Monument located near a spot where Burns would have fought on July 1st. (Faber)

"Look at that old man, come out to fight with us. If that is the kind of people in that town we are here trying to protect, it is certainly worth our while."

Lieutenant Rood took Burns to Lieutenant Colonel Collis, and told him about Burns, saying:

"Sir, this is Mr. John Burns. He wants to fight with us today. I have outfitted him with a rifle, cartridges, and given him an oath. He is ready."

"Can he shoot?"

"Not sure. Let's find out. Mr. Burns, you see that Reb riding yonder mounted on a gray horse? Looks like he is having trouble with it and it is bringing him within range. See if you can hit him."

Burns aimed the rifle and shot at the Rebel, who was bounced from the saddle. The horse continued and rode through the Union lines riderless. The men cheered.

"Well, Mr. Burns, it seems as you can shoot after all. Welcome to the Iron Brigade. Now, take a position and get ready as the Rebels will be coming."

About a minute later, Rood yelled:

"Alright, steady boys. Here they come!"

CHAPTER 36

JACOBS

PROFESSOR MICHAEL JACOBS was up early on Wednesday July 1st. He was anxious as he expected at any time a knock on his door from General Buford and Captain Keogh. Yesterday, Buford and Keogh requested he join them in the cupola of the Lutheran Seminary to give his advice on the ground northwest of the town. This advice would come in terms of strategic placement of Buford's Union Cavalry in order to best defend against, and to deter, the Confederate offensive. Buford explained to him they needed to hold the ground in order to await help from General Reynolds' First Corps. So, strategic placement of men and artillery, plus the movement of the men on the field of battle during the fight was very crucial. Upon understanding this need, he spent a couple of hours the previous evening going over the ground and also potential scenarios of attack by the Confederates so he could point out countermeasures and locations affording the best opportunities for counterattack, if feasible. He knew the historical importance this battle would play in repelling the Confederate invasion of the North, in fact maybe of the war itself, as he told his son Henry about that yesterday. Further, as he might play a part in it with his help interpreting the ground for the army, he decided to keep good notes and good records for history's sake. And, so he was ready.

After seven o'clock, the knock on the door came. He rushed downstairs to answer, and upon opening the door, saw Captain Keogh.

"Good morning, Professor. General Buford is expecting you in the cupola," Keogh said in his thick Irish accent.

"Very well, Captain. I am at your's and the general's disposal."

"Please follow me."

They left the Jacobs' property and walked the short distance to the Seminary. They climbed the steps and then Keogh opened the front door and gestured with his hand:

"After you, Professor."

The professor entered the building pausing to allow the captain to take the lead. Once he did, they walked down the long hall and up the stairs leading to the cupola. They reached the top and stepped out onto it. The view was fantastic. It was higher than the windows of his attic. Plus, he could see the whole field of the pending battle. He also could see, as he

The Lutheran Seminary as is today. Buford would have been looking toward the west on the morning of July 1st, toward the spot the photo was taken. (Faber)

turned, a full, unobstructed view in all directions. He saw the town and all the way south to Round Top Mountain and the large field in front of Cemetery Ridge. For a moment he marveled at the view, but then remembered why he was here. Captain Keogh approached General Buford, who was busy looking through his field glasses.

"Beggin' your pardon General, the Professor is here," Keogh said with a salute.

"Very good, Captain," Buford said while returning the salute. He turned to Jacobs:

"Good morning, Professor. Beautiful day, wouldn't you say? Warm and sunny with those beautiful clouds over there. Amazing the size of the shadows they make. Too bad it has to be spoiled by this fight."

"Good morning, sir. Yes, it is a beautiful day."

"Please...," he said gesturing for Jacobs to come and stand by him. This, Jacobs did. Buford continued:

"You should know this ground better than most and being a professor, I had hoped you could supply us with a little local intelligence."

"I'll do my best, General."

"Good, now we expect the enemy, he will approach from the Chambersburg Pike, there...," he said pointing while he continued:

"We have deployed almost three thousand of our men, dismounted cavalry, to cover the approach, both north and south of the road. And, we have extended our right flank to north of that road north of Chambersburg Pike...what's the name of it?"

"Mummasburg Road, sir."

"North of Mummasburg Road to cover our flank. We have a thousand mounted cavalry supporting those dismounted, on either flank. We have positioned artillery pieces there, there, and to our rear there," again pointing. He continued:

"We hope to spread them out from their column of fours once they come over the crest in the road, by hitting them hard with artillery and the rifle," he said and paused indicating he expected the professor to now comment. The professor coughed to clear his throat and said:

"That looks like a fine placement of your men and an intelligent read of the situation."

"Maybe, Professor, maybe. But, the problem is we expect about ten thousand Rebs to come up that road, about three times our size."

"Yes, sir. So, you expect to have to fall back at some time?"

"That may be correct, but hopefully we can hold until General Reynolds arrives."

"Well, sir. It seems as though that group of trees straight ahead, known as McPherson's Woods, and Herbst's Woodpile on your left side would afford good cover. And that hill, Oak Hill, to the north would serve the same purpose. And, if driven from the town, the group of hills to the south and east look like formidable ground for defense."

"That is just what we were thinking. Anything else?"

"Well sir, Seminary Ridge here would also provide some cover and you could fall back and regroup there."

"All good suggestions, Professor. We have thought of these, but it is always helpful to get confirmation from someone who actually lives here, just in case there is something we didn't see or think of. Your assistance has been much appreciated. That will be all."

"I hope truly that I have been able to be of help to you, General. Good luck and God bless, sir."

"Thank you, Professor. Good day now."

And, so Jacobs left the Seminary and returned to his house to await the commencement of the hostilities.

He returned to his house a little after eight and entered to find his son Henry awake and waiting for him.

"Father, good morning to you. Were you up in the cupola with General Buford?"

"Yes, son I was."

"How does it look from up there? Are the cavalry men deployed in good position?"

"They are. It seems the General has a good understanding of the ground."

"Did you suggest anything they had not thought of or done?"

"No, but the General was pleased with my participation. Really, I just confirmed what they were doing and how they could fall back, if and when they need to."

"Father, I am so proud of you. You could be helping to win this battle."

"Well, maybe so. But our boys are tremendously out manned, by a three to one margin. So, all depends on General Reynolds' First Corps arriving on the field in time to assist."

"When are they supposed to get here?"

"I dunno. But, the general is plenty worried about it. Are you joining me in the attic to watch and take notes?"

"I am. Shall we go now?"

"They climbed the stairs to the attic, positioned the telescope facing west toward the Confederate position and waited. It wasn't a long wait.

"Father, here they come," Henry said in an excited voice as he was looking through the telescope. He continued:

"Have a look."

Jacobs took his turn looking through the telescope and saw the Rebels marching in column toward the town on Chambersburg Pike. The point of the column passed over a crest in the road. About five seconds later, a volley of rifle fire greeted the invaders. Some bullets found their targets dropping several Rebels.

"Good shooting," Jacobs remarked and continued:

"Right on the point of the column. Now, they are breaking column and deploying in the field."

After about a half an hour of the sides exchanging rifle fire, and with the Rebels finally completing placement of their lines, the Union cannon began firing.

"Our artillery is pounding them and our boys are giving them good rifle fire," Jacobs described.

He continued: "Henry, here take a look whilst I start making notes."

Henry took his turn and described what he saw:

"Father, they were caught a little off guard it looks. And, our boys are such good shots. They really are breaking 'em up."

They watched, described the action, and made notes for about an hour, noting the Federals were more than holding their own against the superior force of the Confederates. Then, they noticed a group of officers riding north on West Street. Henry was at the telescope and said:

"Father, do you think that is General Reynolds?"

"Sure could."

"If so, then Buford's boys have held."

"Appears so, Henry, appears so."

"Isn't that grand? And, you helped. Oh Father, I am so proud,"

"Thank you, son. But, I really don't think I helped all that much. Besides, this is far from over. The Rebs haven't deployed near half their men."

"Well, the First Corps should bring enough men to continue holding."

"Yes, until the Rebs, if they do, commit more men. General Early's Corps is somewhere around here. And, the rest of Lee's army is around here somewhere, too."

"Father, do you think they will engage more men and fight it out here?"

"I think they will fight wherever our troops choose to. It will be up to our side, and with the arrival of the First Corps, it is beginning to look like right here. Still, it will be up to the enemy to choose to engage fully."

Henry peered back at the battle with the telescope and noticed some movement around the Seminary. He adjusted his view to that direction and saw General Reynolds and his staff riding back south on West Street, strangely accompanied by an older man on horseback.

"Father, General Reynolds is off again. He must be going to hurry his Corps into the battle. Wait...I see a civilian riding with his staff...an old man."

Jacobs was puzzled as Henry continued:

"Why, it couldn't be? Is it? Father, it's that old fool Burns. I wonder why he is with General Reynolds?"

"Are you sure?"

"Look for yourself."

Jacobs did and indeed it was Burns. He said:

"What would they want with *him*? Knowing how daft he is, he probably volunteered to fight the Rebs. But, that wouldn't explain why he is with Reynolds. He must be acting as a guide or something like that."

"What is the matter with him anyway?"

"Awe, he's just a lonely old man trying to figure a way to contribute now that he's not constable anymore. I kinda feel sorry for the old buffoon. He means well, it's just he doesn't know how to be kind to folks, that's all."

Henry hesitated as he didn't know what to say. He had always despised Burns, and thought of him as a jackass, a mean old coot. But, his father had given him a new way of looking at Burns, that with all the foolish things he did, still in spite of these, he had meant well.

Jacobs continued: "Let's get back to the battle and hope whatever he is doing will be of help to our boys."

Within a few minutes, Jacobs saw the First Corps coming up on West Street. They were rushing up the road and upon arriving directly west of Jacobs' home, they were hastily sent west out to the fighting using Middle Street. Jacobs was on the telescope as the troops began to arrive and were sent to the lines for reinforcement. He noticed Reynolds and his staff directing the movement of the men to the battle line. Then, he saw Reynolds separate from his staff and ride to the Seminary. Burns was not far behind.

Several minutes later, he saw Reynolds return from the Seminary and then ride with the men being deployed on the Union left flank this side of the trees making up McPherson's Woods. Jacobs was intrigued by Reynolds, and judged him as a perfect example of an officer, tall in the saddle and very much in command. He watched him for awhile, giving orders to set his men in place to strengthen the Union left.

"Henry, General Reynolds sure makes a magnificent sight. He is very calm, yet in control."

As he was watching him, marveling at the very presence he was displaying in the midst of the chaos of the battle, Reynolds was knocked off his horse. Jacobs suddenly couldn't breathe.

"My God, no," he said in a barely audible voice. He continued: "No, no."

"Father, what's wrong?"

"They shot General Reynolds. He's gone."

"Are you sure he's dead."

"It looks so. His staff is around him now, but he doesn't seem to be moving at all."

"Maybe, they aren't moving him until his surgeon arrives?"

"Henry, he is gone…"

Jacobs stopped looking through the telescope and sat down on one of the chairs he brought up to the attic. For several minutes, the two men didn't speak. Henry broke the silence:

"Father, is there anything I can do for you?"

"No, son. We are up here, safe in our attic, whilst those brave men are dying out there to protect us and our town. You must remember what you see today, but mostly remember those boys out there who will die today. Say a prayer for them…," he said as his voice trailed off.

It took about ten minutes for either of them to want to continue to observe the fight, but then Henry took the telescope and began watching again.

"Father, the First Corps is driving them from the field. Here take a look. Look straight ahead, our boys are pivoting on the left and surrounding the Rebs. They are surrendering."

Jacobs did and saw the Confederates retreating on both sides of the Chambersburg Pike, and on the left prisoners being taken.

"My, God, they are," he said in an excited voice, and continued:

"Hurrah for Reynolds' Corps, hurrah."

The intensity of the battle waned for awhile and Jacobs and his son took this opportunity to clean up their notes.

"Let's see, the first shots were fired at about half-past nine. Buford's men were about four thousand strong; three thousand dismounted and a thousand mounted, covering both flanks. The Rebels came up Chambersburg Pike about ten thousand strong, but were not in place until well after ten o'clock. At ten o'clock, the artillery began. General Reynolds arrived around eleven o'clock...."

"Father, I think it was closer to half-past ten when Reynolds arrived."

"Are you quite sure?"

"Yes, I remember looking at my pocket watch."

"Reynolds arrived at just after ten and a half A.M. He was shot and killed before eleven. After he fell, the Union left advanced, breaking the Rebel right, and capturing many of the enemy, whilst the Rebel center was broken and they retreated from the field. Our right was then driven back, but counterattacked several times until the Confederates finally fell back. Is that what you have noted?"

"Yes, that is about it."

After several minutes and when he and his father finished comparing notes, Henry took a look at the field through the telescope and saw the Confederates reinforcing and reforming their lines near the point of their first attack. The Union troops were continuing to deploy and were stretching their lines north of town in a semi-circle.

"Father, it looks as if we are in for it right here. Our lines are expanding in the north easterly past Carlisle Road, Rock Creek, and over to Harrisburg Road. The Rebels must be threatening from the northeast."

Jacobs scanned the horizon to the north and east and said:

"You are right. It will be here, Henry. This last action was just the prelude to a much bigger battle. Take over and describe what you see. I want to make a map of it."

"Okay."

Henry surveyed the field and began to describe it for his father when he noticed some activity over at the Seminary, some movement of men to reinforce the lines. But, something caught his eye as strange and different. He saw a man with a top hat and squirrel gun walking with the troops to the battle line.

"Father, take a look. What is that man doing, over there?" he said pointing in the direction of the Seminary.

Jacobs took the telescope and said: "Where?"

"Over there, just west of the Seminary. He has a top hat and a squirrel gun. It almost looks like Burns, again."

"Oh, I see him.........it is Burns. I recognize that hat and his old coat."

"What could he be doing? Maybe, as you said earlier, he wants to join the fight?"

"It looks as though that is what he is doing."

"The army won't let him fight, will they?"

"No, they can't let a civilian join them."

Jacobs watched as Burns made it to the rear of the Union lines, but was stopped and confronted by what looked like an officer. He watched for several minutes and then the first officer took him to another officer. He continued to observe as the second officer took him over to Herbst Woodpile, where he was handed off to another officer and then another, who then gave him a rifle and removed his hat. Shortly after, he was taken to another officer, and after a conference between the two of them, Jacobs saw Burns raise the rifle and shoot toward the Rebel lines as they were beginning to form for an attack. He rotated the telescope and saw a Rebel shot off his gray horse. He swung the telescope back to see several men surround Burns slap him on the back and point to a spot on the line. Burns went over to the pointed spot and crouched down next to the soldiers there.

"Good Lord, they are positioning him in their lines, over by the Herbst Woodpile. That stupid, stupid old man won't be satisfied until he gets himself killed, and that will probably be today," Jacobs said.

He stopped looking through the telescope, and shaking his head, sat back down in the chair. Henry took over and looked for Burns among the men, but could not make him out among the masses of blue clad soldiers. Finally, he noticed the funny looking coat that Burns was wearing. He watched Burns for a second or two, and then the first cannon shot was fired.

CHAPTER 37

PIERCE

MATILDA (TILLIE) PIERCE woke early the morning of Wednesday, July 1, 1863. She was still anxious from the events of the previous day and also apprehensive of the events this day would bring. Tillie remembered yesterday when the Union cavalry passed through the town on its way to set up a defensive position on Seminary Hill, and that she and her classmates from Rebecca Eyster's Young Ladies Seminary stationed themselves on the corner of Washington and High Streets and greeted them with songs while they passed. She remembered singing *"Union Forever"* more times than ever in her life making her vocal chords sore all night long. She quickly dressed and came down for breakfast, but could not eat much. She then heard one of her classmates call from outside the troops were coming up Washington Street again and they should hurry to greet them. She cleaned up her dishes, excused herself, and joined her friends.

They went west on Breckinridge Street to Washington Street in time to notice more cavalry riding north. Once the cavalry passed, a long train of wagons followed. The girls decided more singing would be helpful, so they began another chorus of *"Union Forever."*

At this time, around half-past nine o'clock, Tillie began to hear sounds of the battle from northwest of the town. At first the sounds were barely audible. But, they soon began to grow as the cannon fire intensified and Tillie could see in the distance smoke rising from where she judged was the battlefield. The noise became so loud it was almost unbearable for her.

About an hour later, long lines of infantry passed, all heading toward the battlefield. She noticed the men and even heard some say they wondered if they would be back in town soon on stretchers or in ambulances. This frightened her. The battle and the resulting horrors of the dead and wounded might soon be all too real, but having never experienced it first-hand, she really didn't know what to expect.

She and her friends stayed until the last of the wagons passed by around noon, and then she walked home, as she judged it was time for dinner. Her ears were wringing from the noise, but she became almost immune to the sounds as the battle had been raging for over two hours. When she got home, she saw dinner was ready and on the table, and her father, mother, and sister Martha waiting for her. Like breakfast, she again was too excited to eat.

"Papa, do you think our boys will be alright?"

"I don't know. It must be a terrible battle. It seems the Rebels are attacking from the northwest and our troops are trying to hold them off."

"What if they break through? Won't they be taking the town?"

"Yes, and we must be prepared in the event it does happen. At a moment's notice, we must be able to get to the cellar. So, no more ventures out of the house, young lady."

"Yes, Papa," Tillie replied.

Just then there was a knock on their door. Tillie got up to answer it and showed her neighbor Hettie Shriver and her two children, Sadie and Molly into the house. They all made their way into the kitchen area to where the Pierce's were eating dinner.

"Mr. Pierce, so sorry for the interruption, but I just had to come."

"No bother, Hettie. Are you alright?"

"No, I am scared half to death and the children are scared too."

"Well, you and the children can stay with us if it will make you feel better."

"Thanks just the same, but I think I might go to Papa's house and take the children away from this danger."

Tillie got up from table, went over and hugged Hettie and said:

"Hettie, it will be fine. Stay here with us."

Tillie leaned down to the children and said:

"Girls, do you want to stay here with us until the terrible noises are over?"

Both girls said in unison:

The Shriver House Museum as is today located on Baltimore Street, near Breckinridge Street. Note the Shriver House joins the Pierce House by a vertical joint just left of the drainage pipe. (Faber)

"We want to go to Grandpa's."

The six year old girl, Molly was crying and it looked as though Sadie would start crying at any moment.

"Papa, they are really frightened. Perhaps I could go along and help with the children?"

Pierce asked: "Hettie, how far again is your Papa's house?"

"Mr. Pierce, about three miles south of here on east slope of Round Top and on the Taneytown Road. I would be much obliged if Tillie accompanied us to help me with the children."

Pierce turned to his wife: "Well, what do you think Margaret?"

"As always, it is your decision. But, as the battle is north of town, it seems going to the south would be a safer location. And, I trust Mr. Weikert to keep good care of our Tillie until this is over and it is safe for her to return."

"Yes, I agree. Well it is settled then. When would you like to leave Hettie?"

"I am ready to go as soon as Tillie is."

At that time, they heard the hoof noises from a horse at the back of their house, as there was a slight lull in the battle. Pierce got up from the table and said:

"I'll see what that is. In the meantime, Tillie you gather your things you will need to stay a day or two at the Weikert's."

Tillie decided she would travel light, so she didn't have much to gather. But, she decided her best clothes should be moved to the cellar for safe-keeping. She was upstairs in her room, when she heard her father yell for her to come down. At once, she rushed downstairs and out the back of the house, in time to see her father's big smile, and her gray horse waiting to get into the stable.

"Your horse has returned home to you, Tillie," Pierce said, as he knew how fond Tillie was of the animal.

Tillie was so excited to see the horse that tears came down her cheeks as she rushed over to it. She got to the horse and hugged its neck, like she had done before the Rebels took her.

"You're home, you're home. Thank you, Lord for bringing our horse home safely."

Pierce looked at the saddle and saw the "CSA" markings of the Confederate Army. And, he saw traces of blood on it.

"Looks like the Rebels were using her in the battle, and her rider didn't fare so well. Serves 'em right for stealing away our horse. But, we must get rid of the saddle in case the Rebels take the town and see the horse is here. They may not be so kind and forgiving. Tillie, go into the house and get some lamp oil. I'll dig a hole and we can burn this saddle and bury it."

Tillie did as she was told and her father disposed of the saddle.

Within about ten minutes, Tillie said her goodbyes to her mother and father, and after hearing both of them caution about being careful and safe, she and the Shrivers started walking down Baltimore Street toward the Weikert Farm. Hettie was visibly relieved to have Tillie along as she knew how the girls felt about her and how she felt about them. Tillie felt the nervousness caused by the battle begin to melt away as she now had to be strong for the Shrivers, at least until they reached the Weikert's. Hettie had a hold of Sadie's hand and Tillie took Molly's.

"Girls, are you excited to be going to Grandpa's house? It will be fun adventure," Tillie asked.

"Oh yes," Sadie said.

"Me, too," Molly added.

"Well, we should be there in about an hour. What shall we do?" Tilley asked.

"Can we sing a song, Miss Tillie, can we?" Mollie asked.

"Yes, can we sing *Pop Goes the Weasel*?" Sadie added.

Tillie replied: "Alright, who's gonna start?"

"I will, I will," Sadie said and began to sing and the others joined.

They all laughed and then they sang it again. This time, Tillie played like she was the monkey, crouching down and scratching her under-arms and chasing the girls. The girls screamed and laughed and ran from Tillie. Soon Tillie caught up with Molly, grabbed her and hugged her tightly, saying:

"The monkey gotcha."

Molly laughed very hard and Sadie said:

"What about me, monkey," and then ran off.

Tillie caught her too, and said the monkey got her. They all laughed and then continued on their journey. Hettie was very pleased with how Tillie distracted the girls from the danger of the battle.

In a couple of minutes, they reached the Evergreen Cemetery, the local town cemetery, located on Cemetery Hill, between the Taneytown Road to the west and Baltimore Street to the east. They decided the route would be shorter to cross the hill and so they started up the slope. Tillie noticed activity at the top of the hill, where Union soldiers were placing cannons. As they approached, one of the soldiers addressed them:

"Beggin' your pardon, ladies, but you should not be up here. The Rebs will be firing on this position come haste, so you need to get off this hill as soon as you can."

Tillie looked north toward Seminary Ridge and noticed the intensity of the battle had increased. She saw men were moving all about the field and massive rifle and cannon fire, bursting in the air, creating a thick layer of smoke, such that she couldn't make out the lines of the two armies. She said to the soldier:

"Thank you kindly. We will be on our way, as we are headed toward the Taneytown Road and south of the town."

Tillie, Hettie, and the girls commenced running down the hill toward the Taneytown Road. Upon reaching there, she noticed the road was in poor shape as it showed the signs of the movement of the army. Wagon ruts were everywhere in the road and it was muddy. They started down the road mingling with the soldiers headed in the opposite direction as they were continuing to move north toward the battle.

Just then an ambulance wagon approached their position headed south on the west side of the road. The driver slowed the wagon and then stopped it. He asked the women politely to move off the road and let him pass. They did so, and as it went by they noticed it looked very official to them adorned by a yellow flag. The wagon was about ten feet long and about four feet wide. It had about two feet of clearance from the road to the bottom, as it was sunk into the road about a foot up the wheels. It was pulled by two horses and had four officers seated on one side of the wagon.

Tillie wondered out loud who would be in the wagon, and as the soldiers were passing to north, one of them replied:

"It must be General Reynolds. Word tell he was killed about two hours or so ago at the beginning of the battle."

"Oh. I sure am sorry to hear that," she replied.

"Us too. He was a fine commander and a fine man."

In a few minutes, the party reached the Leister farmhouse along Taneytown Road, which was about a mile and a half from the Weikert Farm. The road had become even more muddy, so they had to leave it for the field next to the house. They stood by the gate to the house unsure on how to proceed to their destination. Another soldier asked what they were doing:

"Missy, what is wrong? Where are you headed with the little ones?"

"We are headed to a farmhouse about a mile south of here, but the road is too muddy to continue," Tillie replied.

"It is rather dangerous here, as we expect cannon fire from the Rebels. They are firing on that hill up ahead, so we can expect the fire to make it toward this place. I will see if we can get you a ride on a passing wagon. Please wait here."

The soldier waved down one of the wagons transporting people from Gettysburg south and away from the battle. There was room and so the soldier helped Hettie, Tillie, and the girls aboard. The wagon was cramped, but for Tillie it was much better than walking. The girls were getting anxious and the little one remarked:

"Mama, when will we be at Grandpa's?"

"Soon, sweetie, soon."

And soon it was, as they arrived at the Weikert farm moments later. After saying thanks and goodbye to the driver, the four walked through the gate and up to the house. Hettie knocked on the door and Mr. Jacob Weikert opened the door and with a big smile, said:

"Hettie, girls, why what a pleasant surprise. Are you here to stay?"

Jacob Weikert was around fifty years old, was about five and a half feet tall, had thinning gray hair, cut short so it was above his ears, wore glasses, was clean shaven, had brown eyes, and an average nose and mouth. He was dressed in brown trousers, a white long sleeved shirt, braces holding up his trousers, and brown boots adorned with some dried mud.

"Father," Hettie said and hugged him tightly. She continued:

"The girls and I are so scared, with the battle so close to us."

"Come in, come in. Hurry. Awe, Sadie, Molly, come to Grandpa."

The four went into the house and the girls ran to their Grandfather. He hugged them and said:

Weikert Farm as is today along the Taneytown Road. (Seamon)

246

"Don't be afraid little ones. Grandpa is here and you are with us now."

Hettie said: "Papa, you remember Tillie Pierce? She lives next door, and has been a great help getting us her safely. It isn't a bother if she stays until the battle is over?"

"Yes, yes, Tillie come in. I owe you a debt of gratitude for helping my family get here safe and sound. Our home is your home, and you can stay as long as you like."

"Mighty obliged Mr. Weikert," Tillie replied.

Hettie's mother hugged the girls and said to them:

"Becky, come downstairs. Your sister and the girls are here."

Becky was the daughter still living at home with the Weikert's. She was about the same age as Tillie. She came down the stairs and rushed to her older sister. She was a couple of inches taller than five feet, had long light brown hair, adorned with a light blue ribbon tied in the back, blue eyes, and average nose and chin, and a bright smile. She was wearing a long dark blue dress, tightly buttoned at the neck, and black shoes. A concerned look was on her face, probably because of the battle noises, Tillie surmised.

"Sister, how good of you to come. And, girls, you are getting bigger every day."

"Hi Auntie Becky," the girls said.

After hugging the girls, Becky turned to Tillie:

"Tillie, it is so nice to see you. It's been almost a month since I have been to town to see you and your folks."

The two friends gave a cordial hug. And then Hettie's mother said:

"Would you like something to eat? You all look like you could use it. Hettie, Tillie, a cup of tea?"

"Yes, Grandma," the two girls said. Hettie replied:

"Mama, let me help you with that. Girls come help Grandma," and the four disappeared into the kitchen.

Just then, they heard many horses galloping on the road outside. They rushed to the door, exited the house, and stood on the porch watching more Union artillery go by heading to the battle.

Tillie was excited to see more cannon headed into battle, so she exclaimed:

"How grand a sight to see. Our boys will surely give it to them Rebels, now. Oh, I do hope we can save the town from them. I am worried about our house and Mama and Papa."

"Me too," Becky added.

"Well, I doubt the Rebs can match that type of firepower. Pray to the Lord He will keep our town in his graces. Now, let's go back into the house and have that tea," Weikert said trying to be reassuring.

After drinking a cup of tea, Tillie was too wound up to sit for long, so she went outside to the porch. Her friend Becky joined her, just as great throngs of infantry began to pass by the house. Tillie noticed, as it was a hot afternoon, many of the troops were stopping at a spring north of the house for a drink.

"I know how we can help them, Becky! Let's get a bucket of water and some cups and bring it to them."

"That's a grand idea."

They went into the house and each got a bucket and a cup. Then, they went to the spring, filled the buckets, and took the water to the road and began handing the men a drink. They did this for about an hour, until the spring was dry and then they filled their buckets from the pump located on the south side of the house. As Tillie was returning to the road with another bucket full of water, she noticed a group of officers riding up. They stopped for a drink from Becky. One of the officers removed his hat, wiped his brow with his sleeve, and got off the horse. He was in his mid forties, tall, had thick dark brown hair, cut above his ears, parted on the right side of his head, a thick mustache, a long goatee that extended about two inches below his chin, a slightly pointed nose and thin lips hidden by his mustache. The officer spoke:

"Sure is nice of you ladies to give us this fine water. We have ridden about fifteen miles from Uniontown and are mighty thirsty."

The other officers also dismounted and took turns drinking from the girls' cups. Becky was in awe of their presence, so Tillie did the talking.

"Uniontown is mighty far, sir," Tillie said.

"That it is, and I can feel every mile," he said while rubbing his back side. He continued:

"I hear Gettysburg is about three more miles up this road?"

"Yes, sir it is. Do you think we can turn back the Rebels and save our town?" Tillie asked.

"Well now, that's just what General Meade has asked me to find out."

"Who is General Meade? You mean General Hooker?"

"No, ma'am. General George Meade. He is in command of this army now. And, I am to take command of the field and report back directly to him."

"Sir, to whom am I addressing?"

"General Winfield Scott Hancock," the officer said with a slight bow. He flashed a big, warm smile and continued:

"And to whom do I have the pleasure?"

"I am Matilda Pierce. Folks call me Tillie. And, this is Miss Becky Weikert."

Hancock removed his glove from his right hand and extended it to the girls. They each shook his hand. Tillie noticed that his grip was firm but very light out of respect.

"Miss Tillie and Miss Becky, we are sure grateful for your water on this hot day. You fine young ladies are doing your country a great service by helping our men."

Tillie blushed a little and didn't know what to say, so she just smiled shyly at Hancock.

"Well, we must be on our way so we can save your town. Men, mount up."

He placed his hat back on his head, mounted his horse, turned back to the girls once more and said tipping his hat:

"Good afternoon to you fine ladies."

And with that, he and his officers were gone in a flash. Tillie and Becky were tired, but the visit from the general renewed their enthusiasm and they continued to pass water to the men until the sun was settling in the western sky. Toward the late afternoon, Tillie noticed the sounds of the battle were coming closer to where they were.

"Becky, it sounds as if the battle is getting closer. What do you think?"

"Yes, it is louder."

Just then, the girls noticed men coming from the north, many bandaged up. One approached them, pointed toward the house, and said:

"Do you girls live in that there house?"

"My name is Tillie. This here is my friend Becky. She and her family live there."

"The surgeons have asked me to find a suitable place to treat the wounded men."

He turned to Becky and said:

"Is your father at home?"

"He is and I will take you to him."

Tillie, Becky and the soldier went to the house and up on the porch. Becky said:

"Please wait here and I will fetch him."

She returned less than a minute later with Weikert. The soldier addressed him:

"Beggin' your pardon, sir, but the surgeons asked me to set up an area where we can treat the wounded men. Would it be too much trouble to use that there barn?" he said while pointing over his left shoulder.

Weikert was momentarily stunned. He hadn't thought of this possibility before, that his property would be needed to care for wounded men. But, he quickly recovered and only seconds later replied:

"Of course. Please, please. Whatever you need and any way we can be of service."

"Thank you, sir. At any moment the ambulances will begin to arrive. Also, I am going to direct those who are walking to go to the barn. Might I also trouble you for some clean linens?"

"Indeed you may. As I said, whatever you need."

He turned to the girls and said:

"Run into the house and get some linens, sheets, cloths, whatever you can find, and bring them over, whilst I show this man to the barn."

"Yes, Papa," Becky said.

They disappeared into the house and returned about five minutes later, just in time to see an ambulance wagon arriving. They noticed the soldier who requested permission to use the barn wave down the ambulance and point to the barn. The ambulance turned into the yard, passed the gate, and stopped in front of the barn. Men jumped out of the front of the wagon and quickly picked up a litter containing a man who was moaning quite loudly. The men whisked the litter into the barn, as more men moved another wounded man in a litter out and into the barn. Three wounded men climbed out of the ambulance and walked to the barn. No sooner had they entered, then the two sets of stretcher carriers emerged from the barn, loaded the litters in the back of the wagon and took off back to the north and the battle.

Tillie and Becky approached the barn and noticed many more bandaged men walking to the barn. They mingled with these men and then entered the barn to give the linens. The barn was dark and their eyes took a moment to adjust to the lamp lit interior of the barn. Once their eyes adjusted, they were overwhelmed by the sight of the hustle and bustle. They noticed men rushing about in the barn. Men were lying on the floor of the barn. Some were moaning, some were crying, and some were staring blankly without any expression at all. The girls didn't know what to do. Another stretcher was whisked by them, and they could see a surgeon pointing to an empty space on the floor of the barn.

"I need more tables in here. *Quickly*," he said.

The stretcher bearers went to the spot and gently removed the wounded man from the litter and left as quickly as they came. They saw a nurse swiftly move over to the man and begin to look at his wound. The man was wounded in the stomach, and they saw the nurse open his uniform coat and look at the blood stained bandage around his core. Another nurse approached them and said:

"Fresh linens. That is grand. Put them over there," she said pointing to a table which had been brought into the barn.

They did so and turned to leave just as the wounded man was lifted onto a table. He moaned and cried out in pain as he was moved. They saw the surgeon check the man's wound and then shake his head at the nurse who had cared for him. Two men then lifted the man from the table and put him back on the empty spot on the floor. Just as fast as the man was placed on the floor, another was placed on the table.

They were stunned to the point of silence. Then they heard Becky's father call for them:

"Girls, let us please leave and let these people do the caring for these men."

Without a word they left the barn, just as another ambulance arrived with more wounded. Once they were out of the barn, the girls began to cry softly. Tears ran down their cheeks. Weikert hugged them both at one time and said:

"Let's get back to the house. They need the room to work and if they need something further from us, they will let us know."

As they were walking back to the house, they heard a loud shriek from inside the barn.

The girls entered the house still shook up from what they had seen in the barn. They needed a few minutes to calm down and Mrs. Weikert helped them in any way she could.

"Girls, can you come to the kitchen and help me with supper, please?"

Becky replied in a voice that crackled: "Ma'ma, how can we even think about eating when there are boys dying in our barn, right out there?"

"Now, Becky, we must be strong. There are little ones in our midst that need us to be strong so they won't be scared. It is bad enough for them to have to hear the sounds of the cannons and the rifles."

"Yes, Mama."

Mrs. Weikert hugged Becky very tightly, stoked her head and said:

"That's my girl. Ask God to give you strength and He will. Tillie, are you alright?"

"I guess, ma'am. But, I've never seen anything like that in my life."

"Not many folks have. Let's pray that this ends real soon. Hettie says you are skilled at keeping the girls busy. Can you do that whilst we make supper?"

"Yes, ma'am, I can. I'll have them write their letters."

"That's the stuff."

And so, the family settled down to trying to do normal things in an effort to cope with the living and dying going on just yards from their house. Soon, supper was ready and they sat at the table to eat it. They spoke of mundane things until the children finished and asked to be excused. They were told to go to the living area, just outside the kitchen, and continue to practice their letters. Once they left, Weikert spoke:

"Now that everyone has calmed down, we must make plans for what we need to do. I spoke with several of the soldiers whilst you girls were getting the linens this afternoon. They said our boys were getting the worst of it, and that measures up as we can see with the amount of the wounded right here in our barn. After supper, I want you two girls to go back to the barn and see if there is anything they need. Mother, the soldiers who will be fighting tomorrow are going to need bread to eat, so you and Hettie plan how we can bake as much bread as the flour and baking soda will allow, how you can make it last, and how we can bake it as quickly as possible.

About tonight, the nurses have asked to be able to make beef tea to nourish the wounded, and have asked to use the cellar kitchen for this. Mother, we need to make available all the dried beef we have, and you girls need to bring them water as they need it."

Tillie looked bewildered at the news Weikert relayed about the battle, and said:

"Mr. Weikert, does that mean the Rebels have taken Gettysburg?"

"I am sorry to say so, but the last soldier I talked to just a few moments ago said the Rebs had driven our boys through the town and have taken possession of it."

"Oh my Lord, what of Papa, Mama, and Martha?"

"Now don't you fret none. The soldiers said the town has not been shelled. There was fighting in the town as our boys retreated south to Cemetery Hill and Culp's Hill, but the soldiers said they didn't see any harm to any of the civilians. One thing we know, the Rebs don't pillage property and they don't hurt civilians."

"Yes, sir."

"As I said, we must prepare for tomorrow. Now, let's clean up the table and you girls go to the barn. I know it is dreadful, but it is more so to them, as they cannot escape to the house the way we can."

Tillie and Becky got up their courage and left the house for the barn. It was dark now, and the sounds of the battle died down to an occasional rifle shot, as no more cannon fire could be heard. Along the way, Tillie knew she had to be the strong one, so she tried to comfort Becky:

"Becky, it's gonna be alright. You'll see."

Unfortunately, Tillie's prediction wasn't accurate. As they approached the barn, they could hear the screaming in agony, the crying, and the surgeons yelling orders to the attendants. They saw more ambulances arriving, and more wounded unloaded into the barn. They entered to see the same scene as in the afternoon, just more men in the barn. As their eyes adjusted, they noticed just about every spot on the barn floor was taken up by a wounded soldier. The surgeons were working on men and so they couldn't get anyone's attention right away. After about a minute or so, one of the attendants came over and asked if they were there to help.

"We could use the additional hands," he said.

"I'm sorry, sir, I just can't," Tillie said. She started to cry, and just managed to say:

"The owner of the house wanted us to inquire if you have need of anything?"

"No, thank him kindly. Just more hands that's all."

Becky was also crying and so Tillie decided they needed to leave this place. She grabbed Becky by the arm and marched her out. They ran across the yard and entered the Weikert house through the cellar. They found in the cellar kitchen some nurses making beef tea. One of them addressed Tillie:

"You cannot be crying around the wounded men. They need comfort, strength, and above all happy faces."

"How can you be happy around so much suffering?"

"Well, young lady, you just have to be that's all."

The other nurse said:

"When it overwhelms me, I think of things that make me laugh."

Tillie said: "Like what?"

"Well, once when I was a little girl I saw my older brother riding a horse, and he decided he was going to play the fool, so he started riding it sidesaddle, you know, like a lady. We all laughed at him, until the horse took him under a tree, and because he wasn't looking ahead, a low limb knocked him right off the saddle and on his behind. We rushed over to see if he was okay, and when we found out he was, we started laughing until we cried."

Tillie and Becky started laughing. Another nurse said:

"Once, my father, God rest his soul, had too much liquor. It was winter and there was a lot of snow on the ground. My father had to use the outhouse and when he came back he forgot to pull his trousers up. As he was climbing the stairs, his trousers caused him to trip and fall off into the bushes, where we found him a couple hours later sleeping with his trousers down around his ankles. That one still makes me laugh even after all these years."

Tillie and Becky laughed even harder and the tears started coming down their cheeks. The second nurse said to them:

"See, laughter does make it better doesn't it? So, when you see something that frightens you or makes you feel horrible, just laugh and it won't be so bad."

"I do feel better, thanks," Tillie said.

The nurses took their tea and left toward the barn. As they were leaving, a chaplain entered, saying:

"Ladies, I saw you in the barn just now and how upset you were. I just wanted to come by and say what you do now for these unfortunate men will be rewarded in heaven many fold by our Father."

Tillie, still thinking about the nurse's father sleeping in the snow with his trousers down, looked at the chaplain and laughed. The chaplain was shocked, and so he said:

"I find nothing funny about what I just said!"

"Oh, pardon me," she said trying to get serious. She continued:

"It wasn't. But, the nurses told me to laugh when I see something bad, and so that is what I was doing. I'm sorry if I was inappropriate."

"I see. Laughter is good medicine against pain, so I don't see the harm."

With that he left. Tillie looked over at her friend and said:

"Becky, I don't know that I have ever gone through a day in my life that had so much misery and yet, tired as I am, I feel that maybe I can do it again tomorrow."

"It seems as though we may have to, and it also seems like the battle may be coming this way, right to us."

"I believe you are right. Let's go upstairs and see if we can help anyone."

They went upstairs, reported to Weikert that the nurses were making the beef tea and the attendant said no more help was necessary for the night. He listened and said:

"Why don't you two help get the little ones to sleep and turn in yourselves? It will be a busy, busy day tomorrow."

And, so they did. Tillie slept on the floor in Becky's room while Becky was tucked in her bed just above her.

"Good night, Becky. And, God bless us, your family and mine, and our boys in the battle tomorrow."

"Good night, Tillie."

Tillie heard Becky begin to breathe deeply and knew she was asleep. She wished she could do the same, but she was listening to the sounds coming from the barn, and so these kept her awake for awhile. She finally dozed off to the thought of the man sleeping naked in the snow.

CHAPTER 38

BUTLER

ELIZABETH (OLD LIZ) BUTLER was awake all night long knowing the day would bring a battle between the Confederates and the Union forces on the northwest side of town. She and her husband Samuel could not sleep at all. They had this problem since last Friday when their friend Isaac Moses had hidden them and their two teenage boys from the Confederates in his secret room in the cellar of his house. They escaped that close call, and stayed in the room until the Rebels left town that next day. Originally, they planned on leaving town to escape the invading Rebel army, and heading north, maybe all the way to Canada. But, that plan changed once the Confederates showed up, occupied the town, and then left town headed north and east, just where Isaac's contacts, who were to help them with their escape, lived. So, they were stuck in town and needed to wait for the outcome of the battle before they could know what to do. And, what would they do if the Rebels were victorious? Would they be safe here in Gettysburg? If not, where would they go? All these questions, and more, filled their heads and kept them from sleeping decently at all.

Now, it was about half-past nine in the morning, and Old Liz was in her kitchen making tea for her and Samuel, when she heard the first cannon blast. She paused what she was doing to listen and make sure her mind was not playing tricks on her. In seconds, there was an answer, and then another, and another. The battle had begun.

"Sam'l, deys begun de fight, yes sur," she said.

"Sounds so. Deys close, too. Dem sounds sure close. Maybe we's go to Isaac's again? Hide in dat room?"

It was a plan they discussed at length the previous couple of nights as it became clear a battle would be fought near, and could be fought right here in Gettysburg. Now, they could not agree on whether to go to the Moses' house. Samuel wanted to go, but Liz wasn't so sure, as she thought that room, although a good hiding place, offered no escape if they were discovered. Hence, the dilemma they faced.

"We's stay, least til we see who's winnin'. Dat's sure. You's glimps'd dat fine sulders comin' up Washton Street yestday. Maybe, deys whup dem Rebels, maybe," she replied.

"Maybe. But, we's gots to be 'pared to goes right quick, if needs to."

"I's git da boys 'pared."

They listened all morning to the sounds of war about a mile from their house, not knowing if one side or the other was getting the upper hand in the fight. Around two o'clock, the situation changed rapidly as the Union forces began to give way and retreat through the town, many along Washington Street. Samuel was sitting in the living area of the house with his door open, and Liz and the boys the kitchen area, when Samuel noticed a band of Union soldiers running south on Washington Street, past his house. And, then more and more passed. This scene sent a chill up his spine. He could hardly talk, but managed the words:

"Ol' Liz, jus saw me sum blue sulders run by, lots dem."

They all went to the front door and peeked out to the street. They looked north and saw more Union soldiers running south on Washington Street. Off in the distance, they could see gray clad soldiers giving chase. One of the gray soldiers stopped, raised his rifle, and fired. They saw one of the blue soldiers knocked off his feet and fall into the dirt road. He lay motionless in street. This shocked them and they went back into the house.

"Sam'l, sees that po sulder shot?" Liz asked.

"Yes. We's better git to Isaac's an quick like."

"You's dink it's safe?"

"Hurry, nots much time. Hurry."

And, so the four of them left their house on a run, south to the Moses house. The men ran faster than Old Liz, and as she lagged behind, she became visible to the pursuing Confederates, who had not noticed the men running in front of her. Samuel knew she was lagging behind but also knew he had to get the boys to Isaac's house. He got there and ran into the house with the boys. Liz was still about fifty feet from the house, when she heard:

"Ya, thea, old woman. Ya, halt or I'll shoot ya."

Further, she heard one of the others say:

"We'll keep a followin' these Yanks. Ya get the contraband."

She was horrified and frightened beyond her wits. Her legs stopped running without her realizing and she stopped. She began to cry as she looked at the Moses' house just a few short steps away. Samuel peeked out of the door, and looked at her with a very sad face. He then disappeared into the house and the door closed quietly. She was left on her own. She turned around, with tears running down her cheeks, mixed with the sweat from her running, and confronted her nemesis.

"You's talking to me?"

"I am. What's ya running fo?"

"I's a frighted, dat's all," she said making sure to make no reference to Samuel and the boys.

"Frightened? Well, ya needn't be. I aint gonna hurt ya. I gonna take ya back south where it's nice and warm."

And, so there it was. She was caught and was going back to slavery in the South. She cried deeply, but then a peace came over her, and it strengthened her. If she could lead these Confederates away from the Moses' house and Samuel and the boys would be safe, she would gladly sacrifice herself and her freedom for them. She wiped her tears from her eyes and said as the Confederate approached:

"Yes, sur."

"Now, that's more like it. Hold out ya hands."

She followed his instruction, and he tied her hands in front of her with a rope. Once he finished this, he led her away north on Washington Street toward the center of the town. As they turned to walk away, they heard a voice from behind:

"Who's dat who is takin' my wife?"

They turned to see Samuel standing on street in front of the Moses' house. He was standing with his legs shoulder apart and sturdy. The Confederate soldier looked at him, temporarily startled by the old man's courage. Old Liz looked at him with all her heart. She thought: "My man, he's aint abandon me."

"Well now, whats we have here. Is this ya wife?"

"Yes, sur, its is. To death do us part."

"Well, sir, she is now owned by the Confederates States of America. As are ya. Kindly, put ya hands out where I can see 'em."

Samuel did so, and with Liz in tow, the soldier came over and tied his hands in front of him. He then led them off toward town.

Moments earlier in the Moses' house, after the door had been closed, Samuel said:

"Isaac, Esther, be much obliged if you's get de boys in dat dere hidin' room for safekeepin'."

He turned to the boys and said:

"Boys, I's need you to be strong, as I's know you is. You's go hide agin likes last time. I's can't let ya Mama face dis by her lonesome. We's be alright, but I's got to have you's promise you's do what the Moses tell and mind them likes dey yours Mama and Papa."

Both boys replied with tears in their eyes:

"We's will Papa."

With that he opened the door quietly, stepped outside and shut it noiselessly.

Isaac said:

"Boys, I's want you to watch your daddy dere and member dis all's your lives. He is one brave man, and so's your Mama."

The boys watched from behind the safety of the closed door as the soldier led their parents away, hands tied, but together.

They walked along Washington Street amongst the chaos of the battle going on all around them. They passed more groups of Union soldiers running toward the south of town, with Rebel troops in close pursuit. Rifle shots were heard all around them. They heard cannon fire from the northwest of town, and shells screaming over their heads toward the hills south of town. They saw wounded Union soldiers being overtaken by Confederates and captured. They saw dead men and horses in the street, and the wreckage of a couple of wagons, turned upside down when the horses were killed out from under the wagon. All the while, the soldier calmly instructed them to keep on walking, even poking his rifle into Samuel's back to make the point.

After walking for about five minutes, they came to High Street. As they crossed, their attention was directed west to the intersection of High Street and Franklin Street, where they saw a group of Union soldiers surrounded by Rebel soldiers. They heard a Confederate yell:

"Surrender ya flag."

"Not today, Secesh."

Then, the Union forces opened fire on the Rebels, killing one and wounding another. This was immediately followed by a discharge of the Rebels' rifles, whereby several Union soldiers were killed or wounded. After this, the Federals surrendered.

"Keep movin'," the soldier ordered.

They walked another couple of minutes and made it to Middle Street. Next to Professor Jacobs' house, they noticed a single Union soldier who was walking south. He caught their eyes because he was moving very slowly. He looked not to be wounded, so it was strange to them that he was walking and not running. Just then, they noticed a group of Rebel soldiers behind him. They raised their rifles and then heard the command to shoot, and they did, killing him.

The horrors of the battle startled them beyond the ability to talk, and so they just silently walked north toward the center of town. They reached

Chambersburg Street and were directed to turn east toward the Diamond. They looked up ahead and saw a small group of colored folks gathered in front of the Lutheran Church, on the south side of Chambersburg Street. They looked behind them and saw more coming. Once they got to in front of the church, they were forced to join this group. One of the Confederates said:

"More? Good. But these, they look old?"

"Yes, but they colored, ain't they?" their captor said.

"S'pose so. Take the ropes off, now that they are hea."

Liz heard a violent scream from inside the church and noticed, for the first time, it was being used as a hospital, as she saw an amputated arm thrown out of one of the windows of the church. She looked at the ground below the window and saw a pile of arms and legs, amidst a pool of blood. This sickened her and she felt her stomach turn and bile come up to her throat. She had to turn away from the sight. Samuel noticed and comforted her, hugging her tightly. More and more colored folks were forced into the group and soon their number was around thirty.

"Take them inside and seat them in the pews," ordered one of the Rebels.

And, so the one guarding them said:

"You heard the lieutenant. Inside."

Liz and Samuel were close to the front of the group and so they climbed the steps to the entrance of the church, passed the white pillars, and opened the door. The church was dimly lit with lanterns and oil lamps.

Once their eyes adjusted, they noticed the scene inside. Wounded soldiers, all of them Union, were laid out in the pews. Confederate soldiers were also in their midst acting as guards. A few nurses were attending to the wounded and applying bandages to stop their bleeding. Many were unattended and were moaning from the pain of their wounds. Two surgeons were working on two soldiers on tables at the front of the church, with many more soldiers waiting their turn. One of the surgeons said:

"Chaplain, can you please come over? This one needs you."

The chaplain, a tall man of about forty years of age, with a full beard, long hair, and a large forehead, dressed in a Union army uniform, looked up and said:

"Certainly, I will be there momentarily."

Suddenly, the doors of the church were thrust open and all inside, including their guard were startled. In came a litter with a wounded soldier and the stretcher bearers said:

"Where do you want him?"

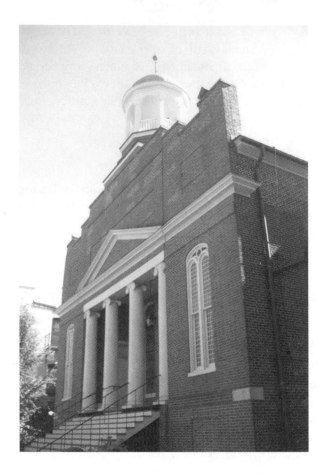

Christ Lutheran
Church as is today,
located on
Chambersburg
Street.
(Faber)

"Over there," one of the surgeons responded, pointing to an empty pew toward the front of the church.

Liz noticed the attention paid to the new wounded man and how it distracted the soldier guarding the group of colored folks. She also noticed the group had drifted close to the stairs leading to the bell tower. Without a word she grabbed Samuel's hand and led him to the side of the group closest to the stairs. She pulled him to slightly separate from the group. He said quietly:

"What's you's doing pullin' me's around?"

"Don't pays no never mind. Just do's what I's do's when I's say."

They stayed in their position for a few minutes and then they heard a loud scream from one of the soldiers being worked on. They looked over in time to see the soldier's leg being cut off. It was a terrible sight, but Liz had now become immune to this type of horror. Her mind was now on escaping. The wounded man continued to scream. She watched as all of the colored folks, and their guards, attention was on the surgeon and his attendants as they removed the bloody remnant of the leg and carried it over to the window. As they tossed the leg out of the window, the church doors flung open again, and another litter was being brought in. Liz noticed the wounded man was in very bad shape and was bleeding profusely, some blood spilling on the church floor as the bearers waited to find out where to put the man. The surgeon pointed again to an empty pew, and so the bearers began to move in that direction, but the rear bearer stepped in the pool of blood and slipped, dropping the wounded man onto the floor. This got the attention of everyone in the church, and one of the surgeons said:

"Be careful, you oaf."

He looked over at the guard of the colored folks and continued:

"You there, help get that soldier off the floor."

The Rebel looked stunned and confused, but set his rifle down, and went over to help with the fallen soldier, who was moaning. Liz saw this was her chance, as all eyes were on the soldier on the floor. She grabbed Samuel by the hand and the two of them quietly made their way to stairs leading to the bell tower. In an instant, they were up the first flight and around the corner and up the next flight. Within seconds they reached the top of the last flight and the trap door leading to the tower. Samuel carefully lifted the door open, helped his wife up into the tower and climbed up himself. He then quietly closed the door.

"We's dun it, Sam'l. We's free again."

"Shhh," he said with his index finger to his mouth. He continued:

"We's don't know if dey follo, so's be still fo awhile."

Sweating from the climb and from their nerves, they listened intently for the sound of footsteps coming up the stairs. After about five minutes of hearing none, they figured their escape was a success. Samuel smiled at his wife, kissed her and whispered:

"Ol Liz, you's foolet 'em. You's foolet 'em."

They lay quietly in the bell tower as the sounds of battle still encompassed them and then slowly died away. They could hear soldiers marching in the street coming from the west. They remained still until around six o'clock when suddenly, they heard shots right out in front of the church. They peaked over the ledge and down in front of the church. They saw a whole brigade of Rebel soldiers in front of the church. Then, they heard the church doors open and heard a voice from inside the church:

"What is going on out here? Can't you see we have men dying in here?"

"Sam'l, dats the Chaplin," Liz whispered.

Then, they noticed one of the Rebels approach the front of the church, put his left boot on the first step and say:

"Surrender, Yank, fore I shoot ya."

"I am a non-combatant and therefore I do not need to surrender as I am not allowed to fight," the chaplain answered.

Liz noticed the Rebel soldier raise his rifle and fire it. After, she saw the chaplain's body fall onto the landing at the stop of the stairs, and heard the Confederate say:

"Now ya a dead non-combatant."

Liz was stunned and she started to scream. But before any sounds came out of her mouth, Samuel covered it with his hand. He looked at her and said:

"What's you see, no matter, be still."

She looked at him and took several deep breaths under his hand and then in a minute she was calmer. Samuel looked back and gave her a glance of whether she was okay. She nodded and so he removed his hand from her mouth.

"Dey killt a Chaplin. Lord have mercy," she whispered.

They heard the commotion in the front of the church, as one of the wounded men from the church shouted:

"You bastard. Have you no shame? You killed a man of God. I hope you rot in hell for it!"

The Rebel didn't know what to say, and so one of the officers said:

"Private, ya get outta hea, now.

They continued to look and saw the man run, only to be knocked down by another soldier, who raised his rifle and was about to strike him when two other soldiers grabbed him and pulled him away. The last thing they heard was the officer say:

"Ya men, back in line."

CHAPTER 39

MYERS

ELIZABETH SALOME (SALLIE) MYERS awoke on Wednesday anxious, like most everyone in town, for what would happen that day. The Confederate Army was seen only a few miles outside of town, the northwest side. Sallie and her sister-in-law, Annie, had been curious last night, so they decided to take a walk out west on High Street to where it ended at West Street and have a look for themselves. Sallie remembered yesterday as they walked, they talked nervously of what would happen the next day. Sallie asked:

"Annie, do you think they will really attack tomorrow?"

"Oh yes, I really do. I hope our boys can give a better showing than at Winchester in June, and be victorious."

"What if they don't?"

"Well then we will have to bear the Rebels in our town again, like last week."

"I don't think our boys, now that Buford's Cavalry is here, will be defeated."

On this day her family was a little apprehensive of the outcome, and even packed up some belongings to leave, but when the time came to go, they couldn't. And, so they decided to ride out the battle at their home. Sallie's confidence with the Union army was high this day, however and so she was excited. This confidence became stronger as more and more troops arrived to join the battle. Sallie wanted to do something to help, so as the oldest daughter of the family, she organized her four sisters to hand water out to the men as they went by on Washington Street. She also gathered food, anything that was practical to hand out, and this too was given to the soldiers.

"Thank you kindly, ma'am," one responded.

"Goin' off to kill me some Rebels; make 'em pay for coming into our state," another said.

And, another said: "Whew, ain't she pretty?"

Sallie blushed, but kept handing out biscuits, slices of bread and fruit, until all she gathered up was given. Once the food ran out, they were left with water to give out and so they continued doing that.

By this time, the battle was raging. Sallie could hear the booming of the cannons and the rifle fire. And, off in the distance, she could see the smoke rising above the battlefield. She knew the battle was intensifying as the men were ordered to pass through the town almost on the run.

They took the cups of water and drank without pausing, and when they were finished, they tossed the cups aside. The girls would gather the cups up, fill them, and repeat the process.

Sallie was filling a cup with water when she looked up and noticed a man walking with a horse toward the rear area. Something was amiss, so she looked closer. To her horror, she noticed the horse was wounded and full of blood, all along its back, its mane and down one of its front legs. She had to look away. Her sister Virginia, who Sallie called Jennie and was two years her junior, said:

"Sallie, what's wrong?"

"Jennie, don't you see the blood all over that horse over there?"

"Yes, how tragic it is for that poor animal. Oh, I forgot, you don't like the sight of blood. It's okay, try not to look."

"How can I not look? I am afraid we will be seeing a lot more of that before long."

"Yes, I am afraid you are right. We are almost out of water. Should we get the youngens out of here before that becomes a common sight?"

"We should. Let's finish the water we have and go back home."

As they were saying this, a group of three men walked by. The one in the middle was limping heavily, and was leaning on the other two for support. Sallie saw his head was bandaged, but it had been done poorly, and so she could see he was bleeding underneath the bandage. She forced herself to look, noticing blood running down his face. She had to look away

The house where Sallie Myers lived during the battle as is today, located on High Street. (Faber)

again, and she forced the vomit coming up from her stomach, back down. She gulped hard several times in order to do this. She also could feel herself becoming light headed. She fought this urge, too, concentrating on hanging onto to her consciousness. She closed her eyes, leaned over and took deep breaths. After a minute, or so, she composed herself and handed out the last cup of water from the bucket she was using. Strengthen, she said:

"Myers, let us go back home."

And so, they did, knowing they had done everything they could to make at least a few soldiers journey to the battle a little easier.

They returned to their home on West High Street not knowing what to do next. All that could be done now was to wait, and so they did. At around three o'clock, Sallie went over to her brother's house to wait and to sit with Annie. She climbed the steps and knocked on the door. Annie answered and said:

"Oh, Sallie, come in, come in. Is there any news of the battle? The sounds seem to be getting closer. Jeff, Jeff, Sallie is here."

Sallie's brother Jefferson was three years older than Sallie, aged twenty-four, was tall, around six feet, had a long face, and eyes wider apart than average. He had light brown hair, parted on the left side of his head, light blue eyes, a pointed nose, and a mustache that extended below the corners of his mouth. He was dressed in brown trousers and boots, a white undershirt and a brown overshirt buttoned tightly around his neck. He had served in the Union army, fought in the war, was wounded and was discharged from the army earlier in the year. He was very fond of his closest younger sister, as she was of him. So much so, that he married her best friend Annie.

Jefferson was in the back of the house, and came immediately upon hearing his sister. He hugged her and said:

"Sallie, are you alright?"

"Yes, I am. A little shaken, though, I'm afraid. I saw a wounded horse and some wounded men coming through the town. It was awful, but I do think more are to come, many more."

"Yes, and we should be prepared. A battle like this is going to result in a lot of wounded men. I was gathering clean clothes to use for bandages."

Annie asked: "Jeff, do you think we will be needed to help care for the wounded?"

"I don't know, sweetheart, but we must be prepared if the need arises. Guess it really depends on if the battle spreads to the town, or if it stays to the northwest."

"I don't know if I can handle seeing a lot of wounded men. I had a hard time seeing that wounded boy bleeding earlier."

"Sallie, we may not have a choice. You may be called upon to help the doctors. We all may be."

"Suppose you're right, Jeff. I need to be stronger."

"You are strong, Sallie, one of the most devoted and strong women I know. Your deep faith makes you that way," Annie said.

"Annie is right. Your faith makes you strong, and clearly stronger than you think you are. We see it. You should, too," Jefferson echoed.

"Let's have a cup of tea and see if we can calm our nerves," Annie suggested.

And so, Annie made the tea and served her husband and her sister-in-law. They drank quietly. When they were finished, Annie gathered up the cups and put them in the kitchen. While she was in the kitchen, Sallie and Jefferson heard loud explosions. Sallie flinched and said:

"Jeff, that one was much closer, wasn't it?"

"Yes, the rifle fire seems closer, too."

Just then they saw a group of Union troops rush by their open door. Then, they saw another group, and then another.

"Jeff, my God, what is going on?"

"It looks like our troops are retreating into the town. That's why the rifle fire is closer. The Rebs must have broken our lines and the battle is coming into the town."

They went to the door, out on the porch, and noticed down the alley to the west more Union troops fleeing the battle and heading toward them. Sallie looked further down the alley and saw a group of Rebel troops chasing the Union troops, then stop and aim their rifles and fire. Sallie saw three Union men fall. She covered her mouth and gasped:

"Oh God, Jeff," she said.

Annie began to cry, and so Jefferson hugged them both tightly and while doing this, walked the women slowly back into the house and closed the door behind them. The ladies were highly upset and so Jefferson had to calm them down:

"Let's stay in here for awhile where it's safe', he said.

The women were crying very hard and so he continued to hug them. After about two minutes of hard crying, the women calmed a little, enough so Jefferson could let them go.

"There, there, are you two okay?"

Annie looked at Sallie and they hugged each other one more time, and Sallie whimpered:

"What an awful sight. Gunned down like that in the street. I don't think I'll ever forget that sight the rest of my life."

"I won't either," Annie said.

"You two stay here, I want to go and see if the Rebels are coming in town in force," Jefferson said.

"No, Jeff, you're not going out there!" Annie said.

"Annie, calm down. Eventually, we will need to go over to Mother's and Father's house and get into the cellar if the Rebs come into the town. I need to know if we should go now or not."

"Jeff, are you sure you should do that? Stay here where it's safe," Sallie said.

"You two listen. I will be alright. Close the door behind me and lock it just in case."

He opened the door and stepped out into the battle. The house was situated right in the middle of the retreating Union forces, which were occasionally being chased by Confederate soldiers. Men were running in every direction, mostly the Union men. Jefferson judged the Rebels hadn't penetrated the town with their main force, just the advance skirmishers, as the amount of Rebels in the town was sporadic. But, he knew it wouldn't be long before the main force would be here. He saw a group of Union men running his direction, and decided to find out what they knew, so he said:

"You men, what is happening?"

One of them stopped and said:

"The Rebels broke our lines both west and north of the town. We are to fall back into the town."

"How soon will they attack the town?"

"Any time. We expect them to start shelling the town, so you should spread the word the civilians should get into their cellars."

With that, he was off. Jefferson looked at his pocket watch. It was half-past three. He had gotten the answer he wanted and now he would go back to his house, fetch the ladies and get them over to his mother's and father's cellar, along with the rest of the family. After he returned, he said:

"Ladies, we have to leave. The Rebels will soon begin to shell the town, so we need to go now."

The three of them left and made it over to the Myer's house in a moment. Within ten minutes, they garnered the family and they all went down into the cellar. After they were settled, Sallie said:

"Jeff, our cellar can hold more. Should we offer it to others?"

"Yes. I will go."

"Jefferson…" his mother said and continued:

"Please, please be careful. I am so proud of you."

"I will mother, I will."

And with that, he climbed the stairs and went outside. Sallie could see him from a cellar window walking up and down High Street offering the cellar space to anyone who needed it. He gathered about ten people and led them down the stairs and into the cellar. By this time, the action from the battle had intensified, so Jefferson made it just in time. As he closed the door, they heard rifle fire very close to the house. They also heard shells flying overhead.

"Jeff, thank God you are back," Sallie said.

Annie just hugged him and kissed him lightly on the lips. Sallie took position at the window and watched the fighting outside. It was a horrible sight and in some instances the fighting was hand to hand. She had a renewed strength after her discussion with Jefferson earlier, but this was more than she could take, so she left the window spot and made her way over near her family. As the battle intensified, the noises became louder and closer. The banging of the cannon and the rifle shots, and the shrieks from the men being killed, or injured, began to take a toll on the people inside the cellar, including several children. There were three little ones in the cellar, two little girls and one little boy. They were all under five years old and their mothers tried to comfort them as best they could, but their screams and cries filled the cellar such that it almost became unbearable for Sallie. So, she decided she would try to distract the children in the hopes it would relieve their anguish. She picked up a pebble from the floor and went over to one of the little girls and got her attention. Once she had it, she showed the girl the pebble and then shook it in both of her hands, which were cupped. Then, she hid it in one of her hands and held them out to the little girl, and said:

"Which one?"

The little girl picked one, and in response, Sallie showed her an empty hand, and showed her the pebble was in the other. The girl stopped crying. Sallie repeated the trick and the girl this time picked the correct hand. Soon, she had all three children playing this game and they all stopped crying and played quietly with Sallie. She kept playing this game with them for a couple of minutes and then the children's mothers took over. Both mothers, as one of the girls and the boy were brother and sister, gave Sallie a grateful look.

Soon, the Union soldiers were retreating in large numbers and were rushing down the alley behind their house, closely pursued by the Confederates. A couple of them decided to escape the alley through the Myers' house. Sallie heard the backdoor to their house slam shut, followed by the same from the front door.

"Mother, father, they are running through the house to get away. How awful."

Annie replied:

"It must be terrible to have to run for your life like that."

"It is not only for their lives. It is not to get captured. The thought of a Southern prison had many of us just as scared as dying," Jefferson added.

Around six o'clock, the sounds of the battle thankfully died down. Sallie made her way back to the window where she was earlier and noticed a group of Union soldiers being held prisoner about ten feet from the window. Sallie opened the window and addressed one of them:

"Have you been captured?"

"Yes, and we are off to a Southern prison. Would you be kind enough to write my family and let them know we have surrendered and will be taken south to a prison?"

"I would be glad to," she replied and continued:

"If you give me your address, I will send your folks a letter hastily."

"I would be entirely grateful, ma'am."

Other captives heard this and asked the same of Sallie and she agreed to send letters for them too. Annie overhead this and came to join her friend. Each of men told Annie and Sallie their name, their unit in the army, and their home address. When the last one finished, the Rebels guarding them ordered them to move, and within a minute they were gone, the last one looking back at Sallie and Annie with a very sad face.

"They are just boys, most not any older than me," Sallie said to Annie.

"Did you see the look on that boy's face? It just breaks my heart to see them being led away like that."

"In some ways it's better than the alternative," Jefferson said pointing to a dead soldier in the road. He said to the group:

"I think it is over, so we can leave here. Please be careful and make it back to your homes as quickly as you can, particularly those of you with the children. Get them off the street before they see too much. You are going to see some gruesome sights, some things you have never seen before, so the less time you are outside, the better off you will be. It looks like the Rebels have the town, so be careful of that too. There will be some of them who it is just better you avoid, so get to your homes."

One by one, they left the cellar and emerged onto the street outside. The parents with the children ran to their homes and disappeared inside. Jefferson, Annie, and Sallie helped Sallie's parents and her sisters up the stairs and into their house. Once they were all in the house, Sallie asked:

"Annie, do you want to go outside?"

Annie looked at Jefferson and said:

"Jeff, is it safe?"

"Probably not, but there are a lot of boys out there that may need our help. Let's see if there is anything we can do."

So, the three of them went out on the porch of their house. They noticed the chaos of the area and the town was full of Rebels. One of them stopped and said:

"Gotcha any Fed troops y'all hidin' in thea?"

"No," Jefferson said.

"Y'all betta not be, for ya sakes."

Sallie looked around and saw several rifles, cartridge boxes, and other debris littering her yard. She then looked over to the street and saw the body Jefferson pointed out earlier. She gasped and said to Annie:

"Annie, that poor boy doesn't have a head. My God."

Annie looked over and was stunned into silence. Just then, a man approached the house from a direction east of there.

"I am Dr. James Fulton, Assistant Surgeon for the 143rd Pennsylvania Infantry. We are using the Catholic Church as a hospital and are in need of fresh linens, beef tea, and fresh water for the wounded. Can we use your kitchen?"

"Doctor, we would be more than happy to assist. Come into our house and tell us what you need from us," Sallie replied.

"Thank you so much. The church is filled with our boys and we are in need of whatever help you can provide us. I will be requiring the same of your neighbors."

Sallie, Annie, and the other sisters spent the remainder of the evening brewing beef tea, boiling blood soaked bandages, and baking bread for the wounded soldiers. It was a long night, but for Sallie the work took her mind off the ghastly sights she had seen today and the fact that the Rebels now occupy her town.

CHAPTER 40

BURNS

JOHN L. BURNS had just gotten settled at his post crouched behind a fence when he heard Lieutenant Rood yell:

"Alright, steady boys. Here they come!"

He had not yet loaded his rifle, so he rushed to do so, mumbling to himself to talk his way through it, making sure he drowned out that awful yell of the charging Rebels:

"Tear open the powder with my teeth, pour it into the barrel, add the bullet, and then ram it down. Cock the trigger and add the charge."

Once he finished, he looked up to see the butternut uniforms of the Rebels within shooting distance, coming in a line, so he raised his rifle, at the same time as a dozen or so of his comrades, and they all fired. He watched the volley tear into the oncoming Rebels and down five or six. He looked around quickly and noticed the fire coming from more of the Union soldiers, both to the left and to the right of him. He also heard bullets whizzing by over his head. He thought to himself: "I should be scared, but I am not. All my life I have waited for this moment, to find myself in a real battle and what better place than to fight for my town, my people, and my home."

He felt the chills all along his spine and the sweat coming from his excitement rolled down his back underneath his shirt. Then, he heard Rood again:

"Reload, boys, let's give 'em another taste of that lead."

So, he had to reload and fire again. This time, he mentally talked his way through the loading procedure. He looked over at his fellow soldiers and noted how fast they loaded and fired their rifles, about twice as fast, so when he was ready, they were ready too with their third shot while he was shooting just his second. He noticed how they waited for the volley from the Rebs and then stood up, aimed, and fired. He did the same, and clearly watched as the Rebel he fired at fell. This was noticed by the soldier next to him, who said:

"Good shooting, Daddie."

Burns just smiled at the boy, who couldn't have been more than twenty, a few years younger than Martha. He went at reloading his rifle. As he was doing this, the men fired again, and then they too had to reload. Again, he finished as they were ready for their next shot. He waited again for the Reb volley, and watched as the men next to him rose up to fire. He did the same and discharged his weapon for the third time. He watched his shot, this time a miss, and noticed more and more Rebels were coming in their direction, more he judged than they could hold off. Just then he heard Rood order:

"Men, fall back to the trees."

And, so they did, running in a crouched position. He followed them and found a tree to use as cover. He was right next to the same man who called him "Daddie."

"The man looked over to him and said:

"Let's keep the fire up, Daddie, or they'll whip us sure."

Burns nodded to his companion and reloaded his rifle. While he was ramming the bullet into the chamber, he looked out from behind the tree and noticed a large group of Rebels coming right for them. He continued ramming and looking as the Rebs came closer, right for him. As he finished and put his ramrod back on his rifle, he heard his mates fire into the group. He looked and saw that all of the Rebs were knocked down but one and that one was coming right for him! He realized the Reb was only a few paces from him as he raised his rifle. The Rebel did the same and fired at Burns from around ten feet. The bullet exploded into the tree and shed bark debris into Burns' face, but he was undaunted and he pulled his trigger.

He watched the scene intently. To him it looked like slow motion, very clear, but lacking of any sound. What was in reality only a fraction of a second seemed to him like several, maybe even ten or more. First, he saw the bullet heading slowly for the Rebel. He could see it in flight. He then saw the bullet penetrate the man's head in the middle of his forehead, causing a big black hole. Then, he saw the expression change on the face of his victim, ever so slowly, from the intensity of his charge to a grimace consisting of painful squinting of both eyes and gritting of his teeth. He then saw the slow motion of his head moving backwards from the blow and his cap float off. Then, dark, red blood came slowly oozing out of the hole. And then like magic, he saw his body lift into the air. He watched, as it seemed like seconds, the Reb airborne before he hit the ground. Finally, he saw his arms and legs shudder as his body absorbed the hit caused by the ground. He stared for what seemed several seconds more and then noticed the man had stopped moving. He was dead. All this happened to him while the sounds of the battle around him were inaudible to him.

He was still staring, when he saw the face of his companion and felt him shaking him. Slowly, he looked up at the soldier, who was talking to him, but he couldn't hear what he was saying. He fought this hard and then he began to hear muffled sounds coming from his mouth. He looked hard at the boy and the sounds finally caught up with the words he was mouthing:

"You're hurt, Daddie, you're hurt."

Burns felt his face and smeared a little blood on his cheek. He rubbed some more and could feel bark chips fall from his face. He said:

"Awe, that is no matter."

He pointed at the Rebel he shot and said:

"That was a brave man, that man there."

The boy was about to respond when he was hit in the back by two shots. The impact of the bullets caused him to fall into Burns, who caught him. The boy looked into Burns' eyes and said:

"Daddie…"

But, no more words would come as he was gone. Burns looked into the boys eyes and saw him pass as his eyes went still. He could feel his body still also. He didn't know what to do, but then he felt a bullet hit him. He slowly let the boy's body drop and looked down at his right side. He could feel the sting, but as yet, there was no blood. He pulled back his coat and looked for the blood, finding it beginning to coat his shirt. He gingerly touched his side, feeling for his ribs, and finding no pain from them, breathed a sigh of relief. He thought: "It must be just a flesh wound. I'll be alright."

Just then, he heard Rood again order the men to fall back. He took one more glance at the oncoming Rebels and noticed the Union line beginning to collapse from both sides. Off to his left, he could see the Union left flank dissolve. And, to his right he could see a gap had formed between his unit's right to the next unit's left, and the Rebels were pouring into this gap. He turned around and in a crouched position ran toward the woodpile. It took him about ten seconds to reach it and he heard, no, he felt the bullets passing him, both to his right and to his left. Once he reached the woodpile, he noticed he was amongst a different group of soldiers, as none of them looked familiar. He heard an officer say:

"Come on boys, let's make a stand right here."

And, so he loaded his rifle, moved clear of the woodpile, and fired. He watched the shot and it downed a Reb coming at him. He repeated and fired again, this time a miss, as the man he was aiming at was downed by another shot. He saw a great Rebel volley tear into the men to his left. He crouched behind the woodpile and heard shots pass above him. He reloaded his weapon and discharged it again, knocking another Rebel off his feet. But, he was slow in getting back to his cover and before reaching it, he felt a twinge in his left arm. When he was ducked behind the woodpile, he looked at his left arm. Again, he felt the sting of the shot, and he could smell the burnt wool from his coat, right at a spot with a black hole in the sleeve. Blood began to appear. He squeezed his arm below his elbow feeling for deeper pain that would be a sign that the bullet damaged one or both of his bones in his lower arm. He could feel no such pain, but did feel the pain from the muscle. He thought: "Again, only a flesh wound. No damage to the bones. I'll be fine."

He heard an officer order the men to fall back toward the Seminary, and so he waited until he thought he could avoid the next incoming Rebel volley. He rose to his feet and began to run, again in a crouched posture. He had taken about ten steps when he felt a fire in his leg and before he could understand what happened, he was knocked down face first onto the ground.

He lay there for about a minute, and then he tried to stand, but he could put no weight on his left leg. He looked down and saw a bullet had passed through his ankle. He knew the Rebels were close, and so he tried to crawl to safety. But, he couldn't move very much without a large effort and he was too tired from the battle, and maybe the loss of blood, to give what would be required, so he laid his head down.

It wasn't long, maybe a minute or two, that he realized the Rebels were running past him. He heard a Rebel officer growl a command, sounding almost like a wild animal:

"Get 'em, shoot 'em, kill 'em, or it will be the death of ya from ou guns."

He felt panicked as he was among the Rebels now, and he was a civilian who joined the battle, making it a capital offense of war. He would be treated as a bushwhacker and hung. His mind was racing. He had to act, but what to do? He decided the first thing was to get rid of his rifle and so he raised himself to a sitting position and flung the rifle as far as he could. It only managed to go about five feet, so he decided he would need to crawl away from it. He painfully pulled his body about twenty feet from his previous position and satisfied he was far enough away, but more, realizing he didn't have the strength to go further, he rested. What next? He thought: "I better bury my ammunition."

So he removed his knife from his pocket and began to dig a small hole in the ground. He cleaned the hole from the dirt and judging it deep enough, he pulled the shot from his coat pocket, tossed it into the hole, and covered it up. The process created a mound of dirt, similar to him to a mole hole, and it would be suspicious when he was found, so he decided he must flatten the mound. He began to roll his body back and forth over the mound and when he thought he had done the job, he rolled away from it about five feet, or so. Once he was clear of the mound, he laid his head back and thought: "What next? A story, I need a story as to why I was here and how I got wounded."

He thought for awhile, going over several scenarios, and eliminated them one by one except the one where his wife Barbara was sick. He mumbled:

"Yes, the old woman is deathly ill and I need to find her some help. Yes, a girl nurse who lives over yonder. I was caught in the battle going for a nurse and received all these wounds. Yes, that's the story."

He laid his head back down and listened as the battle was raging near the Seminary. He lifted his head and looked in that direction. He watched for only another moment and then put his head down, weary from the ordeal. He fell asleep.

He was awakened from his rest by strong hands turning him over. He looked up at the Rebel just as he said to some others:

"Found me a live one ova hea, and he's a civilyun."

His companions joined him, and they stood around Burns as the first soldier said:

"Ole man, what's ya doin' hea?"

Burns was groggy and that helped him tell his sad story.

"My poor, old wife is near death and I need to get a nurse for her. A nurse that lives yonder," he said pointing off toward the west and South Mountain.

The man leaned down and looked at the blood stain coat and trousers and said to his comrades:

"He's a lia. But no matta, he won't be hurtin' us no mo. He's gonna die."

And with that, they went on checking other men lying in the field. Burns felt relieved. Even if his story wasn't quite believed this time, he still was left be. But, he thought he needed a better story, so he pondered this for a minute or two. Then, he thought: "Yes, I have it. I was out here looking for my cows to save them from the battle. That should work."

He lifted his head and looked around him. He judged it to be around six o'clock by the location of the sun to the west. The battlefield was quiet now, save the occasional background shot from inside the town. He tried to move, but found it harder than before as he had lost a lot of strength, from the blood loss, he judged. Still, he decided that moving to another location was best, so he mustered the strength and pulled his body slowly so as not to arise any suspicion from the Rebel party gathering the wounded. He crawled for several minutes and then found himself in the midst of two dead Rebels and one dead Federal soldier. He was so tired from the effort he had exerted that he had to rest again. So, he laid his head back down and let sleep overtake him.

He awoke in pitch black darkness. It was raining and he felt the cool drops kiss his face. He looked up and saw another burial party putting dirt over the three dead men near him. They saw him move and one of them said:

"Hey, Saarg, that one is still alive."

The sergeant came over, looked at Burns and his bloody clothing and said to him:

"What a ya doin' hea, being a civilyun and all?"

Burns decided the new story was what he wanted to try, and so he said:

"I was out looking for my two cows to save them from the battle and got wounded from all the bullets flying around. You fellas with your war did this to me."

The sergeant was taken aback from Burns' accusation and was silent. Burns, seeing his tactic worked, asked:

"I am thirsty and cold. Could I get some water and a blanket? I am cold here."

The sergeant leaned down and looked at Burns' wounds. He lifted Burns' left arm and then he moved his left leg. Burns groaned at the tinge of pain in both movements, and so the sergeant in response said to his party:

"Get this hea man some wata, a blanket, and have the surgeon dress his wounds."

This was done, and as the surgeon left he said to Burns:

"Try not to move too much. The arm has stopped bleedin', but the wound could open up again. Same with that leg. I am sorry I can't do more to get ya outta hea, but I'm afraid we have ou men to attend to."

With that, he left Burns in the field. Burns lay there for several minutes more, but then began to close his eyes again. He used the blanket to cover his head from the light rain, and prior to falling asleep he reflected on his day. His wounds were causing him considerable pain, but that wasn't what he was thinking about. He was proud of his day, and even though his assistance didn't matter to the outcome of the battle, he knew he had at least done his part. He killed several of the Rebels and he fought in a great battle, something he wanted to do all of his life. He thought proudly he had served his country today, and he survived it...so far. This was his last thought as again sleep over took him for the final time of the day.

Earlier in the day Barbara Burns and her daughter Martha were concerned, rightly so, about Burns. The battle turned in favor of the Confederates resulting in the Union soldiers being driven from the field, that very same field Burns told them he was going to be fighting on. The Rebel soldiers had also taken much of the town and by early evening, around six o'clock, the issue was decided and much of the shooting stopped. The Union forces had retreated to Culp's Hill and Cemetery Hill while the Confederates began the occupation of the town, which included a house to house search seeking hiding Union men. Mrs. Burns and her daughter were frantic for news of Burns, but so far there was none. Then, came the sound of footsteps on their stairs outside their kitchen door, followed closely by a knock. At first it was a gentle, polite sounding knock, but quite shortly thereafter it became a thunderous noise.

"Mother, we need to answer," Martha said, over her daughter Mary's crying. Mary had missed her afternoon nap and was extremely cranky about it, making life relatively difficult for Martha.

"Yes, yes. I'll get it. Do you want me to take her?"

"That would be wonderful, and I'll answer the door."

And, so Martha handed Mary to Mrs. Burns and opened the door to see a Confederate officer and two soldiers.

"Evenin'" ma'am. I hate to be of bother to ya, but we must know if ya hidin' any Yankee sulders in this hea house," the officer stated.

"Why no, sir. We sure aren't," Martha replied.

"Iffen ya don't mind, we will be comin' in to search the house just the same?"

"I really do mind. My baby daughter has not gotten much sleep due to you and your infernal army coming up to our homes and starting that battle of yours."

"I do apologize to ya fo that. But, ya mussen remember, it was ya army that came to our houses first."

Martha was temporarily taken aback, but fired back:

"Beggin' your parden, sir but it was your side who fired the first shot."

"Now, ma'am I ain't hea to argue this with ya. We are a comin' in to look fo soldiers whetha ya likest it or not," the officers said in a tone just short of a yell.

While this debate was happening, both the Confederate soldiers and Martha failed to see, or hear, a group of Rebel officers on horseback, which had stopped in front of the house. One of the officers gestured to another and then the second dismounted and came into the yard and over to the foot of the stairs.

"Sageant?"

The sergeant turned around from the door to see who was calling him, and his companions did the same. Instantly, the three soldiers stiffened and saluted.

"Sageant?" the officer from below repeated.

"Yes, sir?"

"The general would like a word, if ya don't mind, now."

"Yes, sir."

He went down the stairs by two's and ran over to a fine looking white horse to address the general. He stopped and stood perfectly still, saluting. The general was in his sixties, Martha guessed, was dressed in a sharp looking uniform, topped off by a wide brimmed hat. He returned the salute, removed his hat, and wiped his brow with a handkerchief. Martha was astonished by this man's authority and wondered who it was. She also found it amusing to see the sergeant, for lack of a better term, squirming at his presence. Then he spoke:

"Sageant, Aye overheard ya conversation with the lady, and find it very inappropriate. We are hea as guests, in a manna of speaking, therefo ya will act accordingly with the propa respect. Undastood?"

"Yes, sir, yes Genrul."

"Now, go back and do ya duty."

"Thank ya, Genrul."

He saluted and then walked calmly back to the stairs, climbed them and came over to address Martha.

"Ma'am, we respectfully request ya pamission to search ya house for enemy sulders."

Martha watched as the officers on horseback rode off toward the town. She turned her gaze back to the sergeant and said:

"If you must. We are not harboring any soldiers in this house."

She stepped aside and allowed the three soldiers to enter. Mary was still crying and Mrs. Burns was bouncing her up and down on her hip. She said nothing to the Rebels greeting her, but instead said to Martha, while handing her the baby:

"She is really upset. Do you want to try and feed her?"

"Alright. No wonder with those soldiers in the house now," she replied purposely staring at the sergeant, who said nothing. So, Mrs. Burns addressed him:

"Sergeant, please do what you came here to do and make it quick like."

The sergeant ordered one of his men to stay with the ladies and told the other to accompany him on the search. After he was gone, Mrs. Burns couldn't help but to ask the remaining soldier about the battle.

"I gather since you are in my home that your side carried the day?"

"Yes, ma'am. We swept them Yankees from the field, thru the town, and down to them hills to the south."

Mrs. Burns became very concerned about Burns, but knew not to ask specific questions. She looked at Martha and then replied to the soldier:

"So, that farm where the battle took place. Is it completely in Rebel hands?"

"Yes, ma'am, as is most of the town, likes I say."

"Did our side lose a lot of men?"

"Well, sum, but the bulk of 'em skedaddled."

Mrs. Burns looked over again at Martha and then back to the soldier:

"And, what of the wounded? Are they being cared for? And, are they prisoners?"

"Well ma'am, ou medical folks a now gatherin' them up. Of course ou boys get first lookin' afta."

"What happens to the Union wounded?"

"They haveta wait thea turn, ma'am, till all ous a takin' care of."

After the soldier finished speaking, the sergeant and the other soldier rejoined them in the kitchen. The sergeant said:

"Let's go. Thea ain't no one else in this hea house."

He turned to Martha and Mrs. Burns and said:

"Thank ya kindly fo ya hospitality. Good day."

Martha handed Mary back to Mrs. Burns and said:

"Sergeant, before you go, I must ask who the general was?"

"Why, ma'am. Ya don't know?" he said in surprise.

Martha nodded her head no.

"That ma'am was Genrul Lee."

After the soldiers left, Martha said:

"Mother, I am very worried about Papa. Maybe I should have a look around? He could be wounded out there with no one caring for him."

"Martha, he chose to go."

"Yes, but what if he is bleeding to death and needs some help? I need to find out. What other explanation is there that he is not back yet?"

"I dunno. Do you think you can get a look around, and are you up to it? You may see a lot you don't want to see."

"I must, mother. I will not be able to sleep atall if I don't."

"Please be careful. I don't want to lose you too, if your father is gone."

"Mother, please don't say such awful things. I will find him if he is there."

So, Martha set off for the battlefield on McPherson's farm. She walked along Chambersburg Pike and saw the destruction left by the battle. She heard the groans of the wounded and saw the Rebel medical personnel treating and removing them. She dared not get off the Pike and therefore she didn't get a good view of the men who were not in close proximity to the road. She began to get more sickened at the site of the bleeding and broken bodies of the soldiers, so much so that she couldn't go on much further. She noticed in the distance a couple of hundred yards away, far enough that they were just figures, shadows really, and not recognizable to her, a party of men looking at one of the soldiers and then they left him. She assumed it was a soldier, who had sometime during the day, lost his blue uniform coat, as he was dressed differently. She saw the soldier begin to crawl away, and felt pity for the man. She said to herself:

"One of ours and they cannot seem to help him."

She mustered up the courage to leave the road and see what she could do to help. She had not gone far from the road when suddenly her leg was grabbed by a Union soldier, who said in a very feint voice:

"Ma'am…water?"

She bent down to look at soldier, who was lying on his side. She turned him and was horrified to see he had been bleeding from a wound in his chest and one in his stomach. She looked at his ashen face, and she saw him smile at her, right before he stopped breathing and the life left his body. He was still looking at her with his eyes fixed squarely on her's and the smile still on his face, when she realized he had just died. A chill went up her spine and she screamed. The scream alerted the Rebel medical folks and they rushed over to see what caused her reaction. While they were coming over, she gently let the soldier's body fall back to the ground, and straightened up with her hands to her face and began to cry, loudly.

"Ma'am, ya shouldn't be out hea," one of them said and gently approached her and gave her a soft hug. He continued:

"This is no place fo a lady. Can ya please return to ya home?"

Martha said nothing, and so he turned to one of his companions and said:

"Corporal, please see this woman home."

The corporal came over to Martha and gently grabbed her shoulders, turning her away from the sight of the dead soldier, saying:

"Ma'am, I's a takin' ya home now. Please let me know the way."

Martha was still crying, but pointed toward her home.

"Alright now, let's begin walkin'."

It took them about five minutes to get to the Burn's home, and upon arrival, the corporal walked her up the stairs and knocked on the door. Mrs. Burns answered and instantly stepped out to hug Martha. The corporal said:

"Ma'am, if ya please. She has seen a little mo than she can handle."

And with that, he left. Mrs. Burns escorted her into the house and said:

"Dear, what happened?"

Martha said between sobs:

"Mother, I saw a man die right in front of me. I saw his life end as he was looking right at me. Right at me; really, through me. He asked me for water and then he was gone. And, he was smiling. I'll never forget that look on his face for as long as I live."

"There, there dear. You just sit right down here and I'll get you a cup of tea."

Martha and Mrs. Burns shared a cup of tea, and it seemed to calm Martha down. She forgot all that she had seen, except the look on the dead man's face. She kept telling Mrs. Burns of it and nothing else. Not even the fact that right before the dying man grabbed her leg, she was headed to see if she could help a perceived Union soldier, which was in reality her father, as he was crawling away. The thought never crossed her mind again, as she didn't know that it was indeed Burns who she was attempting to help.

CHAPTER 40

CULP

JOHN WESLEY (WES) CULP was lounging around in his tent this morning, just as he had done for the past couple of days. It had been twelve days since the regiment crossed the Potomac in Maryland and then entered Pennsylvania. During their time in Pennsylvania, they made stops at Scotland before coming to their current location of Fayetteville, which was about nineteen miles west of Gettysburg, his home town. So far, this was a good thing for Culp as he wasn't very enthused about coming home to Gettysburg, knowing full well he would not be welcomed by many of the town folk due to his enlistment in the Confederate Army.

Culp was a sleeper, so he took every opportunity he could to stay in his tent in the mornings. His best friends B.S. Pendleton and William Arthur had already risen and were about the camp, so he was able to have a little peace and quiet. This was abruptly interrupted when Pendleton stormed into the tent at about noon o'clock.

"Wes, Wes, get up. It looks like them Yanks are puttin' up a fuss near ya town. We need to get ova thea to give 'em our attention."

"What? Near Gettysburg?"

"Yes, the couria just arrived in camp and said we need to move out immediately to Gettysburg."

"B.S., looks like I am going home after all."

"Sure do. Say, maybe we could go to ya house for some home cookin'?"

"Probably not a good idea, you know what they think of me."

"Ya said that about ya friends in Wincheta, 'member that?"

"I do, but those were my friends, some my best. That's different."

"Sure, ya mean the childhood friends ya tryin' to shoot and them shooting at ya?"

"B.S., don't remind me of that. I still don't feel right about that."

"Wes, it is war, so lots is diffaent. But, we a talkin' about goin' home. Ya mean ya family holds a grudge."

"Could be. You know I've written many times and have yet to receive any word in response."

"Ya just wait, it'll be fine. Besides, I wanta meet ya sistas."

"They may be on the other side of this war, but that still doesn't make you good enough for them," Culp said with a smile and threw his cup at Pendleton.

Pendleton caught it with his right hand and said:

"That so? Well, I have it on good word that any friend of their brotha's is a friend of theirs."

They both laughed and Pendleton said throwing the cup back to Culp:

"Get up ya lazy lump and get some coffee. We need to be ready to move out in 'bout twenty minutes, so ya gots to get goin'."

Culp got up and quickly packed his knapsack and the rest of his belongings and went out of the tent just as Sergeant Sheetz came by yelling:

"Men we a movin' out in fifteen minutes. Let's get a goin'. Line up in five."

Culp made his way to the coffee wagon and got a full cup along with three biscuits, two of which he put in his pocket. He went to his tent, retrieved his belongings and made the line next to Pendleton and Arthur. Arthur said:

"Nice of ya to join us. Sorry the wa had to interrupt ya sleepy time."

"Stuff it Bill."

"Awe, a little snappy this mornin'?"

Naw, just a little anxious."

"What fo?"

"Just not excited 'bout going to Gettysburg, that's all."

Pendleton said:

"He doesn't think the town will be too excited to see him."

"Well, they probably ain't gonna be too happy to see any of us, so's ya in good company."

Sergeant Sheetz came by and ordered:

"Alright men, let's move out at a quick step; ou boys need us, so let's get thea."

And, so the Stonewall Brigade moved forward. First, they headed south to connect with the Chambersburg Pike and then they headed west toward Gettysburg. It took a few minutes to get into the marching rhythm, but soon they were making good time.

"Let's see, Gettysburg is nineteen miles away, so we should get there by around six o'clock, at this pace."

Culp, as his usual practice, let his mind drift into thoughts away from the march. He thought of Gettysburg and the hatred of the folks he could be receiving once they arrived and found out he was with them. What would they say? Then, he thought, what if he saw William again? He remembered the look in his eyes at Winchester and how he deliberately shot to kill him. He hoped he could avoid a repeat of that, or this time he might need to shoot back. That thought was too disturbing, so he let his mind drift to happier times at Gettysburg. He thought again of his childhood, walking on the farm and being around the animals. He could smell the fall harvest hay and he almost sneezed because the smell was so real to him. He remembered how much he loved his mother, and thought how a visit there might revive the hurt he still felt when she died.

He smelled bread. Then, he saw his mother looking down at him while he was eating a slice freshly baked. How old was he? Maybe ten? He could see his mother coming over to him at the kitchen table. She said:

"Wesley, do you want Mama to put some apple butter on your bread?"

He heard his answer:

"No, Mama, it's yummy as it is."

"Well, eat up and I'll have some peach pie ready for a treat for my little angel. You'd like that wouldn't you?"

"Oh yes, please Mama."

He remembered her coming over to him, putting her hands gently on his cheek, kissing him on his forehead, hugging him, and saying:

"Wesley, you are my precious, precious boy. Mama loves you so much."

"Me too, Mama."

His thoughts returned to the present. It was a hot day and he was sweating from the exertion of the march, but the moisture running down his cheeks was not from sweat, rather it was tears. He removed his hat and wiped his forehead, his eyes, and cheeks with his sleeve. He returned his hat to his head and pulled it on straight. He tried to think of something different, but to no avail. He was going home so his mind was swimming with images and memories he hadn't thought of in years. He remembered falling off a horse when he was eight years old. He remembered hitting the ground and then he felt the pain in his left shoulder. Pain so real, he could feel it now.

"Wesley, Wesley, are you alright? Are you hurt?" his mother said as she ran to him.

He got up, rubbed his shoulder and then the pain was enough that he couldn't stop himself from crying. His mother reached him and gingerly hugged and rocked him, saying:

"It's gonna be alright, my son, Mama's here. You just go ahead and cry. Go ahead. It will feel better in a couple of moments. Mama's here."

This memory too caused him to shed some tears. His mother was gone, and now he was going back to a place where his love for her, and an emptiness because she was gone, dominated his thoughts.

Within about three hours, they were within about ten miles of Gettysburg and had passed South Mountain to their right about a half an hour ago. It was three o'clock he guessed as he judged the time that had passed so far on this march. The scenery was beginning to be very familiar to him. He had played in these woods many times as a boy, had ridden horses, and had hunted here as a teenager. It all looked just as he remembered it. And, his memory was very vivid and clear. It was as if the background scenery from his memories had come to life. He was thinking of, and experiencing, things just as if they happened yesterday, and the really strange thing is he felt like he was younger too. He thought this must be what it was like to come home after being away for a long, long time. All of his senses became more acute. He heard the sounds of home, he smelled the smells of home, and even the feel of the road beneath his feet was home. On cue, Pendleton said:

"Wes, ya feelin' like home?"

"Yes, and it is remarkable. The sounds, the smells, the sites...all home."

"Well, that's natrul. Hasn't it been five years since ya been back?"

"Almost. It sounds like a long time, but it feels like only yesterday."

Arthur said: "Sua is beautiful country, Wes. I've thought just so eva since we been up hea."

"Tell me again, why did ya leave?" Pendleton asked.

"It seemed like the right thing to do at the time."

"And, now?"

"Of course. If I didn't, I might be shooting at you today instead of with you. And, with that big head of yours B.S., how could I miss?" Culp joked.

Arthur laughed with Culp as Pendleton responded:

"Well, ain't ya the smart one?" He continued:

"Probably so, probably so."

Culp stopped laughing and said in a serious tone:

"We all know we are destined to survive this war no matter what happens, even if I was over there with them," he finished and pointed toward Gettysburg and the Yankees.

They finished talking and in the background they could hear the artillery firing back and forth ahead. They continued their march and by after four o'clock, were less than six miles away. Suddenly, they heard the sergeant again:

"Men, slow down to noamal step."

And, so they did. While they were gradually slowing their pace, Pendleton observed:

"Well, if they don't need us in a hurra, we musta licked 'em."

"Maybe, it'll be like Winchesta where we just mopped 'em up?" Arthur added.

"Don't be so sure, yet. It will be different from Winchester. That's sure. These boys are fighting on home soil now, and it's gonna be quite a fight we got coming, so just keep your heads down," Culp said.

"Ya too. We wouldn't want to see anything happen to ya, specially on your home ground," Arthur replied.

"Wouldn't that be somethin', a Reb killed invadin' his own town?" Pendleton speculated and continued:

"That story would be for the ages. Ya'd be famous, Wes. Or, should I say *infamous*?"

Culp hadn't thought of that before, as he was so concerned about returning home, he hadn't thought what a tale it would make if he were killed here in Gettysburg. He said:

"Just what I wanted to hear, B.S. Another reason to make sure I survive the fight."

"Ya gots plenty reasons to suavive, startin' with that little belle awaiting fo ya at home in Richmond."

Culp's thoughts went back to Catherine. If it wasn't for this war, he could be bringing her to meet his family. Then he thought:

"Not in this lifetime, not in this one."

They finished their march just after six o'clock in the evening. They were told to halt at McPherson's farm. Culp could see the remnants of the battlefield and now the parties of men beginning to gather up the wounded and the dead. Off in the distance, he saw the Lutheran Seminary glistening in the early evening sun. He wondered what had been seen from that vantage point, and speculated probably the whole battle. He continued to look when he saw a glint from field glasses in the cupola.

"Look at the cupola above the Seminary over there," he said and pointed to it, then continued:

"We must be using it as a lookout."

"S'pose it's a good look from up thea," Pendleton said.

At that time the sergeant said:

"Men, we have driven the Yanks from the town. It is ours."

The men broke into a loud cheer and when they quieted down, he continued:

"The enemy has been driven from the town and has taken refuge south and east of it. We a ordaed to proceed to the north and east of town and camp thea to await furtha ordas. We will form the left flank of ou lines on a hill called Culp's Hill. Alright, now let's get ready to move out."

Both Pendleton and Arthur looked at Culp, but each said nothing. So he said:

"Yes, that is my family's land and my second cousin's hill. Remember the picnic on the hill I told you about? Well, that's it. And, my father's farm is just to the north of it."

"My God, Wes, ya truly have come home."

"It looks a though I am. But, there'll be no welcome for me, least not the friendly kind. None for a traitor."

They marched through the town on Chambersburg Street and Culp pointed out the sites for them, feeling a little more comfortable, but still apprehensive in that at any time he could see a familiar face. They reached the corner of Washington Street, and so he pointed off to the left:

"That there fine establishment is the Eagle Hotel. I had my first ale in that there place. Awe, I can taste it now."

"Well if ya can taste it then why don't ya share it?"

"If only I could, my friend, if only I could."

They passed Washington Street and were approaching the Diamond, the center of town. Off to the right was the Christ Lutheran Church. Culp pointed to it too saying:

"Where I worshiped as a boy."

"Ya mean its still standin'? I'd a thought afta that ordeal of havin' ya in thea, it would have fallen down," Pendleton mused.

"So amusing, B.S. So amusing, yet a bunch of bullshit," Culp said and paused before continuing:

"Hey, bullshit. Yeah, B.S., bullshit. Kinda fits, wouldn't you say?"

"Sure do," Arthur added, "Sure do. That's a good one, sure."

They laughed at Pendleton while he was at a loss for words. Suddenly, they heard shots right out in front of the church. Their attention was drawn to the sounds. Then, they heard the church doors open and heard a voice from inside the church:

"What is going on out there? Can't you see we have men dying in here?"

Culp noticed for the first time, the church was being used as a hospital. He noticed a man in Federal uniform appear at the door of the church and step out onto the porch. One of the men, not from his brigade, who appeared to have been part of the fighting for the town as he looked fairly tattered, approached the front of the church, put his left boot on the first step and said:

"Surrender, Yank, fore I shoot ya."

"I am a non-combatant and therefore I do not need to surrender as I am not allowed to fight," the man answered.

Culp noticed the soldier raise his rifle and fire it. After, he saw the man's body fall onto the landing at the top of the stairs, and heard the soldier say:

"Now ya a dead non-combatant."

Culp was horrified. The man was not defending himself and was therefore not a threat. He was trying to help wounded men. He felt anger boil in him.

He then heard a commotion in the front of the church, as one of the wounded men from the church limped out onto the porch, bent down to check on the man, and seeing he was dead, shouted:

"You bastard. Have you no shame? You killed a man of God. I hope you rot in hell for it!"

The soldier didn't know what to say, and so Sergeant Sheetz said to him:

"Private, ya get outta hea, now.

The soldier looked dumbfounded and for a second or two, did not know what to do. Sheetz repeated:

"Did ya hea? I said, get outta hea. Now, move."

The soldier looked at the sergeant again and then began to move toward where Culp was. As he got closer, Culp, who was on the outside of the column of the brigade, separated from the others and moved toward the soldier to intercept him. Within a second, the soldier was in his range, and Culp raised his rifle with both hands and shoved it hard into the soldier. The soldier was completely surprised by the blow and was knocked off his feet. Culp went and stood over him, raised his rifle, and said:

"I oughta beat you to death myself."

He moved his rifle downward preparing to strike a blow, when he felt hands on him stopping him from doing it.

"Wes, Wes...," Pendleton said as he and Arthur pulled him away from the fallen soldier.

Culp pointed threateningly at the soldier and said:

"You are lucky today I am not able to finish the job, but if I ever see you again, I will. I will..."

Sheetz observed this and up until now decided he would not get involved, as the soldier deserved what Culp was giving, but it was time to move on, so he said:

"Ya men, get back in line."

They made their way through the center of town and turned south onto Baltimore Street. Culp was no longer in a mood to point out the sites. He was still shaken by the sight of the man murdered in front of the church. He said:

"I would have killed him. I swear to God I would have killed him right there."

"I know, and if we weren't in front of the whole brigade, we would have letcha," Pendleton replied.

"My God, did ya hea that wounded man say he was a man of God?"

Culp was too upset to say anything, so Pendleton said:

"Yes, I wonda if indeed he will rot in hell?"

"Hope so," Culp mumbled.

They continued walking along Baltimore Street and Arthur, to lighten the mood, said:

"What's the tall buildin', ova thea, Wes?"

He was pointed at the newly completed courthouse, but since Culp was away, he didn't know.

"Not sure. It must have been built since I left. That was where the courthouse was, but it was pretty old. Maybe it's the new one."

They continued south on Baltimore Street and Arthur asked again:

"What's that off to the right ova thea?"

"The Rupp Tannery, and further is the home of John Rupp, one of the most prosperous men of the town."

As they continued past the Rupp residence, they heard shots being fired, and saw Confederate skirmishers shooting at the hill to the south, with more shots coming from the upstairs of several of houses both near and behind them. The sergeant said:

"All halt."

Once the men stopped, the sergeant continued:

"Ahead is Culp's Hill, which clearly is still in enemy hands for now. We will be taking up a position this side of the hill, so move out to the left and advance no furtha until ordas given."

So, the column turned left and down an alley. Culp, Pendleton, and Arthur had not yet passed into the alley, when they saw up ahead a couple hundred yards a young lady run out of a house and bend down to a wounded Yankee. They looked closer and saw she was giving the soldier a drink. Pendleton remarked:

"Is that woman daft, comin' out into the middle of a fight?"

Culp, who had good vision from a distance, noticed something familiar about the girl. Maybe it was the dress, or maybe the posture, but she was familiar.

"She looks familiar," he said.

"Sua, and from this distance ya can see ha? Are ya sure ya not seeing things?"

"I'm telling you she looks familiar. I can see that far," Culp replied as he took another look, this time as hard as he could see. And, then the memory of one his childhood friends became clear, and so he said to no one in particular:

"Ginnie? Ginnie Wade?"

"Who? Ginna Wade?"

"Yes, that's her. You remember Jack Skelly in Winchester? That's his girl."

"I rememba mention of ha. Are ya sure?"

"Mostly. But, it hast to be her."

At that moment, he remembered the letters Jack gave him, patted his chest and felt the pouch he was carrying them in, and took a sigh of relief they were still safe on his person.

Within an hour, they were camped and the sun disappeared over South Mountain to the west. The Rebels knew the Union had yet to place artillery on the hill, so for the time they were out of range of the Federals. They camped north of the hill and within shouting distance of his father's farm. Culp looked over at the house several hundred yards away and remembered the way it looked and smelled inside. He remembered how his room was his refuge as a boy. He would need to visit it while he was here, at least he hoped.

Culp went back into his tent, and after having unpacked his things, he reflected on seeing Ginnie. He was still surprised he had seen her, but he now knew where she would be and would try to deliver Jack's letter to her tomorrow, after the Federals have been driven off Culp's Hill and the area was more secure. He patted the pouch holding the letters, when Pendleton came into the tent:

"Wes, ya got a letta," he said and handed it to Culp.

"Really, I wonder who it is from?"

He looked and saw no return address on it, so he ripped it open and read silently:

"*Private Culp,*

I regret to have to inform you that your friend Jack Skelly, of whom I have been taking care of, has fallen into a sleep of which he has yet to awake from. His condition worsens by the day. The doctor has said it is certain he will pass from this earth in the next couple of days, or so. As I know you would want to hear this sad information as soon as possible, I have posted this letter with the army and asked it be delivered to you in the most urgent of means.

I trust this letter finds you well.
Sincerely,
Elizabeth White
Nurse: Confederate Army of Northern Virginia"

Culp read the letter once and then twice to make sure of the news that Jack was dying, and could be dead already. Pendleton noticed his friend's mood change and asked:

"Wes, what is it?"

"I just got a letter from the nurse taking care of Jack, Jack Skelly, back in Winchester. He is not doing so well, and is going to die, if he hasn't already," Culp said.

He felt tears in his eyes as he remembered the last time he saw his friend in that hospital and the deep look of eternal friendship they shared. He would never see him again. Pendleton noticed and said:

"I'll be outside if ya need anything, anything at all."

"Thanks, B.S."

After Pendleton left, Culp lay down on his blanket and let the tears flow. He thought of the times he had as a boy with Jack. How happy they were. He was one of his closest friends and now he too would be gone. He thought of Ginnie, and how happy he was to see her, and happy that he could deliver Jack's letter of marriage to her. Now, he would have to tell her he was never coming back to fulfill that promise of marriage, and that he was no more. He thought of this and many more thoughts of when he was happy with his friends of this town. All gone, were these, all gone. He fell asleep with still tears running down his face.

CHAPTER 41

WADE

VIRGINIA (GINNIE) WADE awoke early the morning of July 1, 1863. She had not slept well as she knew, as all the townspeople did, the battle with the Confederates would begin today. She had seen the buildup of Union troops with the cavalry moving through town yesterday to take up the defensive position on McPhersons's farm. She hoped it would some-how all go away and so she listened intently for the sounds of the battle, and upon hearing them before ten o'clock in the morning, she knew the battle was at hand. Now, she had to act quickly, as she decided if the battle came, she would move both Isaac and Harry down to her sister's house on Baltimore Street, on the south side of town.

"Boys, boys, it is time we get going to sister Georgia's."

"Has the battle started?" Harry asked excitedly.

"It seems so…shh, and listen."

They were all quiet and then they heard in the distance the boom of the cannons.

"How exciting. Do we really have to go all the way down to Georgia's?" Harry asked.

"Yes, we must. Now, you get yourself ready in case we have to stay a few days. Isaac, have you got your clothes ready?"

"Right here in my knapsack."

"And, your board for your lessons?"

The boy drooped his head and said:

"No, do I really have to bring that old thing?"

"You do and the charcoal too."

"Awe, Ginnie…"

"Isaac, what would your mother think if I let you slack on your lessons?"

"We could just say we couldn't do it because of the battle."

Ginnie bit her lip and thought Isaac had a point and so she said:

"Alright, but when we get back, you will have to catch up with the lessons you missed."

"I will, I will," the boy said excitedly.

"Harry, you lock the door behind me and I will be back for you in about twenty minutes. Isaac, climb on."

She sat down on the bed and Harry helped put Isaac on her shoulders. She carefully went down the stairs and waited for Harry to open the door. He did and she said:

"Now, lock it, please."

She heard the door close and the key turn to lock the door. She walked up Breckinridge Street toward Baltimore Street. She had forgotten how tiny Isaac was. She carried him all the time, but only when he was on her shoulders did she understand what the disease had done to his growth, both in height and in weight. But, what didn't have in his frame, he had in his heart. He continuously proved that to her, one of the reasons why she cared so deeply for him.

"Miss Ginnie, I sure am thankful you take care of me, and I sure am thankful you are taking me to safety away from this battle, as exciting as it sounds."

"I am thankful for you too, Isaac. You must remember, however a battle like this one will harm a lot of people, even kill some."

"You're right, but I have never seen a battle before."

"Neither have I, and I hope I never see one again after today."

Ginnie arrived at Georgia's about ten minutes later and after dropping Isaac off with her mother, returned to fetch Harry. She was back in another ten minutes at the house and then off within a minute, or two. They listened as the battle seemed to intensify and the crackling of the rifles could now be heard. She and Harry walked as fast as they could and presently arrived back at Georgia's house, just as Union soldiers were coming north on Baltimore Street and passing the house. After securing Harry in the house, she paced around wondering what could be done. She decided to bake bread, and so she went about doing this. While the bread was baking, she again paced. She looked out the front window, which faced north, and watched the soldiers go by. She spied a few men drinking from canteens and then throwing the canteen away as it was empty. She decided she could fetch water and give it to the thirsty soldiers as they went by. She said:

"Georgia, where is your water pail?"

"On the back porch, Ginnie, why?"

"I am going to give them water. They look like they need it."

And, so she grabbed three cups from the kitchen and then went to the back porch to get the pail. She went out to the well on the east side of the house and filled the pail. After the pail was filled, she went out to the front and set it down on the grass next to the road. She filled a cup and said:

"Cup of water?"

This filling of cups began at around eleven o'clock and continued for the next two hours, or so. Ginnie went back and forth to the well and then filled the cups of water until her dress was saturated from the spills created by her baling. While she was doing this, her mother took over with the bread baking, and this was handed out as soon as it was cool enough to handle. Then, an odd thing occurred. The men stopped heading north and there were now men headed south from the battle. Ginnie was puzzled, until she decided to ask what was going on:

"Water here. Do you know what's happening?"

"Well ma'am, we were overrun by the Rebs and we are falling back, back to that hill behind you."

Pretty soon, the men coming from the north, retreating, were coming in great numbers. Ginnie continued handing out the water, but soon found it becoming increasingly dangerous being out in the street. She could see the urgency because the men didn't bother stopping for the water, but she was determined to stay as long as possible. She filled the cups and then set two on the sidewalk and held the other out to a soldier.

A few moments earlier, two Rebel sharpshooters, who had taken over the attic in Hettie Shriver's house, the house just to the south of the Pierce house, began to set up for firing at the Union soldiers. One of them began shooting at the retreating Federal troops. He shot and then yielded the window to his partner. The other said:

"Break out some of them bricks round the winda and we can both shoot."

The McCellan House Museum as is today, located on Baltimore Street. Note a statue of Ginnie Wade adorns the front of the museum. (Faber)

He did so, and within a minute they were both shooting as fast as they could reload their rifles.

One said to the other:

"Look yonder, down in front of that red brick house. See the lassy givin' wata?"

"Oh yeah, what of it?"

"See how she holds it out to them? Kin ya hit the cup?"

"What if I hit the girl instead?"

"Don't. I'll shoot at the soldya and ya shoot at the cup. Whatever we's hit, we's hit. She shouldn't be out in the line of fia anyway."

They both aimed and waited for the cup to be filled and handed to a soldier, and when the appropriate moment came, they fired their rifles.

Ginnie was offering a cup of water to a soldier and he was reaching for it when she heard a thump and then she felt the cup fly out of her hand with a sting. She was startled and then she saw the soldier fall right at her feet. She put her hands up to her face and screamed. This was heard by a group of soldiers, who at once came over to her.

"What's wrong Miss?"

By now she was crying, and she said pointing at the man who was shot:

"He was shot right in front of me, and they, they shot my cup out of my hand."

"What? They shot the cup from your hand?"

"Yes, it was awful."

"Miss, we need to get you inside. Can you walk over to the door with us please?"

They surrounded here to shield her from the shooters and walked her to the door. One of them knocked and when the door was opened by Mary Wade, said:

"Ma'am, please don't let her outside again until this is decided. Please keep her safe, as she is very brave and she is very important to us for what she, and you, have done. I am Sergeant Laurence Cook of the 94th New York Infantry. Please remember me. And, you are?"

"I am Mary Wade, Sergeant and this is my daughter, Miss Ginnie Wade."

"Miss Wade, you and your daughter have done a tremendous kindness to us and the only thing we can do to repay you is to get them Rebs who shot at her. This we will do. Now, please close the door and stay safe inside. We will be outside protecting the house."

The sergeant then closed the door before Mary could. Ginnie walked over to the front window and watched. It was about three o'clock in the afternoon and the deluge of retreating Federal troops became a flood of moving men, heading southward, past the house. Ginnie screamed as she saw two more men fall, she suspected from the same men who shot her cup out of her hand. She also cringed as she heard a bullet hit the side of the house a few feet from the window she was looking through.

Her mother yelled: "Ginnie, get away from that window!"

And so, she moved away but not before another shot hit the side of the house, and as she saw several Union men, at the order of Sergeant Cook, aim and fire their guns in the direction away from the house toward the north. She heard the sergeant say:

"Keep a sharp eye, boys. We want those bastards, so find out where they are shooting from. Let's be careful, so use the house as cover. And, where are those sharpshooters we asked for?"

Just then, there was a knock at the back door. Ginnie decided she would get the door, and answered it to find several Union soldiers.

"Pardon us, ma'am, but mighten we have some bread if you have some?"

"We do, and I will get you as much as we have."

She went to the kitchen and sliced the bread that just came out of the oven and handed it out.

"Mighty obliged, ma'am."

For the next couple of hours, she worked hard to bake bread and serve it to the soldiers. The door was constantly being knocked on by soldiers requesting it. And, so she was really busy.

It was after six o'clock, when the sharpshooters Sergeant Cook requested arrived at the house. Ginnie heard the soldiers talking outside, and then heard a knock at the door. She opened the door and saw that is was Sergeant Cook.

"Miss Wade, it seems that the Rebels have decided to halt their advance for the day, but the danger is not over, as this house of yours is right in the middle between the lines. They still have the sharpshooters we have to attend to, so please stay inside and away from the windows. We will be staying as long as needed to protect you and your family."

"Thank you kindly, sergeant."

"Not at all, ma'am."

She closed the door, but heard someone come up to the sergeant, and say:

"Sir, we have located the Rebels who we think have been shooting toward the house. Can you come around to the front so we can show you?"

Ginnie decided to go to the window to see where the shooters were. She saw Cook come from around the house and he and the other soldier look northeast toward the tannery. The other soldier pointed toward the tannery and then they both pointed. Just then, Ginnie saw both of them get hit and fall. She screamed loud and covered her eyes. Mary came over and said:

"Didn't I tell you to stay away from the window?"

"Mother, they shot him. They shot the sergeant."

"Oh, my Lord, Ginnie," she said as she hugged her daughter. They went to the window and peeked out to see if the sergeant was alive. They saw him and the other soldier move a little and so they were still alive, but for how long?

Just then, they heard two shots fire from right outside the door, one from each side of the house, and one right after the other one. Seconds later, they heard a roar:

"Hurrah!" from several of the men outside. One soldier continued:

"Got'em both. Great shooting, boys. Did you see them fall out of the window, both of them, just like a rock being thrown into a pond. Great shooting, that's what that was."

Ginnie went over to the back door, opened it, and asked for one of the soldiers from the 94th New York. In a moment, a private arrived.

"Ma'am you asked for someone from the 94th?"

"Yes, do you know how the sergeant is?"

"Ma'am, I do believe he is alright, but now that we got those Reb bastards, we can make sure."

"Is it safe to go out front? I will like to bring him some water?"

"I s'pose it's alright. I can protect you."

Ginnie said:

"Thank you kindly. I will get a cup of water and meet you here shortly."

She went to the kitchen and got the water. She was headed toward the door, when Mary said:

"Where are you going?"

"Out to give the sergeant some water."

"You will not!"

"Mother, the private said it will be alright. They have taken care of the Rebel shooters, and besides, he said he could protect me."

"Ginnie, you cannot go out there. You were lucky when they hit the cup that they didn't hit you."

"I cannot bear to sit in here worried about my safety, hiding from the Rebels out there, while he is suffering and I can do something about it. Therefore, I am going. I am sorry to disobey you, but I am going."

"Ginnie, please…"

"Mother, I must. I must help him. He was so kind to us. Now, it is my turn."

"I will not lose you."

"You won't, and I promise, when I get back, I will not leave this house until this battle is over."

Mary didn't have the strength to argue anymore and so she just looked away. Ginnie went to the backdoor and stepped out with the private. The private walked her over to the sergeant and once she got there, she leaned down and said:

"Sergeant, how are you doing?"

"Miss Wade," he said in a faint voice, in between breaths. He was breathing shallow and often.

"Sergeant, I brought you some water."

She lifted his head and pressed the cup to his lips. He drank a little, but more spilled out of his mouth. She gave him another drink as he looked up at her with loving eyes. Just then the medical staff showed up and began to work on him. One of them said:

"We have to get him to a hospital, so we need to move him, now."

They lifted him up and moved him back toward the house and beyond, and then loaded him into an ambulance. Ginnie watched as the ambulance wagon rode off south and to a field hospital. She hurried back into the house and when she got in, her mother hugged her tightly.

"Oh, Lord, thank you for protecting my daughter and bringing her back to me safely."

"Mother, it was the Lord's errand that I went out there. I saw it in the sergeant's eyes. It was the Lord."

"Well, remember you promised not to leave the house again, and I am expecting you to honor your word."

"I will, mother, I will."

And, so she went about baking bread and serving it to the soldiers until well into the night, until the knocks at the door ceased, and she, her mother, her sister, the baby, and the two little boys settled for the night. As she tried to sleep from the lounge under the window on the north side of the house, she hoped tomorrow would bring an end to this, but her logic suspected this was far from over, and the horrors of the day would be repeated tomorrow. She prayed to the Lord to give her strength to meet the challenges the day would bring, and be close to her as He was in the sergeant's eyes.

CHAPTER 42

SHERFY, ROSE AND WENTZ

REVEREND JOSEPH SHERFY, his wife Mary Hagen Sherfy, and their six children lived on a farm located a couple miles south of Gettysburg, and next to the Emmitsburg Road, where he and his father before him had developed and grown some of the finest peaches in the county. He was born in 1813 at a location very close to his farm where he grew these peaches, and so he was local to the area and deeply loved the land that was his home. The Reverend was relatively famous because of the quality of the peaches and so his fruit, his peach butter, his peach jam, his dried peaches, and his canned peaches were available for purchase in most of the larger towns and cities of Pennsylvania. Simply, Sherfy was a famous person of his time in this area, and his orchard was a landmark of Adams County, as it appeared on the Adams County map drawn in 1858.

John Rose lived with his family, and many others, on a farm near the Sherfy's place. He was a good friend and neighbor of the Sherfy's, and subsequently the Roses did a great many things with them, such as going to town for shopping, dining, and of course selling the peaches and the peach products. Rose worked his farm along with a tenant named Francis Ogden, and both of them also helped on the Sherfy farm and so with this work there, they both were able to draw an additional wage paid by Sherfy from the sale of his peaches.

John Wentz, his wife Mary, and their daughter Susan lived in a house not far from the Sherfy's. Wentz's place was small in comparison to the Sherfy farm and the Rose farm, but Wentz took great pride in it and the fact that it made him independent. Wentz's son Henry moved to Virginia about ten years ago, as he was a carriage maker. Subsequently, he like Culp, joined the Confederate forces.

The Sherfys spent that Wednesday, July 1st like many other of the folks in Gettysburg, particularly those who lived along the routes to the battlefield taken by the Federal soldiers, in the Sherfy's case Reynolds' First Corps, making water available to the soldiers and baking bread for their nourishment. The Reverend placed a large tub of water along the Emmitsburg Road and spent much of the first half of the day, along with Rose and Ogden, filling the tub. Mary and her mother Catherine spent this time baking and handing out fresh bread to the soldiers passing by. After the First Corps passed, they, also like others, listened intently for news of how the battle was progressing.

At around six o'clock in the early evening, the demand for the water and for the bread had long since ceased and so their work for the Union soldiers had been completed.

"John, Francis, it looks like this is all we can do, but at least we did our part for our boys," the Reverend said and continued:

"Please help me move the tub back to the barn."

Rose replied: "Reverend, we did a fine job. I wonder how the battle is going?"

"It seems to me the sounds of the battle got louder before finally subsiding, which may not be such good news. I pray to the Lord our forces will be victorious, though."

"Make sure you say a good one, Reverend," Ogden added.

Just then, Wentz came up to them. He said:

"Reverend, a mighty fine job of handing water and bread to the boys. If the battle spreads down here to our lands, what are we to do?"

"I dunno. I have worked so hard on this land and to have it damaged or destroyed by the fighting would be a tragic event. Yet, the lives of my family are far more precious to me than any plot of land, even how I do love this land. But, I trust in the Lord. He will protect us."

"I am going to send Mary and Susan to Two Taverns, to friends of ours who live there. I want them safe. I'll be staying to protect my land, however. I cannot afford to lose my little farm, so I will weather the battle however it progresses, even if it spreads to my place," Wentz said.

"I have a lot of kin and tenants living on my property and we will be staying too, unless the fighting comes too close and the danger is too great," Rose added.

Ogden said nothing, but simply nodded while Rose was speaking to indicate his agreement.

Then, they heard riders from the northwest. A group of five men were mounted on horses and were riding toward them.

Rose spoke first: "Wonder why the cavalry is heading this way? Could it be a bad sign of the battle?"

"That is strange," the Reverend replied.

They all stared as the riders came closer. And, then it became apparent to them the riders were not from the Union forces, but were rather Confederates.

"My God, it's the Rebs," Rose said.

"It seems so," the Reverend responded as he was startled and could think of nothing more to say.

In another minute, the riders arrived to where the men were. One of the soldiers dismounted and approached them. He removed his hat, bowed and said:

"Evenin', gentlemen. I am Lieutenant Colonel G. Moxley Sorrel, unda the command of General Longstreet. I am hea to survey the ground. Now, which one of ya can tell me what the names of them hills yonda?"

The men were still in the state of surprise at the sight of the Confederate officer and none of them spoke right away. So, the colonel continued:

"Come, come gentlemen. I do not have all day, hea. By the way, is anyone hea named Sherfy?"

The Reverend was surprised the Confederate knew his name, and so he spoke up:

"I, sir, am Reverend Sherfy. How do you know of me?"

He reached into his pocket and pulled out a map, and unfolding it, said:

"It says right hea on this hea map of Adams County, drawn up in '58, 'Sherfy'."

He approached and showed them the map, pointed and said:

"I believe this map is accurate. See right hea."

He folded the map and put it back in his pocket:

"Now, Reverend, you say...?"

He paused as Sherfy nodded and then continued pointing toward a mountain to the east of where they were standing:

"Being as ya are a man of God, I s'pose ya cannot tell a lie, so I trust ya will just answa the questions truthful. Besides, I am only askin' about simple geographical landmaaks. It says on that map 'Round Top'. Can I assume the larger mountain to the south ova thea is Round Top?"

"You may."

"Good, now I know where's we at."

He tipped his hat, bowed once again, and proceeded to leave, but before he mounted his horse, he turned back and asked:

"Reverend, why is ya place on this hea map of the county? I didn't see any otha farms listed."

"I grow peaches. That's what I am known for in this area."

"Peaches, ya say? We down in Georgia know a few things about growin' peaches. As a matta of fact, my relative owns a peach farm just outside of Macon. I wonda if I might ask a great fava of ya? I haven't had a peach in a couple of yeas and miss the taste of one. Could I try one of ya Pennsylvania peaches?"

Sherfy was surprised at the friendliness of the colonel and realized there may be some common ground with this enemy. Besides, there was

The Sherfy House as is today, located on Emmitsburg Road near Millerstown Road. (Faber)

nothing he liked better than sharing his peaches and seeing the pleasure it brought to those who ate them. He said in polite fashion:

"Colonel, I would be glad to have you try some. In fact, why don't your men ride over to my house where they all can try some?"

"That sir, would be delightful."

And so, Sherfy, Rose, Ogden, and Wentz walked over to the Sherfy house, with the Rebs in tow on horseback. When they arrived, Sherfy yelled:

"Mary, we have some guests. Please come greet them."

Mary came out on the porch and then stopped in her tracks, stunned with the sight she saw. Her hand went to her mouth. Sherfy saw this and hesitated as he momentarily had forgotten these were the enemy. As the moment became a little awkward, the colonel dismounted his horse and approached the porch. He removed his hat and bowed deeply to Mrs. Sherfy and said:

"Evening ma'am. I am Lieutenant Colonel G. Moxley Sorrel at ya service."

Mary looked at her husband and said:

"Joseph, these men are Rebels."

"Now, dear, the colonel is from Georgia where his family grows peaches. He has asked, politely, to sample some of ours. Do you mind going in the house and bringing a jar of canned peaches and maybe a slice of bread with some jam?"

Mary looked bewildered but did as her husband asked. She returned with a jar and a couple of forks. She handed these to Sherfy. He opened the jar and went over to Sorrel, handed him a fork and said:

"Try a slice, colonel."

Sorrel poked a slice of a peach and put it in his mouth. He savored the flavor for about ten seconds and then he bit into it. He chewed ever so slowly relishing every moment of the taste. Then he swallowed it, and said:

"I must say, Reverend, that is the best peach I have eva had. Even the ones back home don't taste that good. Why, it literally melts in ya mouth. How do ya get such flavor from them?"

"Well, I make sure to cultivate the land very carefully, over years, and I prune the trees of excess peaches to make sure they put extra flavor into the remaining fruit, and I continue this for a couple years until the trees put that extra flavor in all of their fruit."

"That, sir, is very wise, and the result is delightful. Do ya mind if my boys have a little?"

"Be my guest."

"What do ya do with the fruit ya prune? Ya don't waste it, do ya?"

"No, we make butter and jam out of it, things we can control the taste of by just adding a little more sugar. Here, try this bread and jam."

The colonel took a bite of the bread spread with peach jam, and said:

"Umm, umm, that is delightful also."

He handed the bread to his men and said:

"Well, we must be on our way."

He placed his hat back on his head, bowed to Mary with a "ma'am," and mounted his horse. His men followed his lead and mounted their horses also.

"Reverend, it has indeed been a pleasua. I cannot wait for this war to end, so I can go home and tell my family ya way of growing peaches so theys can try it."

The Reverend decided he would use this friendliness of Sorrel to get some news of the battle. He feared the news would not be good, but he had to know what was going on in Gettysburg, so he said:

"Colonel, what of the battle?"

"Well Reverend, I am afraid the news is not good for y'all. Ou foaces have taken the town and the enemy, um the Yankees, have retreated to those hills noath of hea. We are also seeing activity on Round Top, so it looks like they a settin' their lines along that ridge, from the hills to the noath all the way south to Round Top. Tomorra, we a fixin' fo a laage engagement, of which some of it could be right hea on ya farm. Ya fine folks might consida clearin' out until the battle is ova."

Sherfy and the others were shocked, specifically that the next day's battle could be right where they were standing, and so no one spoke. The colonel sensed this and also that his time here was over, so he said:

"Much obliged, Reverend. Rememba what I said about clearin' out. This hea is a large, flat area to the ridge yonda, so the artillery fia will be fierce hea."

With that, the Rebels rode off for a closer look at Round Top. Sherfy spoke as the others were still thinking of the coming battle:

"If what he said was the truth, we might be caught up in a tremendous struggle tomorrow. We may need to get our families to safety."

Wentz said: "I am going to send my wife and daughter out tonight. As I said before, I will be staying."

Rose asked: "Where should we go?"

"You are welcome to go to Two Taverns with my kin," Wentz said.

"I think we should all go discuss this with our families and make the decisions with them. As for us, we will be sending the children over to the Trostle's for the evening, and if it gets worse, we will join them and then head to Littlestown. Mary, mother Hagen, and I will prepare to leave, but will only go if we absolutely have to. Let's see what the morning brings," the Reverend said.

"We will be sending our children to safety also. I would like them to go to Two Taverns with your kin, John," Rose said.

He looked over at Ogden, who nodded his agreement.

"That would be just fine. I'll make sure they are at your farm by eight o'clock," Wentz replied.

"Good, then it is settled. We get our children to safety and then we will wait until the morning to decide if we are to leave our lands."

CHAPTER 43

BUEHLER

FANNIE J. BUEHLER spent the better part of the day, until the late afternoon, on July 1st wondering about the happenings of the battle. She had seen the Union troops hurriedly rushing by her house earlier in the day and had subsequently seen them forced back as they were pushed from the northwest side of the town, through the town, and ultimately for the day down to Culp's Hill and Cemetery Hill. On one hand, she was glad that ten days prior she sent her mother, her two nieces, who were visiting, and three of her own children to her sister's house in Elizabeth, New Jersey. She kept her eldest daughter, Kate, and her young son, Allie, with her. On the other hand, she was frightened because Mr. Buehler, her husband the postmaster of the town, had to leave last Friday when the Confederates invaded and took over the town. He had to leave as postmasters who worked for the federal government made "good hostages" for the Rebels. Once caught, they would be shipped to a Rebel prison in the South, and then bargained for. Some had died while this process played out, so the thought of him being in a Southern prison was not their first choice, and made him leaving a necessity. She didn't know where he had gone and prayed he was safe. So, she was alone to face the crisis of the battle and to protect both the two children, and their property. Her friends urged her to leave to get the children to some place safe from the battle, but she of strong stock, had decided leaving was not an option. Besides, where could she go that was safe? And, so in the late afternoon, she wondered what she could do to help the Union cause.

She judged the battle must not have been going well since the soldiers were running through the streets for their lives in order to escape the on-coming Rebels. And, then one of the soldiers said to her:

"Ma'am, please, for the love of God, take yourself and your family and get into a cellar. The Rebels are coming and they could shell the town."

"Is it really that dangerous?" she asked.

"Yes, now do as you are told," he said and ran south toward perceived safety.

She went back into her house. Her three sisters-in-law had come to her house earlier in the day for safety, fearing they would be caught up in the fighting. They lived along Chambersburg Street, near the origin of the battle. The youngest one who was less than twenty, Elizabeth, said to her:

"Fannie, do you think we should go down to one of the cellars?"

"I don't know what we can do to help if we are down there," she replied.

"But, how can we help? This is just so awful," Elizabeth exclaimed in more of a cry than a statement. Tears began to well up in her eyes just after she said this.

Fannie went over to her and gently grabbed her by the shoulders. She pulled her close and gave her a tight hug.

"Elizabeth, I know, I know you are scared. We all are, but we mustn't let that stop us from doing what we can."

She pulled away from Elizabeth, looked her straight in the eyes and continued:

"We must be strong together as a family. Strong for the children so they are not frightened, strong for each other, and mostly strong for those poor boys that will need us to tend to them. You can do this."

Elizabeth looked at Fannie, blinked her eyes a couple of times rapidly, wiped her eyes with a handkerchief, and said as she was dabbing her eyes:

"Alright, what would you want me to do?"

**The Courthouse
as is today.
(Faber)**

Fannie noticed wounded men had begun to come from the battle area and were being taken toward the newly finished courthouse across Baltimore Street from her house, so she said:

"We need to prepare to care for the wounded, so we will need to make bandages, many bandages. Fetch the linens and tear them into strips…" She paused, and then continued:

"Elizabeth, I would like you to care for the children. See to it they are not subject to much of this. Lord knows they are already frightened enough by this fight."

She no more said this than a couple of the wounded men showed up at her alley door. One of them poked his head into the door and said with a rather thick German accent:

"Excus, ma'am, but ve are in neet of bandages and vasser. Might ve trouble you for some help?"

"Oh, please come in won't you?"

She said to Victoria, one of her other sisters-in-law:

"Victoria, come help me with these soldiers. Let's get them in here so we can treat their wounds."

Victoria was a couple years older than Elizabeth and was a lot more of the calm type. She ran over to the door and said to the soldier:

"Here, lean on me and we will get you in here to lie down."

Fannie turned to the third sister and instructed her to also help the soldiers into the house, which she did. They got them to sit down and began to apply some bandages to their wounds.

"Ma'am, ve do sank you kindly for your help. None of us are serious vountet, but ve sure neet your help," the first soldier said.

Fannie replied:

"Are you German?"

"Ja, I am Max Frey, from Berks County, also a private in zee hundret and tventy virst Pennsylvania."

"Well, Mr. Frey, I am pleased to meet you. Where are you hurt?"

"Ma'am, I am hit vright in the leg. It is not too bat, but it hurts and I can't seem to stop zee bleetink."

"Well, you just lay right here and I will fix it up."

Fannie's sisters-in-law took care of the other men and when they were finished bandaging the wounds, another officer showed up at the door and said:

"Ladies, I really need you to get to a cellar. The Rebels are coming and right now we cannot stop them, so please get to a safe shelter. And, close this door and lock it."

Fannie looked around and said:

"Okay, now we are responsible for these men, so let's get them into the cellar."

The four women assisted the soldiers, the two children, and their dog Bruno, to the cellar and there they waited, but Fannie was restless. She was uncomfortable, slightly claustrophobic really, with being in the tight space of the cellar with all of those people. The children too were annoyed. Fannie noticed, but her mind was racing with the urgency of getting out of the cellar, so to fight this, she was concentrating on thinking of ways to help. Then, the German spoke, as he was petting Bruno:

"Ma'am, I am ofer vorty and hafe chiltren ov my own back in Berks County. I lofe zem vis all my heart, and miss zem so much. Voot you mind if I tent to the chiltren? I sink zat more and more voontet will be in neet of your help bevore zis is ofer."

Fannie looked at the kind hearted German and said:

"Mr. Frey, that would be wonderful and beyond what I could ever imagine asking of you."

"Ma'am..."

Fannie politely interrupted him saying to him and the other soldiers:

"Please call me Fannie."

"Miss Vannie, ve are in great det to you vor safing us vrom zee Rebels. Vithout your help, ve vould be prisoners zis fery moment, so vhatever you neet vrom us, please ask."

With that, the German man went over to Allie and began to talk to him. Elizabeth was relieved to know she had the help and then, still shaken by the ordeal, went over to Fannie. Fannie again hugged her and comforted her. They both watched as the German man was entertaining the children, especially little Allie and the dog.

"Younk man, vhat is your name and the name of this vine vatchtog?"

The child spoke in a sweet voice, and annunciated well for his tender age, so much so that Fannie choked up with pride:

"My name is Albert, but people just call me Allie. This is my older sister, Kate, and, this here is my dog Bruno."

"Ah, Bruno. Tid you know Bruno is a goot German name? I too am German."

"You are? What is German?"

"Vell, it is a place in Europe, far, far avay vrom here. It is a lant of many beautivul zings. Vide rivers, zick black vorests, and many, many castles. You know vhat a castle is?"

Both the children's eyes widened, and they each nodded their heads no.

"Vell, it is big house, much, much bigger zan zis one…," he paused and gestured with his hands, bringing them together and pulling them wide apart. He continued:

"It has many vrooms, maybe a hundret, and knights used to leave there."

"What are knights?" they asked.

"Vell, they were soldiers who vore shiney coats of armor, even a large helmut, vith an eye shielt…," again he paused to gesture, moving his right hand down from above his head to below his chin. He continued:

"And, zey vought many battles against bat and evil men, vith svords, like zis…," he began to joust with an imaginary sword, even pretending to joust with Alley, who laughed very loud at the site. The dog even barked in approval. Finally, he put his imaginary sword in his belt, bowed and said:

"I haf now saved the younk Prince Alley, and Princess Kate, vrom ze bad men."

The two children clapped at the performance and Alley rushed over to him to hug him. Kate did also. Fannie was very pleased and said to Elizabeth:

"Well, I do believe we have found proper looking after for the children, so therefore we must see to our boys. I cannot stay in here much longer. I must go up and see what is going on outside."

She said:

"Mr. Frey, I am going up to see what is going on and to see if I can be of help. Do you mind watching the children whilst I am gone?"

"Miss Fannie, it vould be my honor."

To the children she said:

"Children, I will be right back. Now please mind Mr. Frey, as he will be watching you whilst I am gone."

"Yes, Mama, we will," they said but immediately turned their attention back to Frey, and Allie said:

"Mr. Frey, you said "black" forests?"

Frey began to explain to the children about the black forest. Fannie noticed this and turned her attention to her sisters-in-law, saying:

"Please tend to our soldiers here and keep them comfortable, as they are in our care."

With that, she climbed the stairs and went out of the cellar. The noises of the battle ceased and so she thought to herself that the battle must be over. She opened her alley door and took a large gasp of air and put her hand to her mouth as a result of what she saw, several dead soldiers in her alley. She immediately rushed over to one to see if there was anything see could do. She hesitated, but only for a second, to turn him over, not knowing what she would find. As she was doing so, her heart was beating a mile a minute. She heard him groan, and inside she rejoiced saying to herself:

"He is still alive. Praise be to God."

She heard him ask for water, so she rushed into the house and fetched a cup, and then returned. She sat down next to the soldier and gingerly lifted his head onto her lap. She put the cup up to his lips and poured a tiny bit into his mouth. He drank this and then she gave him some more. He looked up at her and said:

"Thank the Lord for you, ma'am."

She said:

"Let's get you in to the house. Are you hurt?"

"No ma'am. I am alright, I just blacked out from the battle, the heat and all…Can you also help my brothers over there?"

"Well, you come with me into the house. I'll get you more water and a place to lie down more comfortable than the streets. And, I will get to your brothers."

She helped him up and into the house, where she motioned for him to lay down on the couch. She said:

"Well, you stay right here and I will fetch your brothers and the rest of the soldiers into our house and out of the elements."

She went back to the cellar to get assistance from her sisters-in-law. She descended down to the cellar and said:

"It looks as though the battle has ended, so let's go back up. Sisters, I am in need of your help. There are several soldiers out in our alley and they are exhausted and in need of water."

With that, she turned around and left the cellar, grabbed another cup of water, and went out to the alley. She repeated the earlier process with another soldier and looked up to see her sisters-in-law coming out with water in their hands. They followed her lead and started giving water to the rest of the soldiers. It took about fifteen minutes for them to get all the soldiers into the house and laid down in the living room. By that time, she said to the women:

"Sisters, please bring our soldiers up from the cellar, whilst I make our boys here comfortable."

The women left and she began to check each of the soldiers. One of them was shivering and sweating at the same time. She puzzled on this as he asked her for a blanket. She fetched one and covered him with it. He looked up in thanks, but could not muster the words. She saw his face was red, like the color of a beet, and so felt his forehead, which was very warm. She said to him:

"Follow me. You should be in bed."

So, she took him and placed him in one of her children's beds, covered him up and said:

"Please, try to rest. I will check on you later."

She looked at the others and they were showing the same symptoms as the one she put into bed, but not as severe, and so she covered each of them with blankets and made sure each had a full cup of water. She looked over at the first soldier she helped into the house and said:

"What happened to you men that got you sick like this?"

"Well, ma'am, we started the day marching at the double quick to get to the battle, and when we arrived, we found this inn was open and was serving whiskey to the men, so we went in and got our share. Each of us got a canteen full before we were ordered out of the bar and into the fight," he paused and then took a drink of water, before continuing:

"Then, we were rushed into battle north of town where we fought for several hours. It was hot and as we had emptied our canteens of water before and filled them with whiskey, we could only drink the whiskey. At the time we thought it was a grand idea, but as the afternoon went on and it got hotter, we began to get weak, I guess from the lack of water. Then, the Rebels broke us and we had to give ground and come into the town. We stopped to fight several times, but were driven back each time. We lost a lot of our number. Finally, we took refuge in the alley outside of your house. Several of the men took sick and fell. The last thing I remember was my head spinning, until I saw your face."

"My Lord, you poor boys. Well, you are safe and there is plenty of water for you, here. And, in a few minutes we will start supper and give you a good meal. That should fix you up."

"Thank you kindly, ma'am. My name is Private James Faber, Jr., ma'am and these two here are my two younger brothers, Joseph and Jacob. We are from the 68th New York."

"Well, Mr. Faber…actually, you three Faber's, my name is Fannie J. Buehler and you are in my home I share with my husband, Mr. Buehler, and our five children. These ladies are my sisters, well sisters-in-law, but sisters just the same, Elizabeth, Victoria, and Lucille."

The Faber's and the rest of the soldiers nodded at the ladies and they smiled back.

Fannie, after having made sure all the soldiers were comfortable, including the soldier she placed in bed, began the job of making supper. It was about seven o'clock in the evening. She went back into the cellar, grabbed two hams, some potatoes, some lard, and some butter. She went into the kitchen to prepare the meal. She was cooking for fifteen people, nine soldiers, her two children, her three sisters-in-law, and herself. She recruited the sisters and together they made a hearty supper. Once it was ready, she returned to the soldiers and said:

"Gentlemen, if you would please make your way to the table? It will be a little close because of our number, but we will manage."

She and the sisters got all the soldiers sat down first and then Alley tugged at her dress:

"Mama, can we sit by Mr. Frey?"

She looked over at Frey as if to ask if it was okay with him. He noticed her and said before she could ask:

"Miss Fannie, it voult be my honor."

And so, Fannie gave her approval and the children expressed their excitement, hugged her and ran to the spots next to Frey. The sisters took their spots at table and then all looked at Fannie who took a seat at the head of the table.

"Shall we say grace?" Fannie asked.

They all took each other's hands and looked over at Fannie to lead. She began:

"Dear Father in heaven, we thank thee…"

Just then, she was interrupted by a loud knock on her front door. Fannie ignored this, but the others looked at the door knowing who was knocking. Fannie continued:

"We thank thee for this food, these men, our family, and ask you keep safe those who are not here…"

Again, there was a loud knock on the door, but this time it didn't stop for several seconds, maybe five. Fannie, who had her eyes closed, now opened them to see all of the others looking at her, wondering what she would do. She became very irritated and said in a voice that reflected it:

"Whoever it is better understand they have interrupted my prayers and our meal."

She went to the door and opened it. There stood three Confederate soldiers. The first addressed her and said:

"Pardon me ma'am, but a ya hidin' any Union soldyurs?"

Fannie was taken mildly by surprise, as she expected the Rebels, but she hadn't expected to have to answer about hiding soldiers. She thought for a brief second, but then her anger took over as she looked back at the soldiers at the table. She snapped:

"Well, pardon me, sir. But, you are interrupting our supper and my saying grace before we eat. This is my home and I will dine with anyone I choose and these gentlemen are my guests for the evening. Do you find issue with this?"

The soldier was stunned and didn't know what to say. He looked at his companions and then one of them said:

"Ma'am, we are ordad to find out if any of the houses in this area are hidin' Union soldyurs."

"Well, sir as you can see, we are not *hiding* anyone and you are welcome to search the house if you must, but you will not interrupt our supper."

"Yes, ma'am, iffen we might, and iffen it's not too much trouble."

She looked at him and said:

"Alright, but I will be accompanying you. Please wait here whilst I finish grace and then we will do your little search."

Much to the surprise of the soldiers, she closed the door in their faces. They looked at each other and then one of them decided to open the door and take a peek into the house. He closed the door as fast as he opened it. One of his companions said to him:

"What's going on in thea?"

"She is sayin' prayers like she say. And, she stopped saying 'em when I opened the door and gave me a look of death."

"Let's get this done hea and move on quick like."

"But, what of the soldiers at table with her?"

"Like she said, they are not in hidin', they are guests. Let's just get this ova with and leave them be. Ya know the ordas about disturbing the civilyuns."

As he was finished saying this, the door opened and Fannie said:

"Now then, gentlemen, shall we get this over with?"

They followed her into the house where she showed them all the rooms on the main floor. In each room, the soldiers searched all the closets and under the beds. She showed them the attic and finally the cellars. She was a little concerned about the soldiers seeing the supplies she had in the cellars, the hams, the flour, and the rest, but the soldiers hurriedly looked around and one said:

"We will be goin' now, ma'am, and let ya get back to ya guests and ya supper. Thank ya kindly and we beg ya pardon for the intaruption."

With that, they climbed the stairs and went into the living room. She followed and as they were about to leave, one turned, tipped his hat, bowed and said:

"Ma'am, pardon us again, enjoy ya suppa. We will be close at hand if ya need anything."

"Thank you, but I do believe we will be fine."

They finished supper and cleaned the dishes. Elizabeth was busy ready-ing the children for bed while Fannie made the soldiers sleeping areas in the living room, both on the furniture and on the floor. The soldier who she placed in bed didn't eat much, and was still red and hot, so she put him back in bed and closed the door behind him. When all was settled, she decided to go outside, but as she didn't want to go alone, she decided to take Bruno. She put the rope around his head they used for walking the dog, and went to the door. Bruno was excited to go outside and so he jumped up on the door and barked in approval. She opened the door and looked outside, where she saw several Rebel soldiers camped on the pave-ment outside her door. They came to their feet when they heard the door open. Seeing her, they came mildly to attention and one of them said:

"Evenin' ma'am."

"I was just going to take the dog for a walk, if you don't mind?"

"No ma'am."

Another said:

"Ma'am I have not walked a daug in two yeas of being in this hea army. I have three of 'em at my faam in Virginia. Would ya mind if I walked yas?"

Fannie hesitated and then thought no harm would come of it, and so she said yes, walked down the stairs and handed the rope to the soldier.

Buehler House as is today. (Seamon)

"Mighty obliged, ma'am. What's his name?"

"Bruno."

The soldier leaned down to the dog, petted and scratched him and said:

"Well now, boy, Bruno, shall we get ya some exacise?"

The dog appreciated the scratching and barked in response. And so, off they went south on Baltimore Street. Fannie didn't know what to do now that the dog was being walked, but she was curious about these Rebel soldiers. How young they were and how much they looked like the boys around the town, just a little dirtier and their clothes more ragged. She decided to sit down on the stairs, as it was a nice evening, so she sat. The soldiers didn't know what to say to her so she said:

"How old are you boys?"

"I am nineteen," one of them said.

"Twenty," said another.

"We are eighteen," said the last as he pointed to the other soldier.

"My Lord, you are just babies. Well babies compared to me. I am in my thirty seventh year."

"Well, ma'am, ya sure don't look it. No, ma'am, not a day over thirty yeas."

Fannie blushed at the compliment and said:

"How kind of you to say. Where are you from?"

"We all from Virginia, ma'am. From Williamsburg, down in the southeast paat of the state.

"What are your names?"

The twenty year old said:

"My name is Corporal Kurtis Dement and this hea is my little brotha Jack. Ova thea is Harold Smith and his twin brotha Henry."

"Well, Mr. Dement, did you see much action today?"

"Yes ma'am. The fightin' was fierce up noath of town, but we finally drove 'em out. Lost quite a few of ou men, though."

"How long have you been in the army?"

"Ma'am, we been in the aamy since the beginning, right afta Virginia joined the Confederacy."

"Really, how long has it been since you have been home?"

"The same amount of time. I am afraid I haven't seen my motha in ova two yeas."

"I'll bet she sure misses you and your brother."

"Yea, but we send lettas back and foath. Jack likes to write and so we get lots from motha and fatha."

"Well, that's grand. It is nice to see they care about you two and you care about them. Family is important."

"Ma'am, ya don't mind me askin', but whea is ya husband? Is he off in the wa?"

Fannie, not wanting to tell the truth, said:

"Well, you could say that."

"Do ya write him often?"

"Well, as we need to. He comes home when he can."

"That's wunderful. Sua wish we could see home again and eat motha's cookin'."

"Well, maybe you can't, for now, but how about I send you out some of my home cooking?"

"Ma'am we would be much appreciative if you reckon."

Just then, the soldier returned with Bruno, and he said:

"Sure do thank ya, ma'am. It was sure like home to be round a fine daug like this."

He leaned down, scratched the dog on both sides of his head and said to the dog:

"Ain't that right, boy? Ain't that right?"

The dog jumped up at the soldier, licked him in the face, and barked in approval.

"Well, ma'am, hea he is, and he has done his business too."

"Why thank you. Now I'll take him back into the house and I will send you boys out some food."

Fannie took the dog back into the house and placed him in his usual spot in the room with the children. The dog went over to his rug, walked in a circle several times, and then sat down, looking as satisfied as he has been in months. He lay down and went to sleep. Fannie closed the door silently and went to the kitchen to make a couple of plates of food for the boys outside. When she was done, she made five plates of ham and potatoes. She carried two of them to the front door, opened it and to the Rebels surprise, brought them down the stairs and handed them to Dement. He took them and handed one to his brother Jack.

"There are three more, if someone could give me a hand and get them?"

Dement said:

"Ma'am this is vera kind of ya. We sure do thank ya."

Two of the other soldiers followed her up the stairs. They waited while she brought two more plates and then the third. She said at the door:

"Well, I must be turning in now. Please enjoy your supper and leave the plates right by the door here when you are finished."

"Yes, ma'am. Goodnight and thanks kindly for this wondaful food. It sure is delicious," Dement said.

Fannie closed the door and went up to her bedroom. It was a warm evening, and so as it was her custom, she opened the window to let some breeze in. While she was dressing in her night clothes, she overhead the soldiers outside talking, and recognized Dement's voice:

"This sure is some good food, just like Mama makes back home."

"Sure is, maybe betta."

"Kinda reminds me of Mama, too."

"Sure do."

She thought to herself how her day was one of many surprises. How much the horror of the battle, the urgency of the Union soldiers, and the sites of the destruction frightened her. How seeing the soldiers in the alley, and thinking they were dead, terrified her. But, seeing the soldiers being brought into the house and taking care of them, nay, being responsible for them, even to the point of challenging the Rebels who wanted to take them away, had given her a sense of fulfillment. And, finally, talking and giving food to the Rebel soldiers had given her a new understanding of them. They weren't the enemy; not at all. They were just boys from somewhere else in this country, very much like the boys around here. They had mothers, too. Mothers who worried about them, and wrote to them, and must be as afraid for their safety as every mother from this town was who has seen a son march off to the war. The war, this damn war, was responsible for all this; all this pain and loss. She lay down in her bed, and thought of Mr. Buehler, how she missed him and wished he was here. The damn war was responsible for his being away, too. The damn war, oh how she now loathed it. She closed her eyes with a prayer to God that it would soon end so all the mothers could have their sons back home with them and that she could have her husband back safe and sound.

CHAPTER 44

WILL

JOHN CHARLES WILL opened the Globe Inn early the morning of July 1, 1863. He knew the great battle would begin today. He heard it from the many Union cavalrymen who ate and drank at the inn the previous night. One of those was Captain Myles Keogh, of General Buford's staff. Although, Buford was staying at the Eagle Hotel, Keogh preferred the Inn as he said it many times last night:

"It reminds me of the pubs back home in Ireland."

Will also knew, from Keogh, that the army would be moving up as fast as they could once the battle began and the Confederates committed to this location to fight. And, a lot of them would be looking for whiskey. So, he and his father decided to open the Inn early, at eight o'clock, to serve these customers. This decision turned out not to be profitable as the soldiers didn't start arriving until around eleven. But, when they started to come, they came in droves. By this time the battle had been raging for over an hour and the sounds were quite loud even at the Globe.

A few minutes after eleven, the bar was full of soldiers, and they were offering any kind of money for a drink, as many of them remarked what good would the money be if they were killed today, anyway?

Will instructed two of his hands to bring up two additional kegs of whiskey from the cellar, which was rather difficult as he missed Samuel Butler's help since he quit last week. He wondered what happened to Samuel, and hoped the Rebels hadn't taken him. By the time the whiskey came up from the cellar, the soldiers were more than ready and each passed their canteens to the bar urging them to be filled. Will accommodated them, but made sure he charged the appropriate prices only, and strictly instructed his employees to make sure this order was followed. This went on for about an hour, when the din of the bar was suddenly silenced. Will wondered what was going on, and he found out quickly, when an officer yelled:

"Men, get on out of this bar. We have a battle to fight and we need all our wits about us."

The men began to file out, and discussing among themselves how to share the whiskey they received. Soon, the bar was empty except for the officer and Will. The officer approached Will and said:

"Excuse me, sir, but I want you to close this bar. I don't want the men tempted to come in here prior to going into action. You may think you are helping these men, but you are not. Men who indulge in the drink usually get it first, so you may have killed a lot of these boys with that whiskey."

Will was stunned. He hadn't thought of it that way, and he suddenly felt very ashamed.

"I'm sorry, I didn't know that. I will close the bar immediately. I am truly sorry. I hope that I didn't bring any harm to any of those boys."

"Okay. Thank you for your cooperation. Otherwise, I would have had to close it for you. Good day, sir."

"Good luck to you today, sir, and God be with you."

"Thank you. We're gonna need it and Him."

Will decided he needed to go see the action himself, as he now had a stake in it, feeling very guilty about the whiskey he sold to the men. By now, the sounds of the battle had become almost intolerable. He walked over to the Diamond and went north on Carlisle Street until he reached the Washington Hotel on the southwest corner of the intersection with Railroad Street. He crossed Carlisle Street where he met David Yount, who was the proprietor of the hotel:

"David, do you know of the battle?"

"Not yet."

Will looked up at the hotel and noticed women in just about every window facing west toward the battle. He heard one of them screaming and others crying. He wondered what they were screaming and crying about. He looked west on Railroad Street and saw men coming from the battle. He saw two men very close, one was limping badly and the other was holding his neck. The one holding his neck then fell. Will rushed over to him and removing his hand from his neck, saw the wound bleeding profusely. The man said to him:

"I've had it. Tell them not to cry for me, as we are trying to save them."

The life then left his body. Will was shaken. He wasn't prepared for this horror. He looked at his hands and saw the man's blood all over them. He had to get the blood off of his hands, had to. He was beginning to lose consciousness, and he fought this very hard. He got up and ran back to the Inn. The run did him some good and it seemed to clear his head, a little.

He arrived at the Inn in less than a minute and immediately went into the kitchen area to wash his hands. He met the cook, who said:

"Mr. Will, are you hurt?"

"No, thank you. I must wash my hands. Can you help me?"

The cook got a tub of water and placed Will's hands into it. He grabbed a scrub brush and a bar of soap and scrubbed the blood, which had begun to harden and was very sticky.

"Here boss, let's get you cleaned up."

Will stayed in the Inn the rest of the afternoon, as the sight of the man dying right in front of him haunted him enough that he didn't want to leave the safety of it. But, he stayed at the open, front door of the Inn. At about half past three o'clock, he began to see Union troops retreating from the battle and running down York Street. At first it was just a few, but then a lot of men were running for their lives. One of them stopped and said:

"Mister, the Rebels are on their way, so you need to get yourself and your family into a cellar."

And, then the soldier ran away, down York Street and disappeared. Will went back inside, dismissed his employees, telling them to go home and protect their families, and gathered up his mother, his three sisters, his sister-in-law, and his little nephew and led them down into the cellar. There they stayed for about three hours or so, while the issue was being decided in the town. Steadily, the noise abated and so the battle about the town was finished. Will led the group out of the cellar, and then he went alone out of the Inn. He went out the front door and noticed the streets littered with debris. He looked across the street and saw a dead horse lying on the pavement. He decided to walk to the Diamond. There were Confederate soldiers everywhere. He turned north and retraced his steps toward the Washington Hotel. There, he saw two dead Union soldiers in the street, one of them was the man who died right in front of him earlier today. The sight sickened him, so again he decided to go back to the Inn.

He entered the Inn and went back to the kitchen. Suddenly, he heard voices in the cellar, and he wondered if one or two of the earlier group stayed down there, or had gone back. He descended down the stairs and entered the cellar. By now it was dark inside as very little light from outside flowed inside due to the time of day, particularly down in the cellar, and he had not bothered to bring a lantern. And, so his vision needed time to clear. Once it did, it still wasn't readily visible as to who was down there with him. But, he still heard the voices, now lower, behind the stacks of old crates. He cautiously walked around the stack of crates, revealing his sister Margaret, who was only sixteen, and a Confederate soldier. They were chatting very close and she had her hand on his arm. They hadn't seen him yet, and he felt guilty spying on them, but was shocked when she leaned up and kissed him. The Rebel returned her kiss and gently put his arms around her. He didn't know what to do as no matter what he did now, he was spying. He decided it was time to interrupt, spying or not, and so he cleared his throat.

The soldier immediately pulled back and so did Margaret. She was embarrassed and was blushing. She fondled her hair and said:

"John, what a surprise. You startled me."

"Well I hope so. What are you doing?"

"I was just down here giving the lieutenant something to eat and drink."

"Looked to me as if you were giving a little more than that."

Margaret again fondled her hair, but didn't say anything. So, Will said to the soldier:

"Do you know this girl is only sixteen? She is barely old enough for proper courting let alone be doing what you are doing."

The soldier hesitated in replying and gave Will a look of disdain. Margaret, sensing the coming conflict, said:

"Now, John. I am old enough to do what I want."

"Really? I don't remember you turning of age yet."

"Well, I am old enough just the same. And, this lieutenant. He's, he's just so handsome. And, the way he talks with that little accent of his."

She blushed again and smiled sweetly at the lieutenant. He turned to Will and said:

"Mista, I do believe the lady can make ha own choices."

Will was rather stunned by the lieutenant's brash remark. He sized him up, knowing all well the soldier was trained to fight, while he hadn't scrapped with anyone since he was a teenager. Nevertheless, he was beginning to anger, an anger caused first by the situation with his baby sister, and now more so because of the clear lack of respect shown by the soldier. He took a step closer to the lieutenant and said:

"Well now, lieutenant, I don't believe your opinion is of any concern here. You have entered my house and you have acted without regard to my respect. I do believe I need you to leave."

The lieutenant looked at Will and decided to size him up as well. So, he also moved closer to Will until the two men were about a foot apart. He was about an inch or two taller than Will, and so he said:

"Mista, I am a memba of the Army of Northern Virginny and I don't have to take any ordas from a Yankee, particulaly from a civilyun. I will stay hea or I will leave as I please."

"Well, sir. Then it is up to me to convince you."

The soldier dropped his gun, and looked at Will and said:

"Make ya move, sur."

At this time, Margaret screamed and said in a frantic voice:

"John, Philip, stop now."

But, it was too late. Will cocked his right arm and threw a punch at the soldier, who blocked it easily and then returned a right cross that connected on Will's jaw, knocking him down. Will hit the dirt floor with a thud, but was not out, so he struggled for a moment and then made it to his feet. He looked at the soldier and said:

"You may whip me, but I will get one shot in on you, so help me."

He then lunged at the soldier, who stepped aside easily and hit Will with a short left fist in the eye again sending him down. Will dropped but the fall was broken by a sack of flour. He rolled over and looked up again at the soldier. He got on his feet again and said:

"I will make you leave my house if it kills me."

Margaret screamed louder now and called for help at the top of her voice. The soldier knew soon he would have a bigger fight on his hands than he wanted and so he said:

"Mista, I tire of this."

He started to leave, but Will grabbed him and threw another right that the soldier again blocked, but the soldier wasn't fast enough to see Will's left coming at his jaw and mouth and it connected. The punch was thrown with as much force as Will could give, which wasn't much to the soldier. It was enough, however to bring blood to the soldier's mouth and anger him.

He spit out the blood and then attacked Will. He threw another left punch that hit Will in the stomach and followed with a right to the side of Will's face. This combination knocked Will down again and this time for good. The soldier stood over Will and said:

"Stay down now, or I will have to make ya stay down pamanent like."

Noticing he was down, Margaret rushed over to him and said:

"John, John are you alright?"

Will was groggy, but said in a not quite coherent voice:

"I'm alright...."

Margaret turned to the soldier and said:

"Now, you get out of here, Philip, right now."

The soldier looked a little stunned, but knew it was time to go, so he said:

"Well, I was finished anyway. Thanks for the kiss. Ya kiss real good."

And with that, he ran up the stairs and out of the Inn. Margaret helped Will to his feet and gingerly up the stairs, as he was still unstable on his feet. They got up to the kitchen, and she set him down in a chair. She went over to the washing area, soaked a cloth in some water and brought it over to Will.

"Here, let me clean you up."

She wiped his face and held the cloth against his right eye, which had begun to swell. He groaned.

"Does it hurt much?"

"Naw, not as much as my pride."

"What are you talking about? He was a trained soldier and you still hit him in the face."

Will thought for a second and then smiled saying:

"I did, didn't I?"

"Sure did and it must have hurt him, because he sure did get mad."

Will just smiled and said:

"Well, my lady, I hope your honor, what you have left...," he said the last part sarcastically and then continued:

"is still intact."

She just smiled and said:

"John, I am sorry for the trouble. He was just so very handsome and I am coming of age. Besides, with all the fellas in the army, I am not exactly getting a lot of callers."

"You will, Margaret, you will. Just give it time. Besides, this way? He could have really taken advantage of you down in that cellar."

"Yes, I know. It's just I have these feelings inside and I cannot control them."

"Those are natural, but you must keep your wits about you and make sure you make smart choices. I think you should talk about these feelings with your older sisters or with mother."

Just then, Will heard a familiar voice out in the restaurant.

"John, are you in the kitchen?"

It was Jones, and he was into the kitchen before Will could get up out of the chair. Jones noticed the swollen eye and the bruising around Will's jaw and said:

"What happened? Are you hurt? Who did this to you?"

He came over to Will quickly and gently took the cloth from Margaret's hands, saying:

"Let me take a look."

He removed the cloth and looked at Will's swollen eye. He dabbed it with the cloth and said to Margaret:

"Can you rinse this for me?"

Then to Will:

"You didn't answer me. Who did this to you?"

"We had a little trouble with one of your men."

"What was his name and rank?"

"Jones, it was handled so we don't need to speak of it anymore."

"If one of our men did this, I want to know who and he will be dealt with."

"No, we don't want that type of trouble."

"Nonsense. General Early will want to know, regardless, so you may as well tell me who it was."

"Don't you think the war is a little more important to the general than my fight? Particularly the way this first day went. I do believe tomorrow will bring more bloodshed than today."

"Maybe so, John, but the general fancies this Inn and is very fond of you. Believe me, he will want to know. Besides he, his staff, and some of his younger officers are on the way for supper."

"They are? Why?"

"For the food of course. He has made arrangements with his staff and wanted me to come and tell you a whole group of officers, about forty or so, will be here by half past seven o'clock. Will you be able to feed that many?"

Jones dabbed the cloth at his eye and then Will decided he was fine, so he politely brushed Jones' hand aside and said:

"Of course, but a restaurant full of Confederate officers? I'm not sure that it is appropriate for me to be feeding the enemy after the battle resulting in so many dead Union men."

"We lost quite the number too. John, I don't see the need to turn away Early's men. Besides, now that the town is in our hands, it could be of great value to have a little security, if you know what I mean?"

"That is true."

He thought for a moment about the need to protect the Inn and all of the supplies, and then thought Early's help would be of great use. So, he said:

"Alright, please tell the general we will be ready."

At precisely half past seven o'clock, Will heard a lot of horses approach the front of the Inn. His father joined him, and they both went out to the front to greet the visitors. Jones and Early led the parade of horses and upon getting to the Inn, dismounted. As they were dismounting, Jones leaned over and said something to the general that Will could not make out. Early brushed himself off and looked over at the Wills. He said:

"Evenin' gentlemen. Aye have been looking faward to suppa at the Inn all day long and have built myself a powaful hunga."

"Good evening, General," Will said.

The general reached out to shake Will's hand, but before he let go, he said:

"Mista Will, what happened to ya eye?"

"General, just a little trouble, that's all."

"Well, I hope ya gave as good as ya got. It wasn't one of my men, now was it?"

"I'd prefer not to say, General."

"Well, ya just did."

He turned to one of his officers and said:

"Colonel Daniel, a word, please."

Daniel dismounted his horse and came over to the general. Early whispered something in his ear and then Daniel replied:

"Right away, General."

"Very good, Colonel, please carra on."

With that the colonel mounted his horse and rode away. Early turned back to Will and his father:

"Charles, how nice to see ya. Aye only wish it was betta circumstances, well at least from ya point of view. My men a famished and Aye explained to them how vera delightful the food hea at the Inn is, so they a all ready for suppa."

"Good evening, General. Please have them come on in," Charles Will said.

Early turned to the men and said:

"This hea is a fine establishment and Aye expect y'all to act accordingly."

And with that, they all filed into the Inn and took seats at the long tables. Jones sat next to Early and once Will came over, he said:

"John, can we have ales all around to start with, and what do you have on the menu this evening?"

"Since you came to the Inn earlier this evening letting us know to expect the general and his staff, we have prepared several hams, have boiled up some potatoes, baked some nice biscuits and have peach pie to top it all off."

Jones looked over at the general, who nodded and said:

"Mista Will, I knew ya would be cookin' up something vera delicious. Please continue as we all will be havin' just as ya say."

"Very well, sir. We will have the ales here in a moment, and we will bring out the biscuits to start the meal off."

Will disappeared into the kitchen and returned a moment later with baskets of freshly baked biscuits. The aroma of the biscuits filled the room and the men began to devour them. The ales were also delivered to the men, who drank them up faster than they could be refilled. The atmosphere was celebratory as many mugs were clicked together in toast. Then, as Will was bringing in the main course of ham and boiled potatoes, he notice Colonel Daniel arrive, look for Early and make his way to him. When Daniel got to Early, he whispered in his ear. Early nodded and then Daniel took a seat next to him, on the opposite side of Early as Jones. Early said:

"Mista Will, when ya finished servin' those plates, might Aye have a word with ya outside this room?"

"Certainly, General."

Will set the last of the plates down and walked over to the general.

"Colonel Daniel, Mista Jones, a moment."

Jones and Daniel rose up with Early and together with Will, they proceeded out of the Inn, where three soldiers were waiting.

"Colonel Daniel, is this the man?"

"Yes, sir, this is Lieutenant Philip Greene. He is from Virginia."

Will recognized the lieutenant as the man he fought earlier in the evening. Early said:

"Mista Will is this the man who caused the trouble with ya earlia today?"

"I'd rather not say, General. The cellar was dark and I didn't get a real good look at him."

"How honaable, Mista Will. Clearly, a snitch ya a not."

Early turned to Greene and said:

"Lieutenant, am Aye to undastand ya had a fight with a civilyun, this man Mista Will, earlia this vera evening?"

The lieutenant was relatively stunned and had nothing to say, which built up a little anger in the General, so he repeated:

"Lieutenant, Aye will not be askin' this again, undastood?"

"Yes, sur. I did have an exchange earlia with this hea man."

"So, ya fought with a civilyun?"

"Yes, General."

Early approached Greene and noticed his right side of his face and his lip were a little swollen. He smirked and said:

"And the marks on ya face, was that caused by this same civilyun?"

"Yes, sur."

"So, not only did ya fight a civilyun, but ya let him get a shot in on ya?"

The lieutenant gulped and said:

"Yes, sur."

"Well, Aye do believe ya owe this man an apology, now don't ya?"

"Yes, sur."

Greene looked over to Will and said:

"Beggin' ya pardon, sur, but I am sorry fo the trouble we had earlia this day."

Will nodded and said:

"No harm done. In fact, it was fun, more fun than I have had in awhile."

Greene smirked in acknowledgement, rubbed his jaw, and said:

"I do agree."

Early laughed and said:

"Lieutenant Greene, now that ya have gotten to know Mista Will in the propa way, I do believe ya can go in and join the men for some suppa, and when ya are done, ya will serve guard of this hea Inn for the duration of ou stay in this hea town."

He looked at Will and said:

"Of course, if that is acceptable to ya, Mista Will?"

"That would be splendid, General."

"Alright then, now that this issue is settled, it is time for some of that ham ya cooked up."

Will served the officers, who ate and then ate some more until they were filled. They consumed a hefty amount of ale along with the meal, and so the mood of the men became very jolly. Early joined in on this and said to Will:

"Have a seat hea, Mista Will, and have ya'self an ale with us."

Will obliged and motioned for an ale to be brought over. It soon arrived and Early stood and said:

"Gentlemen, gentlemen, quiet for a moment, please..."

He paused while the room quieted down and then continued:

"Aye would like to propose a couple of toasts. First, to ou men, who performed brilliantly today. May we have the same success tomorra and defeat these Yankees," he said with a loud emphasis on "Yankees."

The men clapped the tables, stomped their feet, cheered loudly, and then clicked their mugs, saying: "hea, hea."

Early continued:

"As we have done today, we will do tomorra. Now, Aye also would like to propose a toast to Mista Charles Will...," he hesitated and pointed to Charles Will who was tending the bar. He continued:

"And, to Mista John Will, the makas of this fine feast y'all are enjoyin'. Raise ya mugs to the Wills, if ya please."

The men said in unison while clicking their mugs:

"To the Wills."

Early then sat and Daniel stood next. He said:

"And, gentlemen, let us also drink to the general, who without his leadership we may not be enjoying such a fine meal, and having such a fine, successful day. To the general."

The men raised their mugs again and drank to the general, who just waved in acknowledgement. Just then, a courier entered the restaurant, looking for Early. He found him in the crowd and came right over. Upon reaching Early, he saluted and said:

"Genr'l Early, I am Captain William R. Townsend. I bring ya compliments from Genr'l Lee and also a message that he would like ya to join him at his headquartas right away, sir."

Early returned the salute and said:

"Captain, please tell the general I will be along directly."

"Yes sir, but my ordas are to escort ya directly to the gen'rul, sir," Townsend replied.

"Very well, Captain. Colonel Daniel, it seems we must retia from this fine gathrin'. Could ya please pay Mista Will for the food and drink and accompany me to General Lee's Headquartas?"

Daniel rose, wiped his mouth one more time with his napkin and said to Will:

"Mista Will, what do we owe ya?"

"Let's see, forty three men times fifty cents for the meal is $21.50, plus the ales at a dime apiece, should add about another sixteen or seventeen dollars. Should we round it up to an even $40?"

Daniel reached into his pocket and produced a roll of crisp Union greenbacks. He paid Will $50, and said:

"That is a fair price, and hea's a little extra for ya trouble."

Early took one last drink of ale and said:

"Mista Jones. Mista Will, Aye must be on my way. Thank ya for the pleasant meal and drink."

And with that, he and Daniel accompanied Townsend out of the Inn, where they passed Lieutenant Greene, now at his post in front. They each mounted their horses and rode off to see General Lee.

Earlier, the noise of the celebration had alerted many of the townsfolk of the party-like ambiance going on in the Inn. Many reacted rather poorly to the merriment, noting that Union boys were dying that very night in the fields that were fought over that day and in the buildings serving as hospitals just down the street, therefore, to have a celebration in their town seemed to not be the right thing to do, nor the patriotic thing. This would haunt the Will family after the battle and beyond, and many would blame them for making the Confederate officers too comfortable at the Inn. One of these disgruntled townsfolk was none other than Mr. Silas McGee. McGee, himself a coward, had not enlisted in the army, but stayed in Gettysburg. He didn't think very much of himself because of that fact, but justified it because he was saving his skin. During the moments of toasting the Confederates enjoyed, McGee was outside the Inn, listening and plotting. Plotting as to when the right moment to kill Jones would be. He said to himself:

"Maybe tonight, if I can get a good shot."

But, that plan soon became more difficult as he noticed Greene take his post outside the Inn. He would have to wait for another opportunity. He said again to himself, slurring the words as he was not surprisingly drunk:

"Mr. Jones, not tonight; not tonight. But, soon. I promise. Soon you will be cut down by this here rifle."

The Second Day

THURSDAY, JULY 2, 1863 GETTYSBURG, PENNSYLVANIA

CHAPTER 45

JACOBS

PROFESSOR MICHAEL JACOBS rose early again on Thursday, July 2nd and was up in his attic by around eight o'clock. He began taking the day's notes, starting with the weather, noting a sunny and warm day beginning. He was anxious as he expected the fighting this day for the town of Gettysburg to be intense. He was also nervous for the day to begin hoping the Union forces would show better today than yesterday, when they were driven from their positions on McPherson's Farm and from the area north of the town. The Rebels had been successful on both of these fronts in sweeping the Union army back, through the town, and to a position south of town along both Culp's Hill and Cemetery Hill. Jacobs was up most of last night watching the area for the movement of troops from his attic telescope, and making notes of this movement, what little he could see in the darkness. From his vantage point, he could clearly see the Union occupation of the two hills to the north and could see, from the movement of torches, amassing of forces, which extended from these hills in the north, along Cemetery Ridge to the south toward Round Top Mountain. He noted these movements in his journal and speculated the Federal position was being strengthened and they were forming a defensive battle line. He also noted, on Culp's Hill, which was east of Cemetery Hill, much activity as well. So, again he speculated that the north flank was being reinforced and strengthened. These observations were confirmed as he spied the movements of the blue troops with his telescope.

He had been on the street late last night and had overheard many a Rebel soldier boast of their successes of the day and issue promises of another day of whipping for the Yankees coming tomorrow. At first, he was downtrodden last night, expecting another defeat of the Union forces, but this morning this ill feeling turned into one of hope as the more he looked at the Federal preparations forming the battle line and strengthening it, the more he thought this fight would be a bloody one, and one in which the Union could indeed prevail. He took a sip of his morning tea, and heard Henry coming ever so slowly up the stairs and remembered how depressed he was at the outcome of the previous day's fighting, knowing the enemy now occupied the town.

"Good morning, father."

"And to you, Henry."

"I thought I would come up and join you again this morning, even though this may be a disastrous day. Will the Rebels drive our forces away from here today and maybe all the way to Washington?"

"Maybe not. Take a look over there toward Round Top. Our forces are extending their lines there. And, look at Culp's Hill. We are strengthening our position there as well. It is a magnificent line, almost in the shape of a fishhook, and good ground to defend," he said while sweeping right arm in an arc, starting from Culp's Hill and ending at Round Top.

Henry took the telescope and looked first at Culp's Hill and then rotated it to Round Top.

"You are right, father," he said with sheer excitement, and continued:

"It looks pretty impregnable that line the army is building."

"It does indeed. Now if the Rebels hold off their attack for awhile, we might just get a chance to finish reinforcing it."

"Do you think they will?"

"Well, they might. So far this morning, I haven't seen much movement from them. Take a look at their preparations. All I see is them strengthening their lines. See, they are building barricades along Middle Street, just to the south and east of us, but they don't seem to be massing for an attack."

Henry shifted his view to see the Rebel lines and then agreed with his father, saying:

"You are right, father. They don't seem to have much urgency at all. Do you think they are waiting for us to attack them?"

"I doubt it. They had much success yesterday bringing the fight to us, so I expect today to be much the same. They may find we are more ready today than yesterday, however."

"Do you really thing we have a chance in this fight today?"

"I do indeed. One thing General Buford was concerned about yesterday was the ground they were defending and he made a point to say if driven from that ground west of here, how important it was not to lose Culp's, and Cemetery, Hills. Thank the Lord the Rebels didn't take them yesterday, or last night. And, since we are reinforcing them, it will be a tough task today. Now, let's take this opportunity to clean up our notes from yesterday."

And, so they sat down and compared notes on the previous day's fighting.

They stayed up in the attic watching the reinforcement activities of both armies until around half past one o'clock. Henry was finishing a light meal of fruit and biscuits and had tired of looking at the Union lines, so he swung the telescope westerly toward the Hagerstown Road, which extended southwesterly away from town. Suddenly, he noticed troops coming up to the road near Black Horse Tavern. He looked for another minute and then said in a loud voice that startled Jacobs:

"Father, I see the Rebel army advancing to the southwest. Here, take a look. It's a little hard to see because of McPherson's Ridge in between. But, look closely."

Henry vacated the telescope and Jacobs took his spot. Jacobs looked for about a minute and said:

"Well done, Henry. It is hard to see. How did you do it?"

"Father, I saw a glint off their bayonets."

"It looks like they want to hit us in our left flank out by Round Top."

"Does it look like our boys see them yet?"

The professor swung the telescope toward Round Top and observed the movements of the Federals to see if they had been alerted to the march of the Rebels. Seeing none, he said:

"No, our boys don't see them yet. But, wait! It looks like we are sending some men down from Cemetery Ridge down to Trostle's farm, and in front of Round Top," he paused and then continued:

"Why would we do that? Break that marvelous line on the ridge, on high ground, to come down and occupy the lower ground? Maybe we are massing for an attack? Here, Henry, you look."

Henry took the glass and said:

"Father, it doesn't make much sense what is happening. It doesn't seem like enough of a force for an attack. It could be a slaughter if they are exposed to the force the Rebels are bringing."

Henry turned back to watch the Rebel advance. He watched as the Confederates marched past the Taneytown Road and onto a smaller, southeasterly heading road, the Millerstown Road, that would cross Pitzer's Run and Seminary Ridge and ultimately lead to the Sherfy farm and then to Round Top. He watched for about five minutes or so when he noticed something peculiar. The Rebel advance halted and remained still for a few minutes, and then they turned about face and began marching back the way they came.

"Father, take a look. The Rebels are leaving."

Jacobs took the glass and said:

"Thank God. Maybe they noticed something they were not prepared for."

And, indeed they had, as the movement of the Federal forces down from the higher ground, although not a strategic move as it broke their line at the north edge of the small hill north of Round Top, had temporarily surprised the Rebels and had exposed their position to fire sooner than they planned. So, they had to turn around and find another, more concealed route to their objective point.

"Hurrah, they are turning back," Jacobs exclaimed.

"Do you think they are really leaving?"

"No, that would make no sense. They must want to attack our left flank under the cover of surprise and felt that surprise was compromised somehow."

"I sure wouldn't want to be that commanding officer, moving men and then turning them around. It is so much a waste of time and effort," Henry said with a sly smirk.

"That, my son, is a very true statement."

They watched intently looking for the Rebel column and didn't find it until it reappeared around two o'clock again at the Hagerstown Road, only this time westerly of Willoughby Run, about a mile or so closer to the town than the previous spot at Black Horse Tavern. Again, Henry was manning the scope and he again discovered their appearance.

"Father, they are coming again. I see them just beyond Willoughby Run crossing the Hagerstown Road, and this time they look in more of hurry."

"Like you said earlier, someone is in trouble on their side for the wasted march before, so they must be in a might bit of a rush."

They watched them for about the next hour march southerly along Willoughby Run and then turn east at the intersection of the run with Millerstown Road, the very same road they attempted to travel earlier, which led to Round Top, via the Sherfy farm. Once they neared Sherfy's farm, the Rebels deployed their men, about 15,000 strong, with three artillery units, south of the road, mostly, with a few units to the north, all facing easterly. They opposed the Federal units positioned out front of the main body of troops making the defensive line up on Cemetery Ridge. This Rebel deployment took about an hour and while they were taking up position, the Union forces were also preparing for the pending battle. Jacobs was at the glass and said in a very businesslike, but nervous voice:

"It looks like they are readying for an attack near the Sherfy place. Make sure your notes have this correct. Pray to God we are ready."

"Yes, Father, I have it."

"Note the time, around four o'clock in the afternoon."

"Yes, around four o'clock."

Just after Henry finished speaking, the Confederate artillery opened fire with a large roar of their cannon. Soon, the Union cannon answered and the battle was on. The Rebels advanced in a two pronged attack with the forces to the north concentrating on the area north and south of the Millerstown Road, while the south pincer attacked the Union forces in front of the smaller hill north of Round Top. The two sides slugged it out for this area for around four hours, giving ground and then retaking it, several times over. The Jacobs made very distinct notes on the activities of the armies, but mostly witnessed the carnage of the battle.

"Henry, it looks like the Rebels are taking it to us, particularly near that orchard of peach trees just to the south of the Sherfy place. My God…," he paused and looked away from the scope for a moment and then forced himself to look back before continuing:

"The butchery of it. There must be hundreds and hundreds of casualties and dead soldiers. And, that field of wheat near Rose's Woods, the hand to hand fighting is fierce and bloody. Men are going down just like shooting flies in a barrel. Further to the south there is a tremendous rifle dual in, and about, those large boulders northwest of Round Top, along Hauck's Ridge."

Foreground is a portion of the boulders making up Devil's Den as is today. Note Little Round Top in the background. (Faber)

Henry was taking notes and was talking out loud as he was writing as fast as he could:

"The fighting is most vigorous in the Sherfy peach orchard and in the wheatfield by Rose's woods. And, also the fighting extends to the south in the gathering of boulders northwest of Round Top on Hauck's Ridge."

"The Rebels have found the breach in our lines made by coming down from the little mountain north Round Top and are exploiting it," Jacobs observed.

"Rebel forces penetrating the gap in our advance line in front of the little mountain north Round Top," Henry repeated.

"Whoever ordered that placement is probably going to be without a job at day's end, if there is a job to be had," Jacobs said with a sarcastic tone.

Henry looked up at his father and said:

"Do you mean we may lose this battle over some ill advised placement of our troops in advance of our line of defense?"

"I do mean exactly that. If the Rebels get through and up the north side of Round Top, they will have flanked our lines and split them to be gobbled up piece-meal."

"My Lord, what a bungle; a costly bungle…"

"It is so," Jacobs said in finality and then passed the glass to Henry.

The Confederate advance continued as new troops attacked the Union forces north of where the action had been going on at around six o'clock in the evening, opening another area of intense fighting. The locations of combat became hot beds of action for the next two hours or so, until the sun dropped behind South Mountain to the west. As it became twilight, the Jacobs noticed the Rebels began firing on Culp's Hill along the north end of the Union line. Henry was still at the glass and said:

"They are now attacking Culp's Hill in the north and I can barely make it out, but they have advanced and are now also attacking Round Top to the south."

"I see. Their plan all along was to assault both ends of the line. I wonder why they didn't do it simultaneously?"

"Maybe that was their original plan, but the march to the south and the turning back spoiled their coordination?"

"Yes, that is a distinct possibility. That is a very good observation. Make sure it is in your notes."

"Father, can we switch? I want to update my notes accordingly."

Jacobs took his turn at the glass, but the diminishing light of the day, mixed with the smoke on the battlefields made viewing nearly impossible.

He continued to look, but could not clearly make out who was winning the field at any of the four locations of battle. He strained his eyes for one more clear observation, but only saw the flashes of the gunfire and the cannons. The sound of the battle still remained deafening, but as to who was carrying the day became impossible to distinguish. He pulled away from the glass and said:

"Without light, I cannot see if we are holding the field or are losing it. God be with us as this evening's action may indeed determine the outcome of the battle and maybe even the war."

Henry looked at his father, but said nothing as he knew his father was right, that this night's fighting, for all practical purposes, was for it all, and winning and losing the war was being determined right now in the fields out there, unseen except to those who were entrenched in it.

Chapter 46

BURNS

JOHN L. BURNS awaken early the morning of July 2nd. He was cold, he was hungry, he was in pain, but mostly he was very weak and tired. Not tired from lack of sleep, but tired from a lack of his usual good supply of energy. He suspected he was dying and presumed he would have done so during the night if not for the Rebel doctor dressing his wounds and giving him a blanket. He grasped the blanket tightly knowing it had been his salvation last night. He looked around trying to figure what to do. He knew he would need some help today or he would die. He looked to the north and saw his friend Alexander Riggs' house. He judged it a couple hundred yards away, but if he could get to it, he may receive the care he needed and maybe not die after all. He sat up and tried to put weight on his injured leg and finding the pain too intense, plus no real support from it, he knew he would need to crawl. So, he turned onto his stomach, raised up on his elbows and began. At first, it took all the energy he could muster just to move his body, but once he got moving, he found the going a little easier. He decided he would need to rest regularly, so he counted his arm movements and decided ten times would be enough and then he would rest for a moment. He had done this four times, when he heard footsteps be-hind him, and then felt a kick on his leg. He stopped, rolled over on his back, and looked up to see who kicked him. It was the Rebel sergeant who questioned him yesterday. The sergeant said:

"Na, whea ya think ya goin'?"

"My friends live over in that house yonder," he said pointing to the Riggs' house.

"They do, do they? Ya figured ya crawl all that way, did ya?"

"I have no choice, 'cept to stay here and die."

The soldier, for the first time, felt compassion for Burns, and so he said:

"Well, ya a hearty one I haff to say."

He called over to one of the men who was removing the bodies of dead soldiers from the field and said to him:

"Private, ya come over hea, and bring anotha to help this civilyun."

In a moment, two soldiers came over to Burns, and the sergeant said:

"I still think ya lied to us, but since ya still kickin' we'll help ya to ya friend's house."

He turned to the soldiers and said while pointing to the house:

"Carra this hea man to that house yonda."

The soldiers picked him up and carried him over to Rigg's house. It took them about ten minutes to get Burns there, and once there, they climbed the steps to the house and knocked loudly. There was no answer at the door. One of the soldiers tried the door and finding it locked, said to the other:

"Eitha they's not at home, or they's down in thea cella."

"Yes, let's take him to the cella doa and if they's don't answa, let's leave him thea. We has much work to do."

And so, they carried him to the cellar door, placed him on it and knocked on it real loud. They waited a minute or two and then knocked again, while one said:

"Anyone down thea, anyone t'all?"

They waited for another minute and then said to Burns, who was weaker yet from the journey:

"Mista, we reckon we gots to go now. Sorry, but we need to leave ya be hea."

Burns looked up at them, but was too weak to speak, so he laid his head back down on the door. He was in considerable pain, and this pain finally took over his consciousness and he saw blackness closing in on him and he was unable to stop it.

Barbara Burns and Martha Gilbert were up late this morning. The baby awoke at her usual time, rising and announcing she was ready for her morning feeding. Martha was so very tired, so once the baby was fed and changed, she decided to take a nap. Her mother wasn't up yet, Martha judged, as she hadn't heard any movements from her room. If she could get the baby back to sleep, maybe she could too. The baby cooperated and so she fell asleep again, and got a few hours of much needed rest. The baby then awoke again just after noon. Neither of the women slept well at all during the night, and so the added sleep was very much needed. Each in their own way worried about Burns. As the baby cried, signaling it was time to get up, Barbara entered Martha's room and said:

"Good morning sweetheart. Well, afternoon, I guess. Did you get any rest?"

"No, mother, very little. I cannot stop thinking of that soldier's face, and worse, that father may still be out there somewhere. I prayed to God very hard that if he is hurt, he is being tended to."

"I did so also. I am so worried. Something must have happened, something awful, I fear. What it is, I don't know, but it is something awful, I just know it."

Mary interrupted their conversation and Martha looked down at her realizing she needed caring for. So, she picked her up and noticed she needed changing. She proceeded to do so, when the women heard a knock on the kitchen door. They looked at each other, first with a joyful look of news of Burns, but then both of their expressions turned to fear, fear of finding out the truth that may be dreadful. Barbara spoke:

"You finish with Mary and I will get the door."

She then left for the kitchen. Martha finished with the baby, picked her up and hugged her to her body very tightly, trying in vain to stop tears from coming down her cheeks. She walked out of her room and toward the kitchen when she heard a terrible scream from her mother. She ran to the kitchen and found her mother crying deeply and being held by Sallie Broadhead.

"Mother, mother, what is it? Is it father? Is he, is he, dead...?"

Barbara pulled away from Sallie, but was crying too hard to speak, and so Sallie said:

"It seems so, Martha. We don't know for certain, but he was seen shot several times and was wounded severely and left on the field. I was just told this morning and thought you should know."

Martha began to cry uncontrollably and her sobbing affected the baby and the baby began to wail as if she understood the sad news. Sallie saw this and said:

"Let me have her, Martha, I'll take her for awhile."

Without a word, Martha handed the baby to Sallie and then she and her mother hugged each other and cried very loud together. After several minutes, each of the women composed themselves and Barbara said to Sallie, who was rocking and comforting the baby:

"Sallie, thank you so much for bringing us this news and for helping us. You are indeed a good friend..."

She paused and wiped her eyes, and with a quick glance to Martha, continued:

"Do you know if his body has been recovered?"

"No. I was not told that."

"Do you know if it is safe for us to look for it?"

"No, I presume it is not. The Rebels have the town, but our boys are dug in on Culp's Hill and Cemetery Hill. It looks like we are in store for a big fight today, so we need to stay close to our homes, and indoors."

"My God, Sallie, we may not know for sure until this battle is over," Barbara said.

Burns woke up from his sleep on the cellar door by absorbing a kick to his leg again. It was mid-afternoon he judged by the warmth of the day. He moaned and looked up to see who kicked him. He recognized the sergeant again, who said:

"Still with us? Well, the lieutenant wants us to get ya a ride to town. Ya live around hea?"

Burns spoke meekly as he hadn't the strength, saying:

"Yes, not far."

"Well that's good fo ya. I have made arrangements fo ya to ride in that thea wagon ova yonder. They say they know ya. They say they are the Sellingas. Ya know them?"

"I do," he said weakly.

"Well, they's ya ride home. So, let's get ya in the wagon."

The sergeant motioned for the two soldiers, who earlier had carried him to the Riggs' house, to carry him into the wagon. They did so, and placed him between the Sellinger's two children, Michael who was ten years old, and Mary who was about eight. Once there, Anthony Sellinger and his wife, Catherine, came around to the back of the wagon. Anthony was in his mid-thirties, was shorter than average, had brown hair, much of it gone by now, a long beard, blue eyes, and an average nose and mouth. He was dressed in a shabby, old white shirt, black trousers held up by black braces, and old brown boots. His wife Catherine was also in her mid-thirties, was average height, light blue eyes, a strong nose, thin lips, and brown hair covered by a soiled white bonnet, tied under her chin. She wore a tattered and soiled black, long sleeved, full length dress, with a white collar tightly buttoned at the neck. Anthony spoke with a thick, German accent:

"Herr Burns. Ve vill take ja home. Arc ja suitable in there?"

"Yes, Anthony, I am fine. Please take me home."

"Ve vill. I'm sure Frau Burns is vorried zick."

And so, the Sellingers climbed into the seat of the wagon and tugged on the reins of their blind horse, which responded and started pulling the wagon. They started east on Chambersburg Pike and had gone no more than a couple hundred feet, when they were stopped by a Confederate soldier, who said:

"Whoa, thea. Ya can't go this way into town."

"Vich vay, den?" Sellinger asked

"I don't much right care, ya just can't go this way, so turn that thea wagon round."

Catherine asked: "Maybe ve go on Mummasburg Road?"

"Ja, ve try dat vay," Anthony said as he turned the wagon around and headed north through the open fields.

The ride was bumpy, but the blind horse kept a steady pace toward the town and the Burns house. Michael said in a sweet, ten year old's voice:

"Mr. Burns, can I get you a blanket for your head?"

Burns nodded and then Michael said to his sister:

"Mary, hand me that blanket and we will make it into a pillow for him."

He placed the blanket gently under Burns' head. Burns looked up, but could only muster a smile for the little one. He reached over with his hand and motioned for Michael to grab it, which he did. Mary grabbed his other hand and for the rest of the journey to the Burns house, they held his hands tightly.

Burns never noticed these two children before. He thought Sellinger a nice enough neighbor, but had not bothered with the kids. Sellinger was a poor man, and so not many people from the town made the effort to get to know him or his wife, let alone their children. He himself never seemed to have the time, or the interest, to bother with them. And now, here they were holding his hands and making sure his ride was as comfortable as possible. He felt ashamed of himself for his blatant lack of regard for them. So, he just looked at them with a soft and compassionate look for the remainder of the journey home.

Barbara and Martha were busy in their house in the afternoon, trying to do anything to keep their minds off of Burns and their worries for him. It was around half-past four o'clock in the afternoon, when there was a loud knock on their kitchen door. At first, they thought the knock was loud so it could be heard over the cannon fire, which had begun about a half hour earlier, but soon they realized it was something different, as the knock was continuous. Martha looked at her mother and sensing the urgency of the knocker, ran to the door and opened it. She was surprised to see Joseph Broadhead, out of breath and with a huge smile on his face:

"Martha, Martha, love, your father is alive and is on his way in the Sellinger wagon. Come, come look, you can see the wagon coming across the fields."

Martha rushed out to the porch and looked in the direction Broadhead was pointing and indeed saw the Sellinger's blind horse pulling their wagon.

"Are you sure he is in that wagon?"

"Yes, yes, love. I saw him myself."

Martha started crying, but this time the tears were from joy. She ran into the house as her mother said:

"Martha, what is it?"

"Mother, it's father! He is not dead, and is on his way in the Sellinger's wagon. Come see," she said with her voice so excited it was crackling.

Barbara was speechless. She grabbed the baby and followed Martha out to the porch of their house.

"Mother, see. Here's comes the Sellinger's wagon."

Barbara, who was holding the baby with her left arm, put her right hand over her heart and over the baby and said looking up toward heaven:

"The Lord has answered our prayers and has brought him home to us."

"Yes, praise be to the Lord."

Within five minutes, the Sellinger's wagon reached Chambersburg Road and then stopped on West Street, next to the house. Martha had gone down the steps and was there to greet the wagon as it arrived. Once there, she went around to the back of the wagon, and seeing her father, she put her hands to her face and said:

"Father, oh father, you are alive."

Burns could only muster a smile and a slight wave. She then said to Broadhead and Sellinger:

"Can you help him inside? I will get his bed ready for him and send for the doctor."

Martha rushed into the house. Broadhead lowered the wagon door and removed the blanket, saying:

"Mr. Burns, are you in pain?"

Burns nodded and so Broadhead removed the blanket gingerly and said:

"Take my hand and I will help you up."

Burns winced as he was lifted by Broadhead to a sitting position. Broadhead gently pulled him to the edge of the wagon, and he and Sellinger put Burns's arms on their shoulders and gently lifted him down from the wagon. Burns put weight on his injured foot and then it buckled almost causing him to fall, but the two men caught him before he did so. Broadhead noticed and said compassionately:

"John, don't put your weight on it. Lean on us and we will get you into the house."

And so, they carried him to the stairs, each lifting up his legs and having his arm on their shoulders. They stopped at the foot of the stairs, rested a moment, and then proceeded up the stairs, into the house and to his bedroom, where they laid him gently in the bed Martha prepared. Martha propped up his pillow and covered him up with the blankets. She said to Broadhead:

"Joseph, would you be so kind as to fetch Dr. Horner?"

"Certainly, love."

And to Sellinger, she said:

"Mr. Sellinger, thank you so much for bringing my father back home to us. We can never repay the kindness you have showed us today."

"Fraulein Martha, you're friendship ist all ve ask."

"And that you shall have, for the rest of our days."

Within a half an hour, Dr. Horner was examining Burns. He took a thorough look at him and said to Martha and Barbara:

"He has sustained three wounds, one to the ankle, one to the forearm, and one on his side, just below his ribs. They were dressed by a doctor in the field, so they are fairly stable and they are clean. He has lost a lot of blood, but by the grace of God, there are no bone fractures. I am going to redress the wounds. In the meantime, he looks like he could use some nourishment. Can you make him some beef tea, whilst I do so? Let's get some of that in him and let's get him some well needed, and well deserved, rest."

Barbara said: "Oh, thank God. And, thank you, doctor."

Martha said to her father:

"Father, you are going to be alright. You just need rest and some food. I will bring you some beef tea."

Burns said in a soft voice, "Thank you, sweetheart."

He looked at Martha and Barbara as tears flowed down his cheeks. The two women went over to him and hugged him deeply from opposite sides of the bed. He put his arms around them and gave them as much a hug as he had the strength for.

A few minutes before this, the Confederate sergeant who arranged for the ride was curious as to where Burns lived and had followed the wagon to his house. He stood across the street from Burns' house when a young lady approached him. She said, "Sir, what are you looking at?"

"I am lookin' at the house whea that civilyun who was wounded durin' the battle yestaday lives. Do ya happen to know his name?"

"Yes, sir, that's Mr. John Burns."

"How's his wife doin'?"

The girl looked puzzled and said:

"Fine, she is old, but in fine health."

"Realla? I was told his wife was vera sick and he was in search of a girl to nuase hea back to health?"

"No, sir. She is in need of no nursing."

"Well, well, just as I thought, he was a lia all the time. A bushwacka lia. Soon, real soon we'll take caa of him. He'll get what a bushwacka deseaves. I give ya my woad on that."

CHAPTER 47

BUTLER

ELIZABETH (OLD LIZ) BUTLER was awakened just after first light on Thursday, July 2nd. She always was up before Samuel and today was no different even though they were hiding in the cupola of the Christ Lutheran Church in Gettysburg. She looked around and realized she was both cold and hungry, and she had to relieve herself. She saw Samuel still sleeping and saw he had taken off his shirt and wrapped it around his head. She was puzzled by this, but quickly realized he had done this to muffle his snoring. It really didn't matter though, she thought, because the awful noises the wounded men were making below in the church would have drowned out even his loudest snoring. She was surprised that they had gotten any sleep at all because of the sounds of the suffering boys below. She felt so very bad for them, wishing she could do something, but knew her predicament was one of stay quiet to stay free. She tossed and turned on the hard floor and finally fell back asleep.

She awoke again several hours later, in the mid-afternoon she judged as the sun had already moved in the sky toward the west, and there was much activity on the streets below. She looked over at Samuel, who was still asleep and saw how peaceful he looked as he slept. She loved him with all her heart. And, her love grew even stronger yesterday as he had given up his freedom and came out of hiding just so she didn't have to endure the horrible ordeal of being captured by the Confederates alone.

She decided it was time to wake Samuel as she didn't know what they would do at this point. The Rebels had taken the town yesterday and so they were trapped up in the cupola of the church.

"Sam'l, Sam'l wake up," she said while giving him a slight nudge.

"What, what?" he responded, at first rather loud, but as his mind began to clear, much more muffled as he continued:

"Old Liz, what's you's want?"

"Sam'l, what's we's gonna do? De Confedrats have de town and we's stuck up here."

"We's stay put, dat's what. We's stay put," he replied.

"You's sure? Can we's be fine here with no food or water, no blankit, no chambur pot?"

"None's dem needed dings. Freedum's needed ding. You's say's as much when we's a leavin' noth for Canada. You's 'member?"

"Yes, I's 'member. But, dat's before we's stuck up here," she said.

"Ole Liz, now what's dat matta? We's free because of you's and we's gonna stay dat way."

"S'pose you's right. It mattas for our boys, yes sur, it mattas for dem. Dey's the reason we's a leavin' in the first place."

"Yes, dey is. But, also neither you's nor I's wants to go back to slavin'."

"I's sorry Sam'l. I's just tired and hungry, dats all."

"Well, you's never mind dose dings. We's been hungry 'fore and made out just fine, yes ma'am, just fine."

"What's happen if dey's ketched us? Do you's dink we can stay geder?"

"Reckon a couple of broke down folks such as us ain't worth so much, so we's stand good chance to stays geder. But, we's won't be a findin' out, no ma'am."

She asked: "Member the ole Butler place, where's we grew up? Dat fine plantation in Richmon?"

"Dat's longs ago, old woman, longs ago."

"Yes, but Mr. Butler, he's always treated us fair."

"Fair for a slave. Not so fair now dat we knows freedom."

"Member when we jumped the broom geder?"

"Sure do. One of the grandest days of my life, dat day," he responded.

"And, member that awful day when's little Catherine be born and ole Mrs. Butler up and died?"

"Sad day, sad day, indeed."

"Masser Butler, he grieved for months loosting his wife like dat," she said.

"He did indeed. Dat po man."

"Member dat precious, precious baby Catherine? How cutes she was? I's could 'most be fine going backs dere, seeing dat little baby girl against."

"Now, donst you talk dat way, Ole Liz. Donst you. We stayin' free fo our boys and for us folks, and dats de way it be. No mo talk bouts slavin'. No mo, hear?"

Alright Sam'l, alright. I's be still."

As they were talking, they were moving ever so slightly and even with the terrible noises of the wounded, they made some scratching and creaking noises on the boards of the tower floor, and this was heard by a Confederate soldier who was in the church. He stopped by the steps leading to the cupola and listened intently to see if he heard the noises correctly. When he heard them again, he decided he would see what was making these noises, but first he would check with the Pastor, who was helping tend to the wounded men giving them comfort. The soldier approached and said:

"Pasta, I wonda if ya know what might be making noises in ya bell towa?"

"Excuse me, but I am needed here with this man."

"But, Pasta, we was told yestaday to round up all the Union soldyas hidin' in town. Maybe they's one up in ya towa?"

"Nonsense. We have mice that frequent the cupola," he emphasized cupola to the soldier knowing he knew nothing of the proper terminology for church's architecture before continuing:

"And, we have to chase them away all the time. Besides, noises up there are common for this place."

"Just the same, Pasta, I think I need to check."

The pastor was now angry and so he said:

"Young soldier, can't you see this man is dying here, and you are chasing mice? Leave the mice be."

"But, Pasta, like I said, just the same, I wants to check."

"Well, you find an officer to tell me so and I will consider it."

And, so the soldier went to look for an officer and returned with a captain a few minutes later. The first soldier said to the pastor:

"Pasta, this hea captain, he wants to check that bell towa to see if they any Union soldyas hidin' up thea."

"Is this correct, captain...? the pastor asked in a very annoyed voice, then paused and continued:

"Because I have a lot of work to do here and we don't allow persons not of the church up there. It is rather a blessed place to us, you understand?"

"Pasta, maybe ya could have one of ya servas go up and check?"

"Alright, if we must. But, once we prove there is nothing up there will you leave us and the cupola be?"

"Yes, sur, we will."

The pastor went to the back of the church and brought a young server boy to the Confederates, and said:

"This here is Tommy. He will go up to the cupola."

To Tommy, the pastor said:

"Tommy, these soldiers think we are hiding a soldier up there. I told them it was just mice. Can you make sure there are no soldiers up there?"

He finished with a sarcastic look at the soldiers and said:

"I insist you two stay at the bottom of the stairs whilst he goes up."

"Yes, Pasta. That be fine," the captain said and continued turning to the boy:

"Now boy, ya go up them stairs and ya tell us what ya see, undastood?"

"Yes, sir," the boy said and began to climb the stairs to the cupola.

As Samuel finished admonishing Old Liz to be still about returning to slavery, he heard a noise on the stairs. He looked at her with wide eyes. She put her index finger to her lips and said as quietly as she could:

"Shh."

Samuel nodded and they both sat still and kept quiet, listening to see if the footsteps on the stairs below were getting closer. Their hearts began to race, and then beat even faster like they would pop out of their chests, when they realized the footsteps were coming up to the top. They held their breath as the trap door was pushed open. It slammed the floor of the cupola with a thud. There was a pause and then a young boy's head appeared up into the tower. He looked around and saw Old Liz and Samuel. Their eyes locked and he said in a loud voice, loud enough for the soldiers to hear below:

"Shoo, shoo, shoo."

He climbed the last stairs and loudly stomped on the floor at the same time as he looked over at the couple. He continued stomping and put his index finger to his lips and said, smiling at them:

"Ain't no soldiers up here, no sir. Just a couple of mice and they are gone now, too."

"Alright, ya come on down now," the captain said.

The boy turned to go, but then mouthed to them without sound:

"Be back. Stay put and stay quiet."

The Butlers nodded their understanding and the boy went down the stairs closing the trap door behind him. He reached the bottom of the stairs and said:

"Nothing's up there except a couple of mice."

"You see, now can I get back to that boy who so desperately needs me?" the pastor asked.

"Alright and thank ya, Pasta," the captain said.

Satisfied, the soldiers left the boy and the pastor. The boy waited until the soldiers were almost out of hearing and then said winking as he said it:

"Pastor, is there anything more I can do to help you?"

The pastor noticed the wink, paused, and said:

"Tommy, I need some help getting more bandages for the wounded. Could you please follow me?"

"Yes, Pastor. I will help in any way you need."

They left the main body of the church and went to the back, where the supplies were kept, but mainly to be in a place where they could talk without being overheard. Once there, the pastor said:

"Tommy, what's the matter?"

"Pastor, Pastor, there is a colored man and woman up in the cupola."

"There is?"

"Yes, and it looks like they have been there since yesterday."

"Are they alright, you reckon?"

"Looks so, but if they'd been there all night, they must be hungry, thirsty, and in need of a chamber pot. No telling how long they will need to be there."

"That they may, and we must find a way to get them those things. Tommy, think quickly. We need to come up with a reason for you to go up to the cupola, which will not attract attention."

The boy thought for a moment and said:

"Pastor, I don't believe I have swept the cupola in quite a spell. How about I go up and clean it? I could bring them some bread and some water that way."

"Yes, I believe it needs to be swept. And, with the wounded here, it would be better if we did some cleaning of our beloved church."

He thought for a moment and then continued:

"Here's what we'll do. Go to the kitchen and fetch some bread, and then fill a little bottle with some water and pack it in your shirt. Come to me and ask me if there is anything you can do. I will tell you to clean this place for the soldiers. Then, fetch a broom and to not attract attention to the cupola, sweep the stairs outside, work your way inside, and then finally the stairs to the cupola and the cupola itself. Understand?"

"Yes, Pastor."

"Fine. I'll go back to that poor boy who needs me and you go to the kitchen."

And, so they did. In a few moments the pastor was again tending the wounded soldier and Tommy approached him, saying:

"Pastor, what can I do to help?"

The pastor looked up from the wounded man and said:

"Tommy, maybe you could do some sweeping and some cleaning of this place for the soldiers?"

"Yes, Pastor. Do you want me to start outside on the stairs?"

"Yes, that would be fine."

Tommy went to the closet, got a broom, went outside and began to sweep. He kept up this charade for about a half an hour, sweeping the floors, and then he eventually made his way up the stairs to the cupola, sweeping each as he went. The Rebel soldiers in the church paid no attention to what he was doing, as the soldier who made them search it before had left awhile earlier. Tommy opened the trap door and went up into the cupola. He again locked eyes with Old Liz, but kept sweeping the floor of the tower. He did this for a couple of minutes and then made his way over to them. For a moment, he stopped sweeping and reached into his shirt, producing two hunks of bread and a small bottle of water. He handed these to Old Liz and continued sweeping. He soon finished sweeping and looked at the Butlers, saying in a noiseless voice, "Be back. Keep still."

He heard a voice from below:

"Ya up thea, what's ya doin' up thea?"

Tommy looked panicked at the Butlers, but quickly composed himself and said:

"Just some cleaning, that's all. I'm done and am coming back down."

Tommy started down the stairs, closing the trap door as he went, just as the Confederate was beginning to climb the stairs. Tommy met him halfway up and said:

"You can't come up here. The pastor won't allow others to come up here."

"Awe, come now, just a little peak of the view."

"No, pastor won't permit it."

Old Liz and Samuel looked at each other as they overheard the conversation between Tommy and the soldier. A tear formed in Liz's eye as she was again scared they would be discovered. But, also the tear was for Tommy's kindness in protecting them. She never felt they were part of this town, being colored folk. But, today she felt like they were, felt that she and Samuel were just neighbors in need of assistance from the town, and this benevolent boy was providing that support despite the dangers of doing so. For the first time, she felt like they belonged.

She continued to listen and heard the soldier give in to Tommy and the two of them go down the stairs. She listened some more and heard the noise of their footsteps fading away. In another minute she whispered to Samuel:

"Sam'l, dat boy, he a gift from God."

"Sure's is."

"I never feel dis town was our home. Today's I's thinks different. We's part of dis town. That boy, he made us so. He made us so."

As she completed saying this, her next words were interrupted by the roar of cannon fire in the distance south of the town.

They both heard the cannon fire and turned their heads toward that part of town. Samuel said: "I's just hope dey be a town to be a part of."

CHAPTER 48

WENTZ

JOHN WENTZ was in his house alone. His house was located near the Sherfy farm, but on the east side of the Emmitsburg Road, north of the intersection with the Millerstown Road. He sent his wife Mary and their daughter Susan away from the impending dangers of the battle last night; sent them over to the Rose Farm and from there they would go to Two Taverns with the Roses' children. He expected they had gotten there and were safe. And, so he felt comforted with that thought, but now he would be in danger. According to the Confederate Colonel Moxley Sorrel last evening, the battle today could be on this very area where his house stood. He had chosen to stay and do what he could to protect his house and his property, but at what cost might that be? Would he survive it?

It was mid-afternoon when he noticed the Confederates marching toward his house from the west. Earlier, he spied the Union army taking position just to the east, coming down from the little mountain north of Round Top, and forming a line of defense that extended well past his house in both the north and the south directions. He watched intently as the Rebels broke out of their column of fours and began to deploy forming a line of battle. Unknown to him, his son Henry was with them. He was a member

A portion of the foundation of the Wentz House is all that remains today, located on Emmitsburg Road near Millerstown Road. (Faber)

of the Eubank-Taylor Virginia Battery (Taylor Battery), who were at that very moment setting their guns in position on Seminary Ridge just west of the house.

"Gentleman, let's set ya cannon hea at this location," Captain Osmond B. Taylor ordered his men of the Taylor Battery. He pointed to the location he wanted and then the men detached the cannons from the horses and moved them into place. Henry Wentz was among them.

"Henra, which is ya fatha's house?" one of Henry's comrades named George asked while sweating and moving the piece into place.

Once they got the cannon in a proper location and spun it around to face the east toward a peach orchard, Henry replied in a tired voice and pointed toward the house:

"That one over there."

"Why, its right in the line of fia."

"It is, and I am worried my father is still in it. He's so stubborn about the house and his property, he probably is staying behind to protect it. I just hope he has sent mother and my little sister away."

"Now, don't ya fret none. He wouldn't subject the ladies to this, would he?"

"I hope not. I really do."

Just then Colonel Porter Alexander rode up and addressed Captain Taylor:

"Captain, when I give the signal, ya open up on that peach oachad yonda."

"Yes, Colonel, but that cannot be moa than 400 yaads."

"That is accuate, Captain, as I expect ya battea to be. I want to clea them Yankees out of that thea oachad, and I anticipate ya doin' the job."

"Ya can count on us Colonel."

"I knew I could."

Wentz noticed Alexander ride away toward the north to set the artillery up there. He returned about fifteen minutes later and was joined by another general and his staff. Each general had field glasses pressed against their faces. Wentz squinted to see if he could recognize the other general and all at once, he knew who it was. He poked his comrade and said:

"George, look over there, with Alexander. It's Longstreet. He must really be concerned about this battle to be up so close to the lines."

"Why, it ceatainly is. Ya must be right. He doesn't come this close."

"I wonder what's got him so anxious today."

"I dunno. It couldn't be them Yankees. We whipped 'em but good yestaday, and we'll do it again today."

The Peach Orchard as is today, located at the intersection of Millerstown and Emmitsburg Roads (Faber).

They proceeded to load their cannon and Wentz readied himself to pull the lanyard. At that moment Taylor was given the signal by Alexander, and so he yelled, "Fia!"

Wentz was staring out his window toward the Confederate lines at around four o'clock when he noticed a flash and smoke coming from one of their cannons, followed by the loud popping noise. And, then another, and another. He braced himself for the possible impact of the shot with his house, but then noticed the target was Sherfy's peach orchard south of Millerstown Road. Dirt kicked up and several tree branches fell from the impact of the cannon balls. Soon, he heard the Union cannon answer from just behind his house and the battle was on. The sides traded cannon fire for several minutes and Wentz noticed the Rebels begin to advance toward his house and toward the peach orchard. He decided it was time to retire to the cellar and wait the battle out there, and so he descended down the steps and went to the corner where he placed a small cot with a blanket. He sat on the cot and listened as the noises of the battle became more intense. He could hear the whistle of the shots overhead, going in both directions. He decided there was little he could do until the battle was either finished or if his house became directly involved. He prayed it would not be the latter.

"Gentlemen, move up. Move up, now. We got 'em on the run," Taylor yelled about an hour later and continued:
"Let's move to beyond the road and set up nea that house yonda to support ou advance."
He was pointing toward the Wentz house.

George said: "Henra, we are going right up to your house, fightin' on the very ground ya played on as a boy."

"Yeah, isn't that grand? Killing boys defending the very same land I pretended to protect from invaders. And, now I'm the invader."

The irony of the statement caught George by surprise such that he could think of nothing to say, so they worked in silence, hitching their gun to the horse and moving it up to, and beyond, the Emmitsburg Road. They redeployed it just beyond the Wentz house and pointed it northeast toward the retreating Union soldiers and beyond to the Union defenses on Cemetery Ridge. Once in place, Taylor again ordered them to fire, and so the gun became collaboration for the advance of the Rebels northeast and easterly.

All the rest of the afternoon and early evening, they loaded and fired their gun, supporting the Rebel advances and then repelling the Union counterattacks. The fighting was particularly intense as the ebb and flow of the battle engulfed the field between the Wentz house and Cemetery Ridge, and the areas both north and south of that location. The blood spilled was immense and the field was littered with the dead and the wounded on both sides. Finally, darkness came and the action died down to just an intense struggle for the little mountain north of Round Top to the south, and way off toward the north, a struggle for the two hills located southeast of the town. Soon, these too were decided and the stillness of the night took over the field, only to be overtaken by the cries of the fallen. Henry tried not to listen, but it was nearly impossible. He thought of his father.

"George, I've got to see if my father is in the house."

"Well, I am sua the captain will let ya go and see."

And so, after receiving permission from the captain, Henry proceeded over to the house he had grown up in, but had not seen for a long time, as he had moved to Virginia some ten years earlier. Once he got to the front door, he knocked on it loudly. He hesitated and listened for any movement on the inside.

The battle finally calmed down and Wentz was relieved his house had, as far as he could tell without a close inspection, received little damage. He decided to come out from his cellar and he began to climb the steps. He hadn't reached the top when he heard a knock on his door. He froze. What would he do if this was the Rebel army and they wanted his only food stores he had? And, what if they took all his whiskey, drank it up, and began to defile his house? He decided to ignore the knock, hoping it would go away if he didn't answer. But then, his courage grew and he decided he would face the invaders with deliberate purpose and so when the next round of knocking occurred, he pulled the door open with force and yelled:

"Who is disturbing me at my house tonight?"

Once his eyes got used to the night darkness, he noticed it was Henry, who wore a shocked look on his face. Henry said:

"Father, it's me, Henry."

Wentz was now the one shocked, and he looked at his son for several brief moments before he could react. Finally, it dawned on him, and he took quick steps to his son and embraced him, kissing him on the neck.

"Oh Henry. You're here, and you're safe. Let me take a look at you."

He pulled back to an arm's length and grabbed Henry's shoulders:

"You look fine, just fine. Are you alright?"

"Yes, I am, but I wanted to ask the same of you."

"I am fine. A little worse for wear, but I am fine."

"And, Mother and Susan?"

"They are safe. I sent them to Two Taverns last night, so they are fine."

"Why didn't you go with them?"

"I stayed to protect my land. I cannot afford to lose our little farm, so I will stay and face whatever happens," he said.

"Even if it costs you your life? The farm is not worth that."

"It is to me, son. It is to me. Don't stand out there. Come in, come in."

The younger Wentz stepped into the house. Momentarily his thoughts were flooded of images of his childhood. He wondered how many times he passed through that door to enter into the house, and how many times he would see his father, by the fire, telling stories to this little sister, and his mother in the kitchen preparing supper. The smell of house intensified his feeling of being home. But, then his reality returned and so did the concern for his father.

"Father, you could have been killed today. This house was right in the middle of the fighting. It could be hit and burnt to the ground."

"It could and if that happens, well then it is God's will. But, if I can prevent anything else from happening to it, I will."

"Father, you have always been so bull-headed about this house."

"Of course I have. It is all your mother and I have. And, besides, it has the memories we cherish so very much. Memories of you and your sister. I will never let this house, where you were born and where you became a man, be destroyed or defiled. Never," Wentz said emphatically. He continued:

"Now, sit for a spell. I want to look at you and I want to hear all about you. It has been so long since I've seen you. I want to enjoy these moments with you as if these are the last."

CHAPTER 49

CULP

JOHN WESLEY (WES) CULP awoke on Thursday morning July 2nd still shaken and sweaty from a disturbing dream. He had had it before, but not to this detail. He decided this was because he was so close to his old house that the dream must have taken on an extra special energy of its own. Plus, he was so sad when he fell asleep last night because of the news that his good friend Jack Skelly was dying, and really could be dead already. These had to have had an effect on the dream making it so very real. He lay under his blanket and stared at the top of his tent and reflected on the dream. It was of his dead mother, and he was again seeking her forgiveness because he joined the Confederacy. Deep inside he still felt the guilt of turning on his country, his home, and his friends, and so that guilt manifested itself into a reoccurring, and frustrating, dream of him asking his mother's forgiveness, but never getting it.

He tried to suppress the dream as he thought of what he must do today for Jack. He now had the unpleasant duty of informing Jack's mother, his brother Daniel, but most of all Ginnie Wade, of the sad news. He knew Ginnie would take it very hard. He also knew he would have to deliver Jack's letters to his mother and to Ginnie, and this would make the news of Jack's demise even that much more terrible. He leaned over and fumbled through his things finding the two letters. He decided he would deliver these tonight, if possible, after the day's events unfolded and he knew where the regiment would be camped. The talk of the men last night was full of confidence. Confidence that the battle would be won today by the Rebels, and maybe the army would be on their way to Washington tomorrow, so tonight might be his only chance to complete the deed. Besides, he could not bear to keep this sad news any longer than one more day.

Once he finished his thoughts on handling the affairs regarding his friend Jack, the dream of his mother returned front and center to his thinking. It was too real and too vivid, and it was burned in his brain. He recalled it from the very beginning, as if he actually lived it already. He couldn't stop it from coming, so he closed his eyes and let it come, watching as his brain played it as if it were a real memory:

He dressed and then went to look for Pendleton and Arthur. He found them by a campfire drinking coffee.

"Mornin' Wes. Coffee's ova thea," Pendleton said pointing to the wagon where coffee was being served to the men.

Culp nodded and then went to grab a cup. Once he filled his cup, he came back to the fire.

"Wes, woad is the Yanks a entaenched up on ya cousin's hill and that next one," Arthur informed him.

"If that's true, it might be quite a feat gettin' 'em off it," Culp answered.

"Maybe to any otha aamy, but not ous. We are the best fighin' men in the world. An unstoppable foace, that's what we is," Pendleton said.

"I hope you are right, because that hill is pretty steep, particularly on the north side facing us. I remember it well as a boy, sledding down it in the snow."

Culp took a short break from the dream and smiled as he remembered the fun of sledding. This was soon overtaken by the power of the dream again and it continued:

"That must have been excitin'. I haven't thought of sleddin' in so vea long," Arthur said.

Pendleton changed the subject and asked: "Speakin' of ya childhood, ya plannin' on seeing ya motha today?"

It was at this point the dream turned serious. Culp's stomach churned and his hands were even sweaty. It continued:

"Yes. I was thinking of going over this morning. Do you think I can get a quick leave to do it?"

"I don't see why not. Why not go see Sageant Sheetz and see if ya can git an houa away?"

Culp gulped and then took another sip of his coffee, stared into the fire and thought what if he did see his mother? How would she react to seeing him again? What if she wouldn't see him? Well, no matter, he would have to try, try to get forgiveness. So, he took one more sip, threw the remainder into the fire, and announced:

"That's just what I will do."

The dream then shifted to him readying himself to see his mother:

Culp then went to his tent. He combed his hair, tucked his shirt, buttoned his coat, and straightened his trousers. Satisfied with his appearance, he left the tent and walked to his house to see his mother. Once there, he climbed the porch steps and approached the door. He held his hand up and readied to knock. He somehow found the courage and he knocked on the door. He hoped she wouldn't answer, but shortly he heard footsteps approach the door and then the door opened.

His mother opened the door and stared at him. There she was! She looked the same as she always did, not changed or aged a bit. Neither said anything for a long moment. Finally, he spoke as he had to.

"Mother, it is your son, Wes."

She looked at him, but did not speak immediately.

"Mother?"

"Yes, I can see it is you."

"Aren't you glad to see me?"

"S'pose I am. S'pose I'm not. Does it make a difference?"

"Of course, it does. I have missed you terribly. Have you not missed me?"

"S'pose I have," she said as coldly as the rest of her answers had been. And, then she continued:

"What you doing here, in that, that uniform?"

"I have come to see you, that's all."

"Come to see me? Why have you come to see me?"

"Because you are my mother, and I have come to seek your forgiveness for me joining the Confederacy."

"Well, I won't give it to you."

"But, why not?"

She ignored his question and stared off into the distance behind him, and then she carried on her own conversation, saying:

"You should have thought of forgiveness before you put that traitorous uniform on. Thought of how your family would take you being a turncoat and how your family would be treated because of it."

"I'm sorry I have caused you any pain."

"Too late for that."

"I suppose so," he said with tears forming in his eyes.

"Too late for any of it."

"Are you not going to welcome me home?"

"What fur? Haven't you come to take over the town with your army?"

"Well, yes, but it is just because of the war. We had to come north otherwise it might never end."

"Is that how you justify it?"

"It's the truth," he said and the tears now ran down his face.

"Truth, what do you know about truth? Truth is being true to who you are and how you grew up."

"Mother, people change. I changed."

"Not changed in the way you have chosen. That is not truth. You turned your back on us and now you come visiting as if it is old home week. Well, it's not, and I am not welcoming you back here."

"You are not welcoming me, home, to my own house?"

"This is not your house. Not anymore. And, you are just someone that I used to know."

She said this with a very cold look and stared directly into his eyes with that look. This stunned him and hurt him deeply. Yet, he thought he might receive this reaction from her about his decision to join the Confederacy as she was a staunch Union supporter. He remembered he received it many times before, and this made his effort to receive forgiveness from her ever so important to him as it would add legitimacy to his decision. But, she would have none of it, and worse yet, she was very cold to him, enough for him to even question her love for him. This hurt him even more, so much so that he just stood and didn't speak.

"Well, is there anything else you want? Did you get what you came for?"

Still, he didn't know what to say. It was then that he noticed a tear forming in her eye. She turned her head in an attempt to conceal it, but he had seen it and that was enough to give him a little hope of her love for him. It was still there, so maybe this time he would get the forgiveness he sought so desperately. So, he said:

"No, mother. I just wanted to see you again and to tell you that I love you, and that I always will."

"I know that Wes, but you are a traitor. Well, you've seen me and you have said it. Now I must go," she said.

And with that, she shut the door. He was still standing there on the porch and for a moment, he didn't know what to do. Should he knock again? He didn't get what he came for. If she would just forgive him, maybe the rest of the family might also. Maybe even a return, eventually, to the way things were before the war. If he could just survive this war, he might be able to merge his two lives into one; to be able to start a life with Catherine and raise a family with her, and be welcomed with that family at home here in Gettysburg. It just might be possible. So, he turned around and walked down the steps. He would try another time.

With that, the dream rewind ended. He wiped the tears from his eyes and got up to find his friends and to cope with the day's challenges.

A few minutes later he left the tent and looked for Pendleton and Arthur. He found them and Pendleton said:

"Wes, ya alright? Ya must have had some bad dream. Ya moanin' all night."

"Yeah, that one with my mother again."

"Well, soona oa lata ya gonna have to get that one outta ya mind."

"I know, but it is so very hard to do," Culp said and changed the subject: "Have we any orders?"

"Not yet, but I do believe we will be engaged in getting' your cousin's hill from the Yanks some time today."

Pendleton's assumption was correct. Later in the morning the orders came that the Stonewall Brigade would be held in reserve to support General Allegheny Johnson's thrust to take Culp's Hill. The battle for the hill commenced at dusk and continued until it became too dark to clearly identify the enemy. The Confederates had a modest gain of the north face of the hill when the two armies suspended the fighting for the day. The Stonewall Brigade did not see any action as late start of the battle limited the amount of troops the Southerners could send into the engagement. And, so Culp, Pendleton, and Arthur, along with their mates waited the day out wondering and hoping to get into the fight. As dusk approached, it became obvious to them they would not be involved. Culp, anxious about waiting around, said:

"B.S., it looks as though we won't be in this one. It started too late for us to involve our full force. I wonder if we are taking the hill?"

"Looks so. They just gonna haff to win this un without the Stonewall Brigade."

"Yes, sir, it feels nice to sit one ou once in awhile," Arthur added.

"I just hope we took that hill."

"Iffen we did, should we haff a picnic up on it?" Pendleton teased.

"Well, why not. We'll have earned it," Culp teased right back.

"Umm, umm, I can just smell that fresh poak. But, we need some whiska. Now whea will we be getting' that?" Arthur added to the jesting.

"Don't know, but we'll fine some sure enough, even if I have to go to town to get it," Culp said as the finality to their humor.

Pendleton changed the subject saying: "Say, Wes, don't ya have them letters ya need to pass on to ya friend's motha and his betaothed?"

"Yes, I do, and since we are not in the action and are just sitting this one out, I plan on doing that tonight. Plus, I think I'll pay my sister a visit at her house. Care to come along?"

"Nah, I think this family time should be ya's and ya's alone, just the same."

There was no immediate response to his knock. He didn't expect one, though, since it was after ten o'clock in the evening. Eventually, he heard footsteps in the hall behind the door, and a deep, male voice ask:

"Who's there and what do you want?"

It was Jefferson Myers, whom Wes had met a few times before he left Gettysburg, but there was never much of a friendship between them, even though they were the same age. There never seemed to be anything they shared in common, until now. Culp steadied himself, cleared his throat, and said:

"Jeff, it's me, Wes Culp."

Myers opened the door and looked stunned at Culp's presence. It took awhile for him to speak, but eventually he said turning his head toward the back of the house:

"Annie, your brother is at our door."

And, then to Culp:

"Good Lord, I never thought I would see you again."

"Nor, me you. But, here I am and I haven't seen my big sis Annie in over five years."

Just then, Culp heard Annie running down the stairs and then the hall until she got to the door. She stopped and hesitated for a moment, but it was brief, and then she flung herself into Culp, and said:

"Wes, oh Wes, you have come home. I can hardly believe it!"

He hugged her with all his might, and then picked her up and swung her around, all the while maintaining his hug of her. He stopped swinging her and dropped her gently. He pulled away to be arm's length and said:

"Lemme get a look atcha. Annie, you're looking fine. Fine indeed. It seems marriage has agreed with you. And, Jefferson, you look fine, too."

"Wes, you look good. It has been so long since I have seen you. Five years has been a long time and you have filled out. What does that army of yours feed you?"

"Well, we have been eating a lot better these past weeks since we came to Pennsylvania."

"On our meat and dairy I presume," Jefferson said sarcastically.

Culp looked at him, sized him up for a second or two, but then just coolly smiled and said to him:

"That may be, but it is all in payment for our hosting of your boys in Virginia. But no matter, let us not quarrel over the obvious. Rather, I would like to have a pleasant visit with my big sister, if you don't mind?"

He turned back to Annie and said:

"Where's Julia?"

"Wes, it's awful. The wounded men, they are everywhere. Everywhere where they can be cared for. Julia is helping nurse our men in the new Courthouse. She's been there since yesterday and came home, here, for short time last night, just long enough for her to change into fresh clothes and take a bit of supper."

"That's wonderful, Annie. I knew she was the nursing type, every since we were little and she cared for the sick animals on the farm. Remember?"

"Yes, I do. Now, you come in our house and I will fix you some supper. It looks like you could use a little food, too."

Jefferson stepped aside as brother and sister walked past him arm in arm. Annie showed him to the kitchen and had him sit at their dining table.

"Would you care for a cup of tea, whilst I fix you a plate of Minced Pie of Beef?"

"That would be grand, Annie."

Annie turned to her husband and said:

"Jeff, tea?"

He nodded and took a place across the table from Culp, where he stared at him without speaking. Annie noticed the tension, put the tea kettle down, turned to them hands on hips and said:

"I will have no war talk this evening. I don't care that the battle is right here. I haven't seen my little brother in over five years and I intend to have pleasant conversation. Is that clear?"

Both men nodded to her and then she continued:

"You know, Wes, a lot of people are still angry with you over your decision to join the Rebels. Brother William has vowed to shoot you on site, and a lot of our other kin have said the same."

"I know. I saw him at the Battle of Winchester, and he saw me. I couldn't raise my rifle against him, but he did to me. He deliberately took a shot at me, right at my head. Thank the Lord he missed high."

"The Battle of Winchester? You mean the battle a couple of weeks ago?" Annie asked.

"Yes."

"Strange, he didn't mention that to us afterwards. Well, I guess not so strange. He has never spoken of you since you joined. The last thing he said was you are dead to him, and that he has no brother."

She paused before continuing:

"Oh, Wes, I am sorry I have to give you such awful news."

"No matter, sis. I know. I saw his eyes. Cold, black eyes. I know he hates me and wishes I was dead. Better, that he could do the job himself. Where is he, by the way?"

She dished up a plate of minced pie and brought it over and set it in front of him, along with a napkin and a fork. She turned and got the three cups of tea, and settled into a chair between the two men.

"Out east somewhere. York, I think. The regiment disbanded since Winchester and so they were assigned to different units. He has been gone for about two weeks now."

"That's good. I was hoping not to see him on the battlefield again, and even if he is ordered here, Early's forces would block their way, so it is very unlikely I will see him."

There was silence for a moment, while Culp ate a couple of bites of the minced pie. He said:

"This is delicious. I see you have not lost your touch in the kitchen."

Annie smiled and looked at Jefferson, saying:

"Well, I have to make sure my husband is fattened up for the winter."

She then got a serious look on her face and said:

"Wes, what happened to you in Virginia? Why have you turned your back on us up here and have never been home?"

Culp hesitated, and looked at both of them. He then looked down at his food, took another bite and mumbled as he chewed:

"A woman."

"Did you say a woman?"

"I did."

"Really, you have a sweetheart there in Virginia?"

"I do. Her name is Catherine and she is the most beautiful woman I have ever seen, and the most gentle."

"My Lord, little brother. A woman? Why didn't you tell us of her before?"

"She is the daughter of a plantation owner, and they have slaves."

"They have slaves?" she said with a very surprised tone.

"Yes. Her father is very wealthy and very much a successionist. He doesn't approve of me, or at least he didn't, since I was from the north."

Annie was still stunned from his revelation and so she could only say:

"A woman?"

"Yes, and we are to be married after the war is over. He just recently gave his blessing a couple of weeks ago. I have been trying for over three years to get it, and finally, after our victory at Winchester, he yielded."

"Married? Wes, really? I am so happy for you."

He took another bite of food and said:

"Thank you, sis. But, it won't be until after the war, assuming I survive it."

"Now, don't you talk like that. Of course, you will survive it, and you will come home. Maybe even home here to Gettysburg."

"I sure would like to bring her here to meet you. You would love her. She is just a genuinely warm and caring person."

"Yeah, one who owns slaves," Jefferson added.

Culp gave him a sour look and he got the hint that his presence and his comments were creating an unwelcoming air, so he rose from his chair and said:

"Wes, I can see I am not helping the mood between you and your sister, so I am going to retire to bed. I am tired anyway. Glad to see you and that you are well. Goodnight."

And with that, he left the room. Annie looked over at Culp and said:

"Never mind him. He was in the war and got discharged earlier in the year, because of rheumatism of his joints. I guess it was all those cold and wet nights and days in the army. It took a toll on him. But, more he feels he let his unit, and the men, down. Sometimes I think he wants back in the war. Well, no matter. Tell me more about, what is her name, Catherine?"

"Yes. What more can I tell you except that I am so happy she is to be my wife?"

"Well, let's see. Why did you have to join the Rebels because of her?"

"Like I said, her father didn't approve of me right from the beginning. He felt his daughter should be marrying a "propa Southean gentleman" as he would put it. You know me, when I want something, so I kept after her and him. Finally, the war came, and my two best friends from Sheperdstown decided they were going to enlist and urged me to join with them. These two are my brothers, no more, like blood. I am closer to them than I ever was with William, and so imagining them going off to war without me was very difficult. But, I am from the North, so it was expected that I would not be going with them. Still, there was Catherine, and she made a plan and presented it to her father. She asked him if I joined the Confederacy and fought for the cause, would he reconsider his approval of me. He agreed to consider it, and so I had to think about this being my best, and really my only, chance to marry her. And, so after a sleepless night, I chose Catherine, even over my country and my family."

He finished his meal and looked at her for a response. She absorbed it all and said:

"She must be some woman. I really hope to meet her someday."

"I hope so, too. I cannot wait to see her again. I miss her so."

He then remembered his promise to Jack and the letters. So, he changed the subject:

"Annie, do you remember Jack Skelly and Billy Holtzworth?"

"Sure. Ginnie is very worried about Jack as she has not heard from him in weeks, since way before Winchester."

"I know."

Annie looked at Wes with a puzzled look, and so he explained:

"After the battle, I was walking among the Yankee prisoners and I found Billy. He was unhurt, but he took me to see Jack, who had gotten a ball in his arm. The doctors had not seen him yet, so I got him to the hospital. He was taken to Winchester and was immediately taken into surgery where they took his left arm."

Annie put her hands to her mouth and took a deep breath. Culp continued:

"I was there when they sawed it right off. I helped comfort him during the cutting. It was awful to see him like that. I went back the next day and he looked terrible, but he was conscious and he talked of coming home, coming home to marry Ginnie. He was going to properly propose to her when he got back, and it looked like the loss of his arm would bring him home. He had said he had two letters, one for his mother and one for Ginnie. The letter to his mother detailed the news and in Ginnie's, he asked her to marry him. He asked me to either deliver them in person or post them."

"Oh, how wonderful. Ginnie will be so thrilled."

"Yes, but there is more. I asked the nurse caring for him to send me news of his condition, if it got worse. I received a letter last night from her, and she said he is slipping away and feared he may not live more than a couple more days. It was dated last Friday, so he could be gone as we speak."

Again, Annie put her hands to her face. She didn't know what to say to him, so he continued:

"I have to deliver the letters and the news of Jack to Ginnie and his mother, Annie. I have to do it."

"Do you want me to give his mother's letter to her? She has gone to spend time in a neighbor's cellar I heard, but which one I don't know."

"No thanks, I promised I would deliver them personally, and that is what I am going to do. I thought I saw Ginnie earlier today, down on south Baltimore Street across from the Wagon Hotel."

"You probably did. Her sister Georgia just had her baby, and the whole family has been helping her, even Mrs. Comfort."

"Well, then I cannot get the letter to her tonight. The Yanks are putting up quite a fight all around that place. It's a pretty dangerous place to be. I better just come back tomorrow and give the letters."

"Why don't you stay the night here? I haven't seen you in so long and it would be so nice if you would stay."

"I'd love to, sis, but I can't. I have to get back."

He rose to go and looked at her with sad eyes, saying:

"I really wish it were better times. I really wish I could stay. I miss you and Julia so much. But, this is the path I have chosen, right or wrong, and I have to live it."

Annie began to get tears in her eyes and she said:

"What if I don't see you again? I don't know if I could take that. Please keep yourself out of harm's way. Promise?"

"I will."

They hugged each other for about a minute and then walked to the front door. He hugged her again and then after opening the door and stepping onto the porch, said:

"I will be back tomorrow, maybe even the morning."

"Please be safe and please keep your head down. You promised."

CHAPTER 50

MYERS AND PIERCE

On the second day of the battle the fighting was extremely brutal, bloody, and desperate, but desperate for different reasons. The North was desperate to stem the tide of the Confederate advance into their territory and push them back, while the South was desperate for a great victory in the north to show they could indeed win the war, and maybe end it before the real industrial might of the North made it impossible for them to do so. It was fought primarily in two locations, Culp's Hill and Cemetery Hill on the north flank of the Union army line; and Cemetery Ridge, from north of the little mountain north of Round Top to Round Top, on the south flank of the Federal line.

This desperation produced some real acts of heroism and bravery on both sides of the conflict. The Southerners, who were the attackers, charged many times, and in many places, into heavily fortified Union positions, while the northerners, who were the defenders, defied logic by not giving ground even though the circumstances of the fight dictated pulling back. Desperation had replaced intelligence in many instances. So, it went with the soldiers engaged in the struggle, fighting for their lives and fighting with everything they had for their respective countries, in and about this little town in south central Pennsylvania.

Many of the citizens of this town also experienced this desperation; desperate because this horrible event produced a massive amount of casualties needing care in order to survive. Ordinary people, most of whom had no medical training, were required to pitch in and give all they had to save these men, and sometimes this came at great peril to their own safety as the battle raged around them. They were needed to feed, to change bandages, but most of all they were needed to make the men comfortable and to ease their suffering. Two such women, one in town and one in the country southeast of town, did this very thing, and in so doing formed a strong affinity and bond to the men they cared for.

ELIZABETH SALOME (SALLIE) MYERS started the day on Thursday, July 2nd the same way she ended the previous night, cooking beef tea, washing bandages, and baking bread. When the bread was done, she would take it to the church to feed the wounded men. She tried not to hear the cries of the men, but it was difficult for her, so she would leave the church as soon as she completed her delivery of the much needed bread, and gathered bandages to be boiled.

It was about mid-morning when she returned from a trip to the church, only to find Dr. Fulton hurrying behind her. When he caught up with her at her house, he said:

"Sallie, I sure appreciate the work you and your family are doing. I really do, but it is not enough. I need you to come to the church and tend to the men."

"Doctor, what so ever do you mean tend to the men?"

"You know what I mean. You have taken care of a sick person before, comforted them, gotten them nourishment, or whatever their needs are. There are just too many of them and I need all the help I can get."

Sallie, in the worst way, was afraid of this request. She couldn't spend much time in the church as it was, and now she was being asked to spend a lot of time there. A chill went up her spine and her face became pale. This was noticed by the doctor, who put his arm around her and said:

"Sallie, I know you are scared, but they are more so, after all they are fighting to stay alive. Whatever comfort you can give them will be enough. I am desperate."

She thought about saying no, but the word wouldn't come out. God wouldn't let her. Instead, she found herself saying she would go and do what she could.

"That's the spirit. Now you go in and tell your family you will be helping us at the church and then come as soon as you can. I mean as soon as you can," he said emphasizing soon.

Sallie went into her house and told Annie, who was visiting, what she was doing. Annie said:

"You are the bravest, Sallie, and you can do this. If not, God would not be asking you to."

Within ten minutes, Sallie left her house and walked to the church knowing she was doing something that frightened her. It was not just facing the suffering men, but it was the fact she had no idea what to do once she got there. She had no training in nursing, so what could she do? As she walked, she asked God for courage, and for wisdom, and upon finishing this prayer, she climbed the steps and entered the church. She had done this several times already this morning, and avoided looking at the men, but now she had to look. And, the view was even more terrifying. She wasn't more than five feet inside the church when she saw a young soldier by himself. He looked pale and had bloody cloths wrapped around his upper chest. He was struggling to breathe and what breath he could garner was in very short and unsteady intervals. She decided he would be the first soldier she would help. She cautiously walked over to him and bent down to get closer to him. He noticed her, turned his head, and looked deep into her eyes. This startled her, and so all she could muster was:

"What can I do for you?"

He took a deep breath and said with as much energy as he could afford:

"Nothing, ma'am. I am going to die."

This was more than she could take. She was already uncomfortable, and scared, and to get a reaction like this from the first person she talked with made the flight instinct in her take over, and so she rose, turned and ran out of the church. But, upon reaching the first step, she stopped. She couldn't leave, she just couldn't. So, she sat on the first step and cried hard, harder than she had in years, harder than she had in as long as she could remember. And, as she cried, she felt the fear leaving her body with the tears. Soon, she felt alright, renewed, and with considerably more strength that she felt in awhile. She dried her eyes, sat another moment, and then got up and reentered the church, where she found the same soldier. She went over to him and said:

"What is your name?"

"Sergeant Alexander Stewart of the 149th Pennsylvania Volunteers, ma'am. What's yours?"

"Sallie Myers. I live just next door of this church. Where are you from Sergeant?"

The Catholic Church as is today, located on High Street. (Faber)

Stewart seemed very pleased of the attention he was getting from this pretty young lady and even his breathing seemed to stabilize, so he smiled and said with a little more energy:

"Barington, Pennsylvania, ma'am."

"Well, I have never been to Barington, but I am sure it is a lovely place. Do you live there with a wife?"

"Yes, ma'am. Married to a beautiful lady, Miss Elizabeth. My Lizzie. Father and I run the farm in Allegheny County. My younger brother Henry helps best as he can, as he lost part of his foot while serving. He is a good man."

"Do you think they would like a letter from you? I can write one if you would like?"

"That would be fine, ma'am."

"Please call me Sallie, as all my friends do. Can I call you Alexander?"

"I would like that. Say, Sallie I was wondering if you could read the Bible with me? Before I left home, my father and I read a verse. Can you do the same for me?"

He handed Sallie his personal Bible, which she noted had been used quite a bit by its worn appearance.

"I would be honored. What passage would you like to read?"

"Sallie, it is John 3:16."

"Alright, let's see here," she paused and turned the Bible to the gospel of John, found chapter three, traced the page with her left index finger, and began to read:

"For God so loved the world that he gave his only Son, so that everyone who believes in Him might not perish, but might have eternal life."

Stewart closed his eyes as she read this and when she was done, he opened them again. A tear rolled down his cheek. Sallie saw this and said:

"Are you in pain? Can I do something for you?"

"No, you have done a great deal for me already and you have barely met me. That passage will always remind me of my Heavenly Father, and my Lord Jesus. But, it will also remind me of my earthly father, as it is something we have shared together. It is very special to me."

Sallie was moved by this and a tear rolled down her cheek. Stewart saw this and said to her:

"Don't cry, Sallie. I am not afraid. I am ready when the Father is."

With that, he closed his eyes and fell asleep. Sallie checked his breathing to make sure he hadn't passed and finding him asleep, she approached the doctor and said:

"Dr. Fulton, I would like to have some of the men transferred to our house. I think we can make them more comfortable over there and we can get them off the floor, beginning with that sergeant over there."

"Are you sure?"

"Yes, I am. Can you have some of the men take him over? I am not afraid anymore and think I can nurse him better at my home."

"Alright. Why don't you go to your house and prepare a place for him and we will get him over there. Do you mind if I ask his permission?"

"I don't mind at all. He is just resting now. Do you think we should wake him?"

"Yes, we will have to wake him up anyway to move him, so let's do it now."

Fulton walked over to Stewart and gently kneeled next to him. He nudged him awake ever so gently. When Stewart opened his eyes, he saw Sallie again, and he smiled at her. She smiled back, and the doctor noticed this, saying:

"Sergeant, Miss Myers has asked if she could have you taken to her house to be a little more comfortable. Is this alright with you?"

Stewart looked at Sallie again, smiled, and said:

"She is a saint, doctor, and I will go wherever she says."

Just after one o'clock in the afternoon the shooting started, announcing the opening of hostilities for the day. Although the cannon and rifle fire was not coordinated as of yet, it was a reminder of the day's activities ahead. Sallie settled in at her house with Stewart. She made a place for him on her living room floor, had set up linens, blankets and pillows to make sure he was as comfortable as she could make him. She set up a place right next to him for her to sit and tend to him. She could see he was struggling even to breathe, and this saddened her, again. But, his spirits were high and he seemed at peace. She really had never seen death so close before yesterday, and certainly hadn't seen it creep up on someone right before her very eyes, so this was a new and eerie experience. She marveled at Stewart's courage and this gave her more courage to make his remaining time as restful as she could. As she propped up his pillows, she asked:

"Alexander, are you comfortable?"

"Yes, it is very kind of you to have me here like this."

"Can I get you anything right now?"

"Iffen you don't mind, some water would be fine."

She could see he was hot as his face was red and he began to sweat. The beads started to run down his cheeks, so she bundled up a linen cloth and dabbed his face with it. Then she rose and said she would fetch him some water. She returned about a minute later and offered him the cup to drink. She helped him by tilting his head so he wouldn't spill. Once he was finished, she dabbed the cloth in the water, soaking it slightly, and wiped his face again. He smiled at her kindness and said:

"Sallie, you know you looked really odd when you first approached me. You're not used to nursing are you?"

"No, I have never done this before, and I was scared out of my wits."

"I am sorry I said what I did to you. That must not have helped."

"Well, I needed it. I needed to understand that it is not my fears that are important, but rather yours."

"Your fears are important, too. Never forget that. If you don't face 'em and conquer 'em, they will haunt you and hold you hostage until you do."

"Alexander, you are very wise."

He laughed a little, which caused him to go into a fit of coughing. She leaned him up while he was doing so and gently tapped his back. He finished, caught his breath and nodded to her that he was alright and could be laid back down. She gently eased him back to the floor and wiped his face again with the cloth.

"Sorry for that," he said.

"Please do not apologize."

"Anyway, when I first saw you I thought you were a stuffy nurse type, you know the kind that doesn't concentrate on the patient, but only looks to change bandages and move on. I was wrong about that, and so I am sorry for it, too."

"I must have been some site for you? And, to run out like that, well can I say it wasn't one of my better moments."

He smiled and said, "I did watch you run, and you were pretty fast, really."

She laughed, "Well, I thought it was the devil himself chasing me."

"I didn't look like the devil, did I?" he said seriously.

"No, no, it was the devil inside me, that's all."

"Oh, you needn't worry, Sallie. He has no power over you, none at all, not if you don't let him. Seek God, and you will always have all the strength you need."

"I know that now. I guess I always knew that, but I wasn't paying enough attention to it lately. He is always around and in my life and I want, no need, to pay closer mind to Him."

"That is indeed true. I have never been more aware of His presence in my life as I have in these last two days. He is with me and He keeps me strong."

"I can see that in you, Alexander. You are a wonderful witness to the power, strength, and love of our God, and I am certain He is very proud of you."

"Those are very kind words. Do you mind if we read another verse? I think I need to rest for awhile and I want to rest in God's words."

"That would be lovely. Do you have a passage in mind?"

"I do. Do you mind the 23rd Psalm?"

And so, Sallie read the 23rd Psalm to Steward and as he predicted, it put him to sleep. She rolled the blanket back just a little from him, wiped his face gently and rose to see if there was anything she could do in the kitchen. She found her sisters hard at work. She said:

"We need to get a few more soldiers here. Can you help tend to them?"

After getting their commitment of their care, she asked them to watch over Stewart while she went over to the church to inform Dr. Fulton of their intentions. Within about a half hour, three more soldiers were brought over to their house and placed on the living room floor near Stewart. None of the three had serious wounds, such as Stewart, but were in need of a place to rest and recover. She asked each if they were in need of anything, and after getting them water, she settled back next to Stewart.

All afternoon, rifle fire could be heard and some of it was heard hitting the houses near the Myer's house. Around four o'clock the guns of the Southerners opened up south of town. Soon, the northern guns answered. The sound of these found the house and Stewart was awakened from his nap. He looked up and saw Sallie sitting right next to him.

"Did you have a good rest?"

"I suppose so. I don't remember dreaming, so I must have."

"I have some beef tea here, would you like some?"

Sallie helped him down some of the tea and it seemed to ease him a little. He lay back down after a cup and took a deep breath, which caused him to begin coughing again. She helped him through the spell and gave him more water. She began fanning him as the heat was again making him sweat. After dabbing his head, she helped him finish the whole cup of water. Once it was gone, she asked him if he wanted more. With a nod, he answered. She got up to get the water from the kitchen, took a couple of steps, but heard a sound that made her turn around. It was the sound of a minnie ball crackling into the wood floor. She looked at the spot it hit and noticed the path of the bullet crossed right where she was not more than two or three seconds before. It would have hit her. Stewart noticed it too. She looked at him and they exchanged shocked glances. He said:

"Sallie, are you alright?"

"Yes, but I could have been hit by that ball?"

"Yes, you could have, but you weren't. God is with you. Rejoice in that. It is not your time."

She returned and sat by him again, still in shock from the close call. Death seemed to be hunting her, too. But, as Stewart had said, God was with her, and so she would walk in the shadow of death with no fear.

MATILDA (TILLIE) PIERCE spent the better part of the morning of July 2nd handing out water to the soldiers who were coming to the battlefield from the south. The day was hot already and it promised to be hotter. Her service was greatly appreciated by the soldiers passing by, but the demand for the water was great and so she was out about as fast as she set the pail down. Most were polite, some were not, but those that were fortunate enough to get some drank as much as they could.

It was just before ten o'clock, when a group of officers rode up from the south and stopped for a drink. Before Tillie could give them a cup, they were joined by another group of officers on horseback, who came from the north, from the battle lines. The second group stopped abruptly and saluted the first. The second group, Tillie recognized, was led by General Winfield Scott Hancock, whom she had met yesterday. Tillie watched, and listened, to the exchange between the riders. Upon returning the salute, the leader of the first said:

"General Hancock, I trust things are in order for the day?"

"Yes, General. It was a difficult night, but the line is strong."

"And, the ground?"

"It is good ground, General. I would have picked it myself if given the opportunity."

"And, the enemy?"

"They have the town and are coming up in force, both from the north and from the west."

"Will they hit us today?"

"I can almost guarantee it, General."

"Would you hazard to guess where?"

"It could be anywhere, sir. But, you know that wily, gray fox likes to probe at the flanks. That's how we were compromised at Chancellorsville."

"How are our flanks?"

Hancock pointed to the north and answered: "To the north, the flank is strong. We built works all night long and so the position is well fortified.

To the south here…" he paused and gestured with his open palm before continuing:

"We are still building up our forces and are extending them down to that smaller hill to the north of that larger one. As more men come up, we will place them to lengthen the line."

"If old Bobby Lee does hit us on our flanks, we must hold. Here is where we are committing to stop him and send him back south to Virginia, where he belongs."

"We will do our duty, sir."

"I hope it will be enough, otherwise I will have the unpleasant duty of wiring President Lincoln the Rebels are on their way."

"Follow me, sir. We have established a headquarters for you at a farmhouse about a mile or so up this road."

"I'd like a drink of water from that fine young lady over there, first. Care to join me?"

"Certainly, but I am not thirsty just this moment, sir. I have, however had the pleasure of drinking water from that young lady, only yesterday, and it is worth the effort."

"Suit yourself."

The two men separated themselves from their fellow officers and rode the few steps over to Tillie.

"Young lady, I wonder if I might trouble you for a drink?"

"My pleasure, sir," Tillie said while curtsying and holding out the cup.

The officer drank and then handed the cup back to her, saying:

"Thank you, young lady for your kindness to me and my men."

Just then, they heard a commotion on the road. Tillie looked over and saw a soldier fall down and lie for a second or two before trying to get up and walk further. He fell again, and then began to crawl. His comrades broke their formation and came over to help him. But, before they could get him to his feet, a captain came over to them and said:

"Out of my way, I will handle this."

The captain ordered the man to his feet, saying:

"On your feet soldier."

The man tried, but upon rising up on his hands and knees, fell again. This angered the captain, who said while drawing his sword:

"I said on your feet or I will make you stay down permanently."

Tillie watched this exchange with interest and wondered if she should go to try and help the ailing soldier. But, before she could move, the captain raised his sword and struck the fallen soldier, yelling:

"I said get up, soldier."

He hit the soldier several more times, as the soldier tried to cover up. The two generals near Tillie had not paid attention to the altercation, but were quickly drawn to it by the sounds of the sword striking the man. General Hancock reacted instantly:

"You, there, stop striking that man, NOW," he yelled.

Hancock whipped his horse and rode over to the where the captain was hitting the fallen soldier. He stopped his horse, jumped off, and made his way over to the captain before the captain could even react.

"What the hell do you think you are doing, Captain?"

The captain didn't know what to say, and cowered at Hancock.

"Well, speak up."

"I was just, just disciplining one of my men, sir," he said with a sheepish voice.

"Not in my command, Captain."

He turned and addressed Tillie:

"Miss Pierce, isn't it?"

"Yes, sir, that is my name, sir," she said in a rather nervous tone being singled out by the general.

"Miss Pierce, can we get this man into your house where he can get some medical treatment?"

"Certainly, sir," Tillie replied.

"Thank you kindly."

He turned to the men who were trying to help the fallen soldier previously and said:

"You men, get him into that house immediately."

Three of the soldier's comrades picked him up and moved him toward the house. Once the soldier was removed from the area and on his way to the house, Hancock turned back to the captain, who was now visibly shaken and was sweating.

"Captain, I will not have this type of brutality in my army, are you clear?"

"Yes, sir, of course it will not happen again."

"I would like to believe that, Captain, but unfortunately for your sake, I do not."

He went over to the captain and ripped the captain's rank from his uniform. He turned to his staff and said:

"Colonel, arrest this man and take him to headquarters where I will deal with him later."

And then, back to the former captain:

"You, *Private*, are going into battle today, in the location of the heaviest fighting. You may not survive today, but you will have a better chance than with a firing squad, which is what you deserve. Colonel, get this man out of my sight."

The colonel had the captain's hands tied and escorted away from the area. Hancock mounted his horse and rode back to where Tillie was giving the other general a drink. He stopped his horse, tipped his hat to Tillie and said:

"My apologies, ma'am, you had to set this ugly event."

Tillie nodded and said nothing. Hancock turned to the other general and said:

"Sir, let's get to headquarters. No telling when Bobby is going to come out and play today, so we need you briefed and ready."

"General, please lead the way."

And with that, the two groups of riders spurred their horses and sped away. Tillie began serving water again to the men, and inquired of the next one as she handed him the cup, who the other general was. He replied:

"That ma'am was General George Gordon Meade. He is in command of this here whole army."

"He sure is a man of pleasant manners, both he and General Hancock."

"Certainly, ma'am, they are Pennsylvania men."

Tillie continued this water giving for the rest of the morning and all afternoon. Around four o'clock the cannon shots began. The Southern cannons opened the affair and soon the Northern cannons countered. About this time, Tillie saw another group of three riders that caught her attention. The three men came up and waited their turn for a drink. Tillie overheard the one in charge to say one of the other:

"Colonel Chambahlain, we must get the men up as soon as we cahn. You-uh to report to Colonel Strong Vincent."

"Yes, General."

"Well get the men goin'. I must report to General Hancock at headquartahs. Good luck, Colonel. I know you and the men will account you-uhselves well today."

The two men saluted one another and the general rode off toward the Union Headquarters to the north.

The younger of the two remaining men turned to the other and said:

"Lahrence, we might be in ah good fight today. I think the men ah ready. What do you think?"

"Tom, fihst of all, stop cahllin' me Lahrence. It's colonel. Second, they-uh ready. I just hope the remaindah of the ahmy is so prepahred."

Tillie looked at the two men as they waited their turn. The one called Lawrence was of average height, had light brown hair with blonde streaks, parted on the left side of his head above his left eye, was long enough to cover his ears partially; blue eyes; a strong nose; an average mouth and ears; and a thick mustache that extended below his chin. The one called Tom looked very much like Lawrence, except his hair was a darker brown and he had thick sideburns connected to his mustache.

When it was their turn for a drink, Lawrence politely addressed her saying:

"Young miss, it is ahfully kind of you to give us this watah. May I thank you on behahf of all of my men?"

Tillie curtsied again and thanked him. He said:

"I'm Colonel Joshua Lawrence Chambahlain of the 20th Maine, and this hee-uh is my bruthah Tom."

Tom tipped his hat and said:

"Ma'am, and whaht is you-uh nahme?"

"Tillie Pierce."

"Well, Miss Piahce, we ah shortly headed for bahttle, and you-uh as-sistance is verah much helpful to ah cahse. Ain't that right, Lahrence?"

"I am doing what I can, kind sirs."

"And, it is moah than necessahy, Miss Piahce," Joshua said and then he turned to his brother and said:

"Stop cahllin' me Lahrence. Now, let's get goin'. Ah services ah needed. Goodbye Miss Piahce."

And with that they were gone, riding up ahead of the men they were leading into battle.

Around six o'clock in the evening, the battle became intense. Tillie ceased her water giving shortly after the Maine men departed. Soon, the battle in this area had become a desperate fight for control of Round Top and the little mountain north of it, on the Union left flank. The fighting was relentless as the two sides charged and gave way, then counterattacked and fell back, with this cycle being repeated over the course of a couple of hours of bloody conflict.

By evening, the Weikert farm was the recipient of a significant amount of causalities. The barn had been almost filled with the wounded yesterday and so the day's injured spilled over into the house, the outside areas around the house, and the farmhouse further to the rear of the property. Tillie and Becky did what they could to assist the surgeons and the nurses. They were assigned to bringing beef tea and bread to the wounded men. Tillie dove right in and made quick work of slicing bread and bringing it the soldiers. She took some slices down to the cellar and passed them out.

It was then that a soldier sitting in the corner of the room holding a candle called out to her:

"Young lady, could I have a bite of bread for myself and my friend here?"

Tillie walked over to him and knelt down, saying she passed out the last of the slices right before he beckoned her:

"Why, I would be glad to get you some. Please wait whilst I fetch it."

She went up the stairs and into the kitchen, got two slices of bread, and hurried back into the cellar. She found the soldier waiting. She gave a piece to him. He took it and he thanked her, eating it hungrily.

"Have you brought some for my friend, here?"

Tillie handed the bread to the other soldier without a word.

The first soldier said:

"You are a very kind and generous young lady. Could I ask you for a favor?"

"Yes, anything I can do to help."

"Will you watch my friend for a spell, whilst I look in on another of our unit, who is upstairs?"

"I would be glad to."

The first soldier got up, gave her his candle, then left, and so Tillie settled onto the floor he vacated. She looked over at the soldier, who hadn't spoken yet.

"May I get you some water?"

"Yes, that would be fine, iffen it's not too much trouble for you?"

"No trouble a'tall. Be right back."

She returned a moment later and gave the soldier a drink from a cup. He drank what he could and laid his head back down.

"Are you hurt bad?" she asked.

"I am afraid I am, and I don't know if I will live."

"Nonsense, you will live. You mustn't lose hope on that."

"What is your name, deary?"

"Matilda, well Tillie, Pierce. What is yours?"

"Weed, I am from New York."

"I am pleased to meet you Mr. Weed. Can I get you anything to make you more comfortable?"

"Tillie could you wipe my forehead and get me a blanket? I am so cold."

"I will be right back."

She retrieved a linen and a cloth, soaked a cloth in water, and returned to the soldier. She covered him with the linen and dabbed his forehead with the cloth. He looked up at her with kind eyes and said:

"You remind me of my daughter. She is sixteen years old, about the same age as you. And, she is kind like you."

"What is her name?"

"Anna."

"Well, she is a lucky girl to have a father like you. When was the last time you saw her?"

"It has been over two years and I miss her and the rest of the family very much. I am afraid I will not see them again."

"Now, Mr. Weed, I thought we agreed to not lose hope. You cannot, and I will not let you."

He smiled and held out his hand to her. She took it and he said:

"It's a deal if you can stay with me for awhile. I am so tired."

"I am right here."

"Would you mind if I rested for a spell?" I cannot keep my eyes open."

"Please, you need your strength."

And, so the soldier fell asleep. She held his hand and watched him sleep for about a half hour, when the first soldier returned. He greeted her warmly, saying:

"Thank you so much for looking after him."

She rose to leave, which awakened Weed. He turned to her and said:

"Leaving so soon? Well, I know you have others to attend to. Can you promise to return in the morning? I can't imagine a better way to start the day than to gaze upon your face."

"I will, I promise I will be here at first light, or shortly after."

"That will be grand, and I will be waiting very anxiously for it."

Tillie then left saying:

"Until the morning then?"

"Yes, until the morning."

Tillie left the two soldiers and went upstairs to see what else she could do. She found a surgeon and asked him if he treated the soldier downstairs. She described him and where he was currently resting.

"Yes, I did, and I am afraid the news is not good."

"What do you mean?"

"I mean most likely he will not live through the night."

Tillie looked at him and didn't say a word. The surgeon, who was very busy with the other wounded men, said:

"I'm sorry, but his wound is not treatable and so it is just only a matter of time."

She decided it would be better for her to return to the cellar as her company would now be desperately needed by the dying soldier. If she could make his last hours comfortable, maybe he could die in relative peace. And, so she went back down. She went directly over to Weed and the other soldier. The other soldier saw her coming, and said:

"Back so soon? What's the matter? Are you alright?"

Tillie had a sad look on her face, but then instantly realized that is was visible to others, which was not what she wanted, as she learned yesterday. She then thought of the naked man in the snow story and she smiled at that.

"Yes, I just was told I should come back, as everything is in order upstairs."

"That's wonderful. I know he will appreciate you coming back."

She went over and sat next to Weed, then reached for, and held, his hand. He opened his eyes and weakly said:

"You are back? Is it morning already?"

"No, but I just enjoyed being here so much I couldn't wait until the morning."

"I am glad..." he said and then turned his head and fell back asleep.

She took the cloth and wiped his head again, then just sat and held his hand. He looked very pale and she knew he was indeed dying, but she wanted to make sure he held on as long as he could. She would make sure of it. She stayed for two more hours and then satisfied he had not gotten worse, decided she would stow away for a couple of hours, get some sleep, and then return. She got up to leave and quietly slipped away. When she returned, she would find him still living, she just knew it. As she climbed the stairs, she prayed to God for a miracle, and asked that it not be his time. She knew, though, that it was up to God for that.

CHAPTER 51

BROADHEAD

SARAH (SALLIE) M. BROADHEAD, her husband Joseph, and her daughter Mary decided it was safe to leave the cellar. After a full day of evading the battle yesterday, where Sallie had taken Mary to a neighbor's house to wait it out and Joseph stayed home to protect the house, they were at it again this morning, waiting the battle out in a cellar, but this time it was their own. The battle sounds had begun around mid-morning, but had only lasted about an hour, and were not coordinated enough to be the prelude to a larger fight. They were glad about their strategy yesterday, as Joseph, staying home all day, and then Sallie returning in the evening, had done the job of protecting their property. One of their neighbors was not so lucky. Sallie was awakened in the middle of the night by noises coming from the house across Chambersburg Street. The Rebels had broken into the house and had looted it from the cellar to the attic. After this incident, they decided they would not leave their house unprotected, and with the battle moving to the opposite side of the town, this is at least plausible without jeopardizing too much of their safety and well being. As they climbed out of the cellar, they knew this cannon fire just completed was not an ending, nor was it in any way a settlement of the conflict here between the two armies.

"Joseph, they must be massing for a huge attack, as that cannon fire was nothing more than shooting at each other."

"Yes, love, they must indeed. Maybe, it will be tomorrow?"

"Do you think so?"

"I only wish I knew, love. Say, I cannot stand it any longer."

Mary whined and Sallie looked over at her. She held her arms up to signify she wanted to be picked up. Sallie reached down and picked her up, hugged her, and held her tightly. Once she had done this, she turned back to Joseph, saying:

"What can you not stand any longer, Joseph, the hiding?"

"Yes, love, and the thought of being afraid all the time. I cannot stand it. I must do something."

"Well, what can we do?"

"I don't know, pick beans, maybe, love. I don't know, I just don't."

"Pick beans? That just sounds plain odd. Are you feeling alright?"

"No, that's just it, love. Does it really sound crazy to go out and pick beans?"

"Yes, there is still shooting going on out there, so yes it does sound crazy."

Joseph thought for a moment and then a smile, an eerie and crazy smile, broke out on his face.

"That's it, love. I am going to pick all of the beans in our garden, and not let a one be eaten by those traitors. Not a one!"

He proceeded to the back door of the house and opened it. She watched as he stepped out into the back of their house. He turned and looked back to her and said:

"Lock this door behind me, love. I want you safe in here. I'll be out in the garden."

And with that, he closed the door with a loud slam. She went over to the door and looked out the window. She saw him merrily picking the beans from the garden. He went down one row and then another, and when his hands were full and he could carry no more, he dumped his load at the back door and went for some more. When he went back to gather another load, she opened the door and gathered his first load. She heard bullets going by, but they were all aimed higher and were way above them. Still, she was very frightened of the errant shot, so she said:

"Joseph, can you please come back in the house? It is not safe out there. Please…"

"Nonsense, love. Besides, it's a beautiful day to pick *beans*! Let's have some for dinner today."

She couldn't stand to watch, but she did. He continued for another couple of minutes, and then he was finished. He brought his second load over to the back door, and followed her into the house.

"Love, that was fun. I say I did get every one of those beans. None for the Rebels. No, they will have to steal food from someone else, not me, and not you."

She looked at him to see if he had all his wits, which she had doubted for the last few minutes. He noticed her stare and said:

"What, love? Did you expect me to hide the whole time? I cannot. I have to be free from the fear. Well, at least for awhile."

"Are you done now? Done scaring the wits out of me? What if you had been hit? There are bullets flying out there. What would we have done?"

He looked at her and saw that she was genuinely scared. He went to her and hugged her tightly, saying:

"Love, I have been afraid ever since yesterday when Burns went to fight them, and I didn't. I could have gone, but I didn't. I was afraid. Now,

I am tired of that feeling, so I needed to do something brave, or stupid, depending upon how you look at it, to regain my self-esteem."

"Sweetie, Mr. Burns is a crazy old man, and now it probably has cost him his life. That's not bravery. Bravery is staying home and making sure your family is safe. That's bravery to me, and that's just what you did. I am very proud of you and proud to be your wife. Mary is proud of you too. She loves her Papa, but she also wants him around when she grows up, which is a good idea, don't you think? So, no more brave, or crazy, or stupid things, okay? Besides, you can't just decide to join a battle as a civilian because you live close by. That is a real war crime and one that gets you a date with a rope."

"Well, I suppose you are right. Alright, no more stupid things, but, love, I may have a brave one still left in me."

"You have many."

"Well, now that we have fresh beans, how about we have a nice supper and invite the neighbors over for it?"

Around noon, the Broadheads sat down at table with the Gilberts and had a nice meal, the first one either family had since the Confederates showed up on the town's doorstep last Tuesday. Sallie made boiled ham, some shortcake, and they had the beans, which she boiled also. They were very keen to the sounds around them listening and waiting for the battle to start up at any time. But, all in all it was a very relaxing and worry-free dinner, and the five people enjoyed a time away from the battle.

"Mary, sweetie, now you eat all your ham," Sallie instructed the child.

"Mama, do I have to?"

"Of course you do. You want to grow up big and strong like Papa don't you?"

"Joseph, these beans are delicious. I heard they are fresh picked?" Jacob Gilbert asked.

"Yes, picked 'em myself not more than an hour ago."

"At great peril, I might add," Sallie said.

"Gibberish, love."

"Well, I heard that was a very brave thing you did, spending time to harvest them whilst the rifle fire was going on all around you," Elizabeth Gilbert said.

"Really, it was nothing," Broadhead replied with a look of enough to Sallie, so she piped in to change the subject away from him, saying:

"I wonder what's become of Mr. Burns?"

"Oh, that old fool. I heard from one of the neighbors last night that he caught quite a fight yesterday and was hurt in several locations, one of them fatal. Word is that he passed last night from the wounds," Elizabeth said.

Sallie put her hand to her mouth and said:

"Oh my God. I hadn't heard that."

"Well, I heard from the Slentz's that they saw him get hit several times."

"What a shame. I wonder if Barbara and Martha know?" Sallie asked.

"Probably not. I haven't had the heart to tell them."

"Poor Barbara. With all the faults that man had, she sure loved him."

"He wasn't such a bad guy, love, he just didn't know how to be a good guy. I rather liked him and enjoyed the time we spent together. I will miss the old guy, love," Joseph added.

"So will I," Jacob said.

"I guess you are right. He wasn't so bad, but he was so darn obnoxious," Sallie chipped in. She paused and then continued:

"Someone must tell Barbara. I guess I will have to do it, right after we finish our meal. Mrs. Gilbert, do you mind entertaining Mary whilst I do it?"

"Certainly. We will have a nice spot of tea after dinner," Elizabeth said.

She turned to Mary and said:

"Is Ruthie too busy to have tea with me in a few minutes?"

"Well," Mary replied matter-of-factly and continued:

"Let me ask her."

The child held her doll up to her face and whispered something in her ear. She then switched the doll to have it whisper something in her ear. She replied:

"No, Mrs. Gilbert, we are both quite available, thank you."

Sallie looked over at her child and said to Elizabeth while shaking her head:

"It just amazes me how fast she is growing up, and the words she uses are just incredible."

"Sallie, she is a very smart little girl, and you have done a wonderful job working with her."

"Well, you have certainly helped. She just adores spending time with you."

"Not as much as I do. She makes the old woman in me feel young."

The five finished their dinner and then Sallie rushed out of the house to bring the bad news to Barbara and Martha.

After Sallie returned from the Burns' house, she sought Joseph. Finding him in their bedroom resting, she sat down on the bed and said:

"Joseph, that was just so sad."

"I'm sorry, love, you had to be the one to give them that news. Did they take it hard?"

"Very, both cried for a good five minutes. But, then they composed themselves. They are very strong people. People, whom I am afraid, are now going to need our help."

"Well, we will do what we can, love. Mrs. Burns has always been a good friend to us and we will be there for her in her time of need, or whenever she is in want of anything."

"I'm glad to hear you say that. It is indeed the Christian thing to do. It was sad also because they asked if anyone had found his body, and I couldn't answer them. Worse yet, the battle will not allow them to search for him."

"Well, love, he is probably with the rest of the Rebel dead."

"Joseph, that's even a worse thought. What if they up and bury him with their dead and we never find out where?"

"Now, love, they are not savages. They would know he was a civilian and should be returned to his family."

"Are you sure? Maybe they would treat him like a bushwhacker and just put him in the ground somewhere."

"No, love, they won't. When this battle is over, they will return his body."

"I sure hope so. Those women deserve the peace of mind that comes from knowing, and they deserve to bury him themselves."

"Like I said, love, they are not savages."

Around four o'clock in the afternoon, the peace of the town was interrupted by the roar of cannon fire. Joseph decided he was going to stay outside to see if he could get a glimpse of what was happening. He looked off in the distance to the south and saw the cannon fire becoming intense down near Round Top. He looked to the west of his house at the Rebel cannon, stationed near the Seminary, firing on Culp's Hill. He watched for a few minutes, but then something out of the ordinary caught his eye. Off in the distance, in the fields near the Mummasburg Road, he noticed a wagon moving slowly in his direction. He stared at the wagon and recognized it as the Sellinger's wagon, as he identified the Sellinger's blind horse pulling it. Strange, he thought. He went back inside to get Sallie and to show her. They both came out and he said:

"Sallie, love, look," he said pointing at the wagon. He continued:

"It is the Sellinger's wagon. I wonder what they are doing?"

"It sure is. What could they be doing out there?"

"I dunno, love, but I am going to go find out."

"Joseph, no. You promised no more stupid actions, remember?"

"Love, they may need help, and so I am going to offer mine."

"You are right. But, please be careful."

With that, Joseph ran off in the direction of the wagon. I less than two minutes, he approached the wagon, and so he stopped running and said in an out of breath voice:

"Mr. Sellinger, do you need some help? May I be of assistance to you?"

"Ja, Herr Broadhead. Ve haft Herr Burns in zee back, and he needs zome doctring."

"You have John Burns in the wagon?" Joseph asked stunned. He continued as he ran to the wagon:

"Is he alive?"

"Ja, but he needs doctring."

Broadhead got to the wagon as Sellinger stopped the horse. He went around and saw Burns in the back holding the two Sellinger children's hands.

"John, John, you are alive," he exclaimed.

Burns could only manage a smile and a wave and then he went back to holding the children's hands.

"Mr. Sellinger, let's get him home fast so he can be cared for. I'll go and get his wife and his daughter ready for him."

"Ja," Sellinger said and whipped the reins on the horse to get the wagon going again.

Broadhead was off and he sprinted home, all the while the Confederate guns continued their barrage of Culp's Hill. He ran as fast as he had ever run before and reached his home and Sallie in quick manner. He was out of breath, and doubled over to catch some. Then, he raised his eyes to Sallie's and she said:

"Joseph, what is it?"

He smiled and said:

"It's Burns. He is alive and is on his way home in the Sellinger's wagon."

After Joseph helped Burns into his house and bade his goodbyes, he made his way back to his house. The Rebel cannon fire was becoming more intense, and so was the Union's. The sound, even though the majority of the fire was coming from south of town, was deafening. The Broadheads decided to take Mary over to the Gilberts, and they spent the rest of the afternoon and evening, until ten o'clock, in their cellar. While there, they wondered and worried about the outcome of the battle.

"My God, it is like Armageddon out there," Sallie exclaimed as she held Mary very tightly and rocked her.

"Yes, I wonder if we are holding our own against them?" Jacob asked.

"I hope so, and that we were properly reinforced today," Joseph answered.

"This day may decide who the winner is. If we lose, does it mean we may lose the war?" Sallie inquired.

"No, love, but it would go a long way toward that eventual result, as we would have a hard time stopping them for going to Washington and taking over the government."

"Could they do that?"

"Certainly, love, and if that happens, I think we would surrender to them."

"Oh, how awful that would be. I pray to God we win the day and turn those traitors back south where they belong. I don't want them in this town any more. I want them to go away."

"Me, too," Elizabeth stated.

At ten o'clock, the sounds of the battle ceased and so the group decided to come up from the Gilbert's cellar. Sallie had done a good job of keeping Mary entertained and quiet while they were down there and now she was sleeping. Joseph volunteered to take her home, but Sallie said:

"Mrs. Gilbert, do you mind watching her again? Can we put her in the second bedroom for awhile? I just have to know who won the day. Joseph, let's take a trip into town and see what we can find out."

Chapter 52

WILL

JOHN CHARLES WILL spent the day on Thursday wondering when the hostilities would begin. At around four o'clock he got his answer as the shooting started and the battle waged into an inferno. Curiosity had gotten the best of him and so he climbed the stairs to the roof of the Globe Inn and stepped out onto it to see what he could see. He spied the area and noticed the placement of the Rebel artillery, which was pounding away at Culp's Hill. He spent several minutes watching the artillery fire, anticipating a Rebel charge to take the hill, but none was coming, at least not yet. He looked to the south, down the Emmitsburg Road and noticed a lot of movement of Rebel troops in the areas just west of Round Top Mountain. His view was partially blocked by the new Courthouse and by the height of Cemetery Hill, but he saw enough to know much of the fighting would be at that location. He was still squinting to see, when he heard a voice yelling at him:

"Ya, thea, what a ya doin' up thea?"

Will looked around and saw a Rebel soldier with his gun pointed directly at him. He froze, waiting for the Confederate to shoot him.

"I said, what y'all doin' up thea? Get down from that thea roof."

The battle noises absorbed most of what the Rebel said to him, so Will didn't know what to do. Then he saw the Rebel raise his rifle, and he said:

"I'm not goin' to tell ya gain. Eitha ya come down or ya fall down."

Will heard that and raised his hands, saying:

"Don't shoot, I am coming down."

He went down the stairs and out to the front of the inn, where that same soldier was waiting for him, but was engaged in a conversation with Lieutenant Greene.

"I saw him watchin' ou foaces, Lieutenant."

"Now, don't ya neva mind about that. He was just curious, I am sure of that. He is not a threat," Greene answered.

"Well, I do believe Genr'l Early should know about it."

"Don't ya think he has a few moa things to worra about then this civilyun?"

"Well, I don't know, but I think he should know."

"Suit yaself. Are ya gonna be the one to tell 'im? I wish ya luck on that."

The soldier thought it through for a minute and said:

"Pahaps ya right. I guess we can just faget about it."

"Now ya thinkin'. Besides, Genr'l Early really has taken to this man. He loves to eat at his inn hea, so even iffen ya did tell 'im, it wouldn't change that."

And, with that the situation was closed, and the soldier walked off. Greene turned to Will and said:

"Mista Will, ya ought to be a might moa caful. He would have shot ya."

"Thanks, Philip."

"Jus doin' my job. The boss will want a nice meal this evenin'. What have ya got planned?"

"I hadn't thought of it yet. I am so caught up in the battle. Why aren't you?"

"Because, I know we will win. We always do. Besides, how can the battle be more important than ya suppa? Why don't ya go inside and start praparin"? We will be powaful hungry tonight."

And so, Will decided he would do just that. The battle would go on whether he was concerned about it or not, and he would find out soon enough the result. In the meantime, he should do his job and ready the inn for the supper hours.

Around ten o'clock, the shooting finally died down. It was six hours of a frantic struggle, but the outcome was unclear, at least to Will. He was in the kitchen supervising the preparations of some boiled beef and biscuits, when Jones came in.

"John, I thought I would find you here. How's the supper coming? It sure smells good. You know nothing smells as good as freshly baked bread. It reminds me of my mother. She used to love to bake bread."

"Evening Jones. Do you know when I can expect the men to come for supper?"

"Well, just about any time now. Sorry, it's a little late in the evening, but the situation could not be avoided."

"You mean the battle dictates when supper is served."

"Precisely. Say, how are the Currant Champagne sales?"

"Well, not so good these last two days. Same can be said of the general business of the inn. I guess you fellas, and the war you brought, is keeping folks indoors."

"I am sorry about that, John, but it certainly cannot be helped. It is necessary."

"Do you know the result today? Did our line hold?"

"Well, it seems so, although we made some gains on both fronts and softened up the line, ripe for the picking tomorrow."

"I thought you Rebs were going to break our lines today?"

"Me too, but it seems you fellas are giving a better showing than expected. But, tomorrow should be the time for breaking up that line, and moving on to Washington."

"We shall see, Jones, we shall see."

"Now, John, don't get all excited. I don't want the result of this war to get in between our friendship. I have said this before."

"Jones, you are definitely one of a kind."

"That, sir, is true. The pure truth."

As he finished speaking, Will could hear the arrival of the Confederate officers. He and Jones went out of the kitchen in time to hear Will's father greet them and begin to get them to sit down. Early was with them and took his usual spot at table. Jones made his way to the table and sat next to him. Will followed and then the general greeted him:

"Evenin' Mista Will. Aye do trust ya have somethin' special cooked up tonight?"

"General. Yes, tonight we are having boiled beef. We here at the inn prepare it a little differently than you may have ever had it. We add onions, garlic and cook it up, not in water, but in chicken stock. We find adding the chicken flavoring gives it a different taste, one I think you will enjoy."

"That sounds wondaful, doesn't it Mista Jones?"

"It certainly does, John. My mouth is watering just hearing about it. And, the smell from the kitchen, General, is delicious."

"I am glad you are pleased. Shall we start you out with some ales?"

"That would be jus fine, Mista Will. Say, Lieutenant Greene informed me ya had a little trouble today with one of ou men?"

"Nothing I couldn't handle, General."

"Well, ya do be careful, now. And, no mo visits to ya roof. It kinda looks like ya spying, and Aye don't want none of that."

The Confederates were still coming in when the ales began to be served. Each man gulped his first down and soon they were looking for more. This kept Will's father busy. Will brought out the biscuits and then the food. As they were eating, Will decided to join the general to see what information of the battle he could glean from him. So, he sat across the table for him.

"How is the beef, General?"

"It's even betta than ya described. It is so tenda, and I can just taste the hint of chicken flavaing. Mista Will this is the best ya have done yet."

"I am glad you like it. All cooks like to know the food they are serving is being enjoyed."

"What do ya think, Mista Jones?"

"It is every bit as good as anything I have had here. John, you really have outdone yourself."

"Ya know, Mista Jones, ya got a good thing goin' hea with this hea inn of ya's. Afta the wa, Aye will make it a habit of comin' up hea regula like, just to get some of ya cookin'. Aye might even want to go into business with ya hea. Afta the wa."

"Speaking of the war, General, how did the battle go today? Jones says our lines held."

"Yes, sur they did. We did howeva, gain some ground, and we a ready to break it tomorra. Yes, sur, it was a fine fight today."

Just then, the men stopped talking as a man and a woman came into the restaurant. Will looked over and noticed Joseph and Sallie Broadhead. He rose and began walking toward them. Jones recognized them to, and said to Early:

"General, I know these folks. They are really nice people. He runs the railroad in this town, so he probably isn't too happy that we burned the bridge out east of here."

"Mista Will, do ya mind askin' these fine folks to come and join us fo suppa?"

Will stopped, turned around and said to the general: "I will ask."

Will went over and escorted the Broadheads to the general's table. The men cleared a place for them to sit right across from the general, and then Joseph helped Sallie sit. All the men near rose and waited for Sallie to sit first. Once she had, they all resumed the place at the table.

"General Early, may I present Mr. and Mrs. Joseph Broadhead?" Will said.

Early rose again and offered his hand to Sallie, who took it. He kissed her hand gently and said:

"My pleasa, ma'am."

Sallie said: "General."

He shook Joseph's hand and sat back down.

"Mrs. Broadhead, Mista Jones hea says he knows ya?"

"Yes, we did meet a few weeks back, when we thought he was a nice young man trying to earn some money for his family, instead of being a spy for you."

"Sallie, I am sorry about that, but it was necessary to play that part, so I wouldn't be so suspicious."

"Then, Mr. Burns was right about you after all?"

"I suppose so. I guess he is not as dumb as you all thought he was."

"Are you talking about that Mista Burns? He is an interesting fella."

Sallie looked at Joseph, who gave her a look that she should change the subject real fast. She knew what he was indicating, since if the general knew of Burns' involvement in the fight yesterday, he would surely have him shot. So, she said:

"General, forgive a woman for her curiosity, but how did the battle go?"

"Well, first, may Aye offa to buy ya fine folks suppa? When have ya eaten last?"

"Nothing since dinner."

"Mista Will, would ya be so kind as to bring a couple a plates of this hea delicious food to the lady and hea husband?"

Will did as asked and returned a moment later with the food. He placed it in front of the Broadheads and then the general continued:

"Now, where wea we? Ah, yes, the battle today, ya asked. Well, I have to say ya aamy accounted itself quite well. We lost a lot of good men today, but ya lost moa, and we gained some ground and staated the job of sweepin' ya from the field. We will finish the job tomorra."

"Then, the lines held?"

"Aye wouldn't have thought it, but the enemy still controls the heights. Until tomorra that is."

He continued:

"Mista Broadhead, Aye am sorra we had to buan ya railroad. It was necessara though."

Broadhead didn't know what to say, so he just nodded and continued to devour his food. Just then, the meal was interrupted like the previous night by General Lee's courier, William R. Townsend, who found the general and came right over to the table.

"Beggin' ya paadon, Genr'l, but Genr'l Lee requests ya presence at his headquatas as soon as practicable," Townsend said.

"Mista Townsend, please inform General Lee Aye will be along directly."

Townsend saluted and then left. Early rose and said:

"Mrs. Broadhead, it was an extreme pleasa dinin' with ya this evenin'. Mista Broadhead. Mista Will, the beef was indeed delicious. I look foaward to suppa tomorra night."

And, with that he left the inn, leaving the others to finish their meal and enjoy the remainder of the evening, before a very crucial day tomorrow.

The Last Day

CHAPTER 53

JACOBS

PROFESSOR MICHAEL JACOBS rose early again on Friday, July 3rd as he was awakened by the sound of cannon fire about half-past four o'clock. He lit a lantern and proceeded up to his attic to see what he could see. It was still very dark, but he saw the flashes of light made by the cannons over Cemetery Hill, and could hear the booming sounds. He could also see the target of the fire was the north slope of Culp's Hill, and the area north of that hill, Pardee field, as the explosions were visible to him. Fantastic, he thought, as the action of the Union cannons firing northerly from behind the hills, aiming at the north side of the hill, meant the hill was still in Federal control, at least the crest. He looked at his incomplete notes from a couple of hours ago, and began to try to fill in the gaps, at least for the action on the Union right. But, what of the left? He looked through the telescope, pointed it toward Round Top and tried to see if there were any signs of who occupied the two mountains, but it was too dark, so he had to wait. Just then, he heard Henry come up the stairs. Henry was yawning but managed:

"Good morning, father."

"And to you, Henry."

"Do you know what is happening? Can you see anything?"

"Only that our guns are firing at the north slope of Culp's Hill and at Pardee Field, which is a good sign, and means to me we still hold that hill. See?" He said pointing to where the cannon shot was exploding.

"That's certainly good news. Any idea of what happened down at Round Top Mountain?"

"Not yet. It is too dark, but soon we should have the answer. It should be light fairly soon and then we will know. Do you mind going to the kitchen and bringing us a couple of cups of tea?"

"Yes. Do you want your usual two spoons of sugar?"

"Indeed I do."

"Coming right up," Henry said and he disappeared down the stairs. He returned about five minutes later with the tea cups, and then father and son drank tea together in the early morning dawn. They passed the time going over their notes and when they were satisfied they had all in order, they sat back and waited for the sun to make its appearance for the day. This happened right around five o'clock in the morning, and they were ready for it. Henry was at the telescope when he excitedly announced:

"Father, the Rebs are making a charge up Culp's Hill. The fighting is intense, but we are holding our own. Here, take a look."

Jacobs took his turn with the telescope and noticed the heavy fighting for possession of the north slope of the hill.

"Henry, make sure you make a note of the time of the attack. It was shortly after five in the morning."

"Got it, father."

Jacobs watched for a little while longer, and then remembered now it was light enough to see Round Top, so momentarily he swung the telescope to the right and observed that mountain.

"Henry, it looks like we held at Round Top and the littler mountain north of it," he said excitedly and continued:

"Yes, yes, I see our flags still flying on top of it. Hurrah."

He returned the scope to watch the fight for Culp's Hill. He noted:

"Our men are holding their ground and are pouring murderous fire into the Rebels. The casualties are substantial. My God, Henry, the amount of carnage created by this battle is beyond belief. It looks as though the poor Rebs are littering the same field where there are still dead from last night's fighting. It is incredibly tragic. These two armies might destroy each other right here in Gettysburg."

"Father, I do feel a bit awkward taking notes and watching the action as if we are a couple of ghouls."

Jacobs stopped looking through the scope and turned to his son:

"Now Henry, this battle is going to be fought whether we watch it or not. Besides, what we are doing is for future generations to know what happened here, because the losses are so great it will definitely have an effect on who wins this war. We have talked about that. We know the casualties are high, on both sides, but war is that way. You either kill or are killed. As tragic as it sounds, the more wounded and killed on both sides, the better the possibility for our side to prevail. I have studied the numbers and we have a decided advantage there, so we can afford to lose a man for a man. They, however, cannot. I know it is a terrible thing to watch, but the outcome is so very crucial to our country, and even to the whole continent, that we must document it."

"I know, it's just sometimes I cannot bear to think of all those boys, some not any older than me, dying out there. And, what of their mothers and fathers, and the rest of their families, who will never see them again?"

"You are right. It is heartbreaking to think of those who had no choice but to sacrifice themselves here. It is dreadful, but it is for the survival of our country. They are heroes all, even those on the other side."

Jacobs went back to looking through the scope and said:

"It seems the two sides have settled for the moment. We have dug in and it seems are content to wait for the Rebels to attack. Wait, here they come."

The Confederates charged numerous times that morning and each and every charge was repelled resulting in enormous casualties. Finally, around eleven o'clock, the Rebels gave into the obvious fact that they were never going to take the hill and ceased their assaults. Henry was at the glass and noted this:

"Father, the fighting has stopped. The Rebels are making no more attempts to take the hill."

"Just before eleven o'clock. Make sure your notes have this. My Lord, Henry, what took them so long to see how hopeless their position was and how strong our's is? It seems a lot of lives could have been saved if they had come to this same conclusion an hour or two ago."

"You are right, Father."

And, with that the battlefield was still. The smoke cleared from the intense fire, revealing all the wounded and dead. Neither man spoke, as the sight was enough. Jacobs turned away from the telescope and said:

"Henry, let's go down for awhile."

The two men returned to the attic after noon to continue their observations. Still shaken from what they had seen this morning. They had very little to say, as silence seemed the better way of coping. By all rights, they should have been celebrating, as the Union right held against wave after wave of Confederate assault. But, the carnage created outweighed the successful result. Jacobs took the glass, and finding the situation on Culp's Hill the same as they had left it, turned to the south to observe the other end of the Union line.

"Henry, there seems to be quite a bit of activity down near Spangler's farm. The Rebs are moving a lot of men around down there."

He rotated the telescope from south to north looking westerly, and said:

"Oh, my God. They are lining up their guns, a lot of them, all along Seminary Ridge. More than I have ever seen. There must be more than a hundred, and more are being brought up. They are forming an arc with them, a massive arc. Here, take a look."

Henry took the glass and saw the sight. It was an incredible display of artillery, all pointed toward the Union line at Cemetery Ridge.

"It looks like they are massing for a great attack. And, it looks like they are pointing their guns toward our center."

He motioned for Jacobs to look and after he did, he said:

"That's a very astute observation, Henry. I believe they are going to do just that. It all fits, as they are concentrating their forces along the line, but primarily at Spangler's. Let's wait and see."

They didn't have long to wait. Just after one o'clock the Confederate cannons began to fire. At first, the guns were not coordinated, but soon thunderous sounds erupted from them as so many fired at once. The sound was deafening. The Union guns did not immediately join in, and so the damage was being flung upon the Federals.

"Henry," Jacobs yelled over the guns:

"Are you alright?"

"Yes, I am fine. I cannot believe how loud the firing is. It is like thunder right above the house."

Jacobs noted:

"It is seven minutes after one o'clock, and the temperature, let's see…is eighty seven degrees. Take note. The guns are pounding away at our center mostly, so you were right. It looks as though they have given up trying to turn our flanks and want to break our center."

He turned the glass back toward the south:

"Henry, they are sending a lot of men into Spangler's Woods, a lot. Lord, they are forming at the edge of the woods all up and down their line. It must be a mile long. Here, take the glass. I want to catch my notes up," he said with extreme excitement.

"Father, it is an astonishing sight. They must be engaging their entire army on this charge."

"Keep watching. It will probably not be long now."

A couple of minutes later, the Union guns joined the action and began to pound away at the Confederate artillery and men. Henry noted:

"Father, our guns have finally joined the affair. Good shooting, boys," he said in a wound up voice.

He continued to watch and said:

"Father, our boys aim is much better than the Rebs. Their shots are passing over our line and hitting beyond. Our's are right on target. The tide of the battle sure is turning."

"Yes, that may be so, but if they strike a huge blow and break our line, the whole thing will be lost."

"Well, if they don't improve their aim, this barrage may all be for naught. Hey, there is a difference between our's and their's. Our guns are

398

set back and are firing over our men, whilst their guns are firing from in *front* of their men," he said emphasizing over and front.

"That's another very interesting observation. I knew you were smart, but your study of the actions today has been excellent. I have read their gun powder is not as pure as our's, therefore they have a lot of shots that don't quite make the target, and fall well short. They line their men back so as not to get hit by those dud shots."

"So, what you are saying is they have to hold their men back and then on a charge, they have to go further."

"Yes, that is exactly it."

Henry continued to look through the glass and added:

"If that is true, then they will have a long way to go across that field, across the Emmitsburg Road, and then up the remainder of the hill to even get to our lines, all the while we are shooting at them from a strong position. Could it be any different than the assault this morning on Culp's Hill?"

"Probably not. Really, Henry, but this is a much grander scale, so they may have enough men in the attack to actually make it."

They were still watching the artillery match around half-past two, when it suddenly stopped. Jacobs was taking his turn at the glass, and said much too loud now that the shelling ceased:

The fields of Pickett's Charge. (Faber)

"Henry, here we go. They must have stopped firing as they are ready-ing for the attack. Yes! They are coming out of the woods and lining up. Oh Lord, what a line they are making. It stretches from the north end of Seminary Ridge all the way down to beyond Millerstown Road. It must be a mile long. Take a look."

Henry took the telescope and surveyed the Confederate line.

"Father, do you think they have enough men to make it?"

"We'll see. Sure might. I have never seen anything like that. They are throwing everything they have at us."

Henry watched for another couple of minutes in silence, and then an-nounced:

"They are on the move. It looks like a great, gray wave. Why aren't our men firing on them?"

"They will. It must also be a mile they will have to cross, so time and distance is on our side."

Soon, the Union artillery commenced firing, and it was very effective, as Henry noted:

"Our boys are such good shots. They are taking out whole sections of men with each shot. But, the Rebels just close up their lines. They have so many, many men."

It wasn't long before the first Rebels reached the Emmitsburg Road and were stalled by the rail fence along the road. Again, Henry noticed saying:

"Father, they are being held up by the fence along the Emmitsburg Road. Oh Lord, we are picking them off like flies in a barrel. It is tragic."

Jacobs took the glass and watched. He said:

"You'd think they would have taken the fence into account. Sent some men to tear it down. It sure is being costly. What a dumb mistake on their part. It is really slowing them down."

Soon, the Rebels broke through the fence and were making their way up the hill to the Union lines.

"They are very brave men. The losses they are incurring are stagger-ing. Yet, they still go. They still go. Look near the angle in the wall, one of their officers is putting his hat on his sword and is charging. What a valiant man. So many valiant men, and they are all dying. Like that man. I just saw him shot down as he got beyond the wall. Henry, take note, it is almost over. It won't last much longer, the Rebels don't have any more men to send up that hill."

"You mean we have held? Father, we have held and won?"

"It seems so, Henry, it seems so," Jacobs said with a very subdued voice and continued:

"It seems so."

"Father, do you realize what we are saying? We have beaten them. We have repulsed the invaders. We have defended our soil. We have won a great battle for the first time in this long war. We have turned the tide and maybe will have a chance to win this war and stamp out the rebellion once and for all."

Jacobs looked at his son and then realized everything he was saying was true. He walked over to him and hugged him, saying with tears in his eyes:

"My son, never have more true words been spoken. Right here, right here in Gettysburg, Pennsylvania, in the first three days of July, in the year of our Lord 1863, the Union army has been victorious, and has beaten the invaders from the South. Has beaten the Rebels. God bless the United States of America. He has today and He always will."

CHAPTER 54

BURNS

JOHN L. BURNS was resting in his room, recovering from his wounds and regaining some strength when the cannon fire began shortly after one o'clock in the afternoon. The sound awakened him from a short nap as it was so loud he couldn't have ever slept through it. He moved around a little in the bed, trying to get comfortable in an attempt to get more sleep. But, the noises from the cannon fire would not allow it. So, frustrated he turned onto his back. Just then, his wife walked into the room and said loud trying to talk over the cannon fire:

"Oh, John, you are awake. Can I get you something?"

"No, I am alright. What is happening outside? That is more cannon fire than I have ever heard."

"I don't know, but it is thunderous. Do you think we are safe?"

"Yes, the battle is south of here and not in the town. But, with all that fire there must be a huge battle brewing."

Across the street, three Confederate soldiers stood watching his house. It was the sergeant from yesterday and his two companions who had taken Burns to the Rigg's house.

"Well, now, with all them cannons shootin' and makin' noise, it might be jus the time to take ca of that bushwacka," the sergeant said.

"Ya, no one will hea the shots," his companion said.

"He needs to be dealt with," the other said.

And, with that they walked across the street and climbed up the steps to the porch of the Burns' house and knocked loudly on the door.

Burns and his wife were talking when the knock announced that there was someone at their door.

"I wonder who that could be? Who in their right mind would be out with the battle raging? Barbara asked.

"Well, woman, don't just stand there. Go up and answer it."

She gave him a dirty look and left the room to answer the door. A couple of moments later, she returned in the company of the three Confederates.

"John, these men said they know you and were just checking on seeing how you were doing. I told them you were resting, but they insisted on paying you their regards."

"Good aftanoon, John, is it?" the sergeant said.

Burns was stunned and so he didn't answer right away. He looked pale and began to sweat a little. He regained his composure and said:

"Yes, John L. Burns."

"How ya feelin' John? We came by to just check on ya."

"I am getting better, thanks."

"Well, now that ya gettin' betta, maybe ya might answa some questions?"

"Why, what do you want to know?"

"Ole man, what wea ya doin' out thea?"

"Like I said yesterday, my poor, old wife was near death and I needed to get a nurse for her."

"She look fine. Ain't see no signs of sick."

"It was a false alarm. When I got home yesterday, she was well and she has been taking care of me ever since."

Just then, Martha walked in with the baby. She handed the baby to Barbara, and asked:

"What is going on here?"

Barbara replied, trying to diffuse the situation:

"Sweetie, these soldiers are concerned about your father and have come to call on him."

"Well, how wonderful of you, but I must insist you limit your visit to only a couple more minutes. My father is not well and needs his rest."

"Well ma'am, we can, but I wanted to know what ya fatha was doing on the battlefield?"

Burns looked at Martha and knew he had to be the one who answered, so he said:

"Like I said before, I was looking for a nurse for my sick wife. That's what happened. Now, is there anything else?"

"I heard tell ya wantin' to, how was it said: "shoot some Rebs"?"

"Now who would tell you a story like that?"

"Why, one of ya nabors."

"Well whoever that was is a liar. A fool-ass liar."

"Realla now? And, why would they do that?"

"They're copperheads, that's why. Traitors to our country, sympathic toward yours, that's why."

The sergeant looked at Burns and didn't have much to say further, and so the awkward silence was broken up by another knock on the door. Martha looked at her mother and said:

"Are you okay with the baby, you know, in your condition, whilst I go to get the door?"

"Yes, sweetheart, I am fine."

"Good. Papa, you lay down now, you need your rest. Why don't you lay on the couch and I will get you all set up after I return."

And, to the soldiers, she said:

"Gentlemen, I do believe you have your answer. Since my father needs his rest, I would be eternally grateful if you would take leave of us."

The sergeant and his companions decided to follow her request and so they walked after her up the stairs, through the kitchen, and to the door. Martha opened the door and saw Joseph Broadhead standing there. She was surprised he was not flinching from the noise from the cannons, which just seemed to get louder and louder, but she realized the folks in town were, for better or worse, becoming immune to the sounds of the battle. She said:

"Joseph, how pleasant of you to call on us. Won't you please come in?"

She turned to the soldiers and continued:

"These gentlemen were just leaving."

Broadhead entered and stood aside while the soldiers left.

"Thank you for coming by and for your concern for my father," she said to them and then shut the door.

When the soldiers were down the stairs and across the street, she turned to Joseph and said:

"Wow, that was close. They were trying to get father to admit he was in the battle."

"Really, love. What did he say?"

"That mother was sick and he was looking for a nurse for her."

"Fast thinking, love. How is he doing anyway?"

"Well, he is getting ornery, so that must mean he is getting better."

They both laughed and walked down the stairs toward Burns' room. Just then they heard different sounds than the cannon fire. New sounds. They stopped and looked at each other, and then heard Barbara scream, so they ran to Burns' room.

"What happened?" Martha asked.

Burns was on the floor in front of his couch and he needed help getting up. Broadhead rushed over and helped him to his feet. Martha looked over at her mother who was frozen with fright. She saw that the baby was crying, so she rushed over to get her.

"Those dirty Rebs took a shot at me. Two in fact," Burns said.

He pointed at the wall behind the couch and then to the floor, where the two bullets had hit, and said with a smile:

"Too bad for them they are just poor shots. Serves them right, the lousy, traitorous scum."

"John, are you alright?"

Burns sat down on the couch and said:

"I'm alright. I just need some rest. I wish this damn cannon fire would cease."

And it did that moment, as the Rebels, unknown to all in the room, had begun to mass for the great charge. They all laughed, and Joseph said:

"John, you are definitely blessed by God. In fact, you are a hero, the Hero of Gettysburg."

CHAPTER 55

WENTZ

JOHN WENTZ was in his house alone at one o'clock on Friday afternoon when the guns started. He watched from his window the buildup of cannon all around his house. The Rebels even placed a couple of pieces within his yard, and now they were ready, so the cannons began to make war. It was so loud he could not stand it, and so he, like yesterday, adjourned to his cellar. Being down there muffled the sound, but only slightly. So, he took a couple of pieces of cotton, rolled them up and stuffed them in his ears. Satisfied that he had done all he could to muffle the noise, he laid down on the cot and tried to rest. The cannon fire prevented him from falling asleep, and so he reflected on his evening last night when his son Henry had come to visit. He smiled and thought of the nice talk they had until he had to return to his unit. Wentz worried, but just for a moment because he trusted God to care for him, about Henry in this huge artillery battle. He said a quick prayer and this eased his mind, so much so that he fell sound asleep.

"Gentleman, let's pour it into them. Fia," Captain Taylor ordered his men of the Taylor Battery.

George said as they were loading their gun: "Henra, we a fightin' on ya childhood playground again."

"Yeah, how odd it is that I just talked to my father last night and now we are fighting right next to the house again. I hope we can make a break through today," Henry Wentz said to his friend George.

"We will, afta all, this is the Aarmy of Noathern Viaginia."

They loaded and fired their gun for over an hour as were told they were supporting a massive Rebel advance. At half-past two, they were ordered to stop firing. The Rebel army then appeared and lined up for the advance. Henry was in awe and said:

"George, we're engaging a lot of our troops. This is a big show, almost all or nothing."

George was as puzzled as Henry, and replied:

"I wonda why we a usin' so many?"

"Maybe, we think we can sweep 'em off the field."

"Well, of course, or we'd not do it, dumma," George teased.

"Here they go. We have a stunning view of the action from here."

Soon, the Union artillery began chewing up the Confederate lines and the two men's utmost confidence in the Rebel ability to win the day was shattered. In about a half an hour, it was over and those that could, and they were not many as the 35% of the men engaged in the great charge were killed, wounded, or captured, limped back to the safety of Seminary Ridge, while the Union boys yelled in triumph. The battlefield became quiet with the exception of the cries of the wounded and the dying.

"Men, stay sharp in the event the Yankees counterattack," Taylor ordered.

But, there was no counterattack, and so the Rebels were left to lick their wounds and decide what to do next. When it became nightfall, Henry, like the previous evening, wondered about his father.

"George, I've got to see if my father is in the house."

"Well, I am sua the captain will let ya go and see."

And so, after receiving permission from the captain again, Henry proceeded over to the house he had grown up in. Once he got to the front door, he knocked on it loudly. He hesitated and listened for any movement on the inside. Finding none, he tried the door and found it strangely unlocked. He went in and called for his father. When no one answered, he decided to go down to the cellar. The house was completely dark, which would have made it impossible to make his way around had he not grown up there. He went down the stairs and again called for his father. He heard no response again, but he saw a dim light in the corner, made from the stub a candle, which had burnt down almost to the nub. He saw the outline of his father on the cot in the corner. He started over to him, but then heard his loud snoring. He was fast asleep!

Henry debated with himself about waking him, but thought better of it and decided he would leave him a note. He reached into his shirt and produced a small pencil. He looked around and found an old book his father must have liked to read down here. He opened it and found an empty page a couple of pages from the front. He ripped it out of the book and wrote:

Dear Father,

I wanted to check on you once more to make sure you are safe, but I didn't want to wake you from such a sound sleep. I so much enjoyed our time together last night, and look forward to when we can be together again. I hope it will be soon and this damn war will end. It seems your side got the best of us today. I don't know what

that means in terms of the war, but I pray it will be over soon, so I
can come home again and be with you, Mother, and Susan. I love
you all with all my heart and pray for you daily.
Your loving son,
Henry

He folded the paper and put his father's name on the front of the note and laid it by the candle, folded up in an "A" shape. He kissed his father's forehead with tears in his eyes, saying softly:

"Goodbye, Father. I love you and God keep you in His care until we meet again."

Chapter 56

WILL

JOHN CHARLES WILL spent the morning on Friday again wondering when the hostilities would begin. At around one o'clock, he got his answer as the Rebel cannon opened up on the Union position on Cemetery Ridge. The cannon fire was obnoxiously loud and lasted over an hour. Then, there was quiet, but it was only for a few moments. He heard the sounds of more cannon fire followed by musket fire, lots of musket fire. This lasted about a half an hour of continuous fighting and then the quiet was restored again. He judged this to maybe be the end of the affair as it was too early in the day to cease hostilities after such a large show of artillery and rifle fire. He wondered the result, if the Union line held, or if it was broken like Early predicted the previous evening over supper. How would he know? And, then logic took over his brain, and he surmised that if the Union held and repelled the attack, the Rebels would return to the town and set up defenses for a possible counterattack. But, if the Rebels broke the line, then every Southern soldier would be leaving town to press the attack further toward Washington and Baltimore. He waited awhile to see which assumption was coming to fruition.

Between half-past three and four o'clock, he began to see Confederate soldiers entering Gettysburg. At first he saw the stragglers, but soon he saw officers who were giving orders for the men to prepare barricades to block the streets entering the town. He stood outside his inn and looked down York Street to the east and saw a group of Rebel soldiers doing just that. They overturned several wagons and piled crates, and other material, up to reinforce the wagons. He watched for more than a few minutes, with much satisfaction, the satisfaction of knowing the Rebels were the ones who were swept from the field.

He wondered how long it would take for the Confederates, and their spy Mr. Jones, to make their way to the inn, if at all. But, as he saw them setting up defensible positions, he knew they would be here at least the rest of the day and most likely the night. Then, it occurred to him there could be danger in the result of the battle today, and that danger would be if the Rebels decided to stubbornly hold the town and force the Union to retake it. This could be catastrophic to the town in terms of the resulting damage. He hoped this was not the case, and the Confederates would retreat back south without a final stand in the town.

He went back inside the inn to see about the preparations for the supper hours. He wasn't in the inn more than a few minutes when his father came to assist the work.

"Father, it seems our Rebel friends did not fare so well against our boys today?" he said.

"Sure seems the case. For the first time in the last three days, they seem a little scared."

"They do now, don't they? I wonder when our friends General Early and Mr. Samuel Jones are going to make an appearance here at the inn? Do you think they will come at all?"

"Oh, I think they will."

"Do you think there will be a battle to hold the town?"

"I really don't know, but I would think it unlikely. It was a very big showing today. I have never heard cannon and rifle fire like that. It seemed like the whole armies on both sides were engaged. And, for it to end so quickly. It doesn't make much sense unless the Rebels were whipped."

"I am thinking just so."

"Well then, they must have lost a lot of men. Maybe too many to continue the fight, let alone make a stand in the town. Besides, even though they are the enemy, they have treated the town with respect."

"Whilst they were winning."

"That, son, is true."

Just then, they heard a horse coming from the east. They went outside and saw Jones arriving in a relative hurry. He dismounted his horse and came over to them:

"Afternoon John, Mr. Will."

"It is a fine afternoon, Mr. Jones, now isn't it?" Charles Will said.

"Well, it depends on how you look at it I reckon."

"It's been awhile since your side has looked at it like this, huh?" Will added.

"It appears so, and it also appears as though we may be soon leaving this little town of yours."

"Really? So soon? And, just when I was getting use to earning those Union greenbacks you fellas keep spending. Those greenbacks you stole from other towns," Will said.

"Now John, I detect a bit of sarcasm in that. I thought we were getting over the war coming between our friendship?"

"Jones, you may have thought so, but I really can never forget that you lied to me. How can a friendship be built when it starts with lies?"

"Friendships are renewed, they start over, each and every day. It just depends upon whether it is strong enough to rise above petty differences."

"I would say war is greater than a petty difference."

"John, I am going back in the inn to get supper preparations completed," Charles Will said.

"Alright, Father. I will be along in a moment or two."

Will turned back to Jones and said:

"Will the general and his officers be joining us for supper this evening?"

"Indeed they will. They cannot miss a meal from the Globe. They should be here any moment."

"A little early this evening?"

"Well, as I said yesterday, the situation could not be avoided."

"I must go back in and make sure we are ready to receive the group. Care to come in for an ale? It's on me."

"Why certainly. I knew you would come around."

The two men entered the inn. Will said slapping Jones on the back:

"Jones you are an odd one. It seems as though nothing you, or your friends, do has any negative effects on anyone else. Life just goes on."

"Well, it does, doesn't it?"

They walked to the bar and Charles Will poured an ale and gave it to Jones. He took a sip and both he and Will turned to face the door as they could hear the arrival of the Confederate officers. They watched as Will's father greeted them for the evening and begin to get them to sit down. Like the previous night, Early was with them and took his usual spot at table. Jones made his way to the table and sat next to him. Will followed and then the general greeted him:

"Evenin' Mista Will. Aye do trust ya have somethin' special cooked again for tonight?"

"General. Yes, tonight we are having chicken fried. As you know, we here at the inn prepare it a little differently than you may have ever had it. We add onions, garlic and boil the chicken parts some, again not in water, but in chicken stock. Then we drop the parts in a hot vat of lard to make the outside crispy. You will enjoy it."

"Again, Mista Will, that sounds wondaful, doesn't it Mista Jones?"

"It certainly does, John. It is truly incredible how many different ways you cook up food."

"Thank you. As usual, shall we start you out with some ales?"

"Indeed we shall."

The Confederates were still coming in when the ales began to be served. Each man gulped his first down and soon they were looking for more. This again kept Will's father busy. Will brought out the biscuits and the food. He watched them for awhile, as he noticed how different the mood was from the previous evening. It was not celebratory, but very subdued. How could he expect it to be any other way? They must have absorbed a great beating from the Union. He watched the general, but it was hard to tell in his mood. He laughed and joked with Jones just like last night. This puzzled Will, so again he decided to join the general to see what information of the battle he could learn from him. He sat across the table from him.

"How do you like the way we cook chicken here, General?"

The general took a bite of a drumstick and said:

"Vera intarestin'. It is so crispy on the outside yet so tenda on the inside. Aye realla am enjoyin' it. Mista Will ya have again outdone yaself."

"Very good, then."

"What do ya think, Mista Jones?"

"John, you have done it again."

"Ya know, Mista Jones, Aye am gonna miss this place."

"Why, General, are you leaving soon?" Will asked.

"Aye anticipate the need to do so."

"What of the battle today? You are in here awfully early?"

"Well, like yestaday, Aye have to say ya aamy accounted itself quite well. We lost a lot of good men again today. Lots of good men. That is all Aye have to say."

"I see. What will you do now?"

"Aye suppose we will have to regroup and fight anotha day. Let us not talk so much about the unpleasantries of the battle today. Mista Will, what will ya do now that ya favarite customas will no longa be hea to enjoy ya delicious food?"

"General, we will get along just fine, like before you came."

"Ya have to admit ya made a nice profit from ou men, now didn't ya?"

"Yes, General, we did. But, I wonder at what cost?"

"Whatever do you mean, John?" Jones asked.

"Well folks around here have long memories of the events of the day, unlike you Jones. This last three days will forever be burned into their brains. So too how the townsfolk reacted during that time. I wonder what they will feel about us hosting your men, the enemy, as if nothing was happening?"

"It's just business, John, for if we didn't come here, we would have gone somewhere else. Perhaps to the Eagle?" Jones pointed out.

"Yes, we would have, Mista Will."

"That may all be fine and good, but folks around here will not fret on that. They will remember *where* you went and *how* you were treated. I wonder how much this business we did with the Confederate Army will *cost* us."

"Mista Will, Aye don't know much about that, but Aye do know afta these three days, it appears that none of ou lives will *eva* be the same."

The three men looked at each other and understood the magnitude of what was said. No one spoke, except to nod in understanding. Just then, the meal was interrupted like the previous two nights by General Lee's courier, William R. Townsend, who found the general and came right over to the table.

"Beggin' ya paadon, Genr'l, but again Genr'l Lee requests ya presence at his headquatas, but this time it is uagent," Townsend said.

"Mista Townsend, as pa usual ya timin' is excellent. Please inform Genr'l Lee Aye will be along directly."

Townsend saluted and left. Early rose offered his hand to Will and said:

"Mista Will, as per usual, the meal was indced delicious. Aye shall rememba this place with a fondness in my heaat. And, Aye will rememba ya and ya fatha similaaly."

Will took his hand and shook it saying:

"I will remember you and your staff as well, General. Good luck. I mean not with the war, but good luck otherwise."

"Fair enough, and to ya, sir."

Charles Will noticed Early getting up to leave and quickly made his way over to the table. Early offcred his hand and Charles shook it.

"Mista Will, from one gentleman to anotha."

"General, it was a pleasure getting to know you."

He turned to Jones and said:

"Mista Jones, if ya don't mind, come with me."

And to the rest, he said:

"Goodnight y'all."

Jones replied:

"Yes, sir."

He turned to Will and said:

"John, I will be right back."

And, with that Early left the restaurant with Jones in tow.

Early mounted his horse and said to Jones:

"Pack up ya things. One way or anotha we will probably be leavin' this town tonight, or shoatly thea afta."

"Yes, sir I will."

Across the street and in the shadows in front of the David Wills' house, McGee took aim at Jones. He was drunk, as always, so his hands were shaking and his vision wasn't perfectly clear. He waited until Early reined his horse and turned it around to fully expose Jones. He squeezed the trigger of his rifle and it let out a loud pop. He pulled the rifle down just as Jones fell. He saw this and took off running around the corner and south on Baltimore Street. He was gone before the Confederates knew what happened. He said in a voice only he could hear:

"Gotcha, you bastard. Gave you what you deserved."

He kept running while Jones lay bleeding on the street in front of the inn.

CHAPTER 57

WADE

VIRGINIA (GINNIE) WADE was kneading bread on a dough trough at around half-past eight on the morning of July 3rd. She had been up since around four thirty as much work needed to be done today. The day was beginning to warm and shots had been firing outside the little house for over an hour. She was hard at work when the bullet passed through the outside door and then the door to the kitchen before finally hitting her in her back just below her left shoulder blade and passing through her heart. Instantly, she lost her balance and fell to the floor. Her mother, who was at the oven baking bread, saw her fall out of the corner of her eye and instantly yelled:

"Ginnie, are you alright?"

Hearing no answer, her mother rushed to her, knelt down and turned her over, all the while yelling her name. She saw Ginnie's eyes had no spark of life and she screamed. Ginnie's sister Georgia was in the other room, and upon hearing her mother's scream, came into the kitchen instantly.

"Mother, mother…"

And, then seeing Ginnie sprawled on the floor with her head in her mother's lap, she froze, and put her hands to her face, and gasp a huge breath.

"My God, mother, what is wrong with Ginnie?"

Her mother looked up at her with tears in her eyes and said in a very shaky and soft voice:

"She is gone, Georgia."

"Gone, you mean she is dead…?"

"She is gone…she is gone. My precious little Ginnie is gone."

Georgia ran over to her mother and they both cried very hard for a long time. The noise from their grief made its way outside to the soldiers around the house, and instantly there was a knock on the door. But, the knock was only out of being courteous, as three soldiers soon entered the house from the side door that led into the kitchen. One of them asked:

"What is wrong?"

He noticed Ginnie lying on the floor dressed in her blood stained corset.

"What happened? Is she dead?"

Ginnie's mother Mary could not speak, but could only look at him with a blank stare. He and the other soldiers went over to Mary and Georgia and hugged them lightly. After a few minutes, Georgia composed herself and said:

"Thank you for your comfort."

The soldier spoke, saying in a soft voice:

"Ladies, it is not safe here anymore. I would be much obliged if you would move to the south side of the house and into that cellar."

Mary looked up at him, but could still not speak. She just rocked back and forth. Georgia said now calmly, but with no emotion, caused by her being in shock:

"What is your name, soldier?"

"I am Corporal Johnny Brazo, and this here is my younger brother Jace. That fella's name is Avery Smith. We are all from Albany, New York."

"Well, Corporal Brazo, I do agree we must move to the south side, but the only way is to go outside."

"Ma'am, it is too dangerous. We will have to find another way. Jace, let's see what's upstairs. Avery, you stay here and guard the ladies."

The two soldiers disappeared up the stairs and soon there was a yell:

"Smith, come up here, hurry."

The young soldier obeyed scaling the stairs by two. Soon, Georgia could hear the sound of banging. It lasted several moments and then the three soldiers came downstairs to the kitchen.

"Ma'am, we can enter the other house through a hole in the wall upstairs. Can you gather your belongings and follow us?"

Mary screamed: "What about Ginnie. I will not leave her here."

"Ma'am, don't worry. We will bring her," Brazo said.

And, so the soldiers carried Ginnie's body up the stairs, through the hole in the wall and down the stairs of the southern house, then outside the house, and down the stairs to the cellar. Georgia grabbed the baby and helped her mother make the journey. Once there, they laid Ginnie's body on a wooden bench and wrapped it in a quilt. Mary tenderly stroked her head and tussled her hair, straightening it so it looked presentable, all the while crying silently. Her tears dropped onto Ginnie's body. Georgia came over and with the baby, hugged her mother again. They gazed at her lifeless body and more tears fell.

The soldiers also came over and gazed upon Ginnie's body. Smith said:

"We are truly sorry to see this happen to this wonderful lady. She was so kind to us the last few days."

416

Brazo added: "She looks so peaceful, ma'am, so very peaceful."

"Yes, just like an angel," his brother added.

"Yes, she has always been an angel," Mary said softly.

Georgia nodded and Mary continued:

"The angel of Gettysburg. That's what she was. The Angel of Gettysburg."

CHAPTER 58

CULP

"Men, wake up. Up, up, up. To arms. We are being attacked. Get lined up, quickly," Sergeant Sheetz yelled at around half-past four on the morning of July 3rd.

JOHN WESLEY (WES) CULP was awakened not only by the sound of the sergeant's yelling to get ready for an attack, but also to the sound of cannon fire. He was very tired, having gotten only a couple of hours sleep as he was visiting his sister Annie until late last night. He jumped up from under his blanket as his companions, B.S. Pendleton and William Arthur, did the same. They exchanged worried looks as they quickly pulled their trousers up and put on their shirts. The looks on their faces reflected their feelings of danger as they hadn't experienced the threat of a Union attack in their encampment before. Pendleton spoke first:

"Wes, ya think the Yanks a realla comin'?"

"I'd be surprised if they did, and even so, they would have to break through our line to get here. Our position seemed pretty strong when I saw it last night."

Just then, Sheetz came by and said:

"Men, up and at 'em. I expect to see ya lined up and reada in less than five minutes."

And, so they were, and once in line, they were ordered to the barricades and works they completed yesterday while waiting to be sent into the action. They marched at the quick step and soon were in position.

"Men, hold hea until furtha ordas."

The three men went into position behind the barricades and listened as the battle raged on.

"Wes, I realla don't know if we a in such a good position tryin' to take ya cousin's hill again today."

"Well, maybe today is the day, B.S."

"On to Washington, I say," Arthur added.

They waited and listened for more than three and a half hours all the while wondering what was happening. They each were surprised they had not been called into the action, or at least even moved forward.

"I wonder why we just sit here?" Culp said.

"They a call us when they a want us," Arthur replied.

"Yeah, we'll be in soon enough," Pendleton added.

"Well, not soon enough for me. I am tired of sitting this fight out. I want to get in the action."

"Why, so's ya can get kilt right here on ya land?" Arthur asked.

"I am not going to get killed. I just want to go. I am itching to go, for some reason this morning," Culp replied.

"This is realla not like ya, Wes. Ya always the one who keeps us calm."

"Yeah, but we are here, here in Gettysburg, and we need to finish this fight. Here and now."

"We will Wes, we will."

"Well, maybe eventually today, but I want, no I need, to see what's going on."

"Wes, don't ya do it…." Pendleton said, his voice trailing off, but it was too late. Culp stood up for just a second exposing himself above the barricade, but it was enough. The bullet hit him in the head before his friend Pendleton could pull him back down to safety.

"Wes, Wes, can yea hea me?" Pendleton yelled as Culp began bleeding from his wound.

"Wes, Wes, no it can't be," Arthur declared in a broken voice. He looked at Pendleton and said:

"My God, B.S., it actualla happened. He was kilt on his own land fightin' for the Confederacy. He will become infamous."

"Aw, Wes, ya poor soul. I hope ya at peace now."

The words were just a garble for Culp as he lay there in the field of his childhood, dying. He could see Pendleton, but he couldn't communicate, or even move, to let them know he was still here. This feeling lasted for awhile to him, but in reality was less than a second. His mind began to drift in this moment. What was happening to him? And, then he realized he was dying.

He began to think of things he hadn't in awhile. He thought of his brother William, how much he wanted to be like him. He thought of his sisters Annie and Julia, and how they treated him so well as their "little toy brother." He thought of his father, and how sad it was at his funeral. He thought of his mother and her funeral. He thought of the way she loved him and the way she always made the house he grew up in a place of comfort and security; a happy home. He thought of Gettysburg, how much he loved the town. He thought of his friends, Jack and his brother Daniel, and Billy Holtzworth, and of the liquor they shared at the picnic on the hill. He thought of how difficult it was to leave Gettysburg. He thought of his work at the carriage making shop and how much he took pride when the carriage was sold to someone who really thought it grand. He thought of meeting his friends Pendleton and Arthur and how they whipped three older men in an alley. Then, he thought of Catherine, and his thoughts stopped wondering. Catherine, how lovely she was and how he was to marry her at the end of the war. He saw the wedding as clear as if it was a real memory. Lots of sunshine, lots of food, and the most beautiful bride the world has ever seen. His mind stopped on this thought of her in the wedding dress and it stayed just like that new invention, the photograph, only his mind added the brilliant white color of her dress, the red color of her lips, and the yellow color of her hair. He smiled, and tried to hold onto the view of Catherine, but it began to fade away. Where was it going? He concentrated on seeing it until it faded completely from his view. No, Catherine, don't go, he thought. But, she was gone. He began to lose his vision, blackness closing in on him from all sides. Then, he got a warm feeling, a feeling of love and of belonging. The blackness was replaced by a bright light. He concentrated on the light and then he became part of the light, engulfed into it. And, then he emerged on the other side and was standing on the porch of his house in Gettysburg. He looked for a moment and then the door opened. His mother looked at him from the hall. She was so beautiful, not more than thirty years old, he guessed. She spoke in the sweetest voice:

"Why, Wes it is you. We have been waiting for you."

"You have?" He replied.

"Of course. I am your mother. Did you think I wouldn't answer your knock?"

"Mother, am I welcome home?"

"Of course, you are. Why would you ask that question?"

"Mother, will you forgive me for joining the Confederate Army?"

"Wes, of course. You know how much I love you and you could never do anything to disappoint me."

He looked at her and then realized he had been granted the forgiveness he had sought for so long. He no longer needed to carry the burden he carried since he turned his back on his home and his family. Finally, he was at peace.

"Come on in, Wes. I have some freshly baked bread in the oven. And, Ginnie is here. She got here just a few minutes ago. Come, come in. Oh, and Jack is due here in awhile."